INCARCERATION

INCARCERATION

by

John Hudson

The Pentland Press Ltd
Edinburgh · Cambridge · Durham · USA

First published in 1998 by
The Pentland Press Ltd.
1 Hutton Close
South Church
Bishop Auckland
Durham

British Library Cataloguing in Publication Data.
A catalogue record for this book is available
from the British Library.

ISBN 1 85821 592 7

Typeset by George Wishart & Associates, Whitley Bay.
Printed and bound by Bookcraft Ltd., Bath.

Suzanne my wife,
Nicholas and David my sons,
Leasa and Martha my daughters-in-law.

You are my inspiration.

It should be noted that all characters are fictitious and bear no intentional resemblance to persons living or dead.

$\mathcal{O}_{\text{NE}}$

It was a hot sultry Friday afternoon, no different from the weather you would expect in Florida this time of the year. The late afternoon sun was still high and the crowd was beginning to congregate around the Federal District Courthouse. The white stucco building shimmered in the afternoon heat. The crowd waited anxiously outside the building for the outcome of the most important verdict that would ever be handed down by the District Federal Court.

The decision would have dire consequences on political and corporate America.

Judge Robert Hardcastle had been raised in New York and for the past seven years had lived very comfortably at West Palm Beach. He had been appointed to act as trial judge for one of the most heinous crimes the country had ever witnessed – an act of terrorism, the likes of which had never been seen before in the history of America. The final summation by both the prosecuting and defence lawyers had been concluded some two weeks earlier. Today, Judge Hardcastle was handing down his judgement.

Hardcastle was not a stranger to controversy. He had, during one point of his career, been the trial judge in one of America's most publicised kidnap and rape cases. His judgement had split America on racial grounds.

He was a quietly spoken man, in his late fifties, who had been brought up as a practising Christian. His father was a lay preacher and had tried to encourage him and his brothers to join the ministry at a very early age. Despite his father's persistence Hardcastle had other ideas about his future. He had developed some very close relationships with a number of influential people who had a strong belief that the face of American society should change. These were the corporate powerbrokers. The ones most feared by the country's political groups.

The Judge was a short, quite good looking man, with a large scar on the right hand side of his face, running across the cheek to the lower lip. Some say he received the scar in a court room scuffle he once had with one of the country's toughest criminals prior to being sentenced. Truth is that he had an auto accident during the early years of his life and although he had been under considerable pressure from his family to have cosmetic surgery, he believed the scar helped his image as a tough and hard member of the Justice.

It was three in the afternoon. The verdict was due for handing down at four. He sat in his air-conditioned office, oblivious to what was going on outside and carefully pondered over his judgement. It had not been an easy trial. Whatever verdict he gave he knew it was eventually going to have an impact upon the American way of life. He studied the transcript carefully, jotting down notes and highlighting the important aspects.

Maria, his court secretary, entered his office and asked him if he wanted coffee served now. She had worked with him since he first entered the Federal Court system and knew exactly what he would be going through right at that moment. His stress level would be high and all she could do was to offer some momentary distraction from the arduous task of thumbing carefully through his papers. He offered to take the coffee and asked her to lace it with a little tequila. Taking tequila with coffee was a habit he had gotten into since he had come to live in Florida. She never queried his unusual drinking habit and had just come to accept the fact that, if he liked tequila with his coffee, then she saw no reason for her to change his peculiar ways.

The crowd in the street was getting larger and more onlookers took refuge in what little shade could be found around the courthouse building. The courthouse door would be opened at precisely three-thirty. Court security was particularly tight this afternoon. The County sheriff and nine of his deputies had taken up strategic positions around the building and on the steps leading up to the courthouse front door. Federal Bureau Investigators were present, but it was uncertain as to how many had arrived for the afternoon verdict. Court security officers had positioned themselves inside the front door with the latest detection equipment. Everyone that entered the courtroom would have to be screened. This would be a slow process, but the decision had been made by Court security that no one should be allowed to enter without first being thoroughly checked so as to ensure that no weapon or other illegal object found its way into the courtroom.

The decision had already been made that the only people that would be allowed in the courtroom were the prosecution and defence lawyers, certain members of the press and Federal Bureau of Investigation agents.

The crowd had now swelled to over five hundred.

Time was approaching three-thirty. Judge Hardcastle sipped on his tequila laced black espresso. The man that he was to pass judgement on was American born of Italian parentage. There was nothing unusual about that except that the verdict would have such an impact upon America and other parts of the world, that the defendant's ancestors would have turned over in their graves if they'd known of the crime he had committed and what he was about to do. Nothing could stop the events to follow.

In downtown Miami, Bob Wallshot sat pensively at his desk in his large, ostentatious corporate office. The air conditioning was set at seventy degrees Fahrenheit, not a degree warmer or a degree cooler.

Wallshot was one of the most powerful businessmen in the United States and he presided over an international empire of corporate businesses, working exclusively for governments. His friends and business colleagues had always referred to him as BW. Federal and State politicians had direct access to him and he encouraged them to call him BW. After all it was he who influenced the corridors of political power.

BW was not usually at the office on a Friday afternoon, but the Federal Court verdict to be handed down at four was important to him. Judge Hardcastle had promised to telephone him at four-fifteen.

BW was born of American Lithuanian parents during the First World War. He was the youngest child in a family of three. His father had served in the US Army and had been posted to the German front in 1917. Not long after he had been there, he was invalided

3

out, losing his right arm in a secondary explosion. Returning to the United States he found it difficult to find suitable employment and very quickly drifted into petty crime and alcoholism. BW's mother had to save the family from being separated and she worked every hour of the day to keep the family together. It was not unusual to see her day start by cleaning hospital wards and finish by swilling the floor of a local bar. His father died a short time later. He was found mutilated in the back streets of the local neighbourhood. Rumour had it that he had tried to blackmail a local gangster, called Bugs Moran.

BW's mother always told him that he was different from the rest of his brothers. She often said that his other two brothers would turn out no better than their father. When they were old enough they left home and BW never saw them again. His mother died when he was fifteen. The hard life had caught up with her. There was no money in the home for her to get medical treatment and she slipped away rather suddenly, whilst BW stood by helplessly.

From his earliest days he had never known what a normal family life was.

He had developed an inner strength and love for life from his mother. After his mother's death, BW went to live with a family aunt and uncle but he hated every moment that he was with them. They constantly reminded him of the failure of his father and mother and that if he didn't toe the line, he would go the same way. At sixteen he ran away from his foster home. To survive he spent the next twelve months cleaning bar tables at a local pool hall. The few bucks he was paid and the money he made gambling at pool provided him with enough cash to buy a new set of clothes.

Depression was gripping America. There was no work and limited opportunities for a young man of sixteen. Whilst standing on a street corner one day, he saw a parade making its way up the main street. Waiting until it had passed he noticed a group of men carrying signs encouraging young people to join Uncle Sam's Army.

'Why not?' he thought to himself. 'What have I got to lose?' He enlisted in the United States Army, lying about his age.

It wasn't long before he was recognised by the army as having exceptional strategic skills and was encouraged to attend officers' college. Over the next few years he quickly rose to the rank of First

Lieutenant. In 1941 he saw military action in the Pacific. He was on shore leave when the Japanese bombed Pearl Harbour on December 7. Not long after that he was appointed one of General Douglas MacArthur's covert military commanders and spent the remaining part of World War Two serving in various theatres of the Pacific. After the Japanese surrender in 1945, he served as a commissioned officer under MacArthur. BW became America's most highly decorated military strategist. Serving under MacArthur all those years gave him a passionate desire to bring about political and economic change to America.

It was now three forty-five. The Courtroom doors opened and the Sheriff stood on the top of the steps and announced to the crowd that Judge Robert Hardcastle would only allow admittance to accredited press representatives, FBI investigators' and legal representatives. There was a roar of disapproval from the crowd, with a particularly noisy element in the front ready to make a bolt for the front door. The deputies shifted their positions to the front of the building, sensing that a riot was going to take place any moment. They joined arms at the courthouse entrance, standing several feet behind the Sheriff who was doing his goddamn best to quieten the crowd. The heat had taken its toll on those unable to find relief from the afternoon sun. The Sheriff sensed that the crowd was a little restless and continued to plead with them not to cause any disruption. The noise subsided. There was no leadership amongst the protestors. The Sheriff reinforced his position and asked them to be patient for a while longer.

There were about thirty members of the press present, including television and radio news reporters. There was to be no television or radio broadcasting within the courtroom. Slowly the press fraternity made their way up the colonial stairway, slipping behind the cordon of armed deputies. They were confronted by electronic detection and x-ray equipment, carefully positioned, at the entry to the courthouse main foyer. Surrounding the equipment were several courthouse security officers, neatly dressed in their federal court security uniforms of light blue trousers and open neck white shirts. Each officer had strapped to his waist a .38 calibre pistol and had no doubt been instructed to draw and fire should a riot occur.

The press moved in single file, walking slowly through the detection equipment, each person placing metal objects, cameras or other recording equipment that they were carrying, on to the x-ray conveyor belt. There was tension as a courthouse security officer standing at the end of the conveyor confiscated the camera and recording equipment of the guy who was there representing the Los Angeles Tribune. Judge Hardcastle had stipulated that no cameras or recording equipment were allowed in his courtroom. The unenviable task of policing this was left to the front door security. They knew their job and proceeded to give the journalist a receipt for his equipment and moved him rather hurriedly into the courtroom. Those who had similar equipment in their possession gave up their right to it without any disturbance as they were ushered through the detection equipment.

Phil Black was near the end of the queue and was preparing himself to empty his pockets on to the security conveyor. Phil had been a journalist for over 30 years and was currently working on a part time basis for the *New York Herald*. He had been asked by his editor to cover the verdict.

The editor of the *New York Herald* realised the importance of the verdict and did not have to think twice as to who he was going to have report this particular event. Phil might not be as sharp as some of the up and coming younger academic journalists, but what he had was rat-cunning, a survival instinct and a great nose for a story.

Phil was around fifty and had been in New York for the last ten years. He had been raised in Australia and joined the *Sydney Review* as a copy boy in his late teens. At the right time he happened to catch the eye of the Review's newspaper proprietor and within no time after that his days as a copy boy were behind him. He was given an early opportunity to become a trainee journalist. He never looked back. Phil did not need a degree to succeed, he just knew instinctively what to do and say.

Twenty years later Phil suffered a personal tragedy which he never really recovered from. His greatest love, his wife, had been taken from him at a very early age. She died of leukemia. Journalism no longer had any purpose in life for him so he packed his bags and left for the States with no clear direction and the belief that he could lose himself in that immense country.

Phil's mentor, the now ageing newspaper proprietor he had previously worked for, had bought the *New York Herald* and when he became aware of Phil's tragedy, he made it his business to know his every movement. He was indeed the one true great friend that Phil really had.

He offered him a job as a roving reporter. 'No deadlines, no commitments, just help us out when we need you,' he used to say. Phil accepted the challenge and over the next ten years felt very comfortable operating out of his small New York apartment on that basis. When he was needed the editor would call. Phil always responded.

Phil was not surprised to receive a call to cover the Federal Court judgement. He had in fact sat through the whole trial. It was his baby. His boss, the newspaper proprietor, had told him that this was no ordinary criminal case, there was more to it than met the eye. Too many high profile corporate and government leaders had shown too much interest in the outcome. Sniff it out was his instruction.

Phil passed through the x-ray machine and the alarm bell went off. The security officer approached him and politely asked him to raise his hands and spread his legs. The officer slowly moved the x-ray wand over the upper part of his body hoping to detect what set the alarm off.

The meter crackled furiously as he placed the machine over his jacket breast pocket. The officer asked him to remove the object. Phil felt put out that he had been challenged but he also knew that he had been caught trying to smuggle a hidden camera and recorder into the courtroom.

He looked at the officer in dismay and apologised for his oversight. He explained that he was not feeling particularly well. The afternoon heat and the tension outside the courthouse had caused him considerable discomfort. The officer accepted his pathetic excuse.

Phil was on this assignment because he was considered to be more street-smart than anyone else in his profession. He had been instructed to get a photograph of the accused when the verdict was being handed down. The possibility of a contempt of court charge did not concern him.

The courthouse security officer, as Phil would have predicted, did not proceed any further with the physical inspection. He had found out why the alarm went off. He did not need to look any further.

Phil walked into the courtroom with a micro camera strapped to the lower portion of his right leg.

It was only a small courtroom. He hustled himself to the right hand side of the chamber. From there he was able to get a clear and uninterrupted view of the accused. Phil was on his way, not only to submitting a sensational piece of journalism for his paper, but he was going to be the only journalist that would have a series of accompanying photographs.

The courtroom was now packed. On one side of the room was the Nation's press, whilst in front of the Judge's podium sat very quietly a number of Federal Bureau Investigators. On the other side of the room were the prosecution and defence lawyers.

It was three fifty-nine, in walked the court clerk and the remainder of the court staff.

The Clerk of the Court asked everyone to rise, as he announced that the Federal District court was in session with Judge Robert Hardcastle presiding. The words echoed throughout the courtroom as everybody rose.

Judge Hardcastle took his position in the high back leather chair reserved exclusively for the presiding Judge. He looked at the small gathering of onlookers and then fixed his eyes carefully on the accused, Michael Montefiore. He thought for a moment as he stared at the accused. Did he have any idea what the likely judgement was to be handed down? Probably not, he thought.

Hardcastle turned to his written judgement and then asked the accused, Michael Montefiore, to rise before sentencing was pronounced. There was calm in the courtroom moments before he delivered his verdict. Then he announced what everybody had been waiting to hear. 'Guilty of the most despicable act of terrorism that had ever been witnessed in the history of modern America.' Hardcastle had no choice but to impose the severest of penalties and committed him to ten terms of life imprisonment.

Michael Montefiore was never to be released and was to be held in solitary confinement for the rest of his natural life.

As the Judge rose the Sheriff and his officers removed Montefiore from the courtroom.

The press pushed their way through the small courthouse doorway to report the outcome of this long awaited verdict to their newspaper offices. Justice had been completed. The crowd that had gathered earlier were subdued and began to disperse, shaking their heads in disbelief. Ten lifetime sentences.

$\mathcal{T}$wo

There was nothing special about this particular Saturday for Mike Johnston. He had the same routine most weekends. He would get up early Saturday morning and ferry his kid to tennis. On the way to the tennis court he would deviate and pick up another couple of youngsters whose parents were less than enthusiastic about their kids playing tennis on a Saturday morning. If it wasn't for Mike there would not be a team and thanks to him the youngsters were doing particularly well.

Mike Johnston was the Sydney based Chief Executive Officer of a group of service companies operating in the Pacific region. The group was owned by Bob Wallshot. Mike had never met him and most probably was never going to. He dealt directly with some individual out of the Miami office whom he had also never met and really did not think that he ever would anyway. Being twelve thousand miles away made him feel very comfortable, even more so given the time difference between the two countries.

Mike had been with the company for more years than he cared to remember. He often wondered why he was given the job in the first place. He never saw himself fitting in with the entrepreneurial style of most American corporations. In this case it was different, as nearly everyone in the group was incapable of making decisions. This didn't bother Mike, he only referred those matters up the chain that he chose to. He made his own decisions and stood by them. His management and staff respected the independence.

The telephone rang. Mike picked it up rather hurriedly, he didn't want to disturb his wife Elizabeth who was still in bed. It was George Vegas, Governor of one of the corporation's correctional centres. George would quite often ring and advise his CEO that everything was OK. This would particularly happen on Saturday and Sundays.

Mike always believed that it was George's way of letting him know that he was on the job and not off playing golf somewhere. This telephone call was different however. George had never telephoned this early on a Saturday morning. Why the urgency to talk to him first thing?

As predicted George went on to let Mike know that everything was OK and that all prisoners at the morning muster were accounted for. Mike sighed slightly as he was certain that George was going to break some bad news to him. George informed Mike that there had been a few disturbances the preceding evening and an attempted suicide. An aboriginal boy had attempted to take his life. The prison officers had been on full alert all evening and had thwarted the young boy's attempted suicide. Aboriginal suicidal prevention techniques had been applied and on this occasion were successful. Mike was relieved. The last thing he wanted today was to have the press and the Government on his back looking for blood over a suicide, particularly an aboriginal suicide.

George was instructed to pass on management's personal thanks to those prison officers who had prevented the suicide.

He had not quite finished his report, although Mike wished that he had. It was fast approaching eight. He had to get on the road with the kids, otherwise if they weren't there at the stipulated time they forfeited the match. He couldn't let this happen as the semifinals were just around the corner and every match here on in was critical.

George told Mike that he had received a call this morning from the Ministry of Prisons, would not disclose his source within the Ministry but was confident that the information was accurate and that it would impact the Corporation's contract rollover negotiations later in the year. He went on to tell him that it was disclosed at a recent US Senate hearing that the group's parent company in the States had been laundering cash through Swiss accounts and were using the proceeds to acquire arms. The Senate Investigation Committee concluded that there was insufficient evidence and mysteriously dropped the investigation.

George went on to tell Mike that he believed that this was not going to be the last they would hear about it. It appeared a nosy journalist out of New York, who seemed hell bent on getting to the bottom of the whole sordid affair, had recently contacted the Ministry in Sydney looking for information on the local Australian operations.

Mike dismissed the rumours and told George that he should not discuss them with anyone else. He was however, to keep him informed if there were any further developments.

Over the past few years there had been several reports of unusual events emanating from the corporate headquarters. In particular Mike recalled the incident at a nuclear power site in Mississippi. It was reported that the corporation had sent in its special arms squad to quell a union disturbance. The siege lasted three days. The squad finally gained control. During the disturbance three union representatives were killed. The news was plastered over all the national newspapers. The corporation was severely criticised for its actions with calls for any further covert action of that nature to be handled by government agencies. The Department of Energy undertook a low-level investigation and never issued a public report of its findings. No action was ever taken against the corporation. That was not the end of it though. The US Senate, following public pressure, decided to undertake its own investigation. That went on for several months with no conclusion being reached. The inquiry was canned. There were rumours that the President himself had pressured the Senate to drop the hearing.

Mike also recalled the rumour that had been flying around for some months that one of the corporations privately operated Texas medical centres was the centre of a major drug running operation.

Initially Mike dismissed the latest rumour as just that – a rumour. However, on the way to taking his kids to tennis he began to reflect on a series of other bizarre events that had taken place over a long period of time. Perhaps there was substance in the latest story. What was intriguing, was that to Mike's best recollection, all of the incidents had been subject to some form of government investigation. None, however, were conclusive, nor had the corporation ever been held accountable.

Mike picked up his cell phone and dialled the company's public relations consultant, Fran Bright.

Fran was a former Sydney newspaper journalist with the *Sydney Review*. Some years earlier she'd had a difference of opinion over editorial content with her editor. Fran insisted on her own independent style of reporting. The editor had other ideas. The best move Fran ever made was to quit the paper and form her own public relations business. Her first client was Mike's business.

Mike got hold of Fran and proceeded to tell her of the latest rumour that was circulating around the Ministry of Prisons. Her immediate reaction was to protect the company's interest from prying newspaper journalists. She promised Mike that a draft press release would be on his desk first thing Monday morning. Naturally the press release would follow the same line as all the others. Deny the rumours and blame the competitors for releasing defamatory material to the press. It had worked successfully in the past. Mike expressed his concern to Fran, asking her if she had ever considered, as to whether or not the rumours were true. Fran dismissed the comment lightly and reminded him that she had been a journalist too long to believe anything you heard or read.

The morning had passed rather quickly. Mike's interest in the kid's tennis had not been particularly gratifying. This was most unusual. He kept going over in his mind the phone call he had received from George Vegas. What did it mean? Was there any substance in the rumour? Why would the corporation be operating Swiss bank accounts for the purchase of weapons? What were they doing with the arms? Was there a master plan? Stop! This was absurd. He had to convince himself that the stories were all hearsay.

As he drove his car into the drive, his wife Elizabeth came running out to meet him and the kids. Before he could turn the engine off she told him that Bob Kinnear was on the telephone and needed to talk to him urgently. Bob was a former executive of the Wallshot Corporation who had left some months earlier to pursue a lifestyle career of fishing and golf. Bob and Mike had become very good friends over the years and had shared homes from time to time.

Mike picked up the phone to be greeted by a rather anxiously loud speaking Bob. 'What the hell is wrong?' he asked. 'You sound terrible. Settle down,' he demanded.

Bob composed himself and asked Mike had he heard the news. Mike immediately flashed his thoughts, to the early morning conversation he'd had with George Vegas. Before Mike could respond, Bob blurted that Michael Montefiore had been found guilty of terrorism and had been sentenced to ten terms of life imprisonment. What was more, he went on to say that he had been committed to serve his sentence at the corporation's high security correctional centre in Florida. Mike was somewhat bewildered by the news as it meant absolutely nothing to him. Who was Michael Montefiore? Why did Bob make a special call to tell him this news?

Mike found a break in Bob's conversation, long enough to ask him to start from the beginning. He told him that he had no idea what he was talking about and had never heard of Michael Montefiore.

Bob paused, realising that he was chatting with a friend on the other side of the world, who most probably had not been following this particular trial. After all why should he, it would only be of interest to Americans, particularly those who knew Michael Montefiore. Mike Johnson obviously had not heard of him.

Bob's voice relaxed as he gave Mike the full run down leading up to Montefiore's sentencing. 'Montefiore was the regional vice president for Wallshot Corporation's special arms squad,' Bob related. 'He was assigned to Miami International Airport to combat suspected terrorism. He and his squad were instructed to proceed to a sterile section of the airport, where a South American Boeing 747 was laid up pending an investigation. The authorities suspected that the plane was carrying a shipment of arms.' Bob paused for a moment. 'Montefiore and his goons were supposed to provide back up support to the airport's highly trained security team. For no apparent reason that is where it all went wrong. Montefiore and his team of hit men opened fire on the security personnel, killing every one of them and then throwing a number of delayed action bombs into the cabin of the 747. Within seconds the plane exploded, destroying any evidence. His men disappeared in waiting trucks and haven't been heard of since. Strangely enough, Montefiore did not leave the airport. He gave himself up to the authorities. It was though there had been a pre-conceived plan for him to be arrested after the crime had been committed.'

Mike interrupted Bob's graphic detail of the events and asked what was the motive behind the killings and the destruction of the plane. Bob was uncertain but he believed it had something to do with Wallshot Corporation. He went on to tell him that there had been rumours hanging around for some years that Wallshot was providing funds to an overseas arms group. Arms were being smuggled into America, either by ship or air. No one was ever quite certain where they were being stored.

Mike found the story preposterous. Bob didn't necessarily disagree. He questioned Mike, as to why all the government investigations had taken place into the corporation over many years. And why had they all never reached a conclusion? Why had Montefiore blown up the plane? Did it have arms on board and was there a likelihood they would be discovered? Why was Montefiore being sent to one of Wallshot's correctional centres? There were too many coincidences. What Mike didn't know was that Montefiore was very closely connected to the Wallshot family. He would have taken his life for BW.

Mike was pleased to hear from Bob and was quite intrigued by the story that he had just run by him. The way he saw it though, was that this guy Montefiore had committed an inexcusable crime and had been punished severely for it. As for the rest of the allegations he thought it was somewhat exaggerated. Mike promised to keep in touch with Bob and asked him to send his best wishes to the family.

$\mathscr{T}$HREE

BW picked up the telephone. It was 4.15 in the afternoon. He had been expecting a call at that time from Judge Hardcastle. He was not disappointed. He was anxious to know which way the sentencing of Montefiore had gone. Hardcastle spoke rather nervously and told BW that he had had no choice but to put Michael away for the rest of his natural life. He was waiting for some reaction from BW. He was very much aware of the very close relationship that BW and Michael had shared for many years, it would have been like losing his son. There was nothing the Judge could have done under the circumstances, he had to impose the maximum penalty. He only hoped BW understood the dilemma he found himself in. There was a moment's silence as BW cleared his throat. Obviously shaken by the decision, he cleared his throat again and told the Judge that had he been in the same position he would have done the same. The Judge felt a little easier knowing that BW had supported his actions. There was nothing else that Hardcastle could say to BW at this point of time. He felt it would be better if he got off the phone and allowed him some time to mull over the news that he had just delivered.

BW thanked the Judge for the way he had conducted the trial and then suggested that he should come over to the ranch Sunday week to discuss some matters that would be of particular interest to him. 'Come alone,' he demanded. This took Hardcastle by surprise. He was not expecting an invitation to join him at his out of town ranch. In fact he had no idea where the ranch was. BW offered to have the Judge picked up from his West Palm Beach condominium at around noon.

Montefiore left the courthouse in an armoured protected van escorted by several State police officers and two FBI agents. They were not going to take any risks at this stage. They were very conscious that Montefiore's accomplices were still on the run. Would they use this opportunity to free him? They were prepared in case they did. The van had to travel to the other side of town where Montefiore would be detained for processing. A specially prepared detention annex had been built on the side of the local sheriff's headquarters to house Montefiore during phase one of the sentencing process. He probably would not be there for more than a few hours. Afterwards he was to be transferred by FBI helicopter to the Florida State private correctional centre in Saratoga.

The van and escort arrived at the sheriff's headquarters on time, having been monitored all the way by a sophisticated vehicular electronic tracking device. The electronic security controlled gates opened and the van proceeded down the drive under the building. They were now secure from any outside interference. Before the van door was opened, a high security police squad stood on full alert with automatic machine guns cocked ready for firing. Montefiore was removed from the van and escorted to his waiting cell.

He appeared to be calm and relaxed, strange for a man who had just been sentenced to life imprisonment in a maximum security, correctional centre. People began to wonder if the man had any heart at all, or was he just a machine. At no time since his capture had he expressed any emotion. He was a very cool individual.

The county sheriff and the two FBI agents moved into the cell with Montefiore. He was asked to remove his waist belt and all personal belongings from his pockets and place them on the table. There was no hesitation. Montefiore knew the drill. The sheriff watched impatiently as he took off his Rolex watch and placed it on the table. He then turned his trouser pockets inside out revealing a few coins and a silver toothpick. He wouldn't require any of these in the future. The sheriff identified the articles and logged them into a register. The law required that they be held by the State for the term of his imprisonment. In this case Montefiore would never see his possessions again. No one really cared what happened to them.

Montefiore was asked to strip down to his jocks. A doctor entered the room. It was necessary for a thorough medical examination to be given to all prisoners prior to their incarceration. 'Eyesight OK. Ears OK. Blood pressure, normal. No heart irregularities, reflexes satisfactory, no visible identification marks. Internal examination satisfactory, urinal tract clear.' The whole examination had been completed in less than ten minutes. It was routine procedure. The doctor wasn't too concerned as to the thoroughness of the check, as he thought to himself that this was a waste of time and effort on such a vile piece of garbage.

The prisoner was moved to the adjoining room where he was to be photographed and allocated his prison identification number. This would have normally been completed at the institution, but under these very special high security circumstances, the sheriff had been instructed to complete all formalities prior to his removal to the Saratoga correctional centre.

The FBI agents watched intently as Montefiore faced the camera. They had no time for him. It was their buddies he and his gang of terrorists had slaughtered at Miami airport. It was their job to hold and search the Boeing 747, not the Wallshot Corporation's goon squad. The operation would have been successful had it not been for those last few seconds.

Now these two agents faced the perpetrator. The thought of execution flashed through their minds. This was their opportunity as the sheriff left the room for a few brief moments. They looked at each other and fantasised, Montefiore bolting for the door attempting to escape, drawing their pistols and emptying the chambers into the moving target.

The sheriff returned to the room breaking the thought of their brief moment of triumph. They were federal law enforcement officers and understood the responsibilities of the positions they held. Montefiore would suffer a life sentence for his act of terrorism.

The initial processing was now completed and Montefiore was shuffled into a holding pen awaiting the arrival of the helicopter. Tight security surrounded him.

Phil Black had rented a room just around the corner from the courthouse where Montefiore had been sentenced. He had not planned to return to New York for a few days. There was some further investigation work that he wanted to do.

There was knock on his motel room door. He got off the bed and removed the two latch chains to be greeted by a young Hispanic boy. Phil had met the young boy when he had left the courthouse late that afternoon and had asked him to come to his motel room as he had a job for him to do, reminding him that there was a buck to be made.

During the handing down of the Montefiore sentence, Phil had been lucky enough to take a few photographs. Phil felt that he could trust the boy and offered him one hundred dollars to have the film developed and back to him before nine that evening. He had torn the bill in half, giving him half then and the other half when he delivered. The boy had not let him down, handing the developed film to Phil. He had a quick glance at the photographs and was surprised as to how well they had turned out. The young boy waited for his approval and then put his hand out for the other half of the dollar bill. Phil obliged and thanked him.

Phil spent the rest of the evening preparing his story of the events that had unfolded that afternoon. He knew by tomorrow morning every newspaper in the country would be running a front page headline on Montefiore, but none would have photographs from inside the courtroom. He had made arrangements for the company's Lear jet to pick up the story and photographs from the local airport. He could not be late as the plane had to return to New York in time to catch the first edition deadline. Under normal circumstances the photographs would have been sent down the line. This was not a normal circumstance. These photographs were Phil's exclusive, he did not want some hacker intercepting the line.

The jet touched down. Phil was there to meet the pilot and handed the package to him with strict instructions that it had to be delivered to the Chief Editor of the *New York Herald* before the three o'clock deadline.

He returned to the motel feeling pleased that he had not let his editor down. Today had been a personal triumph for him, he felt good about himself. In fact he had not felt this good since his days as a journalist in Australia. Today was a day of adventure. The adrenalin had been pumping through his body. It was just after twelve when he got back to his room, no point in doing any more. His editor promised to telephone him immediately he received the exclusive package. Phil fell on the bed. He was exhausted and within minutes he had gone to sleep.

The helicopter touched down in the grounds of the sheriff's compound no more than a hundred yards from the cell where Montefiore was being held. The sheriff's officers moved into position waiting nervously for the sheriff and the two FBI agents to bring him out of the cell, through the compound and out to the helicopter. They knew that once the chopper had lifted from the compound, their role was over.

The door to the cell opened and standing in the full night light was Montefiore, chained at the ankles and wrists. He was quickly moved across the compound and lifted into the helicopter. The sheriff sighed with relief. His job was nearly finished. The ride to Saratoga was the responsibility of the FBI agents. The sheriff received a signed release for Montefiore. The doors to the chopper closed as the engines thundered furiously. Slowly it began to rise and within minutes it had disappeared into the black horizon.

Saratoga was about a forty-minute ride. The chopper maintained a straight course flying at three thousand feet above the ground. The pilot had been instructed to contact prison communications staff every two minutes to advise them of their precise location. The minutest of detail had been planned carefully for the removal of Montefiore from the courthouse to the correctional centre. Nothing was to go wrong.

The helicopter was in range of the Saratoga correctional centre. Ground communication acknowledged sight of the chopper and authorised its landing, in the south-west sector of the prison compound. The chopper touched down gently as prison officers formed a circle around the craft. One of the FBI agents was the first to jump on to the ground. His colleague pushed Montefiore to the open door and eased him over the side. This was the start of his life-time incarceration at Saratoga.

Ironically it was Montefiore who had helped develop Saratoga prison for the Wallshot Corporation. He had been the special adviser on physical and electronic security and knew every inch of the prison.

Montefiore was transferred to the prison warden. The FBI agents would never see him again – so they thought. They returned to the helicopter and departed.

The reception committee inside the high security prison was very impressive. The Warden, Deputy Warden and Chief of Security were all there to meet Montefiore and escort him to a specially constructed section in Cell Block B. The Wallshot Corporation, with the approval of the Federal authorities had designed and constructed the annex to hold Montefiore. He had to be kept away from main stream prisoners. He was not allowed to mix. That was an order of the court.

The Warden, James Bonham, had been at Saratoga for the past two months. He was in his late sixties and had worked for the Wallshot Corporation over forty years. James knew BW socially. He was one of the very few people that BW called a friend. He trusted him implicitly.

James first met BW in 1956 at a bar in Fort Lauderdale. BW had just resigned from the National Security Agency and had decided to make his fortune in Florida. He was uncertain as to what he was going to do and openly discussed his ideas with James. They both agreed that the business of the future was security.

Since the war there had been a significant change in the economic and social structure of America. Hispanic groups from Puerto Rico and Cuba were entering the country in droves. Most were illegal immigrants and saw the Florida Keys and adjoining coastline as the easiest point of entry. Florida was such an under developed state in those days that the authorities really did not show too much concern. As long as the illegal immigrants crossed the border into Florida it was felt that the problem could be localised. As more and more immigrants made their way into the State crime levels increased. The rich and famous deserted their unsecured beachside homes and migrated up State. This left the southern part of Florida vulnerable. BW saw an opportunity to build an elitist security group, providing protection to the homes of the migrating rich and famous.

Both men dreamed of their future and BW put his hand out and told James that when he formed his security operation, he would like him there at the operational helm. By this time of the evening he could have asked James to do anything. The tequila had taken its toll. James accepted BW's offer moments before he passed out on the bar room floor.

James woke up next morning in the alley behind the bar. He had a painful hangover from the tequila. He had no idea for a few moments what he was doing there. Sitting up he began to recollect his conversation with this stranger he had met the night before. 'What was his name? Bill or was it Bob. That was it – Bob.' He then remembered that he had difficulty with his surname. 'Bob had said call me BW.' What the hell did they talk about? James vaguely recalled security. 'That was right, he offered me a job as his operational man.' He looked around wondering whether BW had experienced the same fate. There was no one else in the alley except him and piles of stinking garbage.

James went about his business for several months after his rendezvous with BW and never really gave him any more thought. It was not unusual to meet someone in a bar, share a story and never see each other again.

BW, to his word, tracked James down and told him of his first contract to look after the winter beachside mansion of one of New York's leading banking families. He was ecstatic and asked James to join him. It was going to be hard work. They would have to run the contract themselves. The upside, BW explained was that they lived in the servants' quarters of the mansion during the year. James had found a new friend. BW had his first employee.

James had grown up with the Wallshot Corporation and was always there whenever BW had that tough assignment to complete. There was no part of the business that James had not been involved in. In fact he knew more about the operational aspects of the corporation than BW did himself. BW was the financial and strategic genius. James always maintained that he knew everyone in political and corporate America. BW had helped a lot of people out over the last forty years. There weren't many names in *Business Who's Who* that didn't owe BW a debt of gratitude. He recognised that was a powerful position to be in and saw that as the underlying strength of the corporation. He always maintained that one day BW would call his debts in.

Being with Michael Montefiore on his first day of incarceration was no accident.

Warden Bonham stood in the high security annex and formally welcomed Montefiore to the Saratoga correctional centre. Bonham reminded him of the crime he had committed and that whilst in this institution he would be housed in isolated quarters and would not be allowed visitation or access to any other prisoner. His point of contact would be the shift prison officer only.

'You will be expected to rise at five every morning, breakfast, exercise, lunch, afternoon exercise, read, evening meal and lights out at 8 in the evening. Should you breach any of the jail conditions you will have your exercise and reading privileges removed and be confined to your cell for a period of 90 days.' Bonham looked straight at Montefiore and asked him did he understand. He acknowledged that he had understood.

Bonham and his deputy warden left the room leaving the chief of security in charge of escorting Montefiore to his newly constructed cell.

Chief of Security, Jim Pike, was not a patient man. He despised any form of life on the inside. Montefiore was just another piece of garbage. He walked towards him, pulled his baton out of its cover, leaned forward and struck Montefiore on the side of the head. He fell to the ground with chains clanging, blood pouring from a large gaping wound. Pike moved forward again and kicked him several times in the side and stomach. He then stood over him and reminded him that his responsibility was to make sure that no prisoner in Saratoga was given privileges. He was going to make life hell for Montefiore.

Pike ordered him to stand up and face him. Montefiore did not move. Pike kicked him again. 'Get up you sonofabitch,' he shouted. Montefiore rolled over and leant on his elbows, looked at Pike and told him, 'If you touch me again, you bastard, I'll kill you with my bare hands.' The worse thing he could have done at that juncture was to threaten Pike. He was uncontrollable as he mercilessly bludgeoned Montefiore with his baton then left him on the floor of the room and ordered two prison officers to clean him up and put him away for the night.

$\mathcal{F}$OUR

The sirens went screaming past the motel at an early hour of the morning. Was it police or fire, Phil sub-consciously thought as he tried to stir and put some life into that body of his. He hadn't slept too well. His editor had telephoned him at a quarter to three to tell him the package had arrived and the first edition would be on the streets by six that morning. Phil hadn't got back to sleep since then. He looked at his watch. It was three thirty Saturday morning. He had to telephone Australia. What time was it there? He reckoned the time difference was fourteen hours with daylight saving. What time did that make it in Sydney? He thought. Five-thirty Saturday afternoon. Was he too late to get in touch with his contact at the Ministry of Prisons, he dialled, there was no answer. He dialled again. Again there was no answer. He dialled again and waited longer. A cheerful voice greeted him. 'Ministry of Prisons,' the voice exclaimed. Phil asked to be transferred to Peter Bent, hoping that he would be working over the weekend. There was silence for a few minutes. 'Just a moment,' the voice came back, indicating that she had located Mr Bent.

Peter Bent picked up the telephone to hear Phil Black introducing himself. He hesitated when he heard Phil speak. 'Just a moment,' he exclaimed, indicating that he was in a meeting with the Minister. He excused himself from the meeting and transferred the call to the adjoining office.

Phil apologised for interrupting him and expressed appreciation for taking the call. He reminded him of their earlier conversation and asked if he had been able to obtain any background information on the Wallshot Corporation's Australian subsidiary.

Bent had worked with the Ministry of Prisons for over twenty years and knew his way around the department. He had taken quite a liking to Phil Black. In some ways he likened his own situation to that of Phil's. He also had lost his wife under very tragic circumstances and was pleased to have shared some of his experiences with Phil. He felt that they were soul mates. Of course Phil was aware of Peter's tragedy. That is what made him a good journalist, his investigative ability. He had to have common ground with a contact in the Ministry. Peter became his target. The next few minutes of their conversation would hopefully tell Phil how successful he had been.

The muffled voice spoke silently into the telephone. Phil strained to hear what Peter was saying. He knew that it was difficult for him to talk openly as his Minister was in the adjoining office. He jotted notes in a hurried illegible manner. 'The Wallshot Corporation ran five prisons, all of them quite independent of the Ministry operations. All of the contracts were due to be re-negotiated later in the year.' Peter told him that the company had kept its nose clean and that was probably due to good management rather than good luck. 'Mike Johnston was the local Chief Executive. He had a good relationship with the Ministry. He was an Australian and had very little time for those in the U.S. headquarters. The business appeared to run reasonably smoothly.'

Peter stopped for a moment whilst Phil caught up and absorbed what had been passed on to him. It wasn't particularly inspiring information. Phil realised that he could have gotten this from any reasonable source. Was this the best that he was going to deliver?

Then the bombshell came. This is what he had hoped to hear. Peter explained to Phil that during his snooping around he had inadvertently come across a locked filing cabinet in the archives. Locked filing cabinets were not unusual but this particular one had a special combination fitted which was only accessible to the Senior Archivist and the Minister. It was the Minister's personal file. With some gentle persuasion he had been able to convince the Archivist to open the cabinet on the pretence that he was doing some confidential research for the Minister. The Archivist did not question his authority as he had known Peter for many years and trusted him.

The filing cabinet contained five files each pertaining to the prison contract negotiations with the Wallshot Corporation. There was one file for each contract, each with tons of correspondence. The paperwork was what you would expect to see relating to contracts of this nature, he explained. One piece of correspondence particularly grabbed his attention. Phil waited anxiously for Peter to make his point. There was an up-front payment made by the corporation to the Ministry for the first contract. The check had been signed by Mr Bob Wallshot and had been drawn on the Banque de Genève of Switzerland. There was a copy of the check in the file. It was for half a million dollars. Peter explained to Phil that was not particular unusual. The Government quite often insisted on up-front fees. However, this didn't appear kosher. The signed agreement that was in the file did not mention an up-front fee and more importantly there was no record of the half million being deposited into the Ministry funds. Phil was now getting quite excited and was beginning to sense a partial orgasm. Was there any more? He asked Peter. On checking the other files he found a similar transaction had taken place except that these were both one million dollar payments to the Minister and drawn on the same bank. Both checks again signed by Wallshot personally.

Phil was stunned by the information. He asked himself why would a Minister accept what appeared to be bribes and then expose himself by keeping copies of the checks in a locked file. Surely he knew there was a risk of being found out. Perhaps not. The first check had been paid over some five years earlier. There would be a reasonable expectation after all that time that his corrupt activity would not be discovered. After all, he thought to himself, had it not been for the lead up to the Montefiore trial and Wallshot Corporation's uncanny luck in walking away from Senate hearings, he probably would not have been asking Peter Bent for information. Phil smelt a story. Too many coincidences he thought. That is what put him on the trail to Peter.

He couldn't believe his luck. Phil asked Peter what he intended to do with the information he had discovered in the confidential locked filing cabinet.

'Nothing,' he snapped back, reassuring himself that he had made the right decision. He explained to Phil that he only had a few more years to go before early retirement. He was not planning to expose the file to public scrutiny and possibly blow any chances he had of receiving his retirement pension. Accepting bribes was not uncommon practice in government circles. Rumours were always rife about who was on the take. This was no different except Peter now had evidence.

Phil was gratified that he had taken the step not to expose the Minister at this stage. He needed time to dig deeper. He assured Peter that the information he had supplied him with would remain confidential for the time being, but could not guarantee what the final outcome may be. Phil had no intention of disclosing his source to anyone.

The telephone call ended. Peter felt somewhat better now that he had eased his conscience and had told Phil of his discovery. Phil fell back on the bed, going over in his mind the startling information that he had just received. This perhaps was the first piece of concrete evidence that the Wallshot Corporation was corrupt. What was he going to do with it?

The glass sliding door to Bob Wallshot's office sprung back quickly. Joseph Markowitz, the corporation's Chief Financial Officer met with his President every Saturday morning. BW greeted him and asked him to take a chair. The agenda for the meeting would be the same as it had always been. They would discuss in detail the weekly financial results, contracts lost and won, margins on those contracts and cash resources. BW was on the telephone when Joseph entered. He had no idea who BW was speaking to, but he heard him refer frequently to the Montefiore sentencing. He occasionally made statements that we were now in a good position to move to the next phase: the government was vulnerable; funding and equipment was nearly finalised. None of this made sense to the CFO. He sat opposite his President staring out of the window making out that he had no interest in what was being discussed. In fact he had no interest. He had only been with the corporation eighteen months and was finding the going pretty tough. He enjoyed autonomy. BW denied him that freedom. Joseph would go home to his wife most nights and discuss his frustration with BW. He believed that BW should be the CFO as well as the President.

The phone was slammed down on its receiver. BW turned to his CFO demanding the weekly results. He turned the financial reports over quickly, smiling when he got down to the bottom line. Good result. What about the contracts lost? Markowitz explained that there had been the normal swings and merry go-rounds, but the loss of sector three of the Texas pipeline contract was of concern. BW sat upright screaming for an answer as to why this very important contract had been lost. He had no explanation. This didn't please BW. He immediately picked up the phone and dialled his Vice President Texas operations, Ron Levine. Ron answered the phone.

'What the hell is going on, Ron?' he shouted. 'My CFO has just told me that we've lost sector three of the Texas pipeline contract.'

Ron shuddered. He had planned to tell BW the news on Monday. The worst had happened. He had found out earlier. Ron told him that the guards had not been performing satisfactorily. The corporation had been warned that if they did not get their act in order, the contract would be pulled. 'We didn't make it,' he exclaimed.

BW wanted to know if they could hold on to sectors one, two and four. Ron told BW the Corporation was under pressure.

'You lose those sectors and I'll have your neck! You hear me?' BW yelled.

Ron cowered. BW was confident that he could turn things around. A telephone call to his very good friend, Governor Sharp, was needed. He told Ron to be on stand-by to move his men back into sector three within 24 hours.

'Expect a call from the Governor's office within the next sixty minutes,' he stated.

The CFO had heard that type of verbal abuse before. He had been on the receiving end many times. BW leaned across the desk and asked Joseph if he was the bearer of any other bad news today. Even if there had been Joseph would have realised that today was not the day to confront BW on any contentious issues.

'What about funding?' BW asked. 'Do we have surpluses in our overseas subsidiaries?'

Joseph knew the importance of having current funding information available for his President. He took some perverse delight in shifting surplus cash around the world. The CFO was always amazed as to how well he controlled cash movements.

'England and Africa are negative,' he answered sharply. 'Australia has a surplus in excess of four million Aussie dollars and South

America is stable. Domestic is seeking funds for next week's operations.'

BW scribbled some notes on his pad. He then instructed Joseph to transfer five million Aussie dollars from the Australian accounts to the Banque of Genève in Zurich first thing Monday.

'There's only four million dollars in the account,' he interrupted.

'Tell them to draw down another million from the Credit Suisse account.'

Joseph found it difficult to understand why you would borrow a million of stand-by at eight and three quarter, deposit it in Zurich and only receive four percentage points. It didn't make sense. One thing he had learned was not to argue with BW over cash transfers.

'Also transfer ten million dollars from our Belize deposits.'

'Where to?' Joseph asked.

'Eight million into domestic operations and two million to be held in the Wallshot Swiss trust account.'

BW indicated that if they were going to win back sector three of the Texas pipeline contract, the Governor's campaign funds would need bolstering. That was the last thing a CFO wanted to hear. He knew how tough the marketplace and the Securities Exchange Commission was on political donations for favours. BW knew also and would not compromise his employees. That is why he handled the offshore accounts.

The meeting lasted an hour. Joseph returned to his office to put in place all the necessary instructions for the movements to take place first thing Monday morning.

Immediately his CFO had left the office, BW locked the door, picked up the telephone and dialled Governor Sharp on his direct line.

Governor Sharp answered and was surprised to hear BW's voice on the other end.

'Ziggy, how are you?' BW inquired.

'Well, thanks, BW.'

The pleasantries out of the way BW was not one to beat around. The Governor knew that.

'What can I do for you?' he asked.

'The Texas Pipeline Contract. How long have we been securing that facility for you Governor?'

BW was fairly confident that he would have absolutely no idea and would take a guess.

'I think about ten years,' he replied.

'Goddamn Ziggy, it has been over fifteen years. Fifteen years of good honest work with absolutely no complaints.'

'I couldn't agree more,' the Governor replied.

'Then why the hell has your office removed us off sector three?'

The governor now knew the purpose of the call.

'BW, I had absolutely no idea that you had been removed.'

'Well, Ziggy, I want to be back in Sector three in twenty-four hours. What are you going to do about it?'

The Governor thought for a moment, knowing that he was the only one who could turn the thinking of his departmental people around. He put the acid straight on BW.

'The election is due to take place early next year. I'm trailing in the opinion polls. My opponent appears to have unlimited resources and he is putting that to good use. He could topple me and that would not only effect sector three of your contract but you would probably lose the rest.'

BW was prepared, that is why he had his CFO move two million into the trust account. He put a deal to the Governor.

'A million dollars will find its way into your campaign funds, with another million going offshore to anywhere you care to nominate. In return you will put us back into sector three immediately and then renegotiate the whole contract for a water-tight term of fifteen years.'

The Governor knew he could get the Wallshot Corporation into sector three within twenty-four hours. With the other demand he saw some difficulty. The temptation of having a million dollars transferred offshore was attractive. He had no guarantee that he was going to serve another term as Governor. He didn't particularly want to go back to being an educator. He hesitated before he answered BW. He knew he could pull it off.

'The deal is done,' the Governor confirmed.

Ron Levine was relieved to receive the call from BW that sector three had been saved, not questioning how he had done it. When he also got the news that the whole pipeline was going to be re-negotiated for fifteen years, Levine was ecstatic. He had convinced himself that BW would hang him out to dry and transfer him to a guarding job in South America. Levine, unbeknown to himself, was as an important part of his master plan and the retention of the pipeline contract was an integral part of the ultimate success of that plan.

$\mathcal{F}$IVE

Phil Black checked out of his crummy hotel early Sunday morning with a copy of yesterday's headlines about Montefiore tucked underneath his arm. All of the national newspapers had run the sentencing on the front page but none had a photograph of an expressionless Montefiore standing before the Judge as sentence was handed down. 'What a scoop,' he thought. It had been a long time since he'd had editorial on the front page, more importantly, front page of the *New York Herald*. Montefiore's photograph would have been flashed around the world by now.

New York was only a couple of hours flying time. Phil was not in a hurry. Why not a leisurely drive down to Miami and catch the early evening flight to Newark. There was no one at his apartment waiting for him. He could catch some shuteye and then head to the office next morning.

It had been several years since he had been in an open top Mustang. He felt as though he wanted the wind blowing through his hair, clearing the cobwebs. Phil had not felt this good for a long time as he thought about the Montefiore trial, the scoop photographs, the sensational news from Australia that the Minister was on the take from Wallshot and the years of buried Senate hearings against the Wallshot corporation that were loosely flying around on the Internet. He hadn't even spent much time investigating those. 'That's a priority first thing Monday,' he thought to himself.

The car hurdled down Interstate 91 en route to downtown Miami. The city skyline appeared in the distance with the normal pollution haze hanging carefully over the top of the enormous skyscrapers. It wasn't much different to New York except that the sun shone in Miami and when it appeared in New York you declared a public holiday.

The Mustang was about to pull off to the right following the signs to the airport when he briefly looked at the clock and realised that he had a few hours to spare before his plane left for Newark. 'Why don't I go and visit the Wallshot Corporation building?' He knew it wouldn't be open on Sunday. 'A few photographs for the files might come in handy for another day.' He pulled back onto the Interstate, leaving the airport turn-off behind him.

The city was no stranger to him. Assignments were commonplace in this neck of the woods. There was an array of glitteratia in Miami. Movie stars, famous entrepreneurs, high profile lawyers. The list went on and on. It was a city of new money. Phil had been down here many times covering suicides, murders, divorces, marriages anything that associated with an American identity and was likely to sell newspapers. Mind you, corporate crime was something quite foreign to Phil. Had he been lucky so far?

He pulled up in the tree-lined boulevard easing the Mustang into the right hand side kerb. He wound down the vehicle window and stared at the seventeen floor building across the road. Emblazoned on the front of the building was the inscription 'Wallshot Corporation – Securing your Future.' Phil viewed the sign cynically, thinking to himself that Wallshot had possibly secured a lot of people's future but not in the way the sign had meant it to be.

The front entrance of the building was in the art deco style with gigantic columns towering above the street-line. The entry floor was richly decorated with mosaic tiles interlaced with the letter "W". No way was Mr Wallshot going to let anyone forget who he was in this town. What was above the columned entrance? Where was Wallshot's suite? Was he up there now? Was he plotting some other scandal? Who else was involved? Questions flashed through Phil's journalistic mind. 'Settle down,' he said. 'This is Sunday. Even a corporate tycoon like Mr Wallshot was entitled to have a day off. Only stupid low paid journalists worked on a Sunday.'

His curiosity got the better of him. He eased himself out of the car and started to take photographs of the building. He walked across the street hoping to get some better shots of the front entry and the mosaic tiling. As he approached the entry of the building he was confronted by a tall statuesque guard unashamedly dressed in a tailored black and white security uniform with several gold bars appearing on his epaulettes. The guard was obviously a senior officer within the Wallshot Corporation and he politely asked Phil to refrain from taking photographs of the building. He moved closer to him exerting his position of authority as the factor to convince Phil that he was not welcome on the site. Phil apologised and explained to the officer that he was a photographer from New York on an assignment for a high profile homes magazine. The guard was obviously suitably impressed and wanted to engage Phil in conversation.

'What magazine do you work for? What issue are the pictures likely to appear in?'

Phil had discovered that the guy had an ego. He offered to photograph the guard if he would allow him to take some exclusive shots inside the building. The guard did not hesitate to oblige Phil. Appearing in a national magazine in his gold braided uniform was more important to him than standing outside a city building on a Sunday.

Phil checked his watch. Time was running out. He had a plane to catch. There was something strange about Wallshot's building. It was instinct. He called it a journalist's nose. Whenever he felt a good story coming on he developed a sixth sense about things around him. He likened it to a smell. He had that feeling now. Stronger than he had ever sensed before. What did it mean?

His afternoon photography expedition had filled in some time for him. He had even been able to elevate the guard to the rank of general. He was the most important person in town today. He couldn't wait to see his photograph appear in a national magazine. Phil hoped he would overcome the disappointment.

By the time the plane touched down at Newark, Phil was exhausted. It had been a hell of a time the last three days. He needed a good night's rest to prepare him for the week ahead.

Warden Bonham summoned his deputy and chief of security to his office. Two things were on his mind. The weekend prisoner incident report, and an update on Montefiore.

The deputy warden assured the warden that there had been no incidents of note over the weekend and handed him his report.

Bonham thumbed through the report noting any exceptional events. There was none of any consequence.

'How is Montefiore?' Warden Bonham asked.

The chief of security sprang to attention, a throwback reaction from his earlier days when he was a Marine drill sergeant.

'Nothing to report, Sir,' he exclaimed. 'The prisoner is confined to quarters, he is comfortable and has not spoken to any of the duty officers since his imprisonment.'

The chief of security then cleared his throat and muttered something about Montefiore resisting orders last Friday evening.

'Speak up,' the warden barked at him.

'Montefiore, Sir, resisted an order on Friday evening and attempted to move towards an exit door. I had to use force to refrain him.'

'What is his condition, Chief?'

'He is comfortable, Sir.'

Warden Bonham was not convinced that his Chief of Security was telling him all the facts and advised him that he wanted to visit Montefiore at ten that morning.

He was appalled at Montefiore's condition. Lying on his bed curled up in the foetal position, the man was obviously in considerable pain. The warden pulled a chair alongside him and rolled him over. His face was so swollen, he could hardly see his eye balls. The massive swelling on the side of his temple had ruptured. The blood had congealed and infection had set in. His stomach was so bruised that it became painful to move even slightly. The warden in all the years that he had been involved in law enforcement had never witnessed anything so brutal. He bent over Montefiore and asked him what had happened. There was no answer. Montefiore knew that it wasn't in his interest to squeal on the chief of security. He rolled over asking the warden to leave him alone.

The warden immediately turned to his Chief of Security and demanded that a full report be on his desk by end of day. He pushed his way past the chief and told him to accompany him to his office. He slammed the door shut.

'What the bloody hell have you done to Montefiore?'

'He refused to take an order, Sir.'

'Don't bullshit me. He no more refused an order than I did. Give me the truth man?'

'Sir, he refused to take an order and I had to use force to restrain him.'

'What force did you use?' the warden asked.

'There is only one way to convince garbage like Montefiore who's boss and that's the stick. I applied pressure with my stick.'

'You mean you belted the living shit out of him, you useless asshole.'

The chief rejected the accusation and reminded the warden who was in charge of prisoner discipline.

'Get out of my office,' he screamed. 'Make sure that you have that bloody report on my desk this afternoon.'

Warden Bonham slumped into his chair. How the blazes was he going to explain this to BW. The first day his boy is in his jail he gets living hell belted out of him. He had to take disciplinary action against his chief of security. He could not be seen to undermine his authority, but as warden he had to ensure the well being of all prisoners. He knew the law entitled all prisoners the right to be safe and secure whilst incarcerated. Not everyone would agree, but the warden was there to uphold the law. The chief had to be disciplined. He could not do anything until after he had read his report.

James telephoned BW's office, the call being intercepted by Marina, BW's personal assistant.

'Good morning Warden, how are things out there at Saratoga? BW was just talking about you this morning. Said what a fine job you were doing. He is very pleased that Michael Montefiore is in your care. As you know Warden, Michael means a lot to him. What can I do for you?'

James felt like hanging up the phone there and then. All this praise being bestowed upon him and he's about to tell BW that one of his closest friends has nearly had his brains belted in.

'Let me speak to BW,' he insisted.

'I'm sorry, BW is not available at the moment.'

She asked if she could pass a message to him. He said no and thought afterwards that perhaps he should have done. He had to get back to Montefiore and get his side of the story.

It was Monday afternoon back in Sydney. Mike Johnston dreaded going to work on Mondays. The morning was the worst. Everyone was trying to get hold of him. The weekends never went smoothly for some reason. He had a theory that senior management should be available to staff on weekends. Too much responsibility was left to second line managers to run the business. The senior executives adopted the same Friday exodus as everyone else. Leave work behind and pick it up on Monday. He believed that senior management abrogated its responsibility over weekends. Great theory he knew but had no hope in changing a long history of corporate culture. You paid the price on Monday mornings. Everything needed to be fixed up first, before you could start a normal day.

He asked his secretary to get George Vegas on the phone.

'Good morning, George, Mike Johnston here. Anything further following our conversation on Saturday morning?'

'Boss I don't think it's a rumour about the arms dealing. I snooped around over the weekend. Spoke to a contact of mine in Defence about arms traders. He came up with some startling news. Did you know that the Wallshot Corporation has a subsidiary registered in Belize? Now wait for it – it's registered there as a weapons trading enterprise.'

Mike could not believe what he was hearing. Who was he working for? Were the operations just a front for a group of illegal money making activities or was this just another normal business activity of the corporation? Whilst he was listening to Vegas he was flicking through the recently released annual report of the corporation searching for any comment on weapons trading. There was none. He then searched the companies that the corporation owned. There was nothing registered in Belize. Surely George had got it wrong.

'George,' he exclaimed, 'I hope your informant has made a mistake. I'll do some checking myself and talk to you later. In the meantime keep this conversation to yourself.'

Following his call to Vegas, Mike left the office to visit Fran Bright. He had received the copy of the draft press release she had promised him and wanted to discuss the format with her. He needed to leave the office for a while and clear a few things up in his own mind. A call on Fran was always refreshing. She had a way of putting things in focus.

Fran was expecting Mike and even had a cup of coffee ready for him when he hit the front door of her office.

'What did you think of the draft press release I sent over this morning?' she asked him.

'It was fine. Covered the issue we spoke about. Hold on to it until we need to release it to the media. There has been nothing published yet about the weekend revelation. Don't want to jump the gun,' he pronounced. 'What do you know about the Internet?' he asked Fran.

'A lot,' she remarked. 'It's a journalist's main tool these days. The bloody cost of accessing is unbelievable, but the information you can retrieve is very helpful at times.'

Mike was encouraged by her comments.

'I don't want to go through the office Internet system. What can you get for me on the Wallshot Corporation?'

'Whatever is listed,' she said.

'Can you get it in hard copy for me?'

She answered positively but made him aware that it was not wise for her to drag it off her service. She could be traced as the receiver of the information and that would automatically tie him back to her. He agreed with her logic and asked if he she had an overseas source not connected to her or the company that could get the information for him. She laughed.

'I can get a number of people to undertake the job. It will cost a few bucks though.'

'That's OK,' he stated. 'Bill it as normal advisory services. I don't want internal audit unnecessarily questioning external charges for web services.'

She agreed to help and asked him what was he specifically looking for. He didn't think it was necessary to tell her too much at this stage and told her he was looking for any connection that the corporation may have with Switzerland. She accepted his rationale but knew there was more to this than what he was letting on.

'Give me about a week and a package will appear on your desk one morning,' she said.

He didn't need to ask any more questions.

When Mike returned to the office he popped into his Finance Director's office. Kev Haslett had been with him for some years. Kev wasn't Mike's choice for the position but he was over-ridden by the corporation's financial controller, who thought he'd better put his stamp on the appointment. After all the guy would have some line responsibility to him. The financial controller had since left. Kev was a pretty ordinary finance director. One day he'd break the news to him and suggest he should look for another job.

Today wasn't that day though.

Kev was a little surprised at Mike's entry. He never had much to do with him except at month end. They seemed to make a point of always avoiding each other.

'What cash have you been sending overseas in the last few months?'

The guilt was written all over Kev's face. Mike had never asked this type of question before. He looked at Mike and told him all the details were in his monthly reports. Mike acknowledged his response and asked him again where the cash had gone and who instructed him.

Somewhat puzzled Kev rather brazenly answered that he received all his instructions for cash transfers from the Chief Financial Officer and he had records to prove it. Mike thought he had rubbed Kev up the wrong way. 'Defensive asshole,' he thought to himself. Mike assured Kev that he did not doubt his integrity. All he wanted to know was where did the cash go.

Kev rumbled through his filing cabinet and removed the cash transfer file. He opened it at the summary schedule. It was a detailed document showing all cash transfers since the company commenced operations in Australia. He handed Mike the file and the summary and asked it be returned when he had finished with it.

Mike returned to his office and removed the summary from the file. He began to thumb his way through each transaction. The summary detailed the amount transferred, the date of the transaction, authorisation detail, cheque signatories and the receiving instructions. Moving through the document there was nothing unusual about the transactions in the first three months. Varying amounts had been moved out to the corporation's main bank account in Miami Florida. Mike recognised the account because that is where his monthly expense reimbursement came from. At the end of the first quarter there was a transaction transferring one million dollars to the Banque de Genève in Zurich. No name just a bank account number. Mike moved through the second quarter rather quickly and again he noticed that at the end of the second quarter another transaction for one million dollars to the Banque de Genève. He skipped to the end of the third quarter, another similar transfer. Fourth quarter, fifth quarter, the same again. A pattern was emerging. Flicking through the next few years hurriedly he turned to the last quarter of the current year and there it was again. One million dollars to the Banque de Genève!

What was all this about? He ran down the corridor and barged into Haslett's office.

'Why is there a transfer of one million dollars every quarter to the Banque de Genève in Zurich?'

Kev's face reddened admitting that he had no idea and exclaiming that he had proper authorisation for the transfers. Mike was now getting annoyed at his finance director's fence sitting. He demanded to be given an explanation as to why regular sums of money were going to Zurich. Kev felt cornered and again admitted that he had no idea and only followed the instructions given to him.

'As the principal accounting officer of this company didn't you feel compelled to know why?' Mike asked.

'No, I am not in the habit of querying instructions from the parent company.'

Mike looked at him, shook his head in disbelief expressing disappointment at the attitude of his finance director.

The matter was not going to stop there. Mike scribbled a facsimile to the parent company's chief financial officer in Florida requesting a satisfactory explanation as to why one million dollars had been transferred every quarter for the past seven years to the Banque de Genève in Switzerland.

'That'll put the cat amongst the pigeons,' he said to his secretary.

$\int$ I X

For some time now Phil had been questioning himself as to why he was still in New York. Nothing had changed over the many years he had been in town, the hustle and bustle; the smog; the city coming to a complete stand still in the peak hour traffic. How much longer could he endure the pushing and shoving on the subway? The trip to the newspaper every day was becoming unbearable.

He had started to think lately about Sydney. He remembered so vividly the cool winters and warm summers. The weekend trips to the beach, the hot sands, the gentle surf and girls in their bikinis. Sydney was a relaxed city, probably not unlike parts of America in the early fifties. How times had changed in the States.

The early morning dreams of Sydney were becoming more and more frequent. Yet New York always continued to capture his imagination. He felt very much at home here and as a journalist it was the centre of international activity. Nothing escaped New York. The thought of returning home writing gossip columns or sports editorials did not offer too much excitement for him.

The elevator concierge greeted Phil as he entered the *Herald* building and told him that the Chief wanted to see him as soon as he put his head through the door.

'Sit down, Phil,' the Chief Editor, Harry Walkinshaw demanded.

Phil threw his coat over the spare chair and flopped into the comfortable single seater. Harry wasn't in the habit of offering Phil this level of courtesy first thing on a Monday morning.

'What's up, Harry?' he questioned.

'The Boss has asked me to speak to you about the Montefiore matter. He thinks there is more to the story than meets the eye.'

'Where's he coming from?' Phil asked. 'Was he happy with the editorial I did for the paper on the sentencing?'

'Delighted, our circulation was up twenty-two per cent.'

Phil was puzzled. He knew he had not given the Boss any inclination of his thoughts or the fact that he had been undertaking his own investigation into Montefiore and Wallshot.

'What about I talk to the Boss about the Montefiore saga?' he asked Harry.

'No, he wants to keep his nose out of this one at the moment. It's best he does and if for any reason we want him to put the heavies on at a later stage, he's clean.'

Phil understood this. The Boss had every confidence in his ability to probe into the matter. Probe he would and so deep it would hurt someone badly. Phil at this stage had no idea what he was letting himself in for.

Harry shut his office door and sat opposite Phil.

'I want you to let me know what you have to date and what you need to get right behind this story? Assuming there is one of course.'

They both knew the Boss was never wrong. There had to be a story.

'You got an hour to spare?' he asked Harry. 'I've done some undercover work already. Let me fill you in. I have been in touch with a Ministry of Prisons official in Sydney to get some background on Bob Wallshot's Australian operations. The informant was more than helpful and came up with some surprise revelations. Mind you, it's going to cost you, Harry. The guy wants to visit New York. I have also done some early research on the failed Senate hearings in recent years concerning Wallshot's American operations. After the Montefiore trial I spent the day in Miami and visited Wallshot's headquarters. Took a lot of interesting pictures and had an amusing conversation with one of Wallshot's security officers.'

Phil outlined his findings in detail to Harry who was surprised how far he had gone with the investigation. He was curious to know why Phil believed that there was a story in there somewhere. Phil eased his curiosity and said quite simply that any person who could escape so many Senate hearings and come up smelling roses like Wallshot had, there had to be more to it than met the eye. Harry agreed with his assumptions.

'Have you got a game plan in mind?'

Phil looked somewhat blank at that moment.

'Game plan. What the fuck are you talking about?' he said.

'Strategy Phil, that's what I am looking for,' he chortled.

He knew Phil didn't have a rat's ass clue what he was talking about.

'What I am going to propose is that we set ourselves a time frame, decide who else we will have to help with the bum work and to what length we are prepared to go to uncover facts.'

Phil was most impressed with the authoritative tone of Harry's voice. It was exactly what he most respected in him, his ability to organise.

An outline plan had already been prepared over the weekend by Harry. He placed it on the table and asked Phil to take it away and come back in the morning with his comments.

'Mr Wallshot, it's Joseph Markowitz here.'

He paused for a moment expecting some sort of response from him. Nothing came.

'I have just received a call from Kev Haslett our finance director in Australia. He's faxing through some draft board minutes for your signature.'

BW interrupted the conversation and asked what sort of minutes did he want signing?

'I'm uncertain, but he mumbled something about having authorisation on record to cover all cash transfers out of Australia. Mike Johnson our Aussie CEO apparently has told Haslett to get it fixed up immediately.'

BW was getting annoyed with Markowitz and told him to stop worrying him with the detail and fix it himself.

'Mr Wallshot, I am not authorised to sign off on the transfers to your Swiss accounts,' he reminded him.

BW hesitated for a moment and then asked his CFO as to why he thought this had now become an issue after all these years. No one had asked for a signed board minute in the past. Markowitz had no idea why this had come to light but at the same time saw no problem.

'I don't want any board minutes relating to Swiss transfers,' he demanded.

'Remind those sonofabitches down-under who they work for.'

The phone was slammed down. The message was loud and clear. Markowitz had to put it to bed.

Markowitz pulled a couple of aspirin from his bottom drawer and threw them down his throat. It was the second lot he had had this morning. Talking to Mr Wallshot was like being let loose with a savage herd of elephants. He could never get him to see reason.

The telephone rang. Markowitz picked it up to hear BW's voice on the other end.

'Joseph, I'm sorry for the way I just reacted. I had no right to do that. You're only doing your job and I'm not making it any easier for you.'

Joseph couldn't believe what he was hearing. Was this his President on the other end apologising? He had not done this before. BW continued, telling Joseph that it was about time he visited the Australian operations.

'It's been a long time since anyone from headquarters has been down-under. Give them the feeling that they are part of the fold. You know, the usual stuff, Joseph. Put all of this nonsense to bed about board minutes and any other issues they may want to discuss.'

Markowitz had never been to Australia. In fact he had never been out of the country. 'Not quite true,' he thought. 'He had been to Belize. The corporation had a security and prison operation there. That wasn't Australia though. What would it be like to be on a plane for twenty-four hours. After all it was only a few hours to Belize. That was far enough.'

When he told his wife the news she was ecstatic. Her husband had finally been recognised by the most powerful man in the corporation. If you measured a trip to Australia as recognition then he had been recognised. BW made a point of not allowing his executives to travel unnecessarily overseas. This way he was able to keep a tighter control on worldwide operations. This suited his plans.

The next day Markowitz contacted corporate travel advising them that he had been authorised by Mr Wallshot to visit the Australian operations. Usually corporate travel would send through an executive travel pack, which had to be finalised before they would even entertain the idea of anyone travelling at corporate expense. Markowitz was surprised to hear that Mr Wallshot had actually contacted the vice president of corporate travel directly advising him to dispense with the normal formalities and push any required authorisations through his office. That was a most unusual procedure.

'When do you propose travelling?' Vice President of Travel asked.

'As soon as you can get me on a flight to Sydney,' he responded.

'I will take care of everything personally.'

He hadn't received attention like this before. Obviously Mr Wallshot's interest in his travel was the influencing factor.

Phil Black had returned to his desk to see an E-mail message from the office of the Chairman. It was a request for Phil to contact him on the direct line when he had concluded his meeting with the Chief Editor.

Amanda the Chairman's personal assistant answered the internal direct line.

'Mr Morphett's office, may I help you?'

Phil loved to hear that voice. She spoke like his late wife, gentle, smooth, confident and extremely inviting. He had known Amanda for nearly ten years. She had looked after the Chairman all that time. Amanda had been very kind to Phil over the years, particularly after he had lost his wife. She had been of great comfort and was always there whenever Phil needed some support.

'Hi Amanda, it's your favourite boyfriend here.'

She laughed.

'Phil Black, you're kidding,' she replied. 'If I didn't know you better I'd say you're doing a line for me.'

'The Boss is after me, Amanda, can you patch me through. How is he today?'

'In a good mood and anxious to talk to you,' she answered.

'Fair dinkum!' he exclaimed.

Amanda chuckled, the only ones in the office who ever used the Aussie colloquialism 'fair dinkum' were Phil and her boss, Rudy Morphett. She always maintained that as the only two Aussies on the paper they had a language all of their own.

'Come up and see me, Phil. I need to talk to you about Wallshot,' the Chairman remarked.

Smiling as he passed Amanda's desk Phil opened the Chairman's door.

'G'day Boss.'

Rudy got out from behind his desk greeting Phil with a firm handshake.

'How ya going, mate? Been a long time since we sat down and had a yarn. Need to talk to ya about that prick Wallshot. He's up to something and I can't put my finger on it', he expressed with concern. 'Harry Walkinshaw filled me in with what you had been doing. What do you think Wallshot's up to?'

Being a little surprised at the Chairman's interest in the Wallshot Corporation, Phil filled him in with everything that he had discussed with Harry earlier that morning.

Rudy was convinced that Phil sensed that there was also something not quite right with Wallshot.

'I'm going to tell you a couple of things that you will not know about and you will have to give me your personal assurance that you won't discuss them with anyone, unless I tell you otherwise.'

Phil knew his Boss well enough to know that any confidences he received would be treated as such.

'Let me fill you in. A few weeks ago Wallshot had a high level corporate meeting somewhere in Florida. That wouldn't necessarily be unusual. What was unusual though was the list of guests, Clark Ford, the Vice President of the United States; General Paul Tyler, former Chief of Defence; Paul Lowenstein, President of First Bank America; Howard Lazenby, President American Telecommunications and Fred Cohen, President of National Oil.'

Rudy hesitated for a moment whilst he took a breath.

'What do ya think of that list of who's who, Phil?'

'Quite impressed, however, ya can't read anything into that,' was his reply. 'You'd expect Wallshot to be mixing with that type of gathering.'

'I'd agree,' Rudy retorted. 'Except for the agenda.'

'What agenda?' was Phil's response.

'One item only,' replied Rudy. 'Operation Incarceration.'

What the fucking hell is Incarceration? Why would the Vice President be at that meeting?' Phil exclaimed.

By this time he was now sitting on the edge of his chair.

'Is there any more to the story?' he asked Rudy.

'Not at this stage but I understand another meeting has been arranged for this coming Sunday. The same party will be there as well as Judge Hardcastle.'

Not wanting to interrupt at that point Phil asked, 'Is that the Judge who just sentenced Montefiore to life imprisonment?'

'That's the same man, Phil.'

'Boss, I know I shouldn't ask but how the bloody hell did ya get all this guff?'

Rudy wasn't going to give out his source just yet but looked at Phil and quietly reminded him that the bush telegraph doesn't only work in Australia.

'The other thing you should know, Phil, is that these people are associated with Wallshot personally. Both Tyler and Lazenby served with him in the Philippines during World War Two, Cohen is married to his sister and it has been rumoured for ages that Ford is on the take from Wallshot. Ford incidentally worked for Wallshot before he entered politics. There are too many coincidences.'

'That's why Hardcastle is attending next Sunday's meeting,' Phil replied. 'Montefiore is a close friend of Wallshot.'

'Why was Montefiore sent to a prison run by his former boss?' he asked himself.

'Hardcastle is in Wallshot's pockets. That's it Boss!' he exclaimed. 'It's all beginning to fit. Perhaps they are moving to steer Ford into the Presidency? No it's more than that. If Wallshot wanted Ford as the next President of the United States he'd go about it differently. Besides he's left his run too late for that. The Presidential election is less than two years away.'

Phil agreed with his Chairman's rationale.

'We have a short time frame to get to the bottom of this,' he remarked to Phil. 'It may be a red herring, but I want it investigated. Shake it up and let's see what falls out. I want you to get back to Oz and do some discreet investigation into Wallshot's Australian operations. You may uncover something. We'll play it low key here, the last thing I want is Wallshot to get wind that the *New York Herald* is investigating his corporation. Australia is far enough away not to upset the apple cart. Report back to me weekly.

'By the way mate I'll square it away with Harry. Don't worry about preparing any fucking game plan for him, just get yourself booked on the earliest flight to Sydney.'

$\mathcal{S}$EVEN

M rs Markowitz was so disappointed that she could not join her husband on his very first overseas trip to Australia, particularly Australia. She had cousins living in Brisbane, cousins she had never met and in fact had never even corresponded with. They were related on her mother's side of the family.

As the limousine pulled up at the departure concourse to Miami airport she reminded Joseph again that he must not forget to contact her cousins when he arrived in Sydney. It wouldn't be long before he was on the plane. The trip from his home to the airport had been one of constant reminder, 'Do you have this, do you have that? Don't forget to do this, don't forget to do that.' The escape was near. She was so excited for him. She felt it was like losing one of her children to a summer camp.

They moved through the terminal looking for the American Airline check in counter. Joining the small queue for premier class passengers he waited patiently for his turn to be checked in.

'May I help you sir?' The attendant asked from behind the check-in counter.

'Yes,' he confirmed. 'I am travelling through to Australia.'

He handed her his tickets and passport, opening it up at the freshly imprinted Australian entry visa. The bags were identified and labelled destination Sydney. He wouldn't see them again for over twenty-four hours. The check-in attendant logged the final flight information into the computer and handed Joseph his boarding cards.

'Sir, you will be travelling on flight 802 to Los Angeles departing Miami at 17.30 hours. You change flights at Los Angeles joining Qantas flight 15, non-stop to Sydney, arriving two days later at 8.00 hours.'

Joseph's wife stepped in and questioned the attendant, 'That can't be right. It's only a twenty-four hour flight from Miami to Sydney. You have him arriving two days later.'

The check-in clerk had been through this so many times before. She looked at Joseph and asked him if this was his first international flight to Australia. He replied that it was, and asked how did she know?

'Sir,' she answered, 'travelling west to Australia, you have to cross the International Date Line, losing a day going over and on your return you pick up a day.'

She looked at his wife and facetiously asked Joseph to explain that to her. An explanation was not required. She got the message.

Last minute shopping at the airport was finalised. He looked at the terminal clock, it was five o'clock. He embraced his wife telling her he would telephone her on his arrival at Sydney. The flight had been called for all premier class passengers, he was on his way to Los Angeles.

Meanwhile, Phil Black had been hurriedly putting together his clothes for his trip to Sydney. He had to be at JFK at 17.00 hours for his United flight to Los Angeles. It was now a quarter to four, how the hell was he going to get there in time. He dived out of the apartment, yelling out as a yellow cab went past. It stopped.

'Mate, get me to JFK by a quarter to five,' shouting at the cabbie through the perspex dividing barrier.

'What the fucking hell do you think I've got on this piece of shit, turbo boosters? I'll do my fucking best in this traffic.'

Phil knew that was a New York cabbies' way of telling you that he would get you there on time. All cabbies were the same. That was a side of New York that Phil really enjoyed.

The cab arrived at JFK at twenty minutes before five. The cabbie knew that would earn him a tip. It did, Phil showed his gratitude and made off like a speeding bullet to get checked in. Fortunately the United counter was still open for his 311 flight to Los Angeles. He was the last to check in.

'Sir, you have been checked right through to Sydney, but you will have to hurry, 311 to Los Angeles is now ready for departure from gate 76.'

Why gate 76? Phil knew that it was at the other end of the airport. He ran like a man possessed arriving at the main door to the aircraft as the staff was getting ready to lock down the aircraft for departure.

'Mr Black, welcome to United flight 311, can I get you a drink, Sir?'

The timing of that question was perfect.

'Double scotch on the rocks,' he replied.

Warden Bonham had not made contact with Michael Montefiore since his first day at the Saratoga prison but he had been receiving progress reports on his welfare. He was thankful that Mr Wallshot had not telephoned him inquiring about his star inmate.

It was time for the Warden to go down to security block B and pay a visit to Michael Montefiore.

He was surprised to see him up and about. Bonham asked the prison officer to leave them for a short time.

'How are you feeling, Michael?' he asked.

'A lot easier now that you've got that goon off my back,' he replied.

The Warden expressed disappointment at what had happened and assured Michael that it would not happen again. Michael appreciated the support and reminded Bonham that he was incarcerated to carry out a mission, not to have shit belted out of him. The Warden didn't have to be reminded why Montefiore was in his prison.

'What can I get for you?' he asked Montefiore.

"I want a full list of all prisoners serving sentences in excess of ten years. I also want a copy of the design drawings for the prison,' he demanded.

'You'll have them by nightfall,' the Warden said.

Both the American Airline flight 802 from Miami and the United flight 311 from JFK touched down at Los Angeles within minutes of each other.

Joseph Markowitz had an hour thirty minutes to get himself off the flight and then take the long trek to the Qantas check-in counter. As his baggage had been checked through to Sydney he thought a brisk walk to the departure terminal would be far more refreshing than sitting on the airport bus. He had been to Los Angeles many times, and he knew that the walk was no more than about fifteen minutes. When he arrived at the terminal he looked for the Qantas business class check-in counter.

It wasn't busy. Handing over his passport and pre-boarding pass the check in attendant asked him if he had any baggage for storage. He replied firmly that he didn't, feeling quite authoritative as he picked up his passport and boarding ticket. The attendant announced that Qantas flight 15 would be departing from terminal 52.

As Joseph left the aisle he bumped into a rather untidy looking guy who was struggling with his baggage and a number of parcels. The man looked up at him and apologised for getting in his way. Joseph acknowledged the apology but before he could finish the man asked him if he was off to Sydney. Joseph reluctantly said yes, hoping to Christ that he would not have him as a travelling partner on the long haul to Sydney,

'May see ya on the plane then, mate,' came the reply.

Phil Black had finally made his way to the Qantas check in counter at Los Angeles International. He was a terribly disorganised person unable to find either his passport or his boarding card. He knew he had put them in his briefcase.

'Must have lost the bloody things on the flight in from New York.'

The girl behind the counter had been through this experience a million times.

'Did you check all of your pockets?' she replied.

Phil began to frisk himself.

'Oops!' he mumbled. 'How the bloody hell did they get in here?'

She smiled. 'I have no idea, Sir,' she replied.

'Your flight is boarding from terminal 52,' she stated. 'By the way I have been able to upgrade you to business class.'

Phil was elated. He hadn't flown business class in all of his years of flying.

'Thank you,' he replied.

'Good evening, Mr Markowitz. Welcome on board. Trust you have a pleasant flight with Qantas to Sydney. Your seat is down the right hand aisle on the left-hand side.'

Phil could never resist last minute shopping at the duty free stores, he picked up some cigarettes and whisky for himself and then made his way to terminal 52. Not surprisingly he was one of the last passengers to join the flight.

'Good evening, Mr Black, please proceed down the right hand aisle, your seat is on the left.'

'G'day mate, told ya I'd bump into ya again.'

Markowitz looked up, couldn't believe his eyes. Over four hundred passengers on board and he had to get the scruffiest.

'Looks like we are going to be travelling companions down to Sydney. My name's Phil Black. What's yours mate?'

'Joseph Markowitz,' he replied hesitatingly.

$\mathcal{E}$ IGHT

'Mr Johnston, there is a courier here to see you,' the receptionist informed him.

'What does he want?' he asked.

'I don't know exactly, Sir. He insists on handing you a package. It's marked confidential and addressed to you personally.'

He had no idea why someone would be delivering him a package shrouded in so much secrecy. He greeted the courier at the front counter to be asked if he was Michael Johnston.

'Yes, I'm Michael Johnston,' he replied.

'Do you have any identification Mr Johnston?'

'Well there's my business card. Or do you want my driver's licence?'

He wasn't amused by the charade. The courier took note of both forms of identification. Satisfied that he had the right person the courier asked Mike to sign his delivery sheet and handed him the package.

Back in his office, Mike noticed that the package had a London postal mark on the front of the envelope. Intrigued, he opened it hurriedly. 'Well good old Fran Bright, she was true to her word. A package would appear within the week with no identification as to where it would come from she said. Except the London postmark, of course.'

He flicked through the documents quickly. There were over one hundred sheets on the Wallshot Corporation. Mike could not believe that the Internet had so much information stored just on one corporation's activities. He picked up the phone and rang Fran Bright.

'Hello Fran, it's Mike Johnston. That package we spoke of arrived this morning, thanks.'

'I don't know what you looking for Mike but if you need any assistance, or even just someone to talk to, you know where to contact me.'

He felt reassured that he had an ally in Fran and acknowledged her offer with appreciation.

The following day Joseph Markowitz was arriving in Sydney. Mike could see no purpose in his visit, but as the Chief Executive Officer he had an obligation to look after him and make sure he went back to headquarters feeling as if he had achieved his goals. Mike knew he was good at that. Keep them feeling warm and fuzzy, he would always tell his senior executives. Give them more than what they wanted but don't tell them more than what they need to know. That was Mike's philosophy. It had always worked in the past and he didn't see the pattern changing with Markowitz's visit.

Haslett had arranged to pick Markowitz up from Sydney airport the following morning. Mike wanted to look through the information he had just received before Markowitz hit the deck. He did not want him to know that he had done a web search on Wallshot as he would not have time to look at the information whilst he was in Sydney.

'Interesting articles,' he thought to himself as he carefully looked through each sheet. He found out that some of the material went back to 1973. A Senate inquiry had been held then into the method of tendering for a nuclear energy site that Wallshot Corporation had won. They were in fact the highest priced tender. There were the usual gripes and moans from the unsuccessful tenderers claiming foul play. 'Nothing has changed in twenty odd years,' Mike thought. 'Why were they awarded the contract as the highest tenderer?' The Senate noted in its findings that they were in fact the highest tenderer but didn't take any further action. Their argument was that it represented the best overall value for money. Mike was aware of that particular site, as he had been there during an earlier visitation program. Wallshot still provided services to the nuclear site he noted in the document.

In 1979 and 1980 there was controversy surrounding the

tendering process for two nuclear reactor sites in the Southern States of America. The Senate inquired into those as well, with no outcome being reached.

"Wallshot Corporation suspected of arms dealings!" The headline caught Mike's eye, as he thought about his earlier conversation with George Vegas. It went on to say that the US government had reason to believe that the corporation had been smuggling arms into the United States via Belize and suggested the evidence was not concrete. There was a Senate inquiry. Mr Wallshot appeared on behalf of the corporation before the Senate, the hearing was dismissed after alleged interference from the White House.

Mike began to think that perhaps what George had told him may have been factual. Why would the corporation be involved in arms? He looked at the date of the hearing, it was less than two years ago.

He now began to thumb through more of the papers, more senate hearings, one, two, three, four, when was it going to stop? Why had the corporation been exonerated on every occasion? All this was too coincidental, Mike thought. No public corporation in Australia would come under so much scrutiny, over such a period of time and still continue to win government contracts, particularly those that were sensitive to the defence of the country. In fact no one company would be allowed to control that number of contracts as it would be considered not in the best interests of the country's security.

Was corruption within the upper echelons of politics? If there was, who was feeding them from within the corporation? Mike continued to chew over in his mind.

"Cash crisis within the Wallshot Corporation." The article read. It was just before Mike joined the company he had heard of the severe cash shortage within Wallshot. Sent shock waves around Wall Street, he recalled. Apparently it appeared to be important enough to warrant a dedicated sheet on the net. It talked about Wallshot filing for Chapter 11 bankruptcy. Audit had picked up a series of unexplained cash transfers of funds from the operating accounts of the company to a Swiss bank account. The analysts somehow or other had gotten hold of this information, spreading panic around the marketplace. The corporation would have gone under had it not been for the US Federal Government injecting loan funds into the corporation.

The government maintained it altered the payment terms on all of its contracts with the Wallshot Corporation. Timing was perfect. There was no further audit investigation into the cash transfers. Instead the audit investigators stated that they had been satisfied with the answers given by the corporation. Particular mention was made of Mr Wallshot's personal assurance that full disclosure would be given in future. All very convenient, as Mike knew that funds were being transferred quarterly out of his operations and to the best of his knowledge there had never been a public disclosure of the transfers.

He always suspected Mr Wallshot was full of shit. This confirmed it.

The more he waded through the documents that had mysteriously appeared from somewhere earlier that morning, the more he began to believe that the Wallshot corporation had questionable business ethics. These were public documents he was looking at. Transcripts from Senate hearings, newspaper articles, documents lodged with the Securities Exchange Commission. They could not all be wrong. This was not a case of not being able to see the wood for the trees. He was touching the wood.

Mike felt as though he should dispose of all the documents. They weren't of concern to him. After all he had his job to do and he was doing it well. The corporation continued to survive despite the rumours and innuendo. Why should he get his knickers in a twist, he thought. He paused for a moment. 'Course it's of concern to me!' he exclaimed, frightening himself as he spoke out aloud. The whole purpose behind getting this information in the first place was because he had been alerted by George Vegas that the Ministry of Prisons was conducting an investigation into the company which could have an adverse effect on the renewal of the company's prisons contracts. This was why Mike was concerned about all of the shit flying around on the net. Obviously someone was taking it seriously within the Ministry. He was not going to be held responsible for losing a major contract without a fight. He needed to know as much about the corporation, if not more than his client knew.

Sipping on his coffee he pondered over what he had been reading. What use was the information to him? What could he do with it? Even if he had an answer there was nothing he could do to influence future events. Should he take Markowitz into his confidence and express his concerns to him? Probably a waste of time, he thought. After all Markowitz was involved and even if he wasn't he was able to access the net as easily as Mike was able to do. Perhaps Markowitz had similar feelings and was also looking for someone to discuss these issues with?

There was uncertainty and until Mike felt a little more comfortable with Markowitz he wouldn't broach the subject with him immediately, perhaps not at all.

Mike collected the papers and carefully placed them in his briefcase, making sure afterwards that it was locked.

Haslett picked up the phone announcing his name.

'Kevvy, what time are you picking up Markowitz from the airport tomorrow morning?'

'Around eight,' he replied.

'You're taking him to the hotel firstly I presume?'

'Yes.'

Haslett's use of monosyllables got right up Mike's nose. 'Can't that idiot engage in any form of conversation,' he thought to himself.

'Good, when he's cleaned up, get him to give me a ring from the hotel. I would like to meet him and have morning tea before he comes to our office.'

'Shall I join you?' Haslett inquired.

'That's not necessary,' Mike curtly remarked.

$\mathcal{N}$INE

The 747 had levelled out at thirty-five thousand feet an hour out of Los Angeles airport en route to Sydney. The captain announced over the intercom that the plane would land in Sydney on time and that the flight would be smooth, with no suspected turbulence. He went on to say that if he or any of his flight staff could be of any assistance then contact the flight director. It was the usual burble that Phil had heard many times.

Looking at Markowitz, Phil suspected that this was his first long haul across ocean. Prior to him falling asleep he had been reading the emergency instruction card. Phil didn't like telling him he was wasting his time reading that because if this plane drops from thirty-five thousand feet no bloody emergency card is going to save him.

Dinner was about to be served. Phil wasn't about to eat alone. He nudged Markowitz on the shoulder. He sat up startled.

'What's wrong?' he exclaimed. 'Is everything all right?'

Panic was written right across his face.

'Yeah mate,' Phil said. 'Everything is OK. Woke ya to join me for dinner.'

'Oh is that all, I was hoping to sleep right through to Sydney.'

'Listen mate,' Phil interrupted, 'this is a fourteen-hour flight. Ya can't sleep that long. Besides you and I have got some serious drinking to do.'

Markowitz was not impressed with being woken and was less impressed with the fact that Phil Black wanted to engage him in conversation.

'What do you do for a living?' Phil asked Markowitz.

'I'm a chief financial officer for a major corporation.'

'Oh! You're a bean counter.'

Joseph deplored being called a bean counter and told him in no uncertain terms that he was not pleased to be called one. Phil backed off realising that he had offended his travelling companion.

'I'm a newspaper journalist,' he piped in. 'Going home for a visit. Haven't been home for ten years.'

Joseph looked surprised and asked him where he was based.

'New York,' he responded.

'Well, you haven't picked up a New York accent, for that matter you don't really have an American accent either.'

'No mate, I guess I don't. I'm an Oz.'

'Who's Oz? Your friend,' Joseph quizzed.

Phil stared at him and said, 'Look here my friend before ya get of this plane tomorrow I'm going to teach you some strine. Yeah some real Aussie phrases. Oz means Australia. Ya got it?'

Markowitz knew by now that he was going to be entertained the whole way to Sydney. In fact he'd even begun to like Phil a little.

They had both finished their meal and were sitting back relaxing with a glass of port. Phil had been telling Joseph all about how he remembered Sydney. He had no idea what Sydney was like today so he knew that he was not giving poor old Joseph a real run down on the Sydney of the nineties. When Phil left Sydney the Opera House hadn't been open for too many years. He couldn't even remember what it was like. As a journalist he loved to fantasise and he kept Joseph entertained for a long time. He assured him that there were no kangaroos down the main street and that the streets were not paved with gold. Phil was surprised to hear Markowitz tell him that he never expected to see kangaroos in the main street. Phil felt somewhat ashamed that he had underestimated the knowledge of his companion.

'What newspaper do you work for?' Joseph asked.

'The *New York Herald*.'

'Rudy Morphett's paper,' Joseph remarked.

'That's right. You know Mr Morphett?'

'Not personally. However, I did meet him once at a function in New York. He was a guest speaker. Spoke about honesty in politics and how he was strongly opposed to corporate interference in the political arena.'

Phil knew how passionate his boss was on that subject. Believed that shareholders elected boards of directors and the people elected Presidents.

'What did you think about his speech then?' Phil asked.

'I was moved by his sincerity,' Joseph responded. 'My boss has completely the opposite view. He believes that corporate America should influence all sectors of government.'

Phil was interested in his remark and asked him who his boss was.

'Bob Wallshot,' he replied. 'You've probably heard of him? He runs the Wallshot Corporation. The largest New York listed services group in the world.'

Phil listened in stunned silence. Did this guy know why he was travelling to Australia, he thought for a moment.

'What's wrong, Phil? Have I said something to offend you,' Joseph asked.

'Um, no! No quite the contrary I was just momentarily reflecting on my earlier days in Sydney. Guess the port is taking its toll,' he replied.

The last thing Phil wanted to do at the moment was to give Joseph an inkling that he had more than a passing interest in Wallshot.

'You said you worked for the Wallshot Corporation, didn't ya? Been there long?' he asked.

'No,' Joseph replied, 'only eighteen months.'

'I'm a pretty nosy journalist always interested in a good story,' Phil proudly boasted. 'Tell me what your corporation does? More importantly what does a CFO do in an organisation like yours? This could prove to be a good feature story for the *Herald*'s weekly financial rag,' he remarked to Joseph.

He had set the challenge up for Joseph. It wasn't difficult he thought. The next few hours were to be an opportunity to bleed as much information out of Markowitz as he could.

Joseph's historical knowledge of the Corporation was really quite remarkable.

He began by telling Phil a little about the corporation's founder, Bob Wallshot. His early life, leaving home at an early age, enlisting in the Second World War and serving with General Douglas MacArthur in the Philippines. He went on to talk about his post military career with the NSA and the frustration he endured continually battling the bureaucracy. During 56 he quit the NSA and formed his own small time investigation and security corporation. Phil was listening intently as he understood that it would take weeks to undertake this type of research back in the States. Joseph continued. 'His first security contract was looking after the winter beachside mansion of Paul Lowenstein of First Bank America. Paul Lowenstein, Phil murmured to himself. It had to be the same guy that his boss Rudy Morphett had referred to earlier? He was one of the powerbrokers that had met with Wallshot in Florida recently? There had obviously been a long relationship between those two.

Joseph was on a roll now, leaving out very little on Wallshot's background.

He continued to tell Phil, about the small contract awards he picked up along the way, until he got his big break in the early sixties. Wallshot apparently called in a favour from an old Marine buddy, who happened to be an adviser to the President. He was awarded several major contracts to provide a range of services for a number of power stations around the country. 'The corporation still has those contracts today, mind you most of them have been converted to nuclear power. After that his business just went from strength to strength. Government contracts just fell in his lap. No one else in the States had the infrastructure to undertake the tasks that he was capable of taking on.' Joseph was very proud of his boss's achievements and no doubt by now thought that he must have impressed Phil, as this was the first time on the flight that Phil had actually remained silent.

He went on to say that the corporation then moved into financing and managing airports, military bases, prisons, oil and gas installations, federal government buildings, communication centres and now had a stranglehold on most of the country's public hospitals. 'It is the only corporate provider of a wide range of facility services to governments in America and most other parts of the world!' Joe exclaimed.

'Stop just for a minute,' Phil asked Joseph. 'I need to go and visit the head. Get us a couple more ports, mate?' he requested.

'Aren't you concerned, Joe [Phil found Joe a lot easier to say than Joseph] that you work for one man that has this type of control over Government?'

'What do you mean?' he asked Phil.

'Your boss provides a wide range of services to nearly every strategic government site in the States. That's what I mean.'

'I hadn't really thought about it that way. Yes, I guess you are right.'

'As Chief Financial Officer, what is your job?' Phil asked.

'Putting it quite simply, my job is to make sure the cash keeps rolling in. Christ, if I don't Mr Wallshot is the first to get on my back about it,' Joe remarked.

'What do you do with the cash that comes in, Joe?' Phil was quick to ask.

'Come on Phil, you know I can't disclose that sort of information to you. Anyway it's not important.'

Markowitz closed further discussion on that subject.

Phil sat back in his seat, contemplating what Joseph had said, wondering how he could extract more information from him without raising suspicion. He decided not to pursue the conversation any further at this point. Maybe in a few hours time.

The lights in the cabin were dimmed. This was probably the best opportunity for both of them to get a little shuteye before their arrival in Sydney.

The first chance Warden Bonham had to read his Chief of Security's report on the Montefiore assault was the day following the reprimand of his senior officer. He read through the report carefully noting and highlighting the pertinent facts. Mr Pike had not left anything out. He strongly believed that he had the right to discipline Montefiore in the way he did and that if confronted with the same situation again he would not hesitate to react in exactly the same way. This concerned the Warden as this was no ordinary prisoner. He could not afford to have one of his officers treating prisoners this way.

Bonham had to get him out of Saratoga. Pike could thwart pre-arranged plans.

Pike was called into the Warden's office. The Warden acknowledged receipt of his report advising him that he was disturbed by its contents.

'I will not tolerate this type of action in my jail,' he told Pike. 'You leave me no choice but to impose the maximum penalty for such damning behaviour. You're dismissed and I want you to hand in your keys and any other company property in your possession to the deputy warden immediately. He will escort you off the premises.'

The Warden telephoned his deputy and advised him of his decision.

It was no use Pike threatening the warden with recrimination. He had handled worse cases than Pike during his career. He was determined to get Pike off site immediately.

With Pike's removal it took away the barrier between him and Montefiore. That line of communication had to be left open.

An announcement echoed through the plane's cabin, advising all passengers that the aircraft was less than two hours from Sydney's international airport. It startled Phil, who had hoped that he would have slept until the end of the journey. He looked across at Joe and was surprised to see him already awake.

'Did ya have a sleep mate?' he asked.

'I dozed for half an hour,' he responded.

'They'll be serving breakfast shortly,' Phil snapped. 'I'm going down to have a wash and shave. Order me a hot breakfast if the girls come along whilst I'm away please.'

'Leave it with me, Mate,' he said laughingly, as he left Phil with his little bit of Aussie slang.

Phil returned about a quarter of an hour later to find his breakfast waiting for him.

'Where are you stopping in Sydney?' Phil asked.

'The Victoria Hotel, in Elizabeth Street,' he replied.

'Before you go back to the States I'd like to catch up with you and perhaps have a spot of dinner one night. How do you feel about that Joe?' Phil asked inquisitively.

'Look here's a contact telephone number. I'm not certain as to what plans have been put in place over the next ten to fourteen days, but I'm sure we can squeeze a dinner in,' he remarked to Phil. 'In fact I look forward to it,' he said. 'Ring me towards the end of next week.'

Phil had every intention of ringing him. He wasn't going to let this big fish get off the hook. He knew he had been blessed. Next week would suit him, as it would give him time to undertake some research and contact a very good journalist friend of his who he hadn't seen for some ten years.

'Ladies and Gentlemen, this is the captain speaking. We are preparing for descent into Sydney airport, would you please bring your seats into the upright position and make sure your safety belt is secured.'

The fourteen-hour flight from Los Angeles was nearly over.

$\mathcal{T}$EN

The explosion was deafening, leaving a gaping hole in the high security perimeter fence, large enough to drive a centurion tank through. The alarm bell rang immediately as the second explosion tore through the central control room, taking out all of the prison's communications and leaving four prison guards dead.

Panic had set in. It was dark and pouring down with rain. The night shift supervisor had been killed in the control room explosion. There was no leadership, no direction. Prison guards ran from the cell-blocks, seeking refuge in the open compound. They had no idea as to whether or not there was going to be another explosion. Safety for themselves was their main priority, leaving the prisoners locked up in their cells unattended.

They had no way of immediately contacting the outside world as communication lines had been completely severed in the first explosion.

Suddenly there was a volley of gunshots coming from security block B.

Prison officers in the compound fell to the ground. What the hell was going on? Had the prisoners in block B freed themselves and broken into the automatic rifle locker. There were more gunshots. Prisoners had broken free from their locked cells and were running in an orderly fashion towards the centre of the compound, led by five others cloaked in black sweatshirts, dark trousers and hooded balaclavas. They fired their automatic rifles into the now dispersing group of prison officers that had been lying on the wet ground in the prison compound. They fired indiscriminately, wounding some of the officers and killing others. This was carnage at its worse.

The compound was alight. A large military style helicopter was descending out of the rain filled low cloud cover, its spotlights directed on its landing target. Two others hovered above. One by one they landed. Their rear doors opening fully. The prisoners and their captors lifted themselves hurriedly on to the choppers. The doors shut and the craft disappeared within seconds into the grey murky night.

The time lapse from the first explosion to the departure of the last chopper had been no more than eight minutes.

The aftershock from the explosion had been felt over twenty miles away. It had been enough to alert the state police and the emergency services. The first police vehicle had arrived at the scene. The police officers were horrified to see the extent of the damage, with fires blazing furiously in three sectors of the prison. At the time of the explosion the police vehicle was on patrol at the other end of the town. They had seen the ball of fire in the southern sky project itself some two hundred yards into the black wet night. They had no idea where the explosion was, but assumed it was in the vicinity of the prison. Before they had left their vehicle to investigate the officers contacted their base to give them a detailed account of what had happened at the prison. Police communications immediately dispatched all available police, fire and state medical services.

As the wounded prison officers lay on the wet ground they could hear the wail of the sirens as emergency services swung into full action, all destined for the Saratoga prison.

Police officers arrived in droves, immediately taking up positions at strategic points within the prison and on the perimeter.

Medical services had arrived at the site. Paramedics drove their vehicles through the main security entry to the prison compound. Police officers supported now by a small number of prison guards directed the vehicles to an open area in the main compound. Bodies were strewn everywhere. Some still, some showing form of life. Paramedics were quick to respond, checking pulses to determine who was alive and who was dead. Covers were thrown over those suspected of being dead. The others were given immediate medical attention. Stretchers moved in, the wounded were hooked up to drips and temporary bandaging applied where necessary. The first of the wounded were placed in the ambulance. Sirens heralded their departure for the Saratoga General Hospital, where emergency hospital staff were on stand-by to take in the first of the wounded.

67

Fire crews had positioned themselves around the central administration building, the communications centre and on the western side of security cell block B. The fires were out of control. Fire hydrants were activated and the long tedious task of pumping millions of gallons of water on to the burning inferno had begun.

Prison officers were still in disarray. No one at this stage knew how many had been killed, wounded or even how many had actually deserted their posts with no intention of returning. It was chaotic.

State legislators had been saying for years that private prison companies were not as well equipped to cope with an extreme emergency situation, as well as the state run prisons. They maintained that public system management was not driven by contract performance and profit greed. The events of the night would support that argument and the call for privately managed prisons to return to state control would figure high on the political agenda in the near future.

The Warden, pulled up at the main sally-port, stalling his vehicle as he hurried to get out of it. He quickly looked around. Perimeter fencing down, administration and communications ablaze and pillars of black smoke pouring out of security cell block B. That summed up the extent of the damage at this point.

The Warden summoned the chief of police and the head of emergency services to a dry room at the rear of cell-block A. His office had now been totally gutted.

'What's the current state of play?' Bonham asked Chief of Police Mark Burrows.

He replied, 'My officers have cordoned off and secured all cell-blocks except cell block B. Remaining prisoners from cell block B have been removed to the medical centre and are being doubled up. Emergency maintenance services are working on providing a temporary fix to the perimeter fence,' he continued. 'Whoever staged this event knew exactly what they were doing!'

Bonham asked Burrows, if he had any idea who was behind the escape.

He replied in the negative, and went on to say that until they had the site totally under control no investigation could take place. Bonham agreed with his observation.

Head of emergency services, Phil Cardonis, had been on the two-way during the conversation between the warden and the chief of police. He was being de-briefed by his crew.

'What do you make of the extent of the damage, Phil?' Bonham asked him.

Phil paused for a moment.

'Warden, cell block B and the communications centre could not be saved. The administration building is down as to seventy per cent,' he remarked. 'Mainly the western end of the building.'

Bonham asked him if there was a likelihood of the fire spreading to other parts of the prison. Phil said no providing the rain keeps bucketing down the way it is now. 'It has been your saving grace. Without it,' he went on to tell him, 'you would have lost the whole centre.'

'Casualties, can you give me an update on what's happening at the moment, Phil?' Bonham asked.

'We haven't got an accurate count at this stage warden, but our latest position confirms forty-two dead. There were thirty-five prison officers and seven inmates. Injuries, last count including inmates, twenty-seven,' he stated.

Warden Bonham slumped into his seat. 'Sixty-nine and possibly still rising you're telling me?' he asked Phil.

'That's correct, Warden,' Phil confirmed.

Bonham then turned his attention to Mark Burrows.

'Do you have any news on the escapees Chief?'

'The latest information that I can give you Warden,' Mark replied, 'is that we have placed the State on full alert. The helicopters they escaped in have to put down somewhere. They'll avoid the normal commercial landing strips. Hopefully some citizen out there will notice something unusual and report in. We have placed a hundred thousand dollars reward for anyone that gives us information that leads to an arrest. If the choppers leave Florida, then we've got little hope of identifying them.'

'Do we know how many prisoners escaped?' Bonham asked the chief of police.

'Your officers have to confirm the numbers yet, but it appears ten,' Burrows replied.

'Do we know the names?' the warden asked.

'Yes I have a list with me.'

Bonham grabbed the list off the chief of police and scrolled through the names. Montefiore was there.

Bonham was quietly relieved. The planned escape had been a success. Montefiore and his hand picked group of lifers had all got away. He knew where they were headed.

The state authorities wouldn't locate them in this weather. By now they were over the Straits of Florida on their way to Belize.

Light was appearing in the eastern sky. Dawn was finally arriving. The full extent of the damage to the Saratoga private prison would be known shortly. The rain had eased and the large black clouds were disappearing over the western horizon. It was going to be another hot steamy day.

Warden Bonham, moved out of his temporary headquarters and walked unescorted to the damaged perimeter fence. Temporary sheets of high tensile mesh wire panelling had been carefully locked into position, with four-foot high rolls of razor wire strapped to the top. Several prison officers stood on post duty, armed with semi automatic rifles.

He then moved across to the administration block. There was hardly anything left. Charred furniture lay sprawled over the ground, surrounded by blackened paper. Cinders were still cracking and popping as the last of the morning rain disappeared.

His office and all of his lifetime memorabilia had disappeared. He was saddened by the discovery. As he approached the communications centre, a lump appeared in his throat. Thirty-five good officers were slain here last night, he thought. 'I hope this mission Mr Wallshot is worth all of this?' he asked himself. In the few months he had been at Saratoga, he had come to like and respect a good number of the officers who served under him. Which ones had been killed or injured he was not certain. Perhaps he didn't want to know.

'Where's cell-block B?' he asked one of the remaining fire officers as he rolled up the last of the hoses.

'Couldn't save any part of it, sir,' he replied.

Bonham noticed the approximate location of where Montefiore's specially constructed cell and compound had been located. He walked across through the ashes, looking for any possible evidence that may not have been destroyed in the fire. None was evident.

On returning to his office, the temporary telephone that had been installed was ringing. He picked it up.

'Warden is that you?'

He recognised it immediately. It was BW.

'Mission accomplished?' he asked.

'Mission accomplished,' he replied.

The phone went dead.

The Deputy Warden, had rounded up all the remaining staff and prison officers, assembling them in the prison gymnasium.

His head slightly bent, he nervously faced his audience expressing his deepest concern and shock at the loss of so many fine officers. He went on to say that a tragedy of this magnitude had never been contemplated and more importantly because of that we were not ready, he told everyone. He asked for the full support and cooperation of every remaining serving officer and requested that they put this tragedy behind them and move forward to a new tomorrow. His speech didn't stir any enthusiasm. A number of the officers turned their backs on the deputy warden and began to walk out of the gymnasium. They'd had enough. Maybe they would feel differently tomorrow. Tonight though twenty-five per cent of their colleagues had been gunned down in cold blood without reason.

Warden Bonham was summoned to the State legislature offices.

When he arrived he was ushered to the second floor, where he was met by the State's Chief Inspector of Prisons, Bob Minosky.

'What a fucking mess Warden,' he exclaimed. 'My arse is right on the line over this debacle.'

That was the last thing that Bonham needed to hear.

He replied in an extremely assertive manner, 'Get off my back on this one. You owe me, remember.'

Minosky backed off for the moment. Bonham was taken into a large meeting room where there was a sea of faces appearing up at him. Some he recognised. Harry Quinn from the State Governor's office; Marcia Hinds from the Prison Action Reform Group; Phil Cardonis from Emergency Services; Mark Burrows, Chief of Police and two others whom he had not met.

'I think you know most of the people sitting around the table, Warden?' Bob Minosky remarked. 'You will not know these two gentlemen. Let me introduce you to Special Agents Lingard and Kowalski. They have flown in from Washington this morning. The President is demanding an immediate investigation into this whole sordid act of terrorism. It's not going to help his re election chances. He wants the terrorists caught immediately or someone's going to fry.'

Threats of this nature didn't faze Bonham.

Special Agent Kowalski was the first to speak, outlining his understanding of the chain of events that occurred the previous night.

'I understand Warden, that it has now been confirmed that at the last count there were a total of fifty-one persons slain and thirty-five are seriously injured. Do you agree with the tally?' he asked.

Bonham answered, 'Yes, regrettably.'

Kowalski went on to say that he had reason to believe that the group who planned the escape of Montefiore and the prisoners were in fact the same group that escaped from Miami Airport after the destruction of that South American 747 sometime ago.

Bonham looked surprised. He knew that his information was accurate, but did not give any indication to the agent that he was correct.

'How do you know it is this group?' Bonham asked.

'We've had information passed to us. We have reason to believe it's reliable,' Kowalski responded.

'Who else would be interested in helping Montefiore escape from Saratoga?' Lingard chirped in.

'Warden, during Montefiore's brief stay under your careful eye, did you notice anything unusual about his activities?' Lingard asked.

Bonham was beginning to feel the heat. He resented Lingard's cynical comment and had no hesitation in bringing it to his attention. Lingard ignored his remarks.

'Did he have any unusual behavioural patterns?' Lingard asked. 'Did he place any undue pressure on any prison officers?'

'Mr Lingard, you have full access to all of our records,' the Warden remarked. 'You will find a fully detailed report on all of Montefiore's activities.'

'Including your discussions with him, Warden?' Lingard exclaimed.

'I resent that comment, Mr Lingard. All activities are recorded,' he re-stated.

'Gentlemen, let's cut out the crap. We have to work together on this. I have to get back to the President within the next two hours to give him an update,' Minosky said.

'Warden, would you clear it with your corporate headquarters? We want access to Saratoga tomorrow morning at sunrise,' Kowalski asked. 'We have been authorised by The President to take full operational control of the institution until further notice.'

The hair on Bonham's neck stood up. He deeply resented the attitude of these two special Dick Traceys. He didn't want the FBI poring over his institution. Christ, what would they find! One small thing could link him to Montefiore.

Bob Minosky looked at Bonham asking for his confirmation that he would allow the FBI to move into Saratoga tomorrow, reminding him of his responsibilities under the terms of the contract. The warden reluctantly agreed to refer the matter to corporate head-quarters, knowing that even they could not refuse a presidential demand.

It was now late in the afternoon, the meeting had finished. A plan of action had to be in place before the Feds moved in to the institution tomorrow.

Bonham wondered where Montefiore would be now. His first drop off was Havana, then pick up a charter for Belize. How long would it be before the Feds knew of his whereabouts? They obviously had a super-grass passing information to them. Who the blazes was it? He rolled it over in his mind time and time again.

$\mathcal{E}$ LEVEN

The early morning sun had just pierced the Pacific horizon as Phil Black made his way out of the Sydney International Terminal. The sudden burst of cold air took his breath away as he reached down to his bag to get his sweater. It had been a hot summer in the States and he had forgotten what the New York winter was like. Sydney may have been cool this morning, but in no way would you compare it with a mid winter day in New York.

Phil was somewhat overcome with his early morning arrival. He stopped for a few minutes, looking around at the activity. People were busily moving in and out of the terminal, taxis and buses loading passengers for their various destinations. The scent of the gum trees jogged his memory of the splendid days he had spent with his wife many years ago in the outback. He was back home. It had been too long.

'Can we give you a lift into the city, Phil?' Joe Markowitz asked.

'No thanks,' he replied. Joe had caught him by surprise. 'I'll call you next week, Joe, and arrange that dinner appointment.'

'Look forward to that,' Joe said.

The taxi pulled up suddenly. 'Where to mate?' the swarthy taxi driver snapped.

'The Old Sydney Hotel at The Rocks mate. No hurry, I've got all day,' Phil informed him.

How things had changed in the last ten years. Phil distinctly recalled that the only trip from the airport to the city was down O'Riordan Street. Not any more though. The taxi whisked around the back of the airport and a few minutes later was on the freeway into town. The skyline was so attractive. He remembered the Sydney tower, it had just been completed when he left. There were new buildings surrounding it, ones that he had not seen before. The taxi turned into Oxford Street. He was amazed at the change in culture, the street was a hive of activity, coffee shops and cafés were doing a brisk early morning trade. Sydney, he thought, had become an international city.

As the taxi turned into College Street, he felt a lump in his throat. He could see through the morning mist the War Memorial sitting majestically in the middle of Hyde Park. He recalled the Anzac remembrance services he used to attend on April 25th each year. The playing of the last post reminded everyone there of those gallant Australians who had died in war. He held back the emotion for a few moments, but was not able to disguise the few tears running down his cheeks. The taxi approached the hotel. Phil had plenty of time over the next few weeks to reminisce. All he wanted to do now was to check in, shower and catch a few hours sleep.

Kev Haslett had been on time to pick Joe Markowitz up from the airport. It was the first time that they had met each other and there was a little caution on both sides.

It was an important day for Haslett, meeting one of the senior executives from corporate office. Markowitz was also somewhat reluctant. He never felt at ease with strangers at first. He knew it would take a few days to get to know this guy.

'Did you have a good flight?' Haslett asked.

'Fine,' Joe replied.

'Mike Johnson would like to meet up with you this morning over a cup of coffee. Is that OK?'

'Look forward to meeting with Mike. I've heard a lot of good things about him in the States,' Joe bragged.

Haslett found it difficult to strike up a conversation with Markowitz and was relieved to see his hotel coming into view as they turned into Elizabeth Street.

The concierge was there to greet him and help unload his luggage. Joe leaned across to Kev and said that he would like to have a chat with him later this evening, asking him if he could join him for an early dinner. Haslett accepted.

'Fran Bright?' Phil asked

'Yes, this is Fran Bright. Who's calling?' she responded.

'Fran, it's Phil Black! I just arrived in from the States. Said I'd look you up next time I was down-under. Well here I am. It's been a long time.'

'Oh Phil, how great to hear from you. Where are you at the moment?' she asked.

'At the Old Sydney Hotel, down in The Rocks,' he replied.

'Sit tight. I'll be down in an hour. Give me time to put on the war paint. We'll have lunch. I know a great quiet little spot, where we can talk. That OK with you?' Giving Phil little opportunity to make other arrangements. He was delighted to be able to share some time with her.

He hadn't seen Fran for over ten years. Had she changed much in that time? He knew she had never been married, although at one stage she was engaged to a young journalist who had been murdered in East Timor whilst on assignment there. Fran had thrown all of her energies into journalism after that tragedy. Reckoned she never had time for men. Phil hoped that time hadn't caught up with her. He shouldn't talk, he thought, time had not been kind to him.

Phil had been sitting patiently in the foyer of the hotel for about thirty minutes, waiting for Fran's arrival. He looked around and noticed several women entering the hotel, but none reminded him of Fran Bright. He glanced again at the front door and saw an attractive red head wearing tight fitting blue jeans and an oversize light blue sweat-shirt. She entered the foyer and made her way to reception. 'She cuts a pretty good shape,' he thought and took no more interest, until he heard someone at reception ask for Mr Phil Black. He got up out of the chair and bounded towards the front counter.

'Fran! Fran, is that you?' he asked.

She looked around quickly and answered, 'Is that you Phil?

They enthusiastically shook hands for several seconds, both extremely pleased to see each other after so many years.

Fran had the bell-hop park her car and then took Phil by the arm, leading him out of the hotel to a restaurant around the corner where she had made arrangements for lunch. They were escorted to a corner table, well out of view of all the other patrons. Fran had been here many times before. The maitre de knew she wanted to be alone with Phil.

'Fran, you look absolutely fantastic,' Phil remarked. 'You haven't changed a bit since we last saw each other.'

'Tell me more, Phil, a woman at my age needs this type of encouragement,' she replied.

Fran wasn't a person that would normally get caught up in this type of flattery. She believed that if a man splurged this type of bullshit, he was only after one thing. She wasn't a one night stand. With Phil it was different. He had been a sincere and good friend for a long time.

They enjoyed a cold bottle of Hunter Valley Chardonnay over lunch and talked about old times, past friends and colleagues and how life had generally been treating both of them. There was an inexplicable feeling that neither of them had experienced for a long time. The banter made them feel young again. The afternoon was dragging on, but who cared. This was a treasured moment for them. The conversation finally got around to what Phil was doing in Sydney.

'Wallshot Corporation has brought me down here,' he replied.

Fran looked at him and remarked, 'I knew the information I'd had passed on to you recently would be put to good use.' It was Fran who had put him onto Peter Bent at the Ministry of Prisons. 'How are you going with your investigation?'

'Since we last spoke,' he replied, 'a lot of water has gone under the bridge. There is no doubt in my mind that Wallshot is up to something big in the States and it involves his Australian operation in some way.'

Fran hesitated for a moment. 'Did you know that Wallshot Australia is a client of mine?'

'No, I didn't. You had not mentioned that last time we spoke,' he replied.

'Phil, I can't say too much. I have to protect my client's confidentiality. You know what I mean. I'd like to set up a meeting for you and me to meet the Chief Executive of Wallshot's Australian operations next week. His name is Mike Johnston. Would you be agreeable? I think you'll find the meeting beneficial.'

Phil did not have to read between the lines. He knew that Fran was giving him a loud and clear message. He graciously accepted and told her he would be available at any time to meet with Johnston.

The afternoon had flown, Phil was beginning to get a little weary, jet lag had caught up with him, or perhaps it was the wine, fun and laughter.

'Can I see you again Fran?' Phil asked rather boyishly. It had been so long since he had asked a lady for a date.

'You don't think I'm going to let you escape me that easily, do you Phil,' she replied. 'We still have a lot to catch up on.'

'What about dinner and a show next week?' he asked.

'Look forward to it,' she said

'I'll make the arrangements. What about next Tuesday?' he asked.

'Can't wait to see you again,' she responded.

Fran walked with Phil to the hotel. She had had a great afternoon and she knew from Phil's behaviour that he had enjoyed himself just as much. She put her arms around his neck and pulled him in tight.

'It's been great to catch up with you,' she remarked. 'Off you go, I'll see you next Tuesday. By the way I'll leave a message as soon as I've teed up a meeting with Mike Johnston.'

Mike Johnston had left a message at the Victoria Hotel that he would be there at midday to meet up with Joseph Markowitz.

It would be the first time that the two had met. Mike had no real idea as to why Markowitz was in Australia, he was astute enough, however, to realise that senior executives don't fly all the way from Florida unless there was an agenda. How much could he confide in this stranger? he thought to himself. He needed to ask some pretty direct questions about the cash transfers to Switzerland and hopefully seek some explanation for the adverse publicity the corporation was always on the receiving end of.

Arriving at the hotel right on noon, Mike was surprised to be welcomed by Joseph Markowitz just inside the main front entry of the hotel.

'You must be Mike Johnston?' Joe asked.

'Yes,' he replied.

'I'm Joe Markowitz,' he exclaimed, putting his hand forward to greet Mike.

'How did you know who I was?' Mike asked.

'My personal assistant showed me a photograph of you before I left the States,' he remarked. 'The photo doesn't do you justice though. You are much younger than I would have imagined.'

Mike thought, nice guy. He's off to a flying start.

'How was your flight?' Mike inquired.

'Good. Hell of a long way from Florida isn't it,' he exclaimed.

Mike agreed.

There was a lounge section in the hotel foyer, which was quiet at the moment. They sat down and began talking about Joe's flight and his first impressions of Sydney. The conversation continued for the next fifteen to twenty minutes.

'What's the purpose of your visit, Joe?'

'The President, Mr Wallshot, asked me to pay you guys a visit. It's been a long time. He didn't want you to think that headquarters had forgotten you,' he remarked.

Mike knew that wasn't the reason. He also knew that this was not the right time to tell him that either, so he decided to let the conversation flow and see where it went.

'Appreciate your interest, Joe. What are your plans whilst you are here?' Mike asked.

'I would like to spend some time getting to know you, Mike. Have a look at your financial controls, visit some of your clients and take a look at a couple of your contract sites. There is no set agenda. As I mentioned earlier the President just asked me to get to know you guys.'

Mike was beginning to feel a little uncomfortable with Markowitz. He was not playing a straight bat. What was even worse he was doing a lousy job of trying to convince Mike that he was here on a goodwill mission.

'I plan to have dinner with Kev Haslett this evening Mike. Trust you don't mind? I'll be spending a bit of time with him over the next few days. Would like to get to know him a little better,' he remarked.

Mike agreed that he should spend some time with him and then asked him to have a closer look at some of the cash controls and procedures, particularly those relating to overseas cash transfers.

'I'll do that,' Joe replied. 'Any particular concerns you may have?' Mike realised that he had now set one agenda item in play.

'We have an exposure with cash transfers to Switzerland,' he stated.

'In what way?' Joe asked.

'The way I see it is that funds are being milked from the Australian operations to a private bank account in Geneva.'

'That's ridiculous,' Joe nervously replied.

'It's not ridiculous. Fund transfers to Switzerland are not going through the corporation's balance sheet. Someone is milking funds and disguising them in the financial records.'

'That's a pretty serious accusation you're making, Mike. You are not thinking it may be Haslett are you?'

'Now that is a ridiculous statement,' he pointed out to Markowitz. 'Haslett is only doing as he's told,' not pushing the topic much more at that point.

'Mike, I'll look into it whilst I'm here. I have no doubts that everything is above board,' he exclaimed. 'Let's talk further, later in the week.'

Markowitz, knew he hadn't handled the outburst too well. That was the reason why Mr Wallshot sent him down-under, to keep the local guys in check and remind them he was paying their salaries. Mike Johnston had got on top from the outset of their meeting. This was going to be difficult to turn around.

Mike asked to be excused. He had a luncheon engagement with a Ministry official to discuss the renewal of the prison contracts later in the year.

$\mathcal{T}$ WELVE

There was a gentle knock at the front door of Judge Hardcastle's palatial West Palm Beach condominium.

'Good morning, sir. My name is Mark Duvall. I'm here to see Judge Hardcastle. Mr Wallshot has asked me to take him to his ranch.'

'I'm Judge Hardcastle,' he replied. 'You are a little early. I'll be ready in a few moments. Where are we going to?' he inquired.

'Mr Wallshot's ranch. It's about two and a half hours from Boca Raton airport.'

'Are we going by plane?' the Judge asked.

'Yes, sir. Mr Wallshot's Citation is fuelled and ready to go.'

Judge Hardcastle was surprised to hear this as he had imagined that Wallshot's ranch was situated somewhere near the Everglades. A two and a half hour flight could put him in any one of a number of states. Why did Wallshot want to see him? This went over in his mind for the umpteenth time. Hardcastle had met Wallshot several times over the years and enjoyed a modest business relationship with him. It was not close, but they had mutual respect for each other. The association had certainly got closer since the Montefiore trial. To have him picked up at his front door and flown by Citation to his country ranch was more than the mark of a casual business relationship. What does Wallshot want of me? he thought to himself.

The stretch limousine eased its way on to Interstate 91, cruising effortlessly towards Boca airport. When they arrived at the airport, Mark showed his security clearance to the airport security officer and proceeded to the southern end of the port, where the Citation was standing. It was an immaculate craft, gleaming white with the letters BW emblazoned in gold on the rear fuselage. An attractive hostess made her way from the plane and opened the rear door of the limousine.

'Judge Hardcastle?' she asked.

'Yes,' he replied.

'Welcome on board. We have a two hour thirty-minute flight to South Carolina, where we will be met and escorted to Mr Wallshot's ranch.'

The Judge at least now knew which state he would finish up in. But that was all. He would just have to wait and see what else unfolded. It wasn't going to be a long meeting as he had told Wallshot previously that he had to be back in town that night as he had a pre-trial hearing to attend in Miami on the Monday morning.

The jet roared into the deep blue sky and immediately turned sharply into the northern sky. They were on their way to South Carolina, expecting to land around three.

The hostess, whose name was Emily, had been selected to attend the flight today as she had a background in law and was seen as a natural fit for Judge Hardcastle. During the flight to South Carolina, the Judge was taken well care of. Pre lunch drinks were served, followed by an exquisite meal of smoked salmon, avocado and caviar. Coffee and tequila was served later. Someone had obviously gone to a lot of trouble to find out what the Judge drank, as not too many people knew that he enjoyed a tequila after a meal.

The Citation was preparing to land. Emily sat next to her charge, leaning over to check that his seat belt was secured. It had been many years since the old Judge had a sweet smelling young woman that close. The soft Dior fragrance captured his imagination. What would it be like to feel the tenderness of such beauty once again. Emily knew that she was turning him on, that after all was part of her job.

'Where are we landing?' he asked Emily.

'Westchester private airport,' she replied.

'How long is the drive up to Mr Wallshot's ranch?'

'Around thirty minutes, I believe.'

'Will you be accompanying us?'

'No, but I will be on the return flight,' Emily insisted.

The Citation touched down without a bump. Judge Hardcastle was amazed at the performance of this craft. It had been luxuriously appointed, with its own twin bedrooms, separate bathing compartment, full kitchen and lounge accommodation. Of course the craft wouldn't have been complete without the monogrammed initials BW appearing on every panel inside the plane.

Harry Selwyn, the Wallshot Ranch Manager, was at the airport in his Jeep Cherokee to pick the Judge up and take him off to the ranch. Harry was a craggy old individual, weather beaten, but apparently one of the finest ranch managers in South Carolina. At least that's what Harry had the Judge believe. Interesting character, had a lot of stories to tell. Within no time at all the Cherokee had pulled up at the front gates to the ranch, the security doors groaned slightly as they opened. The group of security cameras had picked up Harry's Jeep and honed in on the faces of Harry and the Judge, before opening the steel security gates.

The Jeep moved slowly up the winding path climbing at the rate of about one hundred feet a minute. The driveway was carpeted in a red loose stone, complimented by hundreds of mountain ash hugging the side of the road, their branches rocking gently in the mountain wind, touching the side of the Jeep as she picked up speed along the mountain drive. The ranch house came into view just several minutes after clearing the security gate. The mountain behind the ranch house provided a magnificent foil for the timber and stone elongated home.

The Judge got out of the vehicle and looked behind him to see one of the most magnificent sights that he had ever experienced. The valley below was lush green, covered by a carpet of mountain pines with a fast flowing river inter-twined between them. The air was crisp, the day clear.

'Judge, how good to see you. Welcome to Buena Vista Ranch.'

'Why thank you BW. It's a pleasure to be here. I appreciate the opportunity to see this magnificent country.'

'This is my fortress, Judge. This is where I strategise my corporate moves. It gets me away from the hustle and bustle of city life. At my age I need this type of retreat. The young bucks in town will own all this after I've gone.'

The Judge had not seen BW for some time and was surprised to see how much he had aged in that time. He guessed that he was in his late seventies. He had lost a considerable amount of weight since he had last seen him, which had taken its toll on his facial features. The face was drawn and heavily lined. How long would it be before the young bucks, as he put it, moved into the ranch permanently?

'Judge, I'm a troubled man,' he echoed. 'I've seen a lot of change in my lifetime and I'm not happy with the way our country is moving forward. I intend to do something about it before I die. That'll be my legacy to this great country of ours. Come inside the house, it's time you and I had a long talk.'

BW placed his arm around the Judge's shoulder escorting him through the front entrance of the ranch house and into the large open plan sitting room.

The Judge sat down facing the large open window, which displayed the magnificent view that he had just witnessed a few moments ago. It was breathtaking. Next to him was a large wooden framed oak chair, ornately carved with the American Eagle at its head and the uprights carved with the faces of America's heroes. He noticed Eisenhower, MacArthur, Patton and even Custer. BW is a through and through patriot, he thought to himself.

When he sat in his chair, it dwarfed his ageing body, but he sat upright, leaning forward slightly, looking down at the Judge. This was his position of power.

The room was a gallery of his life. There were business leader awards, medals of honor presented by the French and Polish governments; front cover pictures from *Forbes 500* and the *Bulletin*. There were numerous photographs of him shaking hands with world leaders including Gorbachev, Thatcher, Reagan and Chou en Lai. The eastern wall of the room was covered with photographs of him and various members of his executive at the official opening of every one of the contract sites that were managed by the Wallshot Corporation. The Judge's eye caught a particularly large photograph in the middle of the room, which he instantly recognised. It was BW and Michael Montefiore. He estimated that there would have been well over two thousand different types of pictures in that room alone. Bob Wallshot was one of those unique individuals who felt very passionately about everything he did and what it stood for. The Judge recognised that he had a unique ability to influence change.

'Can I get you a drink, Robert?'

'Yes thanks, I'll have a coffee and tequila.'

'Marina, have you met Judge Hardcastle?'

'No sir, I have not.'

'Judge, this is my very close personal assistant, Marina. Marina, this is Judge Hardcastle.'

'Delighted to meet you.'

'Likewise,' the Judge said.

'I'll get you a coffee and tequila, Judge.'

There was a moment of quietness as BW shuffled himself into a more comfortable position.

'You must be wondering why I've asked you up here, Robert?'

'The thought had crossed my mind,' he replied.

'Let me give you some background. Since World War Two we have seen extensive social and political change in this country. Change, I'm of the opinion, has not necessarily been in the best interests of everybody. Republicans have moved more to the left, whilst those cock sucking Democrats have taken the middle ground. Business has suffered, capitalists and the risk takers are losing out. The poor and ethnic classes are benefiting more today from social service support than ever before, the cost of keeping our health and education programs is beyond our means. The country's balance of trade is the worst we have seen in over two hundred years. Businessmen don't want to invest in America's future, they want to take their funds offshore, investing in third world countries. I haven't worked my guts out to see America disappear down the drain in the next few generations. I'm determined to put a stop to this. Now!' he exclaimed.

The veins in BW's neck had reached exploding point. He was visibly exhausted following his tirade.

Marina entered the room bringing the Judge his coffee and tequila. She looked at BW with anger written all over her face, upset that he had got carried away once again with his passion for a new America. She had heard it many times over recent years and knew that he would not settle until he had done everything in his power to bring about change. She looked at him and asked him if he was all right. Could she bring him a drink. He didn't answer her. Just sat silently awaiting a reaction from Judge Hardcastle.

The Judge was taken back by his menacing attack on the political and social structure of America. Many people in this country were of the same opinion and had been for generations. Why the rhetoric, he thought.

'BW, I share a number of your sentiments,' he began. 'As a Judge appointed to the Federal Court, I have been strongly opposed to many changes that have impacted the judicial system of this country. The indiscriminate political interference into the judicial system at all levels can no longer be tolerated. I cannot comment soundly on the economic turmoil we are going through, but I can confidently state that no political party in recent times has had the balls to address the problems. Your sentiments are not yours alone and are not necessarily shared by only businessmen. I am aware of many leading Judges who have expressed the same views privately, not publicly, perhaps that is the problem.'

BW's judgement in inviting the Judge to his ranch this Sunday had been vindicated. He thought that the Judge's passion for a new direction for America had been spawned this day, high in the mountains of South Carolina.

'Let's take a walk through the garden,' he suggested.

The late afternoon was turning cool and the mist was beginning to cover the valley floor. The evening scent of summer flowers spread through the garden blending with the fragrance of the moist laden pine trees. BW and Judge Hardcastle had hardly spoken a word since they had both shared their moments of great passion inside the ranch house sitting room.

'I have a dream for a new and better America, Judge,' BW said unhesitatingly. 'You have been very outspoken in recent times about the future of America. Your sentiments are mine. I would like you to be part of that dream. A group of prominent political and business figures met recently to orchestrate a change. I brought them together. We plan to meet again shortly. I would like you to join us.'

The Judge was uncertain as to what his dream for change was, even less certain as to how he saw change being brought about. One thing he was certain of though, Bob Wallshot could move mountains and probably one of the only corporate figures in America that could achieve a goal of that magnitude. He obviously understood that more would be forthcoming at the next meeting. He agreed to accept BW's invitation.

The evening had drawn in. The judge said to BW that he must return to Florida.

'Harry Selwyn will drive you back to the Citation. Thank you for joining me at Buena Vista today. I look forward to our next meeting.'

The Jeep made its way down the mountain road, with neither Harry or the Judge speaking a word all the way.

What change was BW talking about? Who were the other parties involved? The next meeting was going to be the crux. He mulled it over in his mind time and time again.

The Citation was fuelled and ready to depart. As promised Emily was there to greet him. Her radiant smile and warmth would just finish off a very interesting and exhausting day for Judge Hardcastle.

$\mathcal{T}$HIRTEEN

Lukas Mueller had been head of international banking operations for Banque de Genève for nearly ten years. He had been born on the outskirts of Zurich to a wealthy banking family. His father had been the President of the bank at one time, but had now retired to the northern region of Italy. His son, Lukas, had gained considerable international experience in banking and at one time had spent three years in Miami working for Banque de Genève.

It was during his stay in Miami that he first came across the Wallshot Corporation. The Corporation had been looking to retire some short-term burdensome debt. No one in America would take them on. The asset backing of the business was not sound enough to re schedule a one hundred million dollar loan facility over a ten year period.

Lukas Mueller had been made aware of their plight and arranged through an intermediary to discuss the matter with Mr Wallshot direct. He recalled vividly Wallshot's initial response, which was to reject the notion of dealing with foreign banks in favour of American born and bred banks. Wallshot was not in touch with reality, Mueller thought at the time, and went to a lot of trouble to demonstrate to Wallshot that the ten major banking conglomerates in the States had a high percentage of foreign ownership.

The final wash-up was that after having seen Mueller some two months earlier, he invited him back to his office to discuss a financing deal. Mueller was not surprised. The word had got around the banking community in the States that Wallshot Corporation was a high credit risk. The second meeting did not travel too well at first, with Wallshot demanding that existing debt be extinguished, being replaced with an increased facility at two percentage points lower than the existing structure. Mueller quietly laughed at the preposterous suggestion that the Banque de Genève would even consider such a proposal.

Negotiations continued for several days, without much headway being made. Wallshot was becoming desperate. Mueller knew this. All other options had ceased. Banque de Genève was his last chance. Bankers for his existing loans were expecting repayment in forty-eight hours.

The break-through finally came. Mueller offered a deal, which at first Wallshot found brash and insulting, but after talking through the proposal with his Board came to the conclusion that it had merit.

Banque de Genève offered to repay the outstanding one hundred million dollars to the existing bankers, roll over the facility for a ten year term and provide a further stand-by facility of fifty million dollars to be utilised for future business expansion only. Current prime rate plus one quarter of one per cent rate would apply. This was in fact was one per cent better than the current facility arrangement. The deal was conditional. Lukas Mueller would take up a position on the Board. The corporation would re-assess its international corporate tax planning, using the bank's international tax affairs office out of Zurich. The corporation would also establish a banking arrangement with the bank's headquarters in Zurich. The deal was accepted.

Not long after the arrangement had been consummated, Lukas Mueller was transferred to the bank's headquarters in Switzerland, to head up international operations.

The settlement clerk knocked at Mr Mueller's office door.
'Enter,' he bellowed. 'What do you want?'
'Sir, I need to talk to you about Wallshot's accounts with the bank.'
'Shut the door and sit down.'
Mueller was still on the Board of the Wallshot Corporation and was the only Swiss executive authorised to deal with Wallshot's accounts.
'Mr Wallshot has transferred fifty million dollars from his trust account to the Geneva branch of the Bank of Iraq,' the clerk nervously stated.
'What is the balance of the trust account?' Mueller asked.

'Seventy-five million dollars. I brought the matter to your attention, Sir, as it would be normal for you to authorise such transactions firstly.'

'You have done the right thing. I will speak with Mr Wallshot on the matter.'

Mueller was irate. 'The blithering imbecile,' he yelled out to himself. 'What is he trying to do?'

He picked up the phone and dialled Wallshot's direct connecting line with the bank. Wallshot answered the call.

'My office has just informed me that you transferred fifty million dollars to the Bank of Iraq. What are you doing? That is suicide.'

Wallshot was taken off guard. He was not used to being spoken to in that tone of voice and reminded Mueller to whom he was speaking. Mueller was not fazed about the threat and demanded an explanation.

'I secured a great deal on a shipment of guns from the Iraqi government. They were American arms captured during the Gulf War. The dealer has agreed to ship them to Belize. This will go close to completing our stock-pile of weapons.'

Mueller had calmed down somewhat by now and began to think more rationally. He was the only Board member who was aware of Wallshot's plans and had encouraged him to develop a complex network of offshore companies and tax havens to launder his surplus US dollars through. They had been operating successfully for over seven years. This deal however could bring the whole affair to an end.

'You cannot deal with Iraqi companies,' Mueller reminded him. 'Your government has banned American companies from dealing with the people of Iraq. If this leaks out we are all finished. Incarceration is dead. Swiss regulations compel us to notify the central authority of any US financial dealings with the Government of Iraq.'

This touched a nerve in Wallshot's throat. Incarceration was his dream. It could not fail. What had he done? Had he acted impulsively, letting a deal stand in the way of common sense? That was not his style.

'I was aware of the Government ban on dealing with the Iraqis, but I was confident that with Swiss money being used and shipment to Belize guaranteed it would escape the attention of the authorities.'

Mueller sat quietly for a moment, thinking as to how he was going to untangle this mess.

'Cancel the arrangement with the Iraqis. I will stop the funds transfer. I want you to explain to the Iraqis that a new deal will be struck within the next twenty-four hours. Same delivery arrangements will apply. Never do a deal like this again unless you have firstly cleared it through me,' he reminded Wallshot.

Mueller had to turn this around in the next twenty-four hours. He proposed setting up an arms dealer out of South Africa to buy the equipment for delivery to Sierra Leone, where they could then be forwarded to Belize. This was an escape proof hatch for him. He was going to have to pay a premium, but that was a small price to pay to save Incarceration from total destruction.

Peter Bent had agreed to meet with Phil Black after work that evening. They agreed to see each other in small bar in the back of Darlinghurst, which Peter frequented from time to time. Peter gave him the address.

Phil was running a bit late. That wasn't unusual, he used the excuse to Peter that he had been distracted by gays walking up Oxford Street. He laughed knowing exactly what he meant.

'Thanks for meeting with me, Peter.'

'My pleasure, I needed to put a face to a telephone conversation.'

'I met up with Fran a couple of days ago. I assured her that I would not disclose her as the source of my contact with you. I hope you understand that and I give you the same undertaking. One thing about journalists, Pete, they might stretch the truth when reporting, but they never divulge their source.'

'Any further developments since we last spoke, Pete?'

'Interestingly there are a couple of developments,' he replied. 'The Minister of Prisons has taken particular interest in the renewal of Wallshot Australia's contract renewals later this year.'

'Explain that to me?'

'Well, it's not usual for a minister to take an interest in departmental policy on contract renewals, that decision is left to the Department. The Department wants to screw a better deal out of Wallshot, reckons they've been ripped off for the past five years. Threatening to pull the contracts off them if they don't re-negotiate their price downwards.'

'I can understand that, Pete. That's good business.'

'Don't disagree, but when a minister directly intervenes suggesting to the department that contracts be renewed on the same terms and conditions, then that leaves him somewhat wide open to criticism.'

'Oh! I see where you are coming from. You're saying that old man Wallshot has probably threatened to expose him if he doesn't roll those contracts over.'

'You've got it in one, Phil. The other development is the Minister's trip to the States. He and his wife have been invited as special guests of Bob Wallshot. The Premier is up in arms about that one, obviously concerned about his Minister being compromised. The press will have a field day on that one if he tries to buck the Premier. That round is not finished yet. I'll keep you posted on developments.'

Phil asked Peter if he would like another beer. He didn't refuse. Iced draught beer straight out of the keg had fond memories for Phil during his early days as an up and coming young journalist in Sydney.

'When are you retiring from the Department, Pete?'

'No plans in place yet, but I would hope to be gone by the end of next year.'

'I need your help, mate. Can you hang around for a while longer, I plan to do an exposé on Wallshot Corporation and I need an inside man in the Department.'

'How can I help?'

'Keep you ears to the ground. Any information you can dig up on that bloody corrupt minister of yours and what he's doing with his brown bag takings would be helpful.'

'I'll keep my nose close to the ground for you. I owe Fran a favour. By the way don't forget you said you'd look after me next time I visit New York. I'll hold you to that.'

Phil had not forgotten and assured Pete that he would be looked after.

Peter and Phil rolled out of the Darlinghurst bar just after midnight.

'Can I give you a lift, Phil?'

'Not in your bloody condition, I would sooner walk.'

'Long walk.'

'Mate, I've got all morning. Besides you never know whom you might bump into. My luck might change down Palmer Street.'

'Your luck will have to change if you think you're going to find yourself a whore in Palmer Street. All the brothels were closed down years ago. William Street's the go now.'

'Good, I'm off to William Street then.'

'Talk to you later, Phil.'

Phil was only fooling around with Pete. The last thing on his mind tonight was mixing it with a street walker. He finally made the hotel a little after two. Bed was only a few minutes away. He was ready to crash.

'Could I come around and see you this morning, Mike?' Fran asked. 'I need to talk to you about a journalist acquaintance of mine. I think you'll find it very interesting what I have to tell you.'

'Come now,' Mike replied.

In less than ten minutes Fran was sitting in Mike Johnston's office anxiously waiting to discuss her conversation a few days earlier with Phil Black.

'A journalist friend of mine, arrived from the States a few days ago,' she began telling Mike. 'I've known him for over twenty years. We worked together at the *Sydney Review* and he left for personal reasons and made his way to New York. This is his first time back in ten years.'

Mike was a little bewildered, as he had no idea why Fran would be discussing the background of an old colleague with him. He listened patiently.

'Some months ago, Phil contacted me,' she continued. 'He told me he was doing an article on privately run prisons in America and wanted to talk with a local ministry official about the Australian experience in private correctional management. I put him onto Peter Bent. You know Peter don't you Mike?'

'Yes, I know Peter well. Good guy.'

'Well, Peter and Phil really hit it off. Peter became a source of valuable information for him. However, what I didn't know at the time was that Phil was not doing a cover story on private prisons, in fact he was researching the Australian operations of the Wallshot Corporation.'

'What would be his interest in that?' Mike asked. 'I can't see why we would be of interest to a New York journalist.'

'Sit back, Mike, here comes the crunch.'

Mike was now becoming quite fascinated as to where this conversation was going and sat back in his chair to hear more from Fran.

Fran continued again. 'Phil's boss has asked him to do an exposé on Bob Wallshot.'

'What! What exposé?'

'Rudy Morphett believes that. . .'

'Sorry to interrupt Fran. You are you talking about Rudy Morphett the American newspaper magnate?'

'The same man,' she replied.

'Oh! go on.'

'OK. Rudy Morphett believes that Bob Wallshot and a group of prominent American businessmen and politicians are planning something mighty big. He has no idea what it is, but he's confident that whatever happens it is going to happen soon and it could have major repercussions.'

'Fran, why are you telling me all this? I've got enough of my own bloody problems with Wallshot. I don't need to listen to this crap.'

'I don't think it is crap. That's why I'm telling you this, because both you and Phil are drawing the same conclusions about the corporation. There are things not quite right. Remember the Senate hearings, the Swiss bank transfers, the arms purchases? Don't lose sight of these,' as she reinforced her point with Mike.

Mike got the message. He was up to his eyeballs in his own little private investigation on Wallshot. He asked Fran to keep on going.

Fran was only now beginning to warm up. She was as excited about the whole sordid affair as Phil was.

'Have you heard of Michael Montefiore?'

'Yes, as a matter of fact I have. A good friend of mine rang me from the States recently and told me that this character Montefiore was an ex corporation employee and had been involved in the sabotage of a 747. Apparently he was jailed for life.'

'Hold it there! Mike. Listen to this,' she went on. 'He was jailed for life, in one of the corporation's jails. What's more, part of the prison burnt down last week and Montefiore and a bunch of other inmates escaped and haven't been heard of since. Montefiore apparently is a very close friend of Bob Wallshot.'

Mike asked Fran to pause for a moment. He asked his secretary to get them both a cup of coffee, he needed a breather.

'Fran, I need to talk to this Phil Black. Can you arrange it?'

'Phil has already indicated he would like to meet up with you. When are you free?'

'Just set a time and place. I'll make myself available.'

'Well not Tuesday tonight, he's promised to take me out for dinner. Can you make it tonight? Say dinner at 7 at my place. That way no one will see us all together.'

Mike agreed. He was looking forward to the opportunity of sharing notes with Phil.

He was in for a busy week. Joseph Markowitz was still on his mind. Had not heard from him since his coffee meeting on the day of his arrival. Haslett would no doubt be taking good care of him, jumping under every rock that he can hide himself under would be his style, he thought.

Mike asked his secretary to get hold of Markowitz and set up a dinner for the Tuesday night.

$\mathcal{F}$OURTEEN

Special agents Lingard and Kowalski and a team of special enforcement officers had been at Saratoga for a few days.

They had taken up residence in a makeshift mobile, the nerve centre they called it. Most of the inmates had been transferred to other institutions, those that remained were housed in Cell-Block A. The block had not been damaged during the terrorist attack and with doubling up was capable of holding two hundred and fifty six prisoners. Additional temporary security had been installed in the block's central control pod. Fortunately all cell door-locking devices were still functional. Guard numbers had been beefed up to cater for the increased loading.

Warden Bonham felt like a prisoner in his own institution. He had limited authority whilst the FBI were there. He resented this and did very little to make their job any easier.

Lingard and Kowalski had full operational control, until their investigation was over.

Teams of special enforcement officers were assigned to various duties. Prison personnel had to be interviewed to determine what they knew about the attack. Other groups had to investigate the reasons as to why the perimeter was breached and why were prison officers not capable of repelling such an attack. The investigation was going to be exhaustive.

Both Lingard and Kowalski had not endeared themselves to the staff at Saratoga. This slowed down the investigation.

Lingard asked Warden Bonham to join him at the temporary headquarters.

'This investigation is not going as well as we would like it to go, Warden. We need your cooperation. The quicker the job's done, the sooner you can get back to re-building the prison. You get my drift,' he roared.

'This is the first time since you've been in Saratoga that you have asked for my help. Why should I bend over now?'

'You ain't got a choice Warden. The President is breathing up my ass for results. I don't like the President of the United States putting that sort of pressure on me. Either you toe the line or I'll bust your ass.'

The Warden felt some sympathy for the lousy job they had to do. He had been an enforcement officer himself for most of his life. Mind you, on the other side of the fence, private sector, not with the Federal Agency.

'We'll cut a deal. I'll give you all the help you need, providing you get off my site in the next seventy-two hours. You can have access to all remaining records and my officers will co-operate fully with your special agents. Do you agree?'

Lingard had little choice. He wanted the President off his back.

'I'll agree,' he stated.

'Tell me what you've got so far?' Warden Bonham asked.

'We've got good reason to believe that the attack was orchestrated by the same men that Montefiore used to blow up the South American Boeing 747. What we are not certain of is how they knew where the weakest point on the perimeter was. Someone with that knowledge must have passed in onto them. You got any ideas on that, Warden?'

'Any one that had been involved with the design and construction of Saratoga would have known that,' he stated confidently.

'Not anyone organises the escape of the country's most wanted inmates,' Lingard replied. 'You can do better than that, Warden.'

'Where do your suspicions lie?, agent Lingard.'

'Montefiore of course,' he replied.

'How the hell could Montefiore tell the terrorists where the most impregnable point is?'

'Montefiore worked on the security design of the prison, didn't he?'

'He did, but that's not answering my question.'

'Montefiore got a copy of the plans to the outside.'

'Ridiculous,' Bonham shouted.

'Someone had advanced knowledge on the weakest point of the perimeter, how the central control functioned and knew the exact layout of where Montefiore was housed. The others that escaped with Montefiore were no accident. It was planned! It was deliberate! Putting it bluntly, Warden, someone in you organisation, has helped Montefiore mastermind this mass escape.'

Warden Bonham was not impressed with Lingard's conclusions.

They were right about one thing though, Montefiore had planned the escape from the inside. He knew the FBI agents were only speculating at this stage, but it concerned him greatly that they had reached this conclusion.

'If your suspicions are correct, Lingard, who helped Montefiore?'

'I'm not certain of that. Could be any one of a number of people. Could be you, Warden!'

That sent shudders up his spine as he tried not to show any reactionary signs to the comment.

'I'll ignore what you said Lingard. You're frustrated that you have not found the answers. Quite frankly, I think your judgement is being clouded by the fact that you are under pressure from the President. You want a quick answer and you don't care a damn what you destroy on the way through.'

'I apologise, Warden, the remark was uncalled for.'

'Well let's get on with it then. What further information do you want from me?'

'Let me have a comprehensive background on all of your employees. I've got seventy-two hours to check them all out. I propose doing federal and state checks, fingerprints, Interpol, anything that will totally eliminate them or give me the answer I'm looking for.'

'I'll have that information with you within the hour,' the Warden stated.

'I also want full checks done on yourself, Warden, and every one of your senior officers.'

Senator Harry Groves, Democrat Senator from Ohio had been in his chamber when his assistant informed him that Mr Rudy Morphett was on the telephone for him.

'Rudy, you old son of a gun. How are you going?'

'Seen better days, Harry.'

'Harry, I need to talk you about a little matter that keeps getting in my way.'

'Give it to me straight, what can I do for you?'

'How many Senate hearings have you chaired over the last ten years involving the Wallshot Corporation?'

'Every hearing that has been conducted into his sordid affairs.'

'How many have you concluded, Harry?'

'None of them became public record. You know that.'

'Why?'

'White House interference. I can speculate, but I'm not elected to speculate. The White House office has arranged to close down every hearing. They've used their republican numbers on the committees to beat me every time.'

'Do you think the President has had anything to do with the close downs, Harry?'

'God damn it, no! It's that running mate of his, Vice President Clark Ford.'

Rudy Morphett knew Harry Groves before he was a state senator. He used to work for one of Rudy's mid western newspapers, before he stood for the Senate. Rudy always maintained that he was a lousy journalist, but would make a good senator. He hadn't been wrong. The trouble with Harry was, he was too honest and took his causes too far.

Failure to get hard evidence against Wallshot Corporation over the years had not pleased his Democrat colleagues, they believed he was not a finisher. Wallshot had been a prime target for the Democratic Party for years. They always maintained that it had been his influence that had kept them out of The White House for most of the last twenty years. Harry Groves had not delivered his head for them.

'Harry, could we get together shortly? I need to talk to you more about Wallshot. I've got a theory and I need your help.'

'It must be a bloody big theory if the country's most important newspaper magnate is interested in Bob Wallshot. I'll help you,' he said.

'Good. When are you in New York next?'

'Next week. I'm attending the International Grain and Stock Feed conference at the United Nations Centre.'

'Keep a night free. Let my secretary, Amanda, know where you're staying. I'll have my driver pick you up. We'll meet at my Central Park apartment.'

'See you next week,' Harry finished up.

$\mathscr{F}$IFTEEN

The price of freedom for Montefiore did not come cheaply. He had now been in Belize for several days. He neither enjoyed the place nor the company he had to share his new life with. After leaving Saratoga, the helicopter with its cargo of human flesh had made only one stop en route to Belize. In Havana they put down for a few brief moments to transfer to an awaiting chartered DC3.

Belize sat comfortably between the Guatemala and Mexico borders, a small country previously a British protectorate until it gained independence. The country had its own democratically elected government and like most newly formed independent nations, needed to develop a growing economy to ensure its survival into the future. Banking and the registration of international shipping, were its two major commercial focuses. A number of American and European corporations were using Belize tax minimisation schemes. Representative offices of major international banks were being established in the capital, Belize City.

The government of Belize was attempting to develop a burgeoning industry in honest commercial practices. Countries like the United States and Britain were pouring investment dollars into the country as they had confidence that the country would provide a sound link between themselves and future trading opportunities with the South American continent.

The Wallshot Corporation used Belize primarily as a tax haven. It had also found some unscrupulous dealers in the country that had agreed to offer a safe haven for their arms dealings. Montefiore's presence in Belize was not a coincidence. He had been there many times over recent years, spoke the local dialect and was well connected with a number of prominent locals.

After their arrival from Saratoga, Montefiore and his fellow escapees were shipped by covered truck to a remote part of the country some forty miles from Belize City. Their home for the next few months would be a group of timber huts nestled deep in the rainforests of Belize. Power to the camp would be provided by a battery operated generator, food would be basic camp rations, no alcohol, no women and death to anyone that left the camp were Montefiore's orders. He described it as sheer hell. Montefiore had a mission and he had a short time in which to complete that mission.

Operation Incarceration was his passion. It would be given his total focus.

The first night in the jungle camp had been an unpleasant one. The escapees that had left Saratoga had come voluntarily. Montefiore had outlined his expectations to them during his imprisonment. They all knew and understood what was expected after their arrival in Belize. Since then attitudes had changed. They were now free and saw this as an opportunity to go back on their commitment and disperse into the Belize community, free men. Montefiore left them alone on the first night. He knew they needed to burn some energy, get rid of their frustration. Tomorrow was another day.

The door to the weatherbeaten timber hut was kicked open. The stench from the sweating escapees literally filled the air. Montefiore stood in the doorway quietly with a semi automatic rifle tucked under his arm. Standing alongside him were two ugly looking individuals, dressed in jungle greens, also carrying semi automatic rifles. The escapees stirred and looked towards the door. They screamed abuse for being disturbed so early. The sun hadn't yet risen. Montefiore was going to stamp his mark on this uncouth, filthy bunch of rabble.

'Get your asses off the floor,' he yelled at them. 'I want to see you outside this hut in sixty seconds.'

He stepped back to let them pass. They moved slowly, he waited patiently giving them the full sixty seconds to obey the order. He looked at his watch, the time had expired. Two of the escapees had not moved off the floor of the hut. Without a word being said, Montefiore's accomplices moved swiftly into the room, bent over, picked them up and dragged them into the compound kicking and swearing.

Montefiore had to establish control immediately. There were two wooden stakes hammered in the ground. His men dumped the escapees between the stakes and began to tie their hands and feet to them. It was dark outside at the moment but in less than one hour the sun would be rising and by mid-day it would be overhead. The heat would be intolerable. There they would stay until sunset. If they died it was too bad. If they lived, Montefiore knew they would obey an order next time.

Eight men stood in a bunch facing Montefiore. They had not said a word at what they had just witnessed. They knew they were not here for the ride. The man had expectations of them and he would be looking for them to deliver.

'The next man who disobeys an order will be dumped from a helicopter in the middle of the Belize rain forest. Believe me, gentlemen, when I said this was going to be tough, it's going to be tough. Over the next twenty-four hours you are going to tell me all about yourselves. I'll tell you why you are here, what your chances of survival are and give you an outline of our mission. You have no option to leave,' he went on to say. 'You are here for the duration. You will listen to everything I have to say, you will obey my orders and you will never question my authority. Do you understand?'

The escapees all stood silently, wondering for a moment if they would have been better off in Saratoga. They looked towards Mickey Ryan, for a signal. Ryan shuffled his feet a few times, looking downwards, sensing that the group was looking to him for direction. He faced Montefiore.

'We have given you a commitment. We are all better off here than being in Saratoga. None of us would have seen daylight ever again, had we not escaped. We have a chance here. We'll toe the line, including the two on the ground if they survive the day.'

Montefiore had established his presence. Now to get them trained and organised.

'Ryan, you seem to carry some weight around here. Tell me who you are and why you were in Saratoga?'

'Michael Ryan's my name. I prefer Mickey. Irish background. Served with the IRA until I came to this country. Caught three years ago by the cops for extortion. Threatened to blow up a British Airways Jumbo. Serving thirty years on the inside for the crime.'

'What experience have you had in making bombs?'

'I told you, Mr Montefiore, I served with the IRA. Bombs are second nature to us Irish.'

'Who's next? You over there!'

'Bobby Moxham. I'm not Irish. I blow the fucking Irish up. Come from the Bronx. Got caught by the Feds on armed robbery. I have had no experience in bombs, but I'm the best gun-man you'll ever see. Been in Saratoga for three years. Still got twenty-two years to go.'

A small guy at the back of the group shot forward, yelling out he was next.

'My name is Jerry Springer. Serving forty years for kidnapping and murder. That's one kidnapping and seven murders. Was on death row for five years. The Governor pardoned me. I don't want to go back to jail. I'll die out here fighting for you Mr Montefiore.'

'They call me Hoss Abrams. I was going to die in jail. I blew up a Miami subway. I can move anything for you.'

'What about you, Shorty?' Montefiore asked, pointing his finger to the escapee standing behind Ryan.

'There's not much to tell. I was in Saratoga for life. Electrocuted my wife and mother in law. I'm known as Pete Quinn. I was an electrical engineer, before I fell out of love with my wife. Couldn't stand a bar of her and her mother. Made life easier for myself. Did away with them both.'

'Who's next?'

'I'm Chuck Parzsos. Worked with the New York Mafia. I was a hit man. The Feds picked me up fifteen years ago for blowing up a federal building. I say I was innocent. They say I was guilty. Who am I to argue, they found me guilty. Put me away for thirty years. I have the best fingers in the country. I can make any bomb sing and dance.'

'Parzsos and I have been in jail for the same time. They call me Fuzzy. Don't know what my other name is. You just call me Fuzzy. I'll do anything for you Mr Montefiore. Just don't ask me why I was on the inside.'

'You, sitting over there in the shade. Who are you?' Montefiore asked.

'Everyone knows me,' he boasted. 'I was the one who robbed the

Federal Bank in Washington back in eighty-eight. I managed to take three of the staff hostage. Had to shoot them later. The President wanted me dead. Well I ain't dead yet.'

'What's your name?'

'Oh! Tony Cranna. Anything else you'd like to know, Mr Montefiore?'

'Nothing else now, Cranna,' he replied.

Montefiore looked at the two on the ground.

'If they survive the day, we'll learn all about them as well,' he thought.

There were ten in the group, all hardened criminals. This was a lifetime opportunity for them to secure freedom. They had all the skills that Montefiore was looking for.

Bomb experts, firearm specialists, all with guts and determination.

His team was now fifteen strong, not including himself. He had the ten new recruits and also his own squad that he had worked with many times over the years. They would form the backbone for Operation Incarceration.

'You'll be split up into two groups of four. The other two will join you if they make it. Before you leave here you will learn all there is to know about terrorism and bomb manufacturing. When you're finished you will be sent out on assignment. Any questions?' Montefiore asked.

'I have a question.'

'What is it Ryan?'

'Who are you working for and what do you intend doing with us at the end?'

'Good question, Ryan. It's not important that you know whom I am working for, as far as you're concerned you work for me. When you've completed your training I'll tell you then what your assignment is. Split into two groups of four. Two of my men will accompany each group. Training starts today.'

$\mathcal{S}$IXTEE EN

Fran had done well for herself. Her apartment was on the eastern side of Elizabeth Bay overlooking the harbour. She had a magnificent view of the Sydney Harbour stretching through to the Sydney Heads.

It was just on seven as the security intercom chimed. She answered, it was Phil Black.

'Come straight up Phil.'

She was at the elevator to greet him.

'Come inside. I'll pour you a drink. What will you have?'

'Double scotch on the rocks.'

She poured herself a gin and tonic and then took Phil by the arm, leading him out to the apartment balcony.

'How's your day been?' she asked.

'Haven't got too far,' he responded, sounding rather disappointed.

'Let's see what Mike's got to say when he arrives. I think you'll find him very helpful. You'll like him.'

The chime went again. This time it was Mike Johnston. Fran asked him to come up.

'Mike, let me introduce you to a very good friend of mine, Phil Black.'

'Pleased to meet you, Phil.'

'Likewise. I've heard a lot about you from Fran.'

'What can I get you to drink, Mike?'

'Beer will be fine, thanks.'

The three of them sat on the balcony talking about the view and how much Sydney had changed over recent years. Mike maintained it was one of the finest cities in the world, but he would have been hard pressed to have a different view anyway. He loved Sydney. Phil, was not going to disagree with him as he was a Sydney-sider, although America had been his home for the past ten years, he was taking a real liking to the new Sydney.

They idly chattered on for over an hour. Fran had been in and out taking care of the evening meal. She also knew it was important to give them breathing space. They needed to get to know and trust each other.

'Dinner is ready. Phil, will you do the honours and serve the wine please?'

Phil obliged.

Fran had gone to a lot of trouble. She had prepared roast duckling served with an orange glazed sauce. There was a terrine of piping hot potatoes, snow peas and pumpkin. He had forgotten the last time anyone had cooked him a meal like this.

'Fran tells me you out here doing some research on my parent corporation, Phil?'

'Yeah, what started out being an interest is now becoming an obsession. Have you any idea what Wallshot has been up to over the years, mate?'

'I'm just beginning to find out it seems. Fran was giving me an outline last week of what you had uncovered. Frightening isn't it. How much truth is there in the stories you've heard, Phil?'

'More and more I'm convinced that Wallshot is up to something and he is going to show his cards soon. Whatever he is up to involves a lot of prominent people.'

'Where does Australia fit into the scene?'

'Don't know yet. I was hoping you and I could share some thoughts this evening.'

'I'll do what I can to help you feed your passion for Wallshot.'

'By the way, did Fran tell you that I've got one of my American trumps in town for a week or two?'

'No she didn't but let me guess who it might be?'

'Jeezus, if you knew that I would begin to worry.'

'Oh, let me see. His name wouldn't be Joe Markowitz, would it?'

'Christ, how the hell did you know?'

'I'll put you out of your misery mate. I flew into Sydney with him. We sat next to each other on the plane.'

'That explains it then.'

'Interesting guy. He gave me a mountain of information. He'll be helpful. I'm having dinner with him shortly.'

'I didn't know that, Phil.'

Mike was now beginning to feel quite comfortable with Phil. Their common interest in Joe Markowitz was encouraging, although Mike felt a little differently towards him than Phil did. Still, Mike hadn't sat on the plane with him for fourteen hours, he thought. Joe could turn out to be quite a surprise package.

'I indicated to Fran that I had been concerned that my finance director had been shipping funds to Switzerland on a regular basis for some years,' Mike began to tell Phil. 'I only found out about a couple of weeks ago. I questioned the States on the transfer and they swept it under the carpet and instead sent Joe Markowitz out here, no doubt to tell me to pull my head in.'

Phil wanted to know more. Mike told him everything that he knew and also led the conversation into what he had uncovered on the Internet, without alluding to Fran's involvement.

'You must have a view on what's going on, Mike?'

'I'm concerned, although it's not my business. Cash transfers are being made off balance sheet, the auditors are being misled. That does concern me. It's fraud.'

'Let me add a bit more to what you have told me. Your contracts come up for renewal later in the year. Correct?'

'Shit, do you know that as well?'

'Mate, that is not all. I have a friend in the Ministry who has told me on good authority that the Minister has been taking bribes for several years now. Guess where the money is finishing up? A nice cosy account in Switzerland. My informant also told me that the same corrupt Minister is off to the States shortly as a guest of your boss, Bob Wallshot. What does all this mean at the end of the day? I don't know yet. Maybe there is nothing. But let's assume it is true. If that's the case it goes to indicate that Wallshot is corrupt and he must have so many people in his pocket in the States. He has never been found guilty of an offence yet. People are protecting him. That's what I want to uncover – why?'

'What you're saying then Phil, if the suppressed Senate hearings had been concluded they could have found against him?'

'That's correct.'

Mike was beginning to believe that there was substance in his earlier suspicions about Wallshot. What more could he do to help Phil, he wondered.

'I told you I'm having further discussions with Markowitz. Should I bring any of these issues up with him?'

'Why not! You put him on the spot firstly and when I see him I'll hit him right between the eyes. Let's see what we can dig up. Quite frankly, I'd be surprised if he knew anything. He's a fairly innocuous joker.'

'Where do we go from here, Phil?'

'Let's keep our channels open whilst I'm in Sydney. As long as Fran doesn't mind we could use her as a conduit to each other. You're happy with that?'

'Suits me fine, Phil.'

The evening had been a success. Fran felt more at ease now that both of them had got on so well together. It was a gamble and it paid off. The biggest surprise of the evening was Mike's willingness to cooperate with Phil. She had now guessed that the Wallshot issues had been troubling Mike for some time now. He had found someone with whom he could confide in and share his problems with. He trusted Phil implicitly.

The discussions went on through the early hours of the morning. The trio had covered a range of topics, American politics, football, NBL and of course cricket. What evening wouldn't be complete without cricket, particularly the first Ashes Test between England and Australia. They were all confident that the Aussies could turn the match around.

Mike looked at his watch.

'Have you guys any idea what time it is? It's a quarter to three. I'm off home. Big day ahead of me.'

'Guess that's a signal for me then.'

'I'll see you out, Mike. Don't rush off just yet, Phil. I'd like you to stop for a while longer.'

Fran thanked Mike for coming and expressed her delight that the evening had been helpful to both of them. She indicated that she would set up another meeting with Phil next week. He thanked her.

Shutting the door behind her, she noticed Phil was out on the balcony enjoying another glass of the Hunter Valley red they had been quaffing all night. She joined him. Feeling a little chilly, she nestled up to him. He responded, putting his arms around, bringing her very close to his body. It had been a long time since they had felt this way. Fran looked up at Phil asking him if he was in a hurry to go. He was comfortable and indicated that he wasn't.

'Don't go back to your hotel tonight.'

'I'll have to leave soon.'

'Stop with me. It's been a long time since I've had a man in my bedroom.'

Phil was moved by her passionate desire to have him spend what was left of the evening with her. He put his glass down and moved in closer.

'I would love to spend the remainder of the evening with you.'

They moved slowly towards the bedroom door, their hearts pumping furiously. They were like young kids again. Would they be disappointed? Phil kicked the bedroom door shut and the two of them fell on the large bed, his arms still around her. They looked at each other, their eyes closed and their lips met for the first time. Was this the start of an everlasting friendship, Phil thought for a moment.

'Amanda, where the blazes can I get hold of Phil Black?'

'I'm sure he'll be at his hotel, Mr Morphett.'

'Get him for me sweetie.'

'Mr Morphett, it's the early hours of the morning in Sydney. Do you really want me to disturb him now.'

'Amanda, I need to speak with Phil.'

'Yes, Mr Morphett.'

Amanda telephoned the hotel. No answer from his room was the reply. She left a message on the voice mail for him to ring Rudy Morphett urgently.

'Mr Morphett, I'm unable to raise Mr Black at his hotel.'

'Find him, I need him now. Harry Walkinshaw and I want to have a conference call with him.'

'I'll do my best, Mr Morphett.'

She tried the cell phone. There was no answer. Little did she know that Phil had had enough sense to turn it off, not long after Fran asked him to stop the night.

The evening had not been particularly exciting for either Joe Markowitz or Kev Haslett.

They had arranged to meet at the hotel restaurant for an evening meal. The conversation was all business, with long pauses between each topic. Only once did Markowitz attempt to move him to another area of possible interest. That failed miserably. Markowitz feigned jet lag around nine thirty, apologising to Haslett that he would have to get to bed.

Seventeen

'Good afternoon, Amanda, I've just returned to my hotel room. I received your message on the voice mail. Does the boss want to talk to me?'

'Where were you, Phil Black?' she asked jokingly.

'Now Amanda, you know that you never ask a journalist where he's been when he is on assignment.'

'I hope you got your research right then? It was after three in the morning when I telephoned. Mr Morphett nearly had my head, when I told him I couldn't find you.'

'I'll smooth it over with the boss for you. Leave it with me. OK.'

'Hold on, Phil, I'll patch you through to Mr Morphett and Mr Walkinshaw.'

'Is that you Phil? It's Rudy here. I have Harry on the other line.'

'Hi Phil, how are things going down under?'

'Interesting few days. Uncovered a lot of information on Wallshot and his corporation. I'll send you a report later in the week.'

'Phil, we needed to get hold of you. We're running a front page tomorrow which will blow the socks off you,' Rudy said rather excitedly.

'Yes Phil,' Harry chimed in. 'We've had it checked out for accuracy and had the lawyers pore over it. It's a bit close to the bone. The lawyers will have a field day with this one.'

'What are you guys on about. What headline?'

'Governor Ziggy Sharp from Texas has been caught taking electoral funding bribes from Bob Wallshot.'

'What! How did you get on that?'

'It fell into our laps, this afternoon,' Rudy said. 'Apparently one of the Governor's confidants had a falling out with the governor's office. He wants to tell all. He telephoned us firstly as he knew we were the only non-politically biased paper in the country. It's going to cost us a bundle.'

'It'll be worth it, Rudy,' Harry stated.

Phil was pouring himself a drink as he began to absorb what the boss was telling him. This was dynamite! It would have to bring Wallshot to the surface now. How was he going to deny these allegations. The exposé had to be stepped up, he thought.

'Is it running in the *New York Herald* only?'

'No Phil, we are going to release it to all of our national newspaper affiliates. It'll hit the New York streets first though.'

'What about Governor Sharp, has he any idea what he's about to be confronted with?'

'Not yet! We're saving that until the first paper hits the streets. I plan to ring him direct at that moment.'

'Are you going to ring Wallshot at the same time?' Phil inquired.

'Harry plans to ring Wallshot.'

'Shit, why did this have to happen whilst I'm twelve thousand miles away?'

'Don't worry Phil. The ball's rolling. What you come up with down under will only add weight to this release.'

'I'd love to be in Sharp's office when the shit hits the fan,' Phil retorted.

'Wouldn't we all.'

'Boss, E-Mail a copy of the release to this number. It's OK, belongs to an old journalist mate of mine.'

'I'll do that. The first copy leaves the press in an hour's time.'

'Phil, either Harry or I will keep in touch on progress.'

'Governor Sharp's office.'

'I'd like to speak to the Governor please.'

'Who may I say is calling?'

'Rudy Morphett calling from New York.'

'Just a moment, Mr Morphett. I'll connect you with the Governor.'

There was a pause whilst Rudy waited. Normally he wouldn't have this type of patience, but this call was going to be different.

'Mr Morphett, how nice of you to call. What can I do for you?'

'Governor, I'm not the bearer of good tidings.'

'Why's that, Mr Morphett?'

'My *New York Herald* has just gone to the streets with a front page headline alleging that you have accepted electoral bribes from Bob Wallshot. I wanted you to know personally from me, before one of your staff members broke the news to you.'

'What are you talking about? This is preposterous. I'll sue the pants off you, you sonofabitch!'

'Governor, I'm not here to argue with you. I'm telephoning to tell you that you've got some explaining to do.'

'Who fed this crap to you? I'll deny everything. It is not true. I have never accepted a bribe from anyone. Do you hear me, Mr Morphett?'

'Governor, we have good reason to believe that Bob Wallshot recently dropped two million dollars your way to secure the Texas Pipeline contract. I'm not here to debate the rights and wrongs of this Governor. I'm here to tell you once again that I've just published the allegation.'

'I'll see you in court, Morphett.'

'Happy hunting, Governor,' Rudy replied and put down the phone.

Governor Sharp sat in his chair stunned by the revelation. How the hell did Morphett find out about the two million? What concerned him more, was that one million had been placed in a Swiss account for him personally. His political career would be over by the following morning. The whole country would be aware of the allegations by then.

Instinctively the governor picked up the phone to ring Wallshot. The line was busy.

He rang again a few minutes later. It answered.

'Is that you BW?'

'It is. Who's this?'

'Governor Sharp. Have you heard the news?'

'If you are asking me have I had a telephone call from the *New York Herald*, then the answer is yes, I have heard the news.'

'What the hell's going on BW, has there been a leak from your office?'

'Not this end, I handled everything myself. Must be your office Governor.'

'I'll get to the bottom of it.'

'One thing at a time, Governor. We'll have to prepare ourselves for the press onslaught tomorrow morning.'

'There will be an investigation by the State legislature. If they find out I've accepted funds from you, I'm finished.'

'You're finished anyway, Governor. The people of Texas won't forgive you over this allegation.'

Governor Sharp didn't want to hear that. He was looking for support from Wallshot, not to be buried by him.

'I will offer a million dollars to the Democrats tonight to balance the political funding in Texas. No one can then argue that I didn't donate generously to both parties. The other million I transferred to an account for you in Switzerland is untraceable. You must have told someone about that? Think man, think.'

'The only person who could have known was one of my closest aids. I had to terminate his services last week for not carrying out my instructions. That's probably who blew the lid on this.'

'Governor, deny any knowledge of the million offshore. It can't be found. Acknowledge that you did receive a million for electoral funding. I will cover the offset to the other party. Remember, keep very cool about everything.'

All they could now do was to wait until the revelation hit the national press and television.

Wallshot tried several times that evening to get hold of the Chairman of the Democrat Party. He had not been successful. The media would construe it as somewhat cynical to say after the event that he had offered to put a million with the Democrats. He would have to ride that one out. Blame someone else, he thought for untidy administration within his own corporation.

The first copy of the *New York Herald*'s headlines hit the *Texas Star* and the *Miami Chronicle* approximately an hour after the news was buzzing around New York.

The headlines read, "Governor Ziggy Sharp of Texas bribed by one of America's most powerful businessmen, Bob Wallshot."

The first call arrived just before six. It was Eddie Irvine, Chairman of the Texas Republican Party. He was looking for the Governor. His wife answered the call in the private quarters.

'Where is he?'

'Is that you Eddie?'

'Give me the Governor immediately.'

Governor Sharp was determined not to field any telephone calls until his press staff had arranged a media release and television interview. He couldn't avoid the Chairman.

'Ziggy I warned you about doing business with Wallshot. Why didn't you listen?'

'There was nothing wrong with what I did. I accepted a donation to the election funding campaign, nothing more.'

'What about the allegation that he dumped a million in a Swiss account for you?'

'There's no truth in that story.'

'I hope not for your sake, Ziggy. I'll help you, but if I find you've fed me crap, you'll hang.'

'Can we save my re-election?'

'I doubt it. We were battling before. This has put us in a hopeless position.'

The Governor was more interested in saving his own neck. He knew that if it were ever discovered that he had accepted a bribe from Wallshot, he would probably do time in one of Wallshot's prisons.

Bob Wallshot had decided to leave early that morning for Buena Vista. He knew that no one would know where to contact him. He had organised for Marina to meet him at the airport. Everyone would be looking for him. He needed some space to determine what course of action he had to take next. With all the controversy that had surrounded him over many years, leaving the scene of the crime for a few days would allow the whole affair to go off the boil. Marina would protect him from the jaws of the television and the national press.

The *New York Herald* had planned to do a follow up on their latest headline. Rudy Morphett and Harry Walkinshaw were now up to their necks in a damages claim. One more startling headline wouldn't weaken or strengthen their position.

The cover story had been E-mailed to Fran Bright's office. She called Phil to let him know. He had told her earlier to expect a message from his New York office. She couldn't help but read the front page review and was startled to see the allegations. It appeared that it was true about Wallshot and what he had been up to for decades. This time the press had nailed him first and was not just reporting yesterday's story, as they had on each previous occasion.

Phil read through the article rather quickly. He was unable to contain his excitement. To be back in the States now would have been his wish. This was his story and he should have been there when it hit the streets. He impulsively picked up the phone to ring his boss, not thinking for one moment to ask Fran if it was OK. She would understand a journalist's knee jerk reaction.

'Sensational headline, boss!'

'Phil, we plan to run a follow up story in the next edition, what can you let me have on Wallshot's Australian affairs?'

'Bribery seems to be Wallshot's way of buying business. He has a real knack for it. Why not let his bribing of an Australian politician fly? Don't mention his name at this stage. We'll hold that one for another edition.'

'Now you're certain that the politician is on the take?'

'The source is good, boss.'

Rudy Morphett trusted Phil's judgement implicitly. They decided to run with the story.

'What a day,' Phil sighed. 'Fran, how can I get hold of Mike Johnston urgently?'

'His cellphone is the best bet. Here is his number.'

'Mike Johnston,' the voice answered.

'Phil Black here, Mike. Have you caught up with the headlines to break in the American papers on your boss, Wallshot?'

'Christ no. What's happened?'

Phil gave him a detailed outline of the front page cover story of the *New York Herald*. He was stunned by the news. This would probably mean the gradual demise of the Australian operations, once the news hit the local press. The anti privatisation groups would have a field day. They would be like a frenzied bunch of alligators.

The immediate concern that Mike had was minimising the impact upon the business. He needed Fran to help him. She would know the full story by now, as he was certain Phil had given her the article to read.

The only person Phil thought he owed it to was Peter Bent. He had to give him a call and tell him what was happening. Peter was not surprised to hear the news about the Wallshot allegation and thanked Phil for telling him what had happened.

'That's not all Pete. I need to let you know that my newspaper is going to run the story on your Minister into tomorrow's edition.'

'Why would you want to do that now?'

'We needed to get a much wider coverage. My boss was concerned that Wallshot might try to bury the story in the States. Bring in a few favours. You understand what I mean? We know he can't do anything down here. No one knows him after all. We are not proposing at this stage to identify the Minister. That will be left for another day.'

'Where does that leave me, Phil?'

'Nothing changes, mate. Just keep your eyes open and keep me informed as we had discussed. I promise you again, I won't blow your cover.'

Peter had expected this day to come sooner or later. His Minister was corrupt. He felt pleased that he would play a part in exposing him.

'You've been very helpful today, Fran. Thanks for your support. By the way I enjoyed last night.'

'Phil, we have tonight. You have not forgot that you're taking me to dinner, have you?'

'Oh! Certainly not,' he replied. 'Where would you like to go?'

'Surprise me.'

In the excitement of the events that had unfolded, Phil had forgotten that he had promised to take Fran out for dinner. He was due to go back to the hotel shortly. The concierge would be able to recommend a nice quiet spot, he thought to himself.

'I'll pick you up from you apartment. Say around eight.'

'I will be ready at eight.'

$\mathcal{E}$IGHTEEN

The time has come to confront Joe Markowitz, Mike Johnston kept saying over and over again in his mind. The news that had just been broken to him by Phil had to be put on the table and ironed out. There was no point in raising the issue direct with headquarters, as he knew that they would be scurrying around like chooks with the heads cut off. They could not handle such an issue.

How could he approach Markowitz? He thought for a moment, the bonding between them had not cemented, they hadn't known each other long enough to trust one another. The wrong approach could see him scurrying off to his corner. Mike knew he had to get Markowitz out in the open and openly give his opinion on the events of the day.

Mike's style was one way only, up front and honest had worked for him most times. 'Let's give it a go,' he mumbled to himself. Markowitz was in the office, no time better than right now.

'Joe, can I interrupt what you're doing? Would like to have a chat with you.'

'Sure Mike, that's no problem. What's on your mind?'

'I have had a call this morning from a journalist I met recently. I believe you may even know him?'

'Oh yeah, who's that?'

'Phil Black.'

'Yeah, Phil. I met him on the plane coming down to Sydney. Good guy. Plan to meet him again whilst I am in town. How did you meet him?' Joe inquired.

'A mutual friend.'

Mike was not going to bring Fran Bright into this conversation. Joe did not need to know the connection.

'What I want to tell you may not be news. You may already have heard?'

'Heard what Mike?'

'Wallshot and Governor Sharp of Texas are allegedly involved in some sort of bribery scandal. The news is all over the States today.'

'Shit, how much more can you tell me?'

Mike went through the story piece by piece, just as Phil had told him. Markowitz sat in stunned silence. Could not believe what he was hearing. Mike finished the story and turned to Joe and asked him if he had any idea what was going on.

'This is the first I've heard of what you've just told me, Mike. I can vouch for that. Mind you it doesn't surprise me. Tell me, does it have anything to do with the Texas Pipeline contract?'

'I have no idea. Phil didn't mention that to me. What's the significance of that contract and the bribery scandal?'

'You mentioned something about a million going into election funding and a million being deposited in a Swiss account for Sharp.'

'Yes, that's correct.'

'Well, just before I came to Australia, I was in Wallshot's office. I overheard a conversation between him and our Texas Vice President about a problem with the Texas Pipeline contract.'

'What was the problem with the contract?' Mike asked.

'We had lost part of it for poor performance. To carry on, Wallshot asked me to transfer two million dollars into a Swiss account. He did mention at that meeting that he was going to give the Governor of Texas a million to bolster his election funding account, if we retained the contract. Ironically the corporation retained the Pipeline contract. Perhaps, Wallshot did set the Governor up personally with another million out of his offshore account.'

Markowitz was now freely opening up. His credibility was obviously in question. How much more does he know, Mike asked himself.

'What's the story on the Swiss account? There's been rumours flying around for some time that the account is being used to fund the purchase of arms.'

'That's not correct. At least I don't think so.'

'Are you sure?'

'No, not exactly.'

120

'That's what brought you to Australia, wasn't it?'

'Yeah, I guess that was one of the prime reasons. Mr Wallshot had asked me to keep your inquisitiveness at bay. He was concerned that you were asking the wrong questions, after you sent that facsimile to me demanding an explanation as to why a million dollars had been transferred out of Australia every quarter for the past seven years.'

'You know where the cash was going, don't you?'

'Banque de Genève, Zurich.'

'I know that, but do you know why?'

'No I don't.'

'You know the transactions have all been off balance sheet? There is no record appearing in the local financials and I haven't been able to see any record of the transfers appearing in the American SEC accounts.'

Markowitz was now on the ropes. Had he carefully evaded answering the questions put to him, or was it because he really did not know? Mike was uncertain. One thing he was certain of, Markowitz was visibly upset by the latest revelation.

'Mike, I am concerned about what you are telling me. I wouldn't want our discussions to go any further.'

'Only if I let you know first,' Mike chimed in, 'This is a very serious matter, we stand to lose our local contracts if Wallshot is found guilty of bribing a government official.'

'What can I say. You have to ensure that the whole matter is played down.'

'I'll do my best.'

Mike had been toying with the idea of suggesting that the two of them and Phil Black should get together and swap some notes on the Wallshot Corporation. There were a lot of unanswered questions. Mike and Joe were obviously in the firing line. If there was any fallout from the Wallshot bribery scandal, it would impact both of them dramatically, particularly Joe as he was the Chief Financial Officer for the Corporation. He would be expected to give some pretty good reason as to why he had condoned offshore cash transfers and sizeable donations to political parties. After all he signed off on the year-end accounts to shareholders and the SEC. The wolves would be knocking at his door.

There was no option, he had to get the three of them together.

'You mentioned that you had met Phil Black.'

'Yep that's right.'

'Did Phil tell you why he was in Australia?'

'Um, no, sort of. Mentioned he hadn't been home for ten years. Probably that was about all, I think.'

'His paper is working on an exposé of the Wallshot Corporation. Australia figures in there somehow.'

'Jeezus, I thought he had shown a lot of interest in my job and what the corporation did. That bastard was using me.'

'No, I don't think so, Joe. What he did was to put his journalistic skills to the best use. You happened to be there at the time to feed him information. There would be nothing personal in it, I can assure you. Well, where I am getting to with this conversation, is that I would like the three of us to meet and get our heads together. We are all involved, one way or another, in some type of bloody mess that Wallshot has got us into. Let's share our knowledge and get the best result for each of us.'

Joe remained silent. He had no choice but to join forces with these two guys. He was not in a position of strength and should the bribery scandal be found to be factual, he had to protect his own position. After all he did not know if Phil and Mike had any more knowledge than he had. He agreed to meet with both of them.

Mike had Fran set up a meeting the following day.

Fran opened the front door for Phil. He was on time. She liked that in a person.

He had come prepared for a romantic evening. In his right hand he had a magnificent bunch of red roses, whilst in the other he had a small parcel carefully wrapped in yellow and blue ribbon. She was ecstatic. It had been a long time since a man had brought her gifts. She ushered him into the lounge room, helping him to take his jacket off and place it on the back of a chair. She thanked him for the roses and then fossicked around the cupboard looking for a vase to place them in.

The gift intrigued her. What would he be getting her on their first formal date, she teased him as she opened the package. It was small box. She lifted its lid. The pendant was stunning. A small gold frame of intertwined leaves with a setting of green emeralds in the middle greeted her. She was overcome with excitement, asking him what she had done to deserve such a wonderful gift. He was forceful with his explanation, telling her that their meeting had brought a new dimension to his life and he wanted to remember it with a special token of his friendship for her.

Fran was overcome by his caring and thoughtful words and moved close to him, putting her arms around his neck, kissing him firmly on his lips. She felt the same way towards him and wasted no time in letting Phil know how she cared for him.

He helped put the pendant around her neck. The green emeralds sparkled in the reflection of the down lights. It was made for her. It fitted perfectly.

'I have a taxi waiting downstairs to take us for dinner,' Phil remarked.

'Let me change my dress. This outfit is not going to work with green emeralds.'

'Take all the time you need, I'll have the taxi wait a little longer.'

She disappeared into the bedroom, whilst he slipped downstairs to put the cabbie on standby. By the time he returned, she had changed. Absolutely stunning, he thought to himself.

'Where are we going?'

'A small restaurant I'm sure you'll know down in Rose Bay.'

'Oh, and where's that?'

'The Pier.'

'Fantastic, let's go. I've never been there.'

The taxi pulled up at the front door some seven or eight minutes later. The maitre de had been pre-warned by the hotel's concierge to give Phil and his guest royal service. He would not be disappointed.

'Good evening, Mr Black, how lovely to see you and your guest tonight. Let me show you to your table.'

The maitre de had reserved a special table for them both, in a secluded part of the restaurant, overlooking the harbour.

'May I get you a drink, sir?'

'Yes, we'll have a bottle of your 1986 Dom Perignon.'

'Fine choice, sir.'

Phil had been told by the concierge to order the Dom. The Pier was the only restaurant in town that stocked a 1986 vintage. The restaurant prided itself on its choice of only the finest champagnes.

They toasted each other's good health, as they slowly sipped the smooth aromatic champagne. The evening together had just begun. Tonight was their night. Business or Wallshot would not be discussed, that could wait for tomorrow.

'I'll have the John Dory, lightly grilled, garnished with the lobster tails,' Fran ordered.

'Good, then I'll stick with Balmain bugs and calamari.'

'Can I get you a salad, sir?'

'Yes, why not. A fresh green salad would be superb.'

The evening meal was about thirty minutes before it was served at the table. Phil now understood why the concierge had recommended The Pier. He could have sworn that he could still smell the salt water in the fish. It was that fresh.

As they were finishing their coffee, they simultaneously praised the chef's culinary skills. The John Dory and the Bugs had been a great choice to cement their first evening out together.

It was time to leave. Phil asked the maitre de to phone for a cab. As they waited, Fran, clutching Phil's arm asked him to stop the night at her apartment again. He was hoping that the offer would be there. He wanted to stay and told her that he would not have it any other way. This had been one of the most memorable evenings both of them had had for more years than they could ever remember.

Tomorrow would be another day. Phil was going to have to break the news to Mike Johnston that Wallshot appeared again on the front page of the *New York Herald*, this time for bribery and corruption in Australia.

$\mathcal{N}$INETEEN

FBI special agents, Lingard and Kowalski, had completed their preliminary report on the tragic disaster that had occurred at Saratoga prison. The President of the United States had demanded the matter be wrapped up as a priority. They had interviewed every prison officer who had been on duty one month prior to the arrival of Michael Montefiore through to the day of his escape. There was no doubt in their minds, the whole disaster had been planned by Montefiore. They had comprehensively studied each of the criminal records of the prisoners that had escaped with him. A pattern had emerged, the escapees had been individually identified by Montefiore. They each had a background in arms, bomb preparation and violence. Each prisoner was serving long term sentences, some never to be released. He had picked his targets carefully. The only part of the equation that they hadn't been able to determine, was the reason for the escape.

It crossed their minds that there was a new force rising in America in the area of domestic terrorism. It had surfaced in Oklahoma and Atlanta recently. Of course there had been the World Trade Centre in New York some years earlier, however that had been linked to a foreign fundamentalist group.

There was no trace of Montefiore or the escapees. One thing was certain they were no longer on mainland America. Three unidentified aircraft had been picked up on radar leaving the southern tip of the Florida coast a short time after the escape. It was fairly safe to assume that the unidentified craft were the helicopters used in the removal of the prisoners from Saratoga.

Agents Lingard and Kowalski had given Warden Bonham an undertaking that they would be out of his jail within seventy-two

125

hours. They had concluded their findings a little earlier. The Warden was asked to join them in their temporary control centre to be debriefed on their findings, prior to an interim report going to the President.

Agent Lingard advised the Warden, that they had concluded their preliminary findings. In summing up he expressed grave concern at what they had uncovered. A number of prison officers were of the opinion that the disaster was waiting to happen. Officers were untrained and not capable of handling such an event. Fraternisation between prisoners and officers was rife. Drugs and alcohol had found its way into many sectors of the jail, visitation rights were abused, court rulings were disobeyed. High security cons like Montefiore were given greater access to the prison than directed by the courts. Supervision was virtually non existent.

Lingard paused for a moment to get his breath.

'How much do you want to hear, Bonham?'

'You're full of shit. This is a report to save your ass. The corporation will fight this through the courts if you or the President release it in this form.'

'I'd expect you to react in this way Warden. Trying to find a way for you to get off the hook is not my concern. I'm expected to provide the facts. These are the facts. Let me tell you more Warden,' Lingard began again. 'Not one of your officers has confidence in your ability to manage this institution. They all categorically state that old man Wallshot gave you this job to see out your retirement. I've got to believe them. You had no idea what was going on in the place.'

The Warden was feeling that his world was now caving in around him. Although he wouldn't admit it to these vultures, they probably had hit a nerve. He never wanted the job in the first place. Wallshot insisted he take it, so that someone he could trust would look after Montefiore.

'Before we leave, Warden, there's one final thing I would like to say to you. You were involved in Montefiore's escape from Saratoga. We have evidence that you gave him plans of the institution and supplied him with names and the criminal background of those prisoners that escaped with him.'

Bonham was stunned by the revelation.

'You have no evidence of that,' he retorted.

'Yes we do. I have a taped conversation between you and Montefiore, when he asked for the material and your promise to deliver.'

'Impossible, you're bluffing.'

'Nothing's impossible. You had an extremely disgruntled Chief of Security who taped the conversation without you knowing. We have no further use for you at the moment, Warden. I suggest you consider your next move, don't leave Saratoga.'

Warden Bonham was shattered. His options were slowly sinking. He knew it was only a matter of hours before he would be formally arrested and charged. He had let BW down. He had failed, exposing the corporation to further investigation. It wouldn't finish just there. He knew that this trigger would open up a Pandora's box.

The choices were narrowing. He left the compound and made his way to his vehicle. He locked the doors and pulled out his point thirty-eight revolver. He reflected for a split second before placing it to his temple and pulling the trigger.

Word had reached Bob Wallshot. He was devastated. His closest friend, James Bonham had taken his life. Why? he asked himself a thousand times over. Had it been the pressure of Saratoga? Had he expected too much from him? Wallshot was not aware of the FBI de-briefing that had taken place a short time prior to his suicide.

In the past he had always found peace at his mountain retreat. Buena Vista was a place to think and plan. Times were now troubled. He had to confront a bribery scandal in Texas and now the loss of his best friend. He turned to Amanda for consoling. There is nothing that she could do but offer support in his moment of crisis. The time was drawing near to execute Operation Incarceration. He had fought adversity in the past and he would continue to do so until he achieved his new America. 'The fight must go on,' he kept saying to himself.

'Mr Wallshot, I have Richard Green on the phone.'

'Patch him through, Amanda.'

'Bob, I heard the news about Warden Bonham. If there is anything I can do you know I'm here to help.'

'I appreciate your kindness, Richard.'

Richard Green had been a stalwart of BW's for nearly fifteen years.

He was his principal legal adviser. He had graduated from Miama University in Law in the early eighties and had been approached by the Wallshot Corporation to join them not long after graduation. Richard was a brilliant negotiator and legal tactitioner, a strength that BW admired as he reminded him so much of himself. The only difference being, BW did not have the legal prowess that Richard had.

'I'm trying to get more detail on what led up to Bonham's suicide. I believe the FBI may have laid something on him. I have a contact in the Miami office that may be able to shed some light on the matter. I'll keep you posted.'

Richard had no idea the role Warden Bonham had played in the escape of Montefiore from Saratoga prison.

'The other matter I need to discuss, is the Governor Sharp affair. Did you bribe him, BW?'

'Of course I did. I needed the Texas Pipeline contract renewed. Sharp was not going to interfere in the decision making process unless I made it worth his while. Let me remind you that it's not the first time I have had to sling cash at that bumptious upstart.'

'It's going to be tough one to fight, BW. The *New York Herald* appears to have its facts right. I've been waiting for a visit from the FBI. It'll be a federal matter. Corrupt state governors are moved from the state criminal court jurisdiction. It's too hot for the local judiciary to handle. The only saving grace may be the million bucks into a Swiss account. They'd have to be wrong on that issue. Wouldn't they?'

'You're right, Richard. I have no use for Swiss accounts.'

'Good. We've got somewhere to start our defence.'

Richard explained to BW that he did not want him talking to the press or anyone else for that matter. He told him that if he made any form of statement it could be prejudicial to any future hearings.

BW knew the procedure. Richard had always been by his side. His contacts in Washington and in the federal and state judicial system were quite impressive. He had been able to get the corporation and Wallshot out of many tight situations over the years.

Harry Groves, State Senator for Ohio was ecstatic when he unfolded his copy of the *New York Herald*. To see Bob Wallshot's picture plastered over the front page and the corruption caption attached to the photo, was like music to his ears. He had been chasing this man down for years. This is justice, he thought to himself. A call to Rudy Morphett would be appropriate. Congratulations would be in order.

'Rudy, you did it. I love to see Wallshot's picture in the newspaper, particular when it's front page. Do you really have something on him?'

'He won't crawl out from under this rock, Harry. Trust me.'

'What can I do for you here in Washington? I want to nail this bastard. He's never answered any charges before my Senate hearings. Now it's my turn.'

'How well do you get on with the President?'

'We don't dine together, but we do have a healthy respect for each other. Does that help you?'

'It should do. What I would like you to do is to get in the President's ear and suggest to him that he should re-open the Wallshot Senate hearings that the White House closed down on you. Will he listen to you, Harry?'

'He's going to damn well listen. He owes me a favour,' Harry exclaimed.

'I've got Wallshot in my sights, Harry. I know he's up to something and I want to nail him before he explodes.'

'You're bloody serious, Rudy. All the years I've known you I have not heard you speak like this before.'

'Believe it. There's more to this man than meets the eye.'

Harry Groves had an ally in Morphett, a powerful one at that. The President would not be able to refuse his request to re-open the hearings. He would drop Morphett's name on his desk. That would spur him into action. The last thing a President would want running to a Federal election was to have the country's most influential newspaper offside. There was now enough smoke around with the bribery scandal and the Saratoga disaster. Although Harry did not know that the President had demanded a full investigation into the prison debacle.

'Rudy, the President is not the easiest man to get hold of. Leave it with me for a few days. He'll see me.'

'Before you go, I need to tell you that there will be another front page on Wallshot in the next edition. This is a good story and will help you convince the President.'

'What's coming next?'

Don't ask me. Just buy up a copy of the paper. You won't be disappointed.'

$\mathcal{T}$WENTY

"Wallshot Bribery Down Under."

The headline in point thirty was blazoned across the front page of the *New York Herald* and had been transmitted to every newspaper in the country. Wallshot had captured the paper's attention for the second day in a row.

The Chief Editor had claimed responsibility for the cover story. It went on to report that evidence had come to light that the Wallshot Corporation had successfully bribed an Australian politician to secure a number of prison contracts in the early nineties. The detail was graphic. Everything that Peter Bent had told Phil Black had been reported. The article went on to discuss the payments to the Minister and details of the bank on which they were drawn. This was the first time that Wallshot had been connected with a named bank in Switzerland. There had been allegations in the Sharp bribery exposure of connections with a Swiss account. This article had taken the fight right up to Wallshot. It was going to be hard for him to deny offshore banking transactions.

A copy of the headline had been wired to Phil Black in Sydney. He had been anxiously waiting for it, following a call from Harry Walkinshaw that it was on its way.

He thumbed through the article carefully to make sure that the reporting had been exactly what he had faxed through to his New York office. It had Phil's trade mark all over it. The article was as he had reported. Phil was concerned that he had not shared his exposé with Fran the night before, but at this stage he was doing everything possible to keep her and his other Australian contacts out of the press.

The Australian television news had got on to the exposé sooner than Phil had expected. He had been sitting in his hotel room going over some of the information he'd collected during the few days he had been in Sydney, when a news flash came across the television screen. An Aussie TV journalist who had picked up on the story was outside Parliament House with his roving eye camera, trying to get a one on one interview with either the Minister, who had not been named in the story, or the Premier.

The Minister of Prisons had just arrived at the front gates to Parliament building when the journalist confronted him. He thrust the microphone in his mouth and asked the Minister if he had anything to say on the New York report that he had accepted bribes from a wealthy American industrialist to secure government contracts. The Minister was stunned by the remark and vehemently denied any association with the alleged affair. He pushed the reporter to one side to be met by another group of journalists who had congregated at the top of the Parliament steps. He ordered them to get out of his way and called upon security to forcibly remove them from the premises.

Mike Johnston had telephoned Phil's hotel several times and left messages for him to return the calls. Phil was in his room but had asked the hotel operator not to patch any calls through until further notice. He was getting most anxious as he had been telephoned by the Minister's office for an explanation. Mike needed to know more from Phil. Even Fran couldn't raise him.

She was convinced he was still at the hotel. The easiest way for her and Mike to get hold of him was to front up at his hotel door. She had his room number, so it was easy enough to slip by reception and go straight up without being announced. On the way to the hotel, Fran picked up Mike.

When they arrived they made their way to the fifth floor of the hotel. Phil's room was not that far from the elevator door. Fortunately for them it was slightly ajar. The hotel cleaner was inside tidying up the room. Fran unannounced, pushed the door open and called out for Phil, whom she could see sitting at the desk bashing away on his desktop word processor. He looked up to see both Fran and Mike heading towards him.

'Where have you been all morning Phil?' Fran asked. 'Mike and I have been leaving messages at the hotel and you won't return them. What's going on?'

There was no escape for him. Phil knew they were here for an explanation on the story that had just hit the Aussie press. He felt somewhat guilty that he had deceived both of them.

'My paper is going to be doing a series of articles on Wallshot over the next few days. I'm sorry I couldn't pre-warn you on this one. My boss is convinced that Wallshot is no good. He won't give up until he has nailed him to the cross.'

'What do I tell the Minister's office about the allegations, Phil?'

'Oh, sorry Minister, I just happened to have a meal with this journalist the other night who just happened to say he was doing a story on Wallshot and during his investigations he just happened to stumble on the fact that you were corrupt. Come on, Phil, you not putting all your cards on the table. If you want my help, you're going to have to trust me. If you can't do that I walk out now and you are on your own. Have it you way.'

'Mike's right, Phil,' Fran blurted out. 'I'm beginning to wonder if I can trust you.'

That brought Phil to his senses. The last thing he would ever do was to hurt Fran. Even the Wallshot story was too high a price to pay for losing someone he had grown very attached to.

'Hey guys, I'm sorry. Sit down, let me bring you up to date.'

The tension had eased, the atmosphere in the room had settled down.

'You know I've been working on this story for some time now. You pick up a snippet of information here and a little there. I'm not sure how good my sources are from time to time, but what I do know is that a pattern is forming and pieces of the jigsaw are being put into place. My boss, Rudy Morphett, is the driving force behind the exposé on Wallshot. He had a run in with him some years ago. Wallshot put financial pressure on him and his newspapers, which nearly brought him down. He's never forgiven him for that. We got on to a source here in Sydney that was willing to help me. I can't tell you, Mike, who it is but I am confident that it's a reliable informant.'

Fran breathed a sigh of relief. Phil hadn't mentioned her as the contact with his source. She was now feeling guilty herself.

'What's happening here in Sydney is only the tip of the iceberg,' Phil continued. 'Wallshot, as you both know, has been under suspicion for years now for irregular business activities. No one has been able to nail him. Morphett has good reason to believe that something big in the States is about to go down. The exposé will either bring it to the surface or bury it forever. It's a race against time. One hell of a gamble too. If the paper is wrong, then Wallshot wins and finally drags Morphett and his papers to the ground. You couldn't put enough zeros on how much he would sue the paper for.'

'Is there anything else we need to know?' Mike asked.

'Mate, I do need your help. The shit will hit the fan today and a lot of good people are going to get hurt along the way. Even you Mike! You'll have to take instructions from your corporate office. I would like you to tell me which way they bounce. Your operations are an important part of their international network. The Wallshot Corporation media machine will be in full flight after today.'

'Phil, don't cut me out again. I will work with you. Understood?'

'Understood, mate.'

They shook hands on their agreement. Fran put her arms around Phil, thanking him for taking Mike and her into his confidence. She assured him that she would do everything possible to help him as well. Phil didn't need that reassurance. He had never felt uncomfortable with Fran.

By the time Mike had returned to his office, there were dozens of messages for him to ring various people, including five now from the Minister's office.

Joe Markowitz was stomping around the office, yelling at the receptionist to try his Miami office again. He had caught up with the revelation and was trying to get hold of the corporate media group for an explanation. The lines were overloaded each time the receptionist tried. He saw Mike return to his office.

'Where the hell have you been? Are you aware of what's happening?' he bellowed at Mike.

'Sit down and behave yourself. We are in this together. You know as much as I do. Have you been able to get on to the States yet?'

'Those sonofabitches are not taking calls. They've jammed the lines.'

'Well, put that to one side at the moment,' Mike said. 'We have enough problems in Australia. You'll have to put your mind to those. I need to ring the Minister's office. Will you handle the press? If you need assistance I suggest you use Fran Bright, our media relations adviser.'

Markowitz needed direction. He had never been in the firing line before. Mike understood how to handle these situations, although this was different to anything he had had to handle previously.

'It's Mike Johnston here from Wallshot Australia. Is the Minister available? I understand he wishes to talk to me,' Mike asked calmly.

'I'll put you through, Mr Johnston.'

'Have you any idea what position your Corporation has placed the government and me in? These accusations are preposterous. This will mean the end of your contracts with the Government.'

'Minister, can we keep a level head on this? I have no idea what the whole sordid affair is about. Let me assure you it has not been generated out of this office.'

'Johnston, that doesn't help me.'

'Minister is it you I should be concerned about, or my company losing its contracts?' he asked facetiously. 'What can we do for you?'

'Deny the allegations, you fool.'

'Minister I can't do that. How can I deny something I know absolutely nothing about.'

'For God's sake then talk to the Premier.'

'Minister I would be delighted to talk to the Premier and reassure him that the press release did not come from this office. Is that what you want me to do?'

Mike was now feeling very sweaty. He had pushed the Minister as far he dare at this point of time. In the back of his mind was Phil's graphic description of what this minister had been up to over many years. All of it had been going on behind Mike's back. The Minister had been dealing direct with Wallshot. Why should I feel responsible, he thought.

If he had to fall, Mike was going to make sure he came down in a heap.

'Minister, if you tell me the allegations are untrue, then you have nothing to fear about. Now have you? I'll telephone the Premier and let him know that we will offer what assistance we can to bed down these scurrilous accusations,' Mike said tongue in cheek.

The Minister slammed the phone down, obviously having no desire to continue this fruitless conversation any further.

Over the next few hours there had been considerable tension in the office. Markowitz had contacted Fran Bright and she had arranged to put a planned press release program into play. This she told Markowitz would probably take the matter out of the headlines over the next few days. Joe thought she was the best thing since sliced bread. He could not have handled it in the same professional way that she had. Besides that he knew nothing about the Australian press psyche. After Mike's unceremonious dumping of the Minister, he got hold of the Premier's office. The Premier did not want to talk to him. He couldn't do any more than that. He left a message for the Premier to return his call if he wished. An announcement had to be circulated to all management and staff informing them of the day's events and to assure them that there was no truth in the headlines. That had to be said even though Mike knew it was probably untrue.

It was around two when the pressure eased. It was the first opportunity that Mike and Joe had found time to sit down and reflect on the events of the morning. They decided to get out of the office for an hour to grab a sandwich and a cup of coffee.

'What do you make of this, Mike?' Joe asked cautiously.

'It's the truth, the Minister has been on the take.'

'How do you know that?'

'Had we had the meeting with Phil Black, I understand he was going to raise the matter with you. Unfortunately his newspaper needed to run with it beforehand. Bad timing, I guess.'

'Dangerous bastard that Phil Black.'

'I disagree. The dangerous bastard as you put it is our Mr Wallshot. He's the wild card.'

Joe didn't respond to Mike's accusation, but underneath he knew he was bloody well right.

'I need to get back to the States. There are issues hanging around that I'm going to be asked to explain to the New York Exchange and the SEC. The Wallshot stock price fell fifteen and a quarter overnight. The market will be looking for comfort.'

Mike agreed that Markowitz was of no value to himself or the corporation whilst he remained in Sydney. Arrangements had to be made to get him back on the first available flight.

Mike's secretary interrupted him to let him know that whilst he was out the Department of Prisons had telephoned, requesting that he attend a four o'clock meeting at the Department's offices.

That was the last thing he wanted to hear today. Had he pissed the Minister off so much that he had put his threat to cancel the contracts in train? He wouldn't know until he arrived at the meeting.

'Whom am I supposed to see when I arrive?' he asked his secretary.

'I understand the Director and the Deputy Director will be there.'

'Sounds as though they've brought the heavies in,' he remarked.

Mike arrived at the department's offices a few minutes after four. He apologised to the Receptionist as he was being led to the Director's office.

The greeting wasn't particularly cordial. The Director sat on one side of the meeting table, with his Deputy sitting beside him. At the top of the table was another guy, whom he hadn't met before. He was introduced to Mike as the Department's Principal Legal Officer. The Director, whose name was Ray Lee had only been with the Department twelve months. Mike had met him a couple of times but couldn't really say that he knew him too well. The Deputy Director, Frank Bishop joined the Department in 1989. Mike remembered it well, as he was the guy who Mike was involved with when the first contract was being tendered for. Frank was not a political appointee, unlike his boss. He was a career public servant.

'Thanks for coming down to see us at short notice, Mike,' the Director remarked.

'You caught me at the right time. It's been one hell of a hectic day.'

'Mike, I'll get straight to the point. There's no need to beat around the bush. The Minister's made me aware of his discussion with you this morning. He's not particularly happy. I have to point out that he's asked me to find ways of cancelling your contracts.'

'I expected that after he slammed the phone down in my ear. What are you proposing? I believe the contracts are watertight.'

'Legally, the contracts are, Mike. Politically, they are not. The government can close out any time it wishes if there is any suggestion of corruption involving a minister of the crown.'

'The Minister told me this morning he was clean.'

'I'm sure the Minister is right, but the Premier wants a contingency plan in case anything should go wrong.'

Mike picked up the vibes pretty quickly. What the Director was saying that there was a shadow hanging over the Minister's head. The Premier was seizing this as an opportunity to dump him from the cabinet. He had to prepare himself for that eventuality.

'My belief is, Ray, that you don't have a leg to stand on, either legally or politically. The contracts are watertight and will run their full term until renewal. If you tried to cancel them now that would be a knee jerk reaction and would only exacerbate the government's problem with its minister. Let's face it, the government would be pulled down.'

The Director and his Deputy sat silently for a moment. Their bluff had back-fired. They were hoping that Mike would be apologetic and look for ways to get the corporation out of its predicament. He had not fallen into their trap.

'Is there any truth in the allegations that the Minister has been accepting bribes from Wallshot?' The Deputy Director asked.

'Don't look at me, pick up the phone and ask Wallshot.'

'Believe me Mike, we have tried this morning. We've been unable to get through.'

'Gentlemen, I suggest I leave this meeting now. There's no more I can tell you and threats of taking these contracts away from Wallshot Australia before all the facts are on the table is somewhat premature. Don't you agree?'

'We are not saying that we have the same view as the Minister,' the Director stated. 'However, unless you can provide us with some satisfactory answers, we may have to recommend to the Minister that the Department reviews the company's performance.'

Mike was angry and left the meeting hurriedly, leaving the officials bewildered as to what their next move was likely to be.

It was not possible for them to take on the contracts, as their infrastructure would not cope with the additional burden. They had to find a way around the problem. Perhaps, they thought, the easiest and most practical solution was to recommend to the Minister that they wait on an outcome from the investigation into the alleged corruption. This would buy them time and hopefully resolve the problem. They were confident that the Premier would be left with no choice in the interim but to have the Minister step down until the matter was resolved.

$\mathcal{T}$wenty-$\mathcal{O}$ne

'$\mathbf{M}$r President, I have Senator Groves here to see you,' the President's Chief of Staff announced.

'Show him into the Oval Office.'

This was the first occasion that Harry Groves had been in the White House. He had seen it many times over the years but had never been invited to speak with the President of the United States. He was nervous as he was ushered into the office of the President. His first reaction was to the size. It was much smaller than he had anticipated. The President's large oak desk sat prominently in the centre of the room with the American eagle directly behind. The walls of the office displayed pictures of the country's earlier Presidents, a reminder of the struggle that had taken place in those early days to put America where it was now.

'Senator Groves, welcome to the White House.'

'Mr President, thank you for seeing me today.'

The formalities out of the way, the President escorted the Senator to the leather faced lounge chairs that were situated in the corner of the office. They both sat down.

'I understand from my Chief of Staff, that you wanted to talk to me about Bob Wallshot. How can I help?'

'Mr President, your staff have no doubt briefed you on the allegations that have surfaced in Texas concerning Governor Sharp?'

'They have, Senator.'

'Mr President, I have chaired many Senate investigations over the years into the Wallshot Corporation. They have all arisen as a result of tendering or other commercial irregularities. Let me remind you that each of the hearings has been terminated by your office, prior to any conclusion being reached.'

The President looked at his Chief of Staff and asked him if that was correct. The Chief of Staff acknowledged the accuracy of Senator Groves statement and went on to qualify his support by telling the President that in fact it was the office of the Vice President that had sought termination of the hearings.

'I'm aware of the Vice President's involvement, Mr President. That's what brings me here today. I believe it is in the best interests of this office and for the sake of the country that those hearings are re-opened.'

'That's a pretty tall order, Senator. What is it going to prove?'

'Mr President, you are facing an election within the next two years. The polls are not exactly in your favour. You have to distance yourself from the Governor Sharp scandal, or else you will not stand a chance of being re-elected. More importantly, the Republican Party will be banished to the wilderness. The voters won't be kind to you.'

The President, was taken aback by Senator Grove's aggressive attack on his future election chances.

'Let's assume that's the case Senator. If I agree to your request, how is that going to benefit my re-election campaign?'

'You are going to have to trust me, Mr President, but I have good reason to believe that Mr Wallshot has not only erred in Texas, but in fact I think he has been involved in the same activities with each of the terminated Senate hearings.'

'Do you mean bribery?'

'I do, Mr President.'

'That's a very serious accusation you're making, Senator.'

'No, Mr President, I am telling you it's more than an accusation. I am confident that it's fact. I urge you to re-open one of the failed hearings only. Let me chair the meeting and give me the opportunity to reach a conclusion. If that proves positive, Mr President, you have one of two options after that. One you don't proceed any further and secondly you re-open all terminated hearings to Senate scrutiny.'

'That's one hell of a gamble, Senator.'

'Mr President, it's no more than the gamble I've taken today, talking to you about these very sensitive issues. You have to be seen to be moving against Wallshot over the Texas matter. Failure to do so will leave you wide open in terms of the electorate.'

The President could see clearly the strength of the Senator's argument. He had nothing to lose. Failure to re-act to the Texas issue was tantamount to weakness and would jeopardise another term for him. If he was to re-open one of the earlier hearings, it would be viewed as a positive move.

'What are your views?' The President asked his Chief of Staff.

'In my opinion, you have nothing to lose.'

'I agree. Senator, I trust this errand of mercy is successful to both of us. If I fail you'll fail. You get my drift.'

'Mr President, you will not be disappointed. I would like you to consider re-opening the Senate Committee's inquiry into the awarding of the contract in 1993 for full facility services at the Island Bend defence establishment.'

'My Chief of Staff will look into your request, Senator, and make arrangements to put the necessary approvals in place for the hearing to be re-opened.'

'Thank you for you for hearing me out, Mr President.'

Bob Wallshot had been frantic during his forced exile to his South Carolina ranch. This was the first time in his life that he felt vulnerable. With the Texas situation blowing up in his face and now hearing that the press was running wild in Australia, accusing him of bribing an Australian politician, he kept asking himself, when would it stop. He was convinced that his Swiss accounts would not be discovered. Where his weakness lay was in the strength of the two characters that were desperately fighting for their political lives. There was no doubt in his mind that he had bribed each of these politicians, but how long could he stave off the onslaught from the world media. It wouldn't be long before other allegations would be raised. If that were to happen, the Corporation would collapse around him. He knew he was close to achieving his lifetime dream. Operation Incarceration had to be stepped up immediately.

His direction was now clear. He had to bring his trusted friends together, to prepare a plan for the execution of Incarceration. Michael Montefiore had to be de-briefed. His involvement was extremely critical to the success of the plan.

'Amanda, I want you to get me General Tyler on my private line. After that I need to talk to Howard Lazenby, Fred Cohen and Paul

Lowenstein. Later, you can also get me the Vice President and Judge Hardcastle.'

'Yes sir,' she replied.

General Tyler had been retired for some years from public life but continued to play a significant role in international and domestic defence affairs. Since his retirement as Chief of Defence, he had been extremely active on the lecture circuit, particularly in the Middle East. He was well regarded in most Middle Eastern countries and was seen as an important roving ambassador for the American government. His career in the American defence forces was unquestionable. He was held in high esteem by all defence force personnel.

'Paul, thanks for taking my call. I believe you're in Washington at the moment?'

'That's correct, BW.'

'You've no doubt caught up with press coverage I've been receiving?'

'You've let yourself open to criticism, BW.'

'I realise that. That's the reason for my call. I need to meet with you and the other committee members at the ranch next Sunday week. We are going to have to accelerate Incarceration, before an outcome on the Texas scandal is reached.'

'I couldn't agree more.'

'We'll need to finalise the detail and prepare for execution,' Tyler confirmed.

'I'll contact the other members and have them meet us at Buena Vista,' Wallshot said.

During the course of the day he had managed to get hold of Lazenby, Lowenstein and Cohen. Lazenby had been en route to England, but Wallshot had been able to have a discreet conversation with him on his cell phone. Lowenstein was interrupted at a World Bank meeting being held in New York. He had no hesitation in taking the call as he understood from the message given to him, the urgency. Fred Cohen was on vacation in the Caribbean. He had left his telephone number with Wallshot in case an emergency should arise. The principal committee members that would drive the execution of Incarceration were all available to meet with Wallshot at his ranch on the nominated day.

Judge Hardcastle, was not contactable as he was in Court. A message had been left with his court secretary for him to contact Wallshot urgently.

The Vice President, Clark Ford, was encouraged to hear the news that the plan would be accelerated. He stood the most to gain if it was successful and faced the death penalty for treason if it failed. Despite this he had been one of the greatest advocates for change in America and had spoken publicly on the topic many times, much to the chagrin of the President.

Montefiore was in the Belize jungle when he received a coded message from Bob Wallshot. He was unable to talk to him until he returned to base camp, later that afternoon.

The group had been in the jungle for several days under the watchful eye of Montefiore and his squad members. Taking an undisciplined bunch of rabble and converting them into a well oiled human machine, was no easy feat. They were a bunch of raw recruits committed to success or death. There was no misunderstanding as far as they were concerned. They had been given an opportunity to be free men. That was a better option than being locked up for the rest of their lives. They knew the risks and the consequences of their decision.

The group was being trained in jungle survival, high explosive assembly and weapons use.

Montefiore had anticipated their readiness within the next ninety days. His call to Wallshot later that afternoon would mean an acceleration of his training program.

Ninety days was no longer reality.

The news from Senator Groves was music to Rudy Morphett's ears. He was not confident that the Senator would have been able to convince the President to re-open the Senate hearings into Wallshot. He was a little disappointed that he was only able to secure the opening of one hearing at this stage, but was comforted by the Senator's assurance that the Island Bend Defence contract would secure a positive result for them.

'When is the hearing likely to commence?' Morphett asked.

'The President has assured me that he will act immediately and instruct the Senate Leader to have proceedings commence immediately. I'm anticipating that we'll start taking evidence early next week. I will be looking to wrapping the whole matter up within two weeks after that.'

'Christ, that's one hell of a ride.'

'I'm confident we can do it. You have to remember that we have a lot of evidence on file. Wrapping up the tail end won't be difficult.'

'I'm impressed with your confidence. When can I go to print on the story?'

'As soon as the Senate Leader has given us the green light, I'll let you know. That's the time.'

Morphett did not want to let Wallshot off the hook. He was on a roll now and wanted to keep the pressure on him. The first shots had been fired in the war against Wallshot and he was aware that the momentum from those salvos would keep the front pages of the press occupied for the next few weeks. The next revelation was the important one. This he was confident would stir Wallshot into action.

$\mathscr{T}$WENTY-$\mathscr{T}$WO

The Texas State Legislature had been summoned to debate the allegations that the State Governor had accepted a bribe from Bob Wallshot. Governor Sharp had called a meeting of his close advisers to consider what action he needed to take in the matter.

'Governor, can you categorically deny that the allegations are not factual?' his Chief of Staff stated.

'I am unable to do that. You know as well as I do that we accepted a million dollars from Wallshot for campaign funds.'

'It's not the campaign funds I'm concerned about. We can dump our opponents in just as deep. They've been accepting funding from the trade union movement for years. That's not the issue. Did you take cash from Wallshot and place it overseas?'

'You're beginning to sound like the press,' the Governor heatedly remarked. 'You believe I'm guilty?'

'Governor, I want to get to the truth. If this is just a damn smear campaign orchestrated by your opponents, I need to know. I'll ask again, did Wallshot offer to give you money?'

The political pressure was right on the governor. His conscience was not clear. He had now been confronted by one of his senior members of staff to confess. He felt humiliated. The time had come to face the truth. He turned to his other senior advisers in his office and asked them to leave the room. The Chief of Staff was asked to remain.

'I've been very foolish. Wallshot did arrange to set me up with funds using a Swiss account. It secmed so easy at the time. He assured me no one would ever know. How was I to know that one of my former staff members would leak information. You wanted him fired. Should I blame you now the damage has been done? How do I handle the explosion?'

The Governor's Chief of Staff sat stunned. He could not believe what he was hearing. The man was corrupt and now the whole country knew about it.

'What's Wallshot's position?' he asked.

'I spoke to him, shortly after the press announcement was made. He assured me again that I did not have to worry. No one could trace the cash through the overseas account.'

'Assuming he's correct, we probably don't have to do anything at this stage. The only issue we have to face is your acceptance of the campaign funds. The other party, I'm convinced won't push that one too far. They have enough of their own skeletons. There is a slim chance you may come out of it with your political future in tact, although a little tarnished.'

'Are you sure, we can pull this off?'

'I'm not, but I'll give it my best shot.'

The Governor was now feeling as though he had been castigated by the Almighty.

'The legislature is debating the matter as we speak,' the Chief of Staff said. 'You have to appear before them and categorically deny any knowledge of the offshore funding. You will have to acknowledge your acceptance of the campaign funds and say you erred in your judgement and with hindsight perhaps you should have refused the donation. Then we'll turn the attack on the opposition, slating them for their non-disclosure of political donations. That'll shut them up.'

'What a brilliant idea! If we pull this off, I owe you.'

'Yes, Governor, you'll owe me. I want half of those funds sitting in Switzerland.'

The Governor looked at him with dismay. He could not believe what he was demanding. What were his alternatives? He obviously had none.

The debate in the legislature was extremely heated with both slides slamming each other with accusations of foul play and corruption. The leader of the house was unable to control the debate and in the best interests of good government ordered a recess.

Governor Sharp's office had informed the legislature that he had an announcement to make and planned to address the house within the hour. The timing of the announcement coincided with the recess being called. The Governor was certain that by the time he faced the members, a considerable amount of heat would have disappeared out of the debate.

It had not been easy for Montefiore to get hold of Bob Wallshot. The jungle of Belize was not the best environment to place a long distance telephone call. The local telephone operator only spoke Spanish and was not particularly helpful with trying to understand Montefiore's demands. The message he had received to telephone Wallshot did not indicate where he could be located. Firstly he tried corporate headquarters. No one was able to tell him where he was. The only other place he thought he could be was up in the mountains at Buena Vista. The Belize telephone operator had spent nearly half an hour trying to patch him through to the Miami office and was not particularly cooperative after that connection failed and she was then asked to try the ranch number.

Finally he got his connection.

'BW, it's Michael, I'm calling from Belize.'

'Michael my boy, it's lovely to hear your voice again. It has been so long since we sat down and had a chat.'

'We haven't spoke since before the trial.'

'Don't remind me.'

'Is everything OK for you in Belize? Remember if you have any problem, pick up the phone and call the President of Belize. Mention my name and he will help you.'

'Everything's fine, BW.'

The conversation stopped for a moment. BW had become quite emotional. Michael's trial and imprisonment had taken its toll on him.

'Michael, forgive an old man for feeling upset at not seeing his favourite son for so long.'

'I understand. Tell me why did you need to get hold of me?' Michael asked.

'We are running into difficulty in the States. We have to remove a number of obstacles. You don't need to worry. I'll take care of them. Incarceration has to be executed earlier than originally planned. When will you be ready in Belize?'

'I can't complete the training in less than three months.'

'That's too long, Michael.'

'What time can you give me?'

'I need your operatives in position one month from today.'

'That's not enough time. These recruits are the worst types. They cannot be ready.'

'Michael, they have to be. I want you to offer each of them a million dollars if the plan is successful. That will have them ready.'

Montefiore knew the importance of the plan. He had been an integral part of Incarceration since its inception. He was not going to place obstacles in its way now. His operatives would be ready and in position at the time nominated by BW.

'The team will be ready, BW. They will not let you down.'

'I know, Michael. I will give you the final operational plan within the next few weeks.'

The Governor of Texas was ready to address the assembly. There was still hostility in the air. The mood had not tempered during the recess. There had been intense lobbying on both sides of politics. There were those that wanted to see an end to the governor's domination of state capital hill and there was the other group that owed their political survival to him remaining in power. The governor took up his position in the chamber and began reading from a speech that his chief of staff had prepared for the occasion.

He assured the assembly that the allegations in the national newspapers were not true and at no time had he ever accepted a bribe for favours. He did, however, tell the assembly that he had accepted campaign funds from Wallshot and saw no harm in his actions and went on to remind the legislature that was common practice on both sides of the house.

He delivered his speech with fervour and passion and constantly reminded everyone in the assembly chamber, that during his period as governor the State of Texas had moved further forward than any other state in the Union. The speech sounded more like a pre-election speech, not one that had been prepared to save him from total political destruction.

He sat quietly at the end of his delivery, awaiting some form of reaction from the legislators. It was not forthcoming at first, then there was a slow monotonous handclap from a few of his detractors, which slowly gathered momentum. He was now concerned that he had not convinced them. The leader of the house brought the legislators to order and turned to the Governor suggesting that he leave the chamber to allow the assembly to vote on his future. The Governor had no option but to agree.

Some two hours later the leader of the house contacted the Governor to advise him that by a majority, of one hundred and seventy three votes the legislature had decided that he should stand down, pending a full investigation into the allegations of his corruption.

For the third day in a row, the *New York Herald* had dedicated its front page to Wallshot. The headline read "President instructs Senate Leader to re-open Senate hearings into the business affairs of the Wallshot Corporation." Rudy Morphett had published a full background on Bob Wallshot. Nothing had been left out. It covered his early childhood, the early business years and the influential position he had created for himself in recent years. Anyone reading the story would have been most impressed with the rise and success of this man. What they would not be able to detect was his manipulative manner and the degree of power that he held over society and political life. Morphett was determined to expose him, as he knew, if his gut instinct was correct, Wallshot was going to make his move shortly.

At the time the *New York Herald* was preparing to roll its presses, the editor was not aware that the Texas State Legislature had asked the Governor to stand down, pending an investigation. The conspiracy against Wallshot was gaining momentum.

Phil Black had not been resting on his laurels, whilst his boss was publishing sensational front-page stories on Wallshot. He had wanted to gain more information on the Minister's involvement in the alleged bribery scandal in Australia. He was having difficulty convincing Peter Bent to give him access to the locked filing cabinet, that he had discovered earlier in the archives.

The cellphone rang as Phil was wandering around Circular Quay contemplating his next move. It was Mike Johnston.

'I wanted to let you know that Joe Markowitz has decided to return to the States,' Mike said. 'He believed it was important that he be there to take some of the heat off the rest of the management.'

'I would have liked to have caught up with him before he returned, still, next time perhaps.'

'Phil, he did ask me to pass on his apologies to you. He said he would telephone you in New York, when you return. The other reason I rang was to ask you to meet me for a spot of lunch. I've been able to get a little more information on the Swiss bank accounts the company is using. Thought it may be of interest to you.'

'Of interest! You'd be joking. That's the sort of news I want to hear about. When and where can we meet?'

'What about Zorllinis, at one?'

'I'll be there,' Phil said.

It was a little after noon. Phil knew he would have time to slip back to his hotel, freshen up and be at the restaurant by one.

When he arrived at the hotel, there were messages for him to telephone Rudy Morphett and Peter Bent. He did not have time to talk with Peter just now, but was delighted that he been trying to contact him. Phil was hoping that Pete had changed his mind and was going to arrange to sneak him into the Department's archives. It was a little late to be ringing Rudy in New York. He could wait until after his lunch with Mike.

Zorllinis was situated on the western side of the city, tucked away in the basement of a high rise office tower. Phil was aware of the restaurant. He had read about it in the hotel restaurant guide in his room. From what he could remember they boasted that it was the best Italian food served in the city. They certainly had a reputation to live up to. Phil was a connoisseur of Italian pasta and was ready to pass judgement on their claim to fame.

The head-waiter greeted him and escorted him to a table in the centre of the restaurant. Mike had been early and was quietly enjoying a beer before Phil's arrival.

'Do you want a drink, Phil?'

'Yeah. I'll have a crown lager.'

'Busy little place, isn't it?'

'You'll enjoy their pasta, you'll find most of Sydney's leading businessmen frequent the place. No one takes much notice of who comes and goes. What I suggest is leave it to the waiter to place your order. It makes it more interesting. That OK with you?'

'Sounds fine to me.'

The waiter was a bubbly character, who spoke English with a smattering of Italian dialect. Mike asked him to order lunch for both of them. This was the customary practice at Zorllinis and you usually found that no one table had the same meal. The only thing you had to watch was that if you were not a regular customer you were likely to be served the same meal each time you went there.

'I told you on the phone that Markowitz has left for the States. I had an interesting conversation with him, before he went. In fact I took him out to the airport and on the way out, he let his guard down several times. I'm pretty sure we've made quite an impression on the guy. It was like confession time.'

'What did he have to say?' Phil asked.

'Well, he confirmed that Wallshot has two bank accounts in Switzerland, both of them held at the Banque de Genève in Zurich. The main account is an overseas operating account, which the Corporation uses to siphon excess funds from its daily worldwide operating accounts. The second account is a trust account in Wallshot's name only.'

'Keep on going, 'Phil asked impatiently.

'Let's take the main account firstly. Wallshot and Markowitz are the only senior executives that know about its existence. For record purposes it is disguised. What is important though, Markowitz is not a signatory to the account, only Wallshot. Markowitz's role is solely to move funds into it. Wallshot has total control of the outward movements.'

'Hang on, just back up for a moment. I'm no bloody bean counter, but tell me how is it disguised in the records?'

'Simple,' Mike replied. 'The cash transfers are treated as a contract development expense and are written off over the life of a contract. That is one of the reasons why Wallshot has insisted on long term contracts with long term renewal options.'

'So how does he get away with it then? Surely an audit investigation would uncover the rot.'

'Your guess is as good as mine. Bribery seems to be a way of life with him,' Mike responded. 'Now, the second account. That's the one that is in Wallshot's name only, Markowitz believes is used for settling favours.'

'The rumours and allegations about Swiss bank account dealings are probably accurate,' Phil said.

'It looks that way. Now the final bit of news that I didn't realise and I should have bloody well known, the guy who looks after the accounts in Zurich is Lukas Mueller, who just happens to be a director on the main Wallshot Board. Don't tell me that's not a coincidence?'

'Mike, I need to get this info back to the paper. Can I release it?'

'Yes, by all means. Don't quote me as the source and that way I can leave my cover open.'

'No, I understand. Are you able to give me the account numbers?'

'I believe so.'

'Good, if you can then I'm hoping to be able to link those accounts to one very corrupt Minister here in your country. I'll let you know how I get on. Can you let me have the numbers after lunch?'

'You'll have them.'

Both men were ecstatic with the events that were unfolding. Lunch arrived at the right time. The conversation was exhausted and the appetites were demanding. Phil gave the restaurant the thumbs up.

$\mathscr{T}$WENTY-$\mathscr{T}$HREE

Immediately Phil had returned to the hotel, he called Peter Bent on his direct line. Peter wanted to see him urgently. He had been mulling over his earlier conversation with Phil and had now decided to help out. Sitting on the fence he had thought was not his preferred option. He had nothing to lose by exposing the Minister. Getting Phil into the archives was a slight problem, but he felt confident that he could arrange for him to get access.

One of Peter's many responsibilities was the management of the archives. He had agreed with Phil that he would engage him as a temporary employee with the task of cataloguing certain records. Phil would then get access to the confidential ministerial records regarding the Minister's association with Wallshot. It had some risks, but they were confident that they could pull off the charade. Phil had to be at Peter's office the following morning.

Rudy Morphett had telephoned Phil again. Fortunately for him he was at the hotel when the call came through.

'Where the hell have you been?' Rudy demanded to know.

'Boss, I've been busy tidying up a lot of loose ends.'

'I need you back in New York. The Wallshot affair is starting to roll. I'm sending you down a copy of the latest front page.'

'What was the story line?'

'Senator Groves managed to convince the President to re-open the Senate hearings on Wallshot and now I've just found out that Governor Sharp of Texas has been asked to stand down. You can see now why I need you back home. I really need you to take charge of this whole expose.'

'I'm flattered to think you need me so much, Boss.'

'Don't give me any of that fucking flattery bullshit. Wrap things up there and get your ass back here, pronto.'

The relationship between these two men was electric. They had enormous respect for each other's ability to contribute significantly to a great story. Rudy, however, couldn't handle the detail. He lost patience very quickly and Phil sensed that in his conversation with him.

'I'll be here for about two more days, Boss. I think I have a lead on the Wallshot Swiss accounts. There could be quite a story in this. After that I have to say a few goodbyes and I'll be on the next plane.'

'By the way Phil, you remember that I told you about the meeting Wallshot had at his ranch some time ago with a group of prominent Americans? Well, there's to be another one next week. Same group as last time except Judge Hardcastle is included. I did a brief background check on their corporations. Interesting mixture of businesses they each have. Lazenby's American Telecommunication's supplied most of the hardware and software for the American Government's defence satellite tracking stations, including the one in Australia. What's even more interesting is that one of Wallshot's enterprises provides security to those sites. Before you leave I want you to check to see who is the service provider for the Aussie installation. My money would be on Wallshot!'

'That shouldn't be too hard,' Phil replied. 'The local manager for Wallshot has turned out to be quite a fountain of information.'

It was not going to be easy telling Fran that he had to return to New York. As a journalist herself she would understand that the story came first. This was different though. They had formed a strong attachment for each other. Phil certainly wanted to continue with their new relationship, but he also understood that it would have to go on hold until his assignment was finished. Perhaps she would come to New York and live with him. That would be unfair, he thought. She had a successful business here in Australia. Maybe he should think about retiring and returning to Australia. It had crossed his mind a few times since he had been back home. Phil telephoned Fran immediately after he had finished his conversation with Morphett. He explained that he needed to meet with her as he had been asked to return to New York. She was not pleased to hear the news but tried hard not to make it too difficult for Phil.

Phil told her that he was going to do some investigative work at the Ministry tomorrow and would like to have dinner with her this evening. She agreed.

Bob Wallshot had been in the mountains for several days and had concluded all of the arrangements for his committee meeting on Sunday week. It had not been an easy task, as he had to take care of everything himself. He had learnt through life that no one could be trusted.

Security was of paramount importance. He had brought in a security team from Miami to give the ranch a thorough going over. The gates to the entry of the ranch had to be re-configured to allow for the installation of a sophisticated electronic monitored detection system. Cameras were installed alongside the road leading up from the gate to the house. The communications control room at the ranch had to be upgraded to cater for the changes. This was going to become the central nerve for Incarceration. Radar detection equipment with a radius beam of ten miles had to be installed to pick up aircraft landings within the boundaries of the property. Everything possible was being done to ensure maximum protection.

On the day of the meeting, BW had planned to fly into Buena Vista over a hundred hand picked private security officers from his own operations. Their task would be to make sure that no one, other than his guests, entered the property.

The meeting was planned to take place over two days. Preparation for the execution of Incarceration would take no longer.

Transportation had been organised for each of the committee members. They had to arrive at differing times of the day for security reasons and sufficient aircraft had to be made available to fly them into Westchester. Getting them from the airport to the ranch was probably going to be the easiest part of the exercise.

BW was considered to be one of the country's leading strategic masterminds. It was a strength he had gained from his many years of service with General MacArthur and had not failed him through his long and successful business career.

This would be the last opportunity that Phil would have to spend with Fran. Their evening together had to be special. He had been fortunate enough to get two tickets to the Opera House. Fran had told him earlier that she was an opera buff but never had the desire to go by herself. She found that most of her male partners could not put their minds around sitting at the Opera listening to sophisticated music. Phil had not been for over ten years. His wife had been a great lover of fine music and through her association, they had enjoyed many performances together. Puccini was playing this evening and he couldn't wait to see Fran's reaction when he told her where they were going.

'You're nice and early,' Fran said.

'It's been a quiet afternoon and besides I wanted to see you,' Phil replied.

'Where are we going? '

'We are having dinner at the Benelong firstly and after that I've been able to dig up a couple of tickets for Puccini.'

'You what! Puccini! Phil Black, what can I say. You're wonderful.'

She did not have to say any more. That was enough for Phil. Her over enthusiastic delight said it all.

'Are you ready?'

'Take my arm and let's go.'

'I have a car waiting for us downstairs. I want people to see you tonight.'

The Benelong had a great reputation for fine food and good service. They specialised in catering for the opera crowds. The table they were escorted to overlooked the Harbour Bridge and the Circular Quay. It was breathtaking. Fran felt very special and she let Phil know how much she cared for him.

They both heard the bells chiming, summoning the patrons to take their seats for the opera performance. You could have been in Paris or London. They were both beginning to get quite excited about their night together at the Opera.

The evening had passed so quickly. The performance had held them spellbound for over three hours. Fran did not want to go home, she wanted to stop to see and hear it all over again. They were slow to leave the theatre, chatting incessantly about the music. The limo was out the front of the Opera House to pick them up and take them to Coluzzi's for coffee.

'You understand the need for me to return to New York?' Phil asked gently.

'I understand, but I'm not very happy about it,' she explained.

'Fran, the job I'm doing at the moment will probably take me another three months. After that, I'm not quite sure where the next assignment will take me. I'm going to stick my neck out and tell you that I'm contemplating returning to Australia when all this is over, to hopefully spend more time with you. There you are, I've got that off my chest!'

'You never cease to surprise me. Are you telling me that you'd give up your career in the States to be with me? You're not suggesting that we should become an item are you?'

'Fran, I want you to marry me, when I return.'

'God, this is all happening too quickly. Are you sure that is what you want?'

'You have made me very happy. I haven't loved anyone for ten years. I want our relationship to go on forever more.'

'Phil, if you still feel the same way about me in three months, I'll accept your proposal of marriage. Can we go home now? I have a wedding to prepare for,' she said laughingly.

The next morning Phil was on a cloud. He could not believe what he had done the night before. When he had woken up he had to pinch himself several times to remind him of what he had said to Fran. He had no regrets. It was a new start for him.

Arriving at the Department of Prison's office he asked the receptionist if he could see Peter Bent. The receptionist had been expecting him and suggested that he make his way to the fifteenth floor. Peter was there to meet him. He whisked Phil into his office and closed the door behind.

'I've been able to get you access to the room for most of the day. I may be struggling to get you in there tomorrow though. I understand that the Department's investigation team will be poring over the records to see what they can turn up on the bribery allegation.'

'Thanks for sticking your neck out for me, mate. I'll be out by tonight. I promise you that. What would the investigation team be looking for? Do you know?'

'Not yet I don't and I am pretty certain they won't until they find it. Whatever it may be they are looking for, that is.'

'Well, I'd better get down to the archives and start the ball rolling.'

Why do they invariably put archives in the basement of buildings, Phil thought to himself as he looked around the large musty room that housed the Department's records. It was probably one of the untidiest rooms that he had seen. His newspaper had an archives room, but compared to this it was a palace. Peter pointed out the Minister's filing cabinet where he had previously found the incriminating check copies and told Phil that he should have a look at the management contracts between Wallshot Corporation and the Department.

Peter assured him that he would have the room to himself and was unlikely to be disturbed. If he ran into any problems he told him to give him a call on his direct line.

The Minister's filing cabinet had been left unlocked. There appeared to be no semblance of order. There had been some attempt in the past to put an organised system in place, but over time it had obviously failed. Files had been broken open and loose papers were strewn around the base of the cabinet drawers. Phil picked the documents up carefully and moved them to the table alongside the cabinet. He began to sift through the paperwork in an attempt to find some useful information.

After a few hours he was beginning to get a little weary. His efforts hadn't provided him with anything to get excited about. The best he had achieved was to tidy the filing system. At least this would be of some benefit to the Investigation team that no doubt would be going through the same cabinet tomorrow.

He opened the top drawer and noticed a series of files all marked confidential. Was he on to something? Each file had been carefully sealed and then tied with a piece of pink cord. He pulled them out of the cabinet. There were five files. The first one was headed up, "Contract to Manage Private Prison Southern Region." Phil was uncertain at this stage as to whether or not he should break the seal and check the contents of the package. What do I have to lose, he thought to himself and began to tear open the top of the file. There were a number of very formal documents between the government and the Wallshot Corporation. The type of paperwork he knew you would expect to see in a file like this. Then to his surprise, there was what he had hoped to find, a copy of a handwritten letter from the Minister to Bob Wallshot outlining the bids submitted from the other tenderers for the Southern Region prison. Phil knew this would have been in breach of government policy. No one in their right mind would give a tenderer a competitive advantage, particularly a Minister of the government.

What about the other files. What was in those? He opened them one by one and discovered that the Minister had written to Wallshot on each occasion. This explained to Phil the reason why the Corporation had been successful in winning the first five awards.

What Phil couldn't find was evidence that the Minister had accepted a bribe. Peter had assured him that he had seen copies of the checks given by Wallshot to the Minister. Had someone else got there before he did and removed the copies from the file?

Phil was frantic. He picked up the office telephone and dialled Peter.

'Peter Bent, can I help you?' came the response.

'You told me that there were copies of the checks in the filing cabinet. I can't find them. Do you know where they might be?'

'They were in the top drawer. I stuffed them behind a book at the back of the cabinet.'

'Just a moment, the cabinet drawer is jammed. I should be able to wrench it open. Got it!' he exclaimed. 'They're here.'

'Why would a Minister hold on to copies of checks?' Phil kept asking himself. There had to be a reason. Peter had been right. The first check copy went back some five years. It was drawn on Wallshot's Swiss account, payable to the Minister. Where had it been lodged? Phil was satisfied that there was enough evidence to incriminate the Minister. Handwritten letters to Wallshot outlining details of other tenderer's bids and check copies, with each payment being linked to the award of a contract.

What Phil had not told Peter, was that he had brought a mini camera with him, it was no good just viewing the documents he had to have hard evidence. He began to photograph the checks and then proceeded to do the same with the handwritten letters from the Minister. From the checks he was able to confirm the account number of Wallshot's Swiss bank account. Time was running out, he had promised Peter that he would finish up around four. That would give Peter time to make sure everything was back in place. Phil was aware of the investigation that was to take place tomorrow. Why should they have it all served upon a plate for them? he thought. He placed the handwritten notes and the check copies in a sealed envelope and carefully lodged it inside a record book that contained correspondence dating back some forty years. They would be safe there, as the dust on the book was as old as the correspondence. He needed time to review the documents and prepare an outline for his newspaper.

It was exactly four when Phil rang Peter to let him know that he had finished. Pete was busy and asked Phil to make sure that everything was back in place. He could not come down as he was waiting on a call. Phil assured him that he had left everything the way he had found it, but did not tell him that he had hidden the checks and the notes elsewhere.

As Phil left the Department's office, he kept rolling over in his mind as to why the Minister had left the check copies in the file. It was as though he wanted them to be found. The Minister had not gone to any lengths to keep the whole sordid affair under wraps. Why? Maybe he was just plain bloody stupid. Why hadn't the material been discovered before Pete found it? There had to be someone else involved. It would have to wait for the time being. Phil had to get back to the hotel and telephone a story through to Morphett.

When he arrived at the hotel, he was surprised to see Mike Johnston waiting in the foyer.

'Hello Phil.'

'G'day, Mate. What a surprise to see you here.'

'Yeah, I was hoping to catch you. Bumped into Fran this afternoon, she told me you have to get back to the States.'

'Yep, unfortunately. Morphett says he needs me to run this story on Wallshot. Reckons he can't do it himself. Who am I to argue.'

'No, I understand. I didn't want you to slip out of the country and not say goodbye and also I wanted to tell you that I am contemplating resigning from the Corporation. When all this shit hits the fan I can't afford to be around to pick up the pieces, because there won't be any pieces to pick up.'

'Mike, I know where you're coming from and I'd probably feel the same way if I were in your boots. Would you do me a favour?'

'I'll try!'

'Don't resign just yet? Wait a short time. I'll keep you posted on what's happening from our end. I'd like your help on exposing Wallshot, but I'll need you in the States to do that. In the meantime I'm going to need more help from you whilst you're still running the business. How about deferring your resignation for a couple of weeks?'

'Fair enough mate. Two weeks it is.'

'Oh, by the way Mike, does your operation do any work for the outback American defence satellite tracking station?'

'What makes you ask that?'

'Rudy Morphett ran something by me yesterday. Asked me to inquire.'

'As a matter of interest, we do.'

'What?' Phil asked.

'The satellite tracking station is actually run by a US government agency. The Aussie government has got some sort of long-term lease arrangement with them on the understanding that no questions are asked. Our contract was organised through our headquarters on behalf of the US government. We look after the electronic main-tenance, provide the ground security and do a few other things.'

'How many people have you on site?'

'Around three hundred I think. Anything else you need to know?' Mike asked facetiously.

'No mate, as I said I was just interested. Listen I'll have to get on, I've got some packing to do and get ready for my flight.'

As he pushed the door open to his hotel room, the telephone was ringing. Who the bloody hell was this, he thought, as he threw his papers on the bed. Surprise, it was Rudy Morphett. Phil was convinced that this guy never slept. It must have been around three in the morning in New York.

'Have you got a flight scheduled?' he asked.

'Boss, you'll be pleased to know I'm booked out of Sydney tonight.'

'Good, the minute you touch down at JFK I want you to get hold of me. I need to bring you up to date.'

'Do you mind if I have a shower first?'

'Stuff the shower, see me as soon as you arrive,' he snapped.

'I want you to keep the front page open for me Boss. I'll have to give you the hard evidence when I see you, but there is no doubt that Wallshot has been bribing an Aussie Minister. I've got check copies and some handwritten notes. It's conclusive.'

'Great stuff. I'll ring Harry Walkinshaw now and tell him to get ready for the story.'

Phil spent the next half an hour on the phone with Rudy going through the detail of his discovery at the Department's archives.

'This is the going to be the biggest thing to hit the press so far,' Rudy said. 'Let's see how Wallshot handles it. When you come back I plan to ease the pressure on him. There's enough going on at the moment to keep the momentum rolling. If he is up to something, then it's likely to break after the next meeting at his ranch. This will give you the time to prepare the full exposé.'

Phil was glad to put down the phone as he had been anxious to call Fran before he left. This would be the last time that he would have an opportunity to speak to her for a few days and he wanted to make sure that she understood that he was going to come back to Sydney after all this was over.

$\mathcal{T}$WENTY-$\mathcal{F}$OUR

The Banque de Genève in Zurich had just concluded its monthly directors meeting. Lukas Mueller had been under enormous Boardroom pressure. The board was extremely concerned at the publicity that the Wallshot Corporation had been receiving in the United States. Although the bank had not been specifically mentioned in the press reports there was an inference, through Mueller's connection as a director of Wallshot Corporation and the Banque de Genève.

The chairman of the bank had directed Mueller to find out what was going on and let him know as a matter of extreme urgency. This made it difficult for him as he was part of the conspiracy and in no way could he let his fellow board members know. He and Wallshot had a business arrangement after the execution of Incarceration. Mueller would become a substantial shareholder in the bank.

Bob Wallshot had not been easy to find but Mueller's persistence had paid off.

'BW, I'm under terrible pressure from the bank's shareholders. You have to help me.'

'We are both under scrutiny my friend. My main concern is to get the *New York Herald* off my back. Morphett is hell bent on destroying me. I can stop him, however, I need your help.'

'If it will help both of us, I'll do what I can,' Mueller said.

Wallshot knew what Morphett's Achilles heel was. He also knew how to exploit it.

'Morphett's *New York Herald* is burdened with excess debt. If there were a run on his stock the market would be sent into a tailspin, pushing his stock price down to untenable levels. He wouldn't be able to sustain that for too long, as he relies on his stock holding as collateral for his own personal debt.'

'Where do I fit in to the equation?' Mueller asked.

'Simple! The Banque de Genève is a large shareholder in the *New York Herald*. Convince your Board to dump the stock. Use the line that you have spoken with me and you are convinced that the paper's allegations are wrong and that I am preparing to sue Morphett for a billion dollars. They'll want to get out of the *Herald* stock very quickly as they know that Morphett hasn't got that sort of money. In the meantime I'll sell short and buy back when the price drops to its lowest level.'

'That's a brilliant strategy, BW. That'll keep the bank off my back and it'll also keep you off the front page of the newspapers for a short time.'

'You're right, it will only be for a short time, but that is all I need. Morphett will be beside himself when he sees me as one of his shareholders.'

For the fourth day in a row the *New York Herald* had run a front-page cover story on Wallshot. Today's issue was going to be the most telling. The headline read, "Wallshot Bribes Foreign Government Official."

The headline went on to give graphic detail of the Wallshot tentacles spreading into Australia and questioned the integrity of a man that continued to deal with American business and government. The article expressed the view that Wallshot had to be brought to justice.

Richard Green had a meeting scheduled with Wallshot to discuss the mounting pressure on him and the Corporation.

'Last time we spoke, BW, you will recall that I told you I had a contact that may be able to shed some light as to why James Bonham committed suicide.'

'I do recall you saying that, Richard. What did you find out?'

'I'll put it straight on the line for you, BW. The FBI has sufficient evidence to suggest that Bonham helped Montefiore and the other prisoners escape from Saratoga. Were you aware of that?'

'How would I be aware?' he asked impertinently.

'BW, I'm beginning to believe that there is more going on that what you are telling me. As your legal counsel, I need to know everything.'

'Bonham was a friend and that's all you need to know,' he answered, blatantly lying to Richard.

'We'll leave that for now. The reason why I wanted to see you is to get your reaction to the latest allegation about you bribing an Australian politician. Did you bribe him?'

'I'm not sure. I may have.'

'What do you mean, you may have? You must know. The paper said you paid this guy millions, using that Swiss account again. The one you denied knowing anything about.'

'Listen you little upstart, don't start throwing shit over me. If you can't handle what's going on, get out. You hear me, get out.'

'BW, you leave me no choice. You're up to something and I don't want to be involved. I'll quit, right now. You're on your own. I'm not going to be around to pick you up after all this is finished.'

Richard stormed out of the meeting, leaving Wallshot dumbfounded. He had never been spoken to like that before. The pressure was beginning to tell on him. In differing circumstances he would not have reacted that way. Richard was right but he hadn't trusted him enough over the years to take him in to his confidence.

The flight from Sydney to Los Angeles seemed particularly long this time for Phil. He remembered when he came down to Sydney sitting next to this strange character, Joe Markowitz. By the end of the trip he had grown to like Joe and hoped that he'd meet him again. The return flight was uneventful, except for the little old lady sitting next to him who was intent on telling Phil her life story and the sordid details of the many lovers she had conquered over the years. He could hardly believe that this tiny, frail, heavily lined woman had even held hands with a man, let alone have a life of complicated love entanglements. She would rattle on for about ten to fifteen minutes, then begin to yawn and settle back into her seat for a sleep. When she awoke she got straight back into the story, starting exactly where she had left off. That was an achievement in itself. The break gave him time to have a snooze and also reflect on his whirlwind romance with Fran.

Phil was still struggling, searching for an answer why the Aussie politician had left copies of the bank checks in his confidential files. Over and over again, he asked himself, why. Had he missed something in the files? Had something been taken out by another party?

The old lady who was sitting next to him had dozed off again. He reached for his travelling bag and pulled out the photographed correspondence and checks that he had printed just before he left the hotel. There was nothing there that stood out and hit him between the eyes. Maybe there was nothing, he thought, and the politician was just plain bloody stupid.

He bolted upright. Peter Bent had said to him before he came to Sydney that it was normal for the government to insist on an up-front fee being paid. In fact he distinctly recalled him saying that half a million dollars had been paid by Wallshot for the first contract. Phil flicked through the check copies and noticed the first one payable to the Minister was for half a million dollars. The other cheques were also for half a million, payable to the Minister. He recalled Peter had said that the Minister had received a million dollars for the other contracts. These checks were only for half a million. Peter was too smart to make a mistake like that, he knew. That was it! That was the missing link. Peter Bent was the other person in the deal. The Minister had taken half a million and Peter had been given a half million each time. It can't be, he kept saying to himself. But it had to be, that's why the whole investigation went so easy. Peter wanted him to find out! But why!

There was nothing Phil could do at the moment. He had to wait until he got to Los Angeles. Should he call Peter when he arrived at LA and ask him straight out, or should he wait for a while? The question kept going over in his mind time and time again.

The flight was still a few hours out of Los Angeles, which gave Phil time to reflect on the chain of events that led up to Pete escorting him down to the Archives. It was all coming into place. Pete had used Fran to get in touch with him. That was no coincidence. He had released a little information at a time. Just enough each time to moisten Phil's saliva glands. The friendly meeting he had with Pete had been orchestrated. The sharing of a few beers in downtown Sydney had also been part of the plot; the visit to the Archives. There was no investigation the following day. Pete had carefully planned the whole scenario.

Phil thought to himself, that assuming he was correct and that he was part of the bribery scandal, then why had he led him by the nose to the scene of the crime?

He had no answer for that. What he did know was that when he arrived in LA he would telephone Pete immediately to seek an explanation for his apparently strange behaviour.

Time had not stood still for Joe Markowitz since his return from Sydney. No sooner had he arrived at Miami airport, he had been whisked off to the corporate headquarters to be de-briefed by the management committee on the events that had taken place since his brief sojourn in Sydney.

The meeting had been organised by the Senior Executive Vice President for Business Development, Wal Fields. The management committee met regularly under normal circumstances with the meeting being chaired by Bob Wallshot. The meetings were invariably a waste of time as Wallshot heavily influenced the decision making process.

Field called the meeting as he had not been able to get hold of Wallshot and was extremely concerned by the events that were unfolding. He was the most ambitious of the management team and saw this as his opportunity to influence the committee in Wallshot's absence and perhaps convince the market that it was time for Wallshot to go. However, the meeting could not be held until Markowitz returned. Field had very little knowledge of the financial affairs of the corporation and relied heavily on Markowitz's financial skills.

Without Wallshot the management committee was absolutely leaderless. Not one of them could make a decision on what step to take next and, perhaps more importantly, not one of them really wanted to go head to head with Wallshot.

Although Joe Markowitz had been away for a week or so, he had been able to bring himself up to date within a short time frame. His major concern was the negative impact the various scandals were having on the stock value. The stock had plummeted to its lowest levels since the corporation had listed on the New York Stock Exchange.

If the falling stock price could not be arrested immediately the corporation would have to seek Chapter 11 protection.

The management committee agreed that Joe should be the one to front up to Wallshot and place it right on the line with him. After all, other than Wallshot, he was the only one who had any financial understanding of the corporation. This meeting was going to be one that he was not necessarily going to cherish favourably. Standing up to BW was not easy and Joe knew he had a daunting task ahead of him.

Wallshot was due to return to the office late that afternoon. Markowitz had to get in to see him then, as he was not confident that the corporation could continue to withstand a further significant fall in its stock value.

$\mathcal{T}$WENTY-$\mathcal{F}$IVE

$\mathbf{T}$he Qantas 747 had touched down at LA airport on time. Phil was hyped up. He could not wait for the plane to pull in to its berth. It seemed like a lifetime before it finally came to rest. He was not due to fly on to New York for about two hours. It would leave him enough time to get hold of Pete Bent. He joined the long queue waiting to be processed through Immigration. At last it was his turn to face the unfriendly immigration officer to be questioned as to why he had left the country, what had he been doing overseas and was he travelling on to another port. It was the same old shit each time, he thought to himself. Why the hell doesn't he finish and allow him to get on with the job of finding a telephone to ring Pete, he kept saying over and over again.

Finally, he departed Immigration and made his way to the nearest exit. He didn't have to worry about collecting his baggage, that had been transhipped to JFK. At least he believed so.

Using his Amex card he swiped the telephone card slot and began to dial the number for Pete Bent. He had no idea what time it was in Sydney and wasn't particularly interested anyway. He was calling him at home and he knew someone would answer.

A quietly spoken voice stammered into the phone saying hello.

'Pete, is that you?'

'Yes it is. Who's this?'

'It's Phil Black, mate. I'm calling from Los Angeles airport.'

Pete's voice had now become more coherent.

'I think I know why you have phoned me!'

'Well I don't need to beat around the bush then, do I, mate? You had me convinced at one stage that you were above board but my journalistic instinct kept telling me something was wrong. It didn't

170

hit me until I was half way across the Pacific. I would have telephoned sooner if bloody Qantas had on-board phones.'

'I deliberately left the trail open for you. You know that, don't you?'

'I do now. It was so bloody easy, I should have picked it up sooner.'

'I'm glad you did. It was only a matter of time before someone caught on to what was happening. I'd prefer it to be yourself. I could not live with it any longer,' Pete said with emotion.

'Why were you involved?'

'I fell into it, quite by accident. At the time that the government was asking the private sector to run its prisons, I was involved in the program, I was actually part of the evaluation team. We recommended another corporation for the job. The Minister decided in his wisdom to overturn our recommendation. I was the only one who questioned his decision. He wasn't too happy about it and went out of his way after that to make life pretty tough for me.'

'Go on, there is obviously more to the story.'

'Oh yeah, there's a lot more yet.'

'The Minister had me transferred to another department. He did not want me involved in the selection process. That didn't bother me too much. I was on the back end of my career and had lost interest in work since my wife had died, which you'll recall I shared with you at one point.'

'I do remember,' Phil acknowledged.

'Of all places he could have transferred me to, he had to go and throw me into Archives. I was there for nearly nine months, dutifully carrying on my job, counting down the days until my retirement, when I came across a locked confidential filing cabinet with the Minister's name stencilled over the front. You know the filing cabinet I'm talking about! Well, I found a way of opening it and came across the same file that you were going through. The same handwritten note addressed to Wallshot, that you discovered was in the file, together with a copy of the check for half a million dollars.'

'It's all starting to come into place now,' Phil remarked.

'After that, I sat tight wondering what the bloody hell I was going to do about it. My wife and I had always dreamt of travelling the world to exotic places. She was taken from me before we could ever fulfil that dream. I thought stuff it! I'm going to confront the Minister at an appropriate time. There had to be something in it for keeping quiet.'

'Did you blackmail him?'

'Of course, and what better time to do it when I found out from one of my colleagues he had overturned another recommendation of the evaluation committee.'

'What was his reaction?'

'To use a good Aussie colloquialism Phil, when I told him he acted like a stunned mullet. I put everything on the line with him. Told him what I knew and that if he didn't play ball I was going to place the file in the hands of the Commission against Corruption. CAC would have cut their teeth on that one.'

'Is that why he cut you in for half?'

'Eventually he did. Took some time mind you. At first he didn't tell me that he had put the screws on Wallshot for a million dollars for the second contract. He was getting greedy. I found out by accident. That's another story though! He offered me ten per cent of what he got. I laughed at him and told him fifty or I squealed. He knew I wasn't bluffing. If I had turned him in at that stage, he would have finished up doing twenty years. He wouldn't have lasted five minutes inside. There were a lot of scores to be settled. He knew that and agreed to fifty per cent. I had nothing to lose. Life was one big shit anyway.'

'You both received checks from Wallshot after that?'

'Yes we did and that's why I insisted on keeping the copies in the locked files, so if we were ever caught, we'd go down together.'

'You got away with it for so many years. Why did you decide to expose that mongrel of a minister and yourself?'

'Quite simply I'd had enough. Couldn't live with the deceit any longer. When I knew you were sniffing around on Wallshot and had an interest in his Australian operations, I made life a little easier for you. That's why I took my copies of the checks out of the file. You had to work it out eventually that a million was being paid over but the Ministers' check was for only half of that.'

'It was like a game to you, Pete, wasn't it?'

'In a way I guess so. If you hadn't found out I was going to CAC anyway.'

'If the Minister goes down, you will as well. You know that. What are you trying to do to yourself?'

'When the shit hits the fan, I'll offer to cooperate as State's witness in exchange for immunity or a reduced sentence. They'll cop that.'

Phil by this stage had completely missed the call for his flight to New York. He couldn't believe what Pete had just told him. The carefully orchestrated way in which he had been leading this other life for so long. Phil was feeling a little guilty that he had opened up the Wallshot story. If he hadn't, Pete would have just merrily gone on taking his cut of the action. They had been on the phone for over two hours when Phil glanced down at his watch.

'Shit,' he remarked, 'I've missed my bloody flight to New York. Mate I've got to go. I won't leave you in a mess. I'll help you if I can beat any charges. Just give us the front running on your story. By the way where's the money gone?'

'You won't believe it. Cancer research!'

'Mate you don't surprise me. You're a fucking hero. A modern day Robin Hood.'

With that, Phil said his byes and hung up. He had to arrange another flight, but firstly he thought he better call Rudy otherwise he would be wondering where he had got to when he didn't turn up at New York as planned.

Joe Markowitz did not have to wait to arrange a meeting with Bob Wallshot after his arrival at the office, BW was on the phone asking him to get up to his office immediately. When Joe entered BW's office he was quite surprised to see how well he was standing up to the pressure. He was showing no obvious sign of stress and in fact the glint in his eye told him he was in for the long haul.

Markowitz had prepared himself for the confrontation. He did not want to be caught off guard. He knew exactly what funds were available in all of the domestic and international operating bank accounts and latest stock prices.

'Good to see you again Joseph! How was your trip down under? You sorted those guys out I hope?'

'The trip was fine, even though I had to cut it short.'

'Sorry you had to come back early. We're in some trouble. I needed you here anyway.'

In all the time that Joe had worked for Wallshot, he had never once expressed that type of support for him. Perhaps now was too late, he thought.

'The Corporation is in trouble, Joseph. Morphett is hell bent on destroying my business. He has to be stopped. I've got a plan and I want you to control it for me. I can't be seen to be involved. I want you to use one of our offshore companies to sell short stock in Morphett's *New York Herald*. We're going to buy back when I tell you, with funds that I have arranged. You don't need to know where those funds are coming from.'

The tactic that BW was proposing was a fairly sensible approach in these circumstances and had been used by many conglomerates over the years to take up positions in target companies. This time the tactic was being used for another purpose. That was to destroy Morphett. Joe was not comfortable with the funding arrangements. He did not have to be told where the funds were coming from. He knew, they were tied up with Wallshot's Swiss banking interests. He thought about what BW had said to him momentarily and agreed to put his defence plan in place.

'I've arranged with the Banque de Genève to dump its stock holding in the *New York Herald*. I think they have around twenty per cent. I want you to sell short the same percentage. The market will believe that the institutions are quitting the newspaper. That should send the stock on a downward spiral. We'll buy back a controlling interest at the right price.'

'The right strategy for the wrong reasons,' Joe said to himself.

'We have to talk about the falling Wallshot stock price. The banks are getting nervous. They're holding your paper as security for loan facilities. With the falling price the paper is worth one quarter of what it was before the allegations were flying around.'

'Tell them absolutely nothing. Remind them that they have made a lot of money out of Bob Wallshot'.

'That's not going to keep them at bay. Their argument will be that you have made a lot of money out of them. That won't wash!'

'I need three weeks then all my problems will be over. Can you guarantee you can deliver me that time, Joseph?'

'I'll do what I can,' not questioning what he meant by his statement that all his problems would be over by then.

The meeting with BW had not been a complete waste, even though he had not been able to re-enforce his concern that the corporation was in dire financial straits. One thing Joe had learned about Wallshot, he had always been able to pull miracles out of the bag when least expected.

Two things concerned him about his meeting. Firstly the burning desire to destroy Morphett and his *New York Herald*. This was something of particular interest to him because of the conversations he'd had with Phil Black and Mike Johnston whilst in Sydney. The second matter that concerned him was the reference to everything being OK in three weeks. What did he mean by that remark? It was an unusual comment to make. It was pretty obvious to Joe, that Wallshot did not have a long term strategy in place to combat the wolves and at no time had he taken into consideration the impact should he be found guilty of the allegations that were being thrown around.

He knows something and he isn't going to share it with me, Joe thought.

The Corporation had a non-trading company in the Cayman Islands. It was last used a few years ago to clean up some unwanted tax losses. Joe thought this would probably be the best vehicle to sell short the *New York Herald* stock. No one would be able to trace the ownership of the company as the shareholders were well disguised. All he had to do now was to wait for BW to give him the green light to start selling.

Phil had arrived in New York to be greeted by his own tabloid on display at the front entrance to JFK airport. The headline read, "Wallshot To Appear before Senate Hearing on Bribery Scandal."

The *Herald*'s chauffeur was waiting outside the terminal to take Phil to the office.

Rudy Morphett was anxiously waiting to be de-briefed on his Sydney trip. He had told the driver to make sure that he took him straight to the office and under no circumstances should he deviate from that instruction. Phil wasn't particularly happy with the kidnapping but he also knew that once he had de-briefed the boss he could high tail it for his apartment and put a few hours between his flight and fronting the office the next day.

To be met by the boss and the chief editor was some achievement, Phil thought. He had never felt so important as he did at the moment he walked into Rudy's office. Both he and Harry Walkinshaw offered to remove his jacket and asked him to sit down, relax and get comfortable. Phil was determined to savour this moment of triumph, as he knew he would probably get his ass kicked tomorrow.

'Welcome back to New York, Phil,' said Rudy.

'Thanks boss. It's good to be back.'

'Yeah, nice to see you,' Harry chimed in. 'Your call from Los Angeles! Tell us what that was all about? Fill us in.'

Phil had already given Rudy a brief overview of his discussion with Peter Bent, but for Harry's benefit as well, he filled them in with the full conversation that he had with Pete.

'That's an incredible chain of events,' Rudy remarked.

'Does he realise that we will have to go to press on what he has disclosed,' said Harry.

'He has no doubt in his mind what the consequences are. I covered the implications with him. Quite frankly, I reckon he's glad to get it all over with. It was really troubling him. At the right time he'll cut a deal with the courts and I've said I'll help him if I can.'

Phil went on to tell both Rudy and Harry everything that had happened in Sydney, except his romance with Fran. This was not the time to pop that one out of the woodwork. That would have to be saved for another day. He had been in the office for nearly two hours and he could feel his speech becoming slurry. His eyes were beginning to roll back into his head. The lack of sleep on the long trip had caught up with him. Looking at Rudy he didn't need to ask to go home. The signs were all there. They both knew they were not going to get any more sense out of him tonight. Rudy called the chauffeur and ordered him to pick Mr Black up from his office and make sure he gets home.

By the time the chauffeur had got to the office, Phil had fallen asleep in the chair.

$\mathscr{T}$WENTY-$\mathscr{S}$IX

The Premier of the Government had not been given an option. He had to refer the bribery allegation concerning his Minister to the Commission Against Corruption; CAC as it was commonly known.

CAC had been formed in the eighties by a former government which had come into political power on the promise of a crime free state. It was supposed to be an independent commission for reviewing corrupt activity within government. It was designed to be free of the influence of politicians and the judiciary. It was not a court of law and could only refer its findings to the public prosecutor for legal redress. The powers of CAC were so great that politicians feared that the institution was above the law.

The Minister had been told by the Premier that he had to step down from his position whilst the investigation was being conducted by CAC. As a member of the left wing faction of the incumbent government, the minister was strongly opposed to that action being taken. He was confident that he would not be exposed, as the financial dealings he'd had with Wallshot were offshore transactions and most probably could never be traced. The Premier was under intense pressure to make sure that he did step aside until the matter was resolved. He could not afford to have a scandal of this nature bring the whole government down.

The Commission's hearings commenced straight away. The whole sordid affair had to be brought to a head as early as possible.

Justice Roberts was appointed by the government to head up the hearing into the bribery allegations. He was a fairly impartial character, although over the years he had expressed some fairly radical left wing views. There was a belief within political circles that he favoured the sitting government.

The Commission was to report back to the Government within the next seven days. That was a fairly tall order considering the starting point was no more than a newspaper article appearing in the *New York Herald* some days earlier.

Justice Roberts was able to select a competent group of analytical researchers to assist him uncover as much as he could on the allegations. He hoped that it would not entail a trip to the United States to interview the author of the article, to determine the source of the allegations. His previous experience in investigations of this kind had turned out not to be particularly fruitful as he found that most journalists would not disclose their source, even if they were threatened with contempt of court proceedings. On a couple of occasions in the past he had not hesitated to jail two journalists for not co-operating with the Commission and wouldn't hesitate to take that same course with this hearing if an obstacle got in his way.

The decision to talk to the author of the article had been made by Justice Roberts. One of his researchers advised him that it was the editor of the *New York Herald*, Harry Walkinshaw, who was responsible for the article appearing in the American press. Justice Roberts did not hesitate to pick up the phone at the appropriate time and ask for Walkinshaw.

'Mr Walkinshaw, my name is Justice Roberts. I have been appointed to investigate certain allegations that appeared in your paper concerning one of our Ministers accepting bribes.'

'I'm pleased to talk to you, Justice Roberts. How can I help with your investigation?' Walkinshaw asked.

'I understand that you may have some evidence suggesting the Minister has accepted bribes from a Mr. Wallshot of the Wallshot Corporation?'

'We certainly do have evidence.'

'Are you able to share that information with me?'

'I'll need to talk with our lawyers first. You'll understand our need to be cautious. I'll need you to fax me a request for information.'

'I can do better than that, Mr Walkinshaw. I can arrange for our government representative office in New York to drop that around to your office within the next few hours.'

'Get them to telephone me then and in the meantime I'll see what I can do for you.'

'I appreciate your co-operation, Mr Walkinshaw,' Justice Roberts said and then hung up the telephone.

He felt reasonably comfortable with the relationship that he had established with Harry Walkinshaw. It was cordial and a little formal, he thought, but considering the sensitivity of the matter, he was feeling rather pleased with his initial success. Justice Roberts arranged for the government office in New York to contact Walkinshaw immediately.

In the meantime, the Minister had been requested to appear before the Commission to face questioning over the allegations. This had to take place immediately after he had received a response from the *New York Herald*. Roberts knew the Minister was going to deny the accusations and without any firm evidence on which to question him, the cross-examination was going to be tough.

During the course of the day, the Minister had held a press conference, denying any association with Wallshot and threatening to sue the *New York Herald* and anyone else who muttered a word on the matter.

The hearing was now set to take place.

Senator Groves had wasted no time in forming his Senate Committee to investigate the 1993 Island Bend Defence Services contract that had been awarded to the Wallshot Corporation.

There were six senators appointed to the Committee, three republicans and three democrats. The President had insisted on the committee being of equal representation, as it would appear to the electorate that this was not a witch-hunt on Wallshot. Senator Groves was appointed Chairman.

Senator Groves was an old Senate campaigner. He realised that this was probably going to be the last opportunity he would have to seek justice against Wallshot. He had been a thorn in his side for many years.

Wallshot had been requested to appear before the Senate hearing and give evidence against the allegation that he had offered a bribe to secure the Island Bend contract. He had threatened not to appear and indicated in no uncertain terms that he was strongly opposed to the hearing being re-opened. Senator Groves was confident that he would turn up and do everything possible to clear his name.

Harry Walkinshaw had been in touch with Rudy Morphett to let him know that he had received a call from Justice Roberts requesting information they may have on the Aussie bribery scandal. Rudy was extremely impressed with the way the State government had reacted and told Harry to give the Commission what ever they needed to secure a conviction against Wallshot.

A few hours after he had last spoken to Justice Roberts, Harry received a telephone call from a guy letting him know he was from the Australian Government's New York office. He told Harry that he had been asked to secure some information from him regarding a bribery scandal back home. Harry suggested that they should meet and he would give him what he wanted. The representative agreed to be in Harry's office within the hour.

Rudy was on edge when he contacted Phil Black. Phil just put it down to the fact that the Wallshot affair was getting to him and that was the reason why he had called Phil back from Sydney, so that he could take over the story and take the pressure off him. What Phil didn't know was that Rudy had just received a call from the New York Stock Exchange, asking for an explanation why *New York Herald* stock was being dumped in the market. He had no answer for them. It concerned him greatly that Wall Street had lost confidence in his management and were prepared to quit stock without discussing the matter with him firstly. He had always demonstrated an open door policy for them. Why weren't they returning the same courtesy, he thought.

'Phil, I want you to cover the Senator Groves hearings. They are due to start in Washington tomorrow morning. Introduce yourself to Harry Groves. He's expecting to hear from you.'

'Do you want me there for the complete hearing?' he asked.

'Use your judgement. The interesting part will be the Wallshot evidence. That's assuming he turns up of course. Remember it is a public hearing and we can only print the facts as they are handed down. I don't want contempt charges laid against us at this stage.'

'I'll get the shuttle down first thing in the morning, boss.'

Rudy Morphett was becoming increasingly more anxious as the minutes ticked away. His advisers had informed him that there were two parties quitting the stock at any cost. They told Rudy that they were uncertain whom the selling brokers were representing, but it appeared to be offshore interests. He was not satisfied with the answers they were giving him and demanded that they get off their asses and find out what sonofabitches were putting it up him.

New York was like a lifetime away from Sydney, Phil kept thinking to himself. He had not spoken to Fran since he had returned to the States. All he wanted was a few minutes of privacy where he could have a few precious moments of conversation with her. The only thing he could do to overcome the problem was to slip out of the office and use the pay phone in the lobby. If he hung around much longer, someone was likely to collar him and that would be the end of it for the day.

Picking up his jacket, he had a quick look around and he was confident that now was the time as everyone around him was otherwise occupied. Moving to the elevator, he kept saying to himself, I'll be with you soon Fran. The elevator ground to a standstill. The doors opening vigorously. He was about to step inside, when a voice yelled out across the press office, 'Mr Black, you're wanted on the telephone.'

'Stuff it,' he said, 'I didn't hear you.' In that split second he was on the brink of turning away from the instrument that provided part of his livelihood, the telephone. A journalist never refused to take a call. It could be a story I'm walking away from, he reminded himself. The elevator doors began to shut. He stretched and pushed the open door button. The doors flew open. The office he was so confident of leaving behind for a few minutes re-appeared.

'Who's on the telephone?' he barked.

'Someone called Markowitz. He said he's calling from Florida.'

Phil ran back to his desk. Markowitz was the last person he expected to hear from. He thought he had treated him a bit unfairly back in Sydney and had not really told him everything he was up to. Still, if he had been in the same position, he would have played his cards pretty close to his chest, he kept saying over in his mind.

'Phil Black here. Is that you, Joe?'

'Phil, I haven't got much time, I need to talk to you. Listen to me and please don't interrupt.'

'I understand, mate.'

'When we last met I said I would help you where possible with your Wallshot story. Well, I've been doing a little of my own research and I'm convinced that Bob Wallshot has bought himself many favours over the years. The main purpose of this call, however, is to let you know that you should be aware that *New York Herald* stock is being sold short in the marketplace.'

'Shit, this sort of information could get you and me into a lot of trouble.'

'I know and I also know that I can trust you to use the information discreetly. What you need to know is that Wallshot is selling short using a Cayman's Island Corporation. Naturally you'll have difficulty tracing the ownership. Listen, I'll have to go. The walls have got ears in this place.'

'Joe, I'll use the information carefully. Thanks, make sure we keep in touch.'

The call to Fran would have to wait. He checked his watch. It would be early morning back in Sydney. He convinced himself that Fran could not be disturbed in the early hours of the morning.

Phil understood that selling stock short was a fairly common practice with investors. Why then would Wallshot be selling *New York Herald* stock? Morphett and he had scant respect for each other. There had to be another motive.

The only thing Phil could do with this sort of information was to lay it on the boss himself. If there were a run on the stock, he would certainly know about it. He called Morphett's office and told his secretary that he wanted to talk with him straight away.

'Boss, is there a run on *New York Herald* stock?'

'Yeah. It appears someone's trying to fuck me! What's it to you, Phil?'

'I've just been told that Wallshot is short selling your stock, using a Cayman's Island Corporation.'

'Christ that's all I need. I expected the prick to make some move. He wants to ruin me. There are two sellers in the market. I'm waiting on my financial people to tell me who they are. If one is Wallshot, who the hell is the other?'

'Boss, you didn't hear this from me. OK.'

Morphett acknowledged the sensitivity of the detail that he had just been given by Phil and would do everything possible to protect the source of his information. He had no idea where he had picked up the lead, only assuming that it was a Sydney informant.

The financial advisers to the *Herald* had to be told straight away. They could spend wasted hours trying to dig up this type of information. When Morphett finally got hold of them he let them know that Wallshot was selling *Herald* stock short. He asked them who the other seller was. The adviser said that they were waiting on confirmation but believed it was the Banque de Genève out of Zurich.

The penny then dropped. Morphett was now convinced that Wallshot had made a move to buy the *Herald*, using his contacts in the Swiss bank to dump their stock and push the price down. Him selling short would exacerbate the problem. At the appropriate time, Wallshot would have to come back into the market to buy his short sold stock and then continue to purchase a controlling interest at rock bottom prices. Morphett knew that once there was a run on the stock it would continue for a few days until market confidence was restored. If he was going to checkmate Wallshot, then he would have to make his move now. He instructed his financial advisers to soak up all the available stock in his name. If he could starve Wallshot of stock to satisfy his short selling then he had him snookered. It would also send a signal out to the market that Rudy Morphett had confidence in the *Herald*. This would stabilise the stock price and turn the falling price around pretty quickly.

The *Herald* stockbrokers moved into the market immediately, buying up all stock that was offered for sale. In the first hour of trading the *Herald* stock had dropped seven dollars with over fifty million shares being dumped. This represented approximately ten per cent of the total stock in the Corporation.

By mid morning the stock was still being heavily traded. The price had dropped a further two dollars with another one hundred million shares been traded. This time Rudy was buying and had secured nearly all of the mid morning stock sale. By noon it was estimated that over one hundred and fifty million shares had been traded in *Herald* stock, which represented about thirty per cent of the total capital. Wallshot had sold short twenty per cent as he had instructed Markowitz, but had only been able to buy back a little less than ten per cent. Morphett had picked up twenty per cent.

At the commencement of afternoon trading, movements in the stock suddenly ceased. Apparently the Banque de Genève had removed its sell orders. As small trades began to trickle through the price of the stock began to move upwards. Morphett had won round one of his confrontation with Wallshot. He had left him with a short fall of ten per cent of the capital, which he had to buy back at whatever price he could negotiate otherwise he would find himself in dire straits with the SEC and the NYSE.

By the end of the day the *Herald* stock price had moved to two dollars above the early morning pre sell off price.

Morphett was totally exhausted and at a little after six he flunked backwards in his chair and called to his secretary Amanda to tell Phil Black to get himself up to his office.

Phil just wanted to get back to his apartment, when he heard from Amanda. The last thing he needed this late in the evening was a meeting with his boss. From past experiences he had found that these meetings usually went on to the early hours of the morning.

'You look terrible!' Rudy remarked to Phil.

'I feel bloody awful, boss. Can we keep this meeting short, I do need to get some sleep,' he cheekily remarked.

'Sure. Thanks for the tip off you gave me on the stock. If your source were here I'd kiss his ass. We saved the *Herald* from falling into Wallshot's hands.'

'This may spell the end of an era! He still has to face several allegations of corruption.'

'I'm sure something else will come out of the woodwork.'

'Phil, let me tell you I'm still convinced that we are just seeing the beginning of this man.'

'Well, you had me convinced that he had a tilt at the corporation and failed. That should be the end of him as far as the *Herald* is concerned.'

'No, that was only a side-step. Controlling the paper would have given him editorial clout on what was written about him. There's still something around the corner and I can nearly guarantee that we are going to know all about it shortly.'

'Stick with your instinct, boss. I'll keep the ammunition coming.'

With that Phil left the meeting. The trip to his apartment could not come quickly enough. He fought desperately to keep himself from dropping off on his way home.

He would ring Fran tomorrow.

$\mathcal{T}$WENTY-$\mathcal{S}$EVEN

The CAC hearing investigating the allegation that a Minister of the Crown had acted corruptly was scheduled to commence taking evidence at ten that morning. The hearing would be held in one of the Commission's chambers, probably in one of the smaller units as it was expected that very few witnesses would be called. Justice Roberts had only been given seven days in which to prepare a preliminary report for the Premier. The government's office in New York had been in touch with Harry Walkinshaw of the *New York Herald* and had been given access to a considerable amount of material that no doubt would be used as Commission evidence during the hearing.

Justice Roberts was to be assisted by two junior barristers who would prepare the case and collect whatever research was required to be presented as evidence. There would also be two court reporters and a commission clerk. Security at the Commission was low-key as this particular hearing did not pose a threat to witnesses or any other party that may be involved.

Over the next few days the Commission would call for evidence from the Minister, Mike Johnston, Chief Executive Officer of Wallshot's Australian operations, Director of Prisons and a representative of one of the major accounting firms.

Justice Roberts would be hopeful that at the conclusion of the hearing he would have sufficient evidence to present to the Premier.

Right on the dot of ten, Justice Roberts entered the chamber. Those in the room stood up and bowed as he took his seat.

The Commission Clerk was asked by Justice Roberts to read out the terms of reference for the hearing. The terms of reference had been prepared by the government and approved by the Cabinet. The document was not particularly lengthy with the clerk finishing her recitation after about four minutes. The terms of reference were quite simple, requesting that a commission of inquiry investigate the allegations surrounding the Minister.

With the formalities out of the way, Justice Roberts wasted no time in asking the Minister to take a seat in the witness box. Despite his earlier threats not to appear, he seemed to be quite relaxed as he made his way to the witness chair. The Commission clerk asked him to place his hands on a new edition of the Holy Bible and repeat after her that the evidence he was about to give was the whole truth and nothing but the truth. He followed her command, not faltering once. He was extremely confident that he was not going to have his political career tarnished out of this kangaroo court, which he had referred to earlier in the week.

Justice Roberts looked straight at him and asked him if he understood the reason why he was appearing before this commission of inquiry. The Minister acknowledged that he did and went on to say that he found it to be quite distasteful that his reputation and long years of service to the community had been questioned in this manner. His comments were entered into the Commission records.

'Minister, certain allegations that originated from a New York newspaper, have been brought before this Commission for investigation. Those allegations suggest that you accepted certain financial rewards from a corporation based in the United States, known as Wallshot Corporation. What do you have to say about these allegations, Minister?'

For the first time since his arrival at the hearing, the Minister looked a little distressed. The shock of the formal challenge from the Royal Commissioner that he may be involved in a bribery scandal took him unawares. He sat upright in the witness chair and composed himself, before he answered the Commissioner's opening remark.

'I've read the same newspaper articles as you have and after twenty years in politics if I believed everything that was published in a newspaper I wouldn't be sitting here today. Any suggestion that I have taken a bribe from the Wallshot Corporation is fabricated and totally untrue and I intend to sue the New York newspaper for libel.'

Justice Roberts was not distracted by the Minister's outburst.

'Were you the Minister responsible for awarding Wallshot Corporation contracts for the management of five prisons?'

'I was and I'm proud to say that in doing so the taxpayers have reaped the benefit of my actions.'

'Minister, would you be so kind as to just answer the question. This is not a political rally and answers of a superfluous nature are irrelevant.'

The Minister stared at Justice Roberts for a few moments not quite sure how to respond to such a remark. He thought for a moment before he answered, knowing that the last thing he needed to do was to piss the Commissioner off unnecessarily.

'Your remark is well founded, Commissioner, this is not a political rally, just a political witch hunt!'

'Did the Wallshot Corporation have to compete in the open market place for each of the contracts it was awarded?'

'Yes, there was an open tender system. We encouraged a wide range of experienced companies to submit tenders.'

'I would like you to reflect back on the very first contract that you awarded Wallshot Corporation. Did they have the lowest tender price?'

'They were the lowest tender and they also provided the best value for money.'

'Did you see the tender prices of the other parties before you accepted Wallshot's bid?'

'No I did not. That was the responsibility of the evaluation committee to recommend to me as Minister the winning party.'

'You never saw the tender prices of the other competitors?'

'Commissioner, how many times do I have to tell you. No!'

The question was asked deliberately as the Commissioner had sitting in front of him a photocopy of a handwritten note that the Minister had prepared and sent to Bob Wallshot, outlining the tender prices of each of the competing parties for the first contract. The note also went on to say, 'If you want to win you have to beat these prices.'

'You have told us, Minister, that you did not get to see all the tender submissions and that you based your judgement on the recommendation of the evaluation committee. Did the same procedure apply to the other four contracts that were awarded to Wallshot Corporation?'

'Yes it did, and for the very good reason that a minister had to distance himself from the evaluation process, otherwise he could finish up here answering bloody stupid questions like me. Where is all this leading to, Justice Roberts?'

'To determine the truth Minister, the truth! Did you at any time wonder why Wallshot Corporation had been successful on each occasion?'

'It was a little unusual. It never concerned me. Governments prefer to establish relationships with its suppliers. This I considered to be a good relationship.'

'Did you at any time ever receive any form of gratuity for awarding a contract to Wallshot Corporation?'

Justice Roberts could not wait any longer. He thought it was appropriate to get straight to the point. He knew the Minister was lying as he had evidence in front of him that had contradicted his opening questions. The Minister had now been put into the spotlight.

'I resent the manner in which the question has been put to me, but in the spirit of contributing to the right outcome for this hearing, I again categorically deny accepting any form of gratuity from Wallshot Corporation'.

'Minister, the Commission thanks you for appearing here today. I will however reserve the right to ask you back at a later stage, should it be necessary.'

The Minister breathed a sigh of relief. He was convinced that the Commission had no hard evidence and that it would be only a matter of a few days before all this was over.

During the course of the day, Justice Roberts took evidence from the Director of Prisons. He was particularly interested in learning more about the tender process and the role of the evaluation committee. The Director was only able to give the Royal Commissioner a broad overview of the tender process and the role of the evaluation committee, as he had not been head of the department at the time the contracts were awarded. The previous Director of Prisons could not be asked to submit evidence as he had died a few years earlier.

The representative of one of the leading professional accounting firms had been requested by Justice Roberts to provide an overview on how the Swiss banking system functioned. This was particularly important to him as it had been reported in the *New York Herald* that the Minister had allegedly received cheques drawn on a Wallshot Swiss bank account. The accounting expert stated that it was an extremely easy process, providing funds paid were drawn and deposited in Switzerland. Justice Roberts had also asked the accounting expert whether or not it was possible to trace the existence of funds paid into offshore Swiss accounts. The expert was fairly confident that transactions of that type were nearly always untraceable. The Swiss authorities were renowned for protecting client confidentialities, the expert informed the Royal Commissioner.

It was after four in the afternoon. Justice Roberts had concluded taking evidence for the day and adjourned the hearing until ten the following morning. He planned to put Mike Johnston in the witness box tomorrow, to determine whether or not he had played any part in the alleged bribery scandal.

During the first day of the CAC hearing, Mike Johnston had been spending most of the day at his office, browsing through the old contract files for the five prisons the company managed on behalf of the Government. He had been hoping to find some evidence that might link Bob Wallshot with the Minister. He was fairly certain there would be nothing as he had been involved in every one of the contract negotiations. From what he could recall there had never been a suggestion of any wrongdoing. Mike was not sure what value he would be to the Commission. He was fairly certain in his own mind that any evidence he could offer would be pretty tame. There was nothing that he was aware of that was incriminating.

The Commission clerk had telephoned Mike's office late in the afternoon to ask him to make sure that he was at the Commission chamber by ten the following morning.

Justice Roberts was sitting in his office late in the evening poring over transcript of that day's proceedings. This was the part that he did not particularly like but unfortunately he knew it was part and parcel of the job that he had to do. At the same time that he was reviewing the transcript, the barristers assisting him were going over the documents with a fine tooth comb. They were scheduling the pertinent information and preparing questions for the Royal Commissioner to ask those witnesses that had not as yet appeared before him.

The Commission clerk came into his office looking a little puzzled. She approached his desk and told him there was a gentleman waiting in reception who needed to talk to him urgently about the hearing. Justice Roberts looked at her somewhat perplexed.

'Who is this gentleman and what does he want?'

'I don't know, your Honour. He won't tell me. All he is prepared to say is that he has some information that could assist you with your hearing.'

'This is highly irregular. Ask him in and I need you to join us.'

The clerk left the Justice for a few moments whilst she made her way out to reception. The gentleman who had asked to see Justice Roberts was sitting down, anxiously waiting for some type of response from the Commission clerk.

'Justice Roberts will see you,' she said. 'Would you please follow me to his office.'

He acknowledged her courteousness and followed her to Justice Robert's suite.

'My name is Justice Roberts, I believe you want to see me? How can I help?'

'I have some information that will help you with your hearing. Before I share that with you I need to be assured that you are in a position to grant me immunity from prosecution.'

'I can't do that until I have an understanding how valuable the information is to the hearing. What I can provide you with is my personal assurance that I will do everything in my power to help with your request for immunity. If that's not acceptable then I guess we have nothing to discuss.'

The gentleman thought this over for a moment. He knew the system well enough to know that Justice Roberts could not offer him immunity. He would have to discuss the request with the Attorney General and get his approval to grant immunity from prosecution. There was a gamble, but he was prepared to take it.

'My name is Peter Bent! I work at the Ministry of Prisons.'

During the next four hours, Peter went through the events of the last several years, giving Justice Roberts a detailed account of his involvement in the Ministerial bribery scandal. The Commission clerk had been furiously taking down every word that Peter uttered. As midnight approached, Peter had exhausted himself and was not able to offer anything more to help the Commission. He had cleared his memory of every minute detail. It was a load off his mind. The burden had been lifted. He had finally told someone of the Walter Mitty lifestyle he had been living all those years.

Justice Roberts told him that he would speak with the Attorney General first thing in the morning and request that consideration be given to granting him immunity from prosecution. The one credible thing that Peter had done was that he had donated all of the bribery money to charity.

'I will need to call you as a witness, but I will not do that until I have a clear signal from the Attorney General. By the way, has the Minister been in touch with you?'

'No he hasn't. I've asked myself the same question several times. I have no answer. Perhaps he thinks he's beyond the law!'

'Most politicians do, Mr Bent. Thank you for sharing all this information with me tonight. In a perverse way I admire you for your courage and honesty.'

That had been enough for one night. Justice Roberts had to get hold of the Attorney General first thing in the morning and see whether or not he could strike a deal with him. It wasn't going to be easy.

$\mathscr{T}$WENTY-$\mathscr{E}$IGHT

The Chairman of Banque de Genève had called an emergency meeting of the directors to find out who had authorised the sale of *New York Herald* stock held by the bank. It was scheduled as a crisis meeting and it was expected that all directors would attend.

Of all the directors only two did not turn up. The chairman was aware that one of his colleagues had been recently hospitalised and couldn't be expected to attend the meeting. The other missing director was Lukas Mueller.

The meeting was held in the main boardroom of the bank's headquarters just off the Bahnofstrasse. The building had been built in the late eighteen hundreds and had been carefully restored internally to reflect the period architecture. No expense had been spared in the use of European timber panelling interlaced between the light beige Italian marble walls. The main foyer led to the oversize marble staircase, which was the main entry to the first floor of the ornate building. On the first floor there were only two rooms. At the top of the staircase was the office of the President of the bank, which had been richly decorated, with all the fine furniture of the period. Adjoining his office was the bank's principal boardroom. The boardroom was used exclusively for the directors. In the centre of the room was a large oak table, decorated in gothic style. Around the table were sixteen chairs, each ornately carved with lush leather seat panelling. The one wall was covered with a fourteenth century tapestry depicting a Franco-Swiss battle scene, whilst two of the other walls had impressionist paintings by Monet, Manet and Cezanne, hanging majestically. Behind the oak boardroom table was a full size window which allowed full sunlight to enter the room when the drapes were pulled open. Each of the directors had his own seat at the boardroom table and upon their arrival, coffee was served.

The Chairman wasted no time in calling the meeting to order. He expressed grave concern at the bank's action to dump its stockholding in the *New York Herald*. The directors were dismayed. They knew that an action of this kind had to be authorised by the board because of the significance of the transaction. No one around that room had prior knowledge of the sale. The Chairman was quick to point out that the only person who could shed some light on the deal was Lukas Mueller, who, according to him could not be located.

It was the head of investment banking that had been astute enough to realise that the order to sell had been placed and it was only after his intervention that the order was cancelled. The Chairman went on to tell the board of directors that it appeared that Lukas Mueller gave the instructions to sell the stock, with no one questioning his decision or more importantly his authority to do so.

The dumping of the stock had been an international embarrassment to the bank and the bank would have to put special measures in place to ensure that a transaction of this type never happened again.

At the conclusion of the meeting, the Chairman called for the termination of Lukas Mueller's contract with the bank. Given the circumstances the board had no alternative but to terminate his services immediately.

The Senate hearing into the Island Bend Defence contract was due to kick off next morning in Washington. Bob Wallshot had returned to his office, after an absence of several days, to prepare himself to confront Senator Groves. In the meantime his financial advisers had prepared their final report on the likely shortfall of stock to be bought back, to cover his short selling of *New York Herald* stock. Wallshot had been told that the news was not good. There was a shortfall of fifty million shares with the stock price slowly rising.

Markowitz had been summoned to Wallshot's office to discuss how the corporation was going to finance the buy back of the stock.

'Have you read the advisers report on the *Herald* stock shortfall?' BW asked.

'In detail, unfortunately. We haven't got that sort of cash in the corporation. I've estimated we'd have to provide over six hundred million dollars to cover the shortfall.'

'How much can you put your hands on in the next seventy-two hours?'

'If I drain all the domestic and international accounts, at tops fifty million.'

'That leaves us five fifty shy. Has the market discovered that the corporation owns the Cayman Island company that sold the stock?'

'I'd say not at this stage because if they had the Wallshot stock price would be falling. That hasn't happened as yet.'

'How long can we stall telling the SEC?'

'We should be telling them now.'

'That's not what I wanted to hear. I want to know how long can I stall them?'

'You can't. I refuse to be a party to that type of tactic, Mr Wallshot. If you want to play that sort of game, you find some other whipping boy to do your dirty work. You got this corporation in the shit and you sure can take it upon yourself to get the corporation out of the shit, because I won't be here to help.'

The veins in Markowitz's neck were nearly bursting, as he became more and more infuriated. Wallshot had pushed him too far once too often. He stood up and leant over Wallshot's desk shaking his fist at him as he left his office, slamming the door behind and then making his way back to his office to empty his drawers before he left the building.

The sudden change in Markowitz's attitude was not surprising, as he had been preparing himself for this moment for some time now. It had all started after he'd had his first discussion with Mike Johnston, back in Sydney and had slowly developed since then. His phone call to Phil Black to tell him about Wallshot's plan to sell short *New York Herald* stock had brought the whole affair to a head. He knew that after that he could not stay around and see the corporation collapse around him.

Wallshot had only been spoken to once before like that. He wouldn't tolerate that attitude. He looked for excuses, blaming

Markowitz for whatever reason he could lay his hands on. Although he had just been told by Markowitz that he would no longer work for him, he still did not have an answer as to how he was going to finance the five fifty shortfall.

The last thing he needed right now was a diversion of this magnitude. He was due to meet with his colleagues at Buena Vista in a few days to plan the final operational assault for Incarceration. Short term funding was a solution. Perhaps the Banque de Genève would come to the party, he thought. BW impulsively dialled Lukas Mueller to be greeted by a Swiss-French speaking receptionist who very politely told him in broken English that Mr Mueller was no longer with the bank. In desperation he attempted to get some clearer answers from her asking if she knew where he could be contacted. She had been instructed by the Chairman that if anyone should be looking to speak to Mr Mueller, she should put the call straight through to his office. At that moment the Chairman took the call and asked if he could help. Wallshot did not know what to say for a moment. He asked to be put on to Lukas Mueller. The Chairman reinforced the receptionist's earlier advice that Mueller was no longer with the bank and offered to assist. Wallshot explained who he was. Although the Chairman had never met Bob Wallshot, he was extremely familiar with the banking operations of Wallshot and his Corporation.

'Mr Wallshot, I'm aware that Mr Mueller has always looked after your banking affairs, but unfortunately he left us rather suddenly today. Perhaps I can help you?'

'Well, I don't know. I need some short term funding to finance the expansion of my operations.'

'How much is required?' Mr Wallshot.

'Five hundred and fifty million US dollars.'

'What collateral can you offer the bank for this additional funding?'

'My personal stock holding in my corporation.'

'We would also be seeking a charge over your deposits with the Banque de Genève, Mr Wallshot.'

'Listen you sonofabitch, you'll get my personal stock only. You touch those deposits and I'll have your fucking balls.'

The bank had no obligation to advance the funds to Wallshot, but the Chairman did agree after Wallshot's outburst that he would refer the matter to his international banking division for a decision and promised to get back to him within the next day.

A contingency plan was needed. Wallshot had the feeling that the bank was going to knock him back. He knew that Mueller had stuck his neck out many times for him in the past and now that he was not there he could not rely on that support.

The one source that he knew he could tap was his close personal friend, Paul Lowenstein of First Bank of America. He decided to keep that alternative up his sleeve until he had heard from the Banque de Genève. He would only use Lowenstein as a last resort as he was going to need his help to get Incarceration off the ground.

Not long after Markowitz had arrived home and gone through the pain of explaining to his wife that he had thrown his job in, he thought it would be important to let Phil Black know that he had quit his job at Wallshot Corporation.

It had been a restless night for Phil, he had tossed and turned and had found it difficult to get to sleep. Across the street from his apartment was a large flashing neon sign. All the years he had lived there he hadn't particularly noticed the sign or its flashing during the evening. He lay awake for hours thinking about his life and what he had done with it. Had it been wasted since his wife unexpectedly left him? He remembered vividly the pain and sorrow that he suffered for many years and despite help from friends he was never able to come to grips with why she had been taken from him at such an early age.

The years he spent languishing in New York, had it not been for Rudy Morphett, where would he have been? Being away from the office on assignment was his escape mechanism. There he was able to vent his anger by throwing his heart and soul into the job ahead. This provided him with temporary relief only as the pain and misery returned when he was back in his city apartment.

What about kids, he began to think. Would he have had children had his first wife not been taken from him? How many would there have been? A boy and a girl sounded like a good combination. On second thoughts perhaps not, too old.

The neon sign kept flickering. He got out of bed and moved to the window, peering on to the street below. There was little movement apart from a couple of street kids fossicking through the garbage and a road sweeper brushing the previous days filth from the roadside. There were several neon signs in the street. Surely they must have been put up the day before? They weren't there when he left for Sydney. Or were they? Perhaps he had never spent the time to open the window and look outside.

What did this mean? Fran had been on his mind since the moment he had got home. There was purpose to his life, he thought over and over again. Perhaps Fran was the influence. The hills were greener on the other side. He had never felt so strongly about anyone for many years. He even thought for a moment that he felt more passionately about Fran than he had ever felt for his wife when she was alive.

The bedside clock chimed four. That was the first time he could recall hearing the clock chime. 'What a pretty sound,' he echoed. 'Fran, where are you?' he called out, as he picked up the phone and began dialling her Sydney number. 'Hi, it's me. How are you sweetheart?'

'Oh Phil, where have you been? You promised me you'd ring when you got to New York. I have been so worried. It's been nearly three days.'

'Fran, darling, I have no excuses, please forgive me.'

'You're excused. I thought for one terrible moment that our time together had been a dream and that you had forgotten me.'

'Well your dream is broken. I have missed you and let me tell you I have done nothing but think about you from the moment I stepped on that plane.'

'Phil, I can't bear to be apart from you. I'm going to close the business down for a few weeks and come to New York.'

Phil was so excited by the news he couldn't contain himself for a few moments.

'Shit, the bloody neon sign has gone out!'

'Phil, what are you talking about.'

'Oh, nothing just a private joke, between me and a friend who hangs around.'

'When are you leaving?'

198

'I'll try and get on a flight before the weekend. You can put me up?'

'By the time you get here there will be plenty of room.'

The phone was placed gently on the cradle. Fran would be with him in a few days. What were they going to do together? Shopping in New York was top of the list. A visit to the Empire State building; Statue of Liberty; Ferry ride around Long Island; World Trade Centre; the list was endless. Firstly though he had to get the apartment shipshape. In the years that he had lived there, nothing had been done. In fact Phil couldn't even recall the last time he swept the carpet.

'First things first,' he said. Coffee and toast and then a plan of attack before he caught a taxi to La Guardia for his shuttle flight to Washington.

Harry Groves' Senate hearing received a mention on page three of the *Washington Express*. It only covered a few lines and even then the journalist had not got it quite right. That was the *Express* for you. The paper had been living off its reputation since its reporting of the Cuban crisis back in the sixties. The best it could do these days was to cover the events on Capitol Hill or the gossip around the corridors of the White House.

You'd probably find that most Washingtonians had never heard of Bob Wallshot. Those that did wouldn't be interested in the allegations surrounding him. Cynically, most people in the capital were of the opinion that nearly all politicians and bureaucrats were useless and corrupt, so someone like Wallshot would be like water off a duck's back to them.

The Senate Committee hearing was due to kick off at ten sharp. Bob Wallshot had been asked to appear and at this late stage it was still uncertain as to whether or not he would turn up. He had made it well known on several occasions that he had no intention of participating in a kangaroo court. As far as he was concerned the matter was closed.

The hearing room selected was one of the smaller chambers, big enough to accommodate seating for the six senators selected to conduct the hearing, with sufficient seating for an audience although it was most unlikely that many would attend, apart from those that were acting as advisers to witnesses called to provide evidence.

The bells had rung. It was right on ten. Senator Groves and his Committee Members entered the chamber and took up their positions.

A larger than expected audience had gathered. There were representatives from several newspapers including Phil Black scribing for the *New York Herald* and its syndicated papers. At the back of the chamber was a small group of men dressed in business suits, who appeared not to be too interested in what was going on around them.

Senator Groves provided the background on why the committee had been re-convened, without giving any indication as to his discussions with the President and the influence of Rudy Morphett. He indicated to the committee that certain irregularities had arisen in recent times, which could have a bearing on the outcome of the earlier hearing.

The Senators had all been debriefed at the time they were selected to join the Committee and were just going through the motions of displaying an interest in what Senator Groves was telling them and those members of the audience that were present.

Phil Black sat in the section reserved for the journalists. This area was dedicated to them and provided them with sufficient desk space in which to jot down their notes. It also gave them their own exit should they urgently need to get to the bank of phones outside the hearing chamber.

When he entered the chamber Phil had carefully looked around the room to see if there was anyone that he knew. Apart from a number of journalists that he had bumped into from time to time on various assignments, the audience was no more than a sea of unknown faces. He did, however, notice the small group of men sitting in the back of the chamber. They were more than interested bystanders. There were four of them and they each knew one another. Before the day was over he intended to find out who they were.

Senator Groves asked the Senate clerk to call the first witness, Chuck Donnington. Chuck was the site manager at the Island Bend Defence establishment and had been in that job since Wallshot Corporation first won the contract. He had been involved in the earlier hearing and had been greatly relieved at the time that it had concluded, because he found that these types of hearings always made him extremely nauseous. It was nerve-racking to face such powerful individuals and be questioned incessantly.

'Mr Donnington, you appeared at the 1993 hearing into the awarding of the Island Bend Defence contract. May I remind you that the evidence you gave at that hearing will form part of the record for the purposes of this hearing. Do you understand what I am saying to you, Mr Donnington?'

'I do understand, Mr Chairman.'

'Are you still the site manger for that particular contract?'

'I am, Mr Chairman.'

'Has the contract been renewed since the 1993 hearing, Mr Donnington?'

'It was renewed in 1996, Mr Chairman.'

'Did your corporation have to compete in the open market for the renewal of that contract?'

Chuck Donnington was uncertain as to how he should answer the question and leant over to his lawyer to seek advice. The lawyer was an out of town lawyer who had been engaged by Bob Wallshot because of his great depth of experience in handling questions emanating from Senate hearings.

'In answer to your question, I have been instructed to advise you that I am unable to answer, as I have no knowledge of the corporation's procedures in renewing contracts.'

'Surely, Mr Donnington, you would have input into the contract you are expected to manage,' the Democrat Senator from Arkansas asked.

'I'll repeat my previous answer, Senator. I have no knowledge of the corporation's procedures in the renewal of contracts.'

'Mr Donnington, may I remind you that this hearing has been re-opened by Presidential request and I would recommend very strongly that you participate with this Senate Inquiry,' the Chairman demanded.

Again, Donnington edged towards his lawyer for instruction.

'Mr Chairman, I am determined to offer your hearing whatever assistance I can give them, however, I can only provide answers pertaining to operational issues.'

Harry Groves now realised that he had a hostile witness to contend with and was not going to get very far with this type of questioning. Chuck Donnington was excused and instructed not to leave Washington as he would be recalled at a later date. The Chairman then turned his attention to the lawyer assisting the Wallshot witness and let him know in no uncertain terms that he expected to see Mr Wallshot at the inquiry first thing tomorrow morning, otherwise he would take steps to have him subpoenaed.

The lawyer was taken back by the aggressive stand the Chairman had taken and undertook to do his best to have Wallshot at the inquiry the next day.

During the course of the hearing, the committee heard evidence from several witnesses, both from employees of the Wallshot Corporation and from the Department of Defence. Most of the evidence that had been collected was a re-hash of earlier statements made at the initial Inquiry.

The last witness called for the day was a tall slender Afro-American who answered to the name of Molly Nelson. Molly was in her mid forties, had really taken good care of herself and was easily recognisable in a crowd. When she was asked to appear in the witness seat, she moved from the rear benches and slowly ambled down the aisle. Her tight fitting short length dress hugged her body like an elastic suit. Molly was not unaccustomed to making grand entrances. She took her seat opposite Harry Groves and stared at him for several seconds before he spoke to her.

'Miss Nelson, I understand you work for the Defence Procurement Office here in Washington?' The Chairman asked.

'Please sir, call me Molly.'

'Thank you, Molly. Would you be so kind to answer the question?'

'No sir. I am no longer in the employ of the Procurement Office. I did work for that office until two weeks ago.'

'I am sorry to hear that, Miss Nelson, um Molly. Can you tell us what happened?'

'I sure can, sir. I was the Head of Contracts for Defence Procurement. I won that position in 1991 and I did a damn good job. I prepared a report in 1993 recommending that Wallshot Corporation be removed from the Island Bend Defence site.'

'Why was that, Molly?' The Republican Senator from California asked.

'Well, Sir, there were a number of irregularities in the contract file.'

'Tell the Committee, what sort of irregularities?'

'There was evidence of the government paying for services they never received.'

'That's a pretty serious accusation, Molly. Tell us more.'

'Defence Procurement was authorising payment for services that never formed part of the original contract.'

'Did you refer the anomaly to anyone in your Department?'

'I did, Sir.'

'Who was that person?'

'My immediate superior, the head of Defence Procurement, Allan Bayswater.'

'Did Mr Bayswater, take any further action, Molly?'

'No sir. In fact he removed the Island Bend contract from my portfolio.'

'Why do you think he did that?'

'Sir, it was Mr Bayswater who had been authorising the additional services.'

The questioning of Molly Nelson had been carefully planned. Molly had come to the Chairman's office a few days earlier, concerned that the Island Bend Defence hearing was being re-opened. She told the Chairman that she would like to appear before the committee. She maintained that she had information that would be invaluable to the Committee inquiry. The Chairman, after hearing what she had to say, agreed.

'Molly, you mentioned irregularities. Were there other anomalies?'

'Yes Sir, there were. Mr Bayswater would approve the accounts for payment, but the checks that were cut were not in favour of Wallshot Corporation.'

'Who were the checks in favour of, Molly?'

'A Cayman Island trading company.'

'Did you seek to address this with Mr Bayswater?'

'I did, Mr Chairman, and like I said, I had the contract taken off me.'

'Molly do you have the name of the Cayman's Island company?'

'I do Sir.'

'Please write it down for me and hand it to the Inquiry Clerk.'

Harry Groves knew exactly who the company was before he even saw Molly's scribbled note to the Inquiry clerk. He was one step ahead of Molly, because he had searched the company and found that it belonged to Wallshot Corporation. What he didn't know at this stage was how Bayswater was getting his cut of the action.

'Molly, before you step down from the witness chair, I would like to ask you one more question. Why aren't you with the Department now?'

'Sir, two weeks ago I was dismissed for poor performance. I know that wasn't true.'

'Who dismissed you?'

'Mr Bayswater dismissed me.'

'Do you think you may have been dismissed, because someone may have been aware that you would appear at this Inquiry?'

'You got it in one Sir.'

Molly Nelson was excused from the witness chair and asked to remain in Washington until the hearing had concluded.

Phil Black was startled by the revelation and the minute Molly Nelson left her seat, he got up and made his way to the exit door. He had to get to a phone before the other journalists. As he scrambled to the exit door, he noticed the four men who had all been sitting at the rear of the chamber were leaving simultaneously.

Picking up the telephone he dialled his New York office and was immediately patched through to Rudy Morphett. He told Rudy the events of the day and the startling evidence that Molly Nelson had given to Harry Groves, just before he wrapped up the day's hearing. Printing the Molly Nelson story had to be delayed for a few days, Rudy told Phil. He and the rest of the media had an arrangement with Harry Groves that nothing would be published until he had taken all of his evidence. There was concern that Wallshot might use the argument that he was being tried by the media and would seek a cancellation of the committee hearing before it had finished.

Phil put down the phone and walked across to security reception. He flashed a badge that had similar markings to a FBI Agent's shield and introduced himself as Agent Black. Looking at the security guard on the other side of the counter he demanded to look at the reception log. The log contained the names of everyone that entered the Senate chambers during a day. The security guard had no hesitation in putting the book under Phil's nose. As he thumbed through the pages carefully, he came across the names of the four men who had been sitting at the rear of the same chamber that he had been in all day. The names didn't mean much to him, but he took a note of them anyway. What did interest him, was the names of the Corporation's they each represented; First Bank of America, American Telecommunication, National Oil and the Wallshot Corporation. He remembered the names of the corporations from an earlier conversation he'd had with Rudy Morphett. These were the corporations whose heads had been meeting secretly with Bob Wallshot at his ranch recently.

$\mathcal{T}$WENTY-$\mathcal{N}$INE

Ten days in the rainforest of Belize had taken its toll on Michael Montefiore and his group of prisoners. The summer heat was unbearable, but he was determined to get every one of his charges fully trained within the time frame that had been given to him by Bob Wallshot.

The men had been rolling out of bed at five in the morning, including the two prisoners who had given him trouble the first day in camp. They were not returning to their quarters until after eight in the evening. The only way that Montefiore was going to complete his end of the bargain with Bob Wallshot was to have them working from sunrise to sunset.

One of the difficulties that he had found in the first few days was getting the group focused on the task ahead. He had still not told them what their final mission was and he planned to keep it that way until he had been instructed to prepare his men for departure.

On rising from their crude sleeping quarters the men would help themselves to breakfast. It would normally consist of eggs, ham and charred toast swilled down with black Colombian coffee.

By six in the morning, they were being transported to a specially selected spot in the depths of the rainforest, some twenty miles from base camp. The trip would normally take nearly two hours. The terrain in parts was nearly inaccessible, making it very difficult for the four-wheel drive vehicles to remain on the jungle track. If there had been an early thunderstorm, the trip would take the vehicles over three hours.

The site had been well prepared, some months before the men had arrived in Belize. One part of the area had been cleared of all vegetation and was being used for weapons training. Selected targets had been installed at various locations and the men would undergo hours of training, using the targets as firing practice.

Away from the firing range, a timber building had been erected. The building was used for the assembly and disassembly of various types of bomb devices. It was important, if the mission was to be successful, that every man involved was capable of arming and disarming a wide range of main and secondary bomb devices.

In selecting the men, Montefiore had looked for those that had experience in weapons or bomb work. Once the operation had begun, the time-frame in which to place the bombs in position was extremely tight. The men had to be capable of handling them under all conditions.

The lawyer representing the Wallshot Corporation witnesses had been in touch with Bob Wallshot to give him a full run down on the first day of the Senate hearing.

When he heard about the accusations that Molly Nelson had made, he could have torn off the head of the lawyer. He had warned Bayswater some weeks earlier that she could be a danger to him and told him to dispose of her. Obviously dismissing her and paying her to keep silent had not worked.

Not appearing before the Senate hearing was no longer an option for Wallshot. The lawyer had nothing to lose in letting him know in no uncertain terms that his survival depended upon his appearance before the committee, refuting the evidence that had been submitted to date. Wallshot was not particularly pleased with the thought of being grilled by a bunch of hard nosed politicians, whom he was convinced were there to see the finish of him. Had Bayswater covered his tracks, he would have not appeared. There was now a loose end and he had to attend to it. The only way to do that was to heed the lawyer's advice and be at the hearing the next day.

The second day of the CAC inquiry was due to take place in Sydney.

Justice Roberts had been able to get hold of the Attorney General early that morning and was able to give the Minister an outline of his meeting with Peter Bent the night before. The Attorney General did not want to discuss the matter over the telephone and asked Justice Roberts to meet with him at his office.

The Attorney General was part of the right wing faction of the government and had never been particularly fond of the Minister for Prisons. This, he thought, was a golden opportunity to bring his career to a blunt end. He knew that the Premier would be particularly interested in the news that Justice Roberts had received and no doubt would support him in finding a solution for Bent to avoid prosecution.

The Attorney General met with Justice Roberts for about an hour. The Minister's chief of staff had joined them and spent the whole meeting taking down copious notes of the discussion.

A decision would not be forthcoming immediately as the Minister had to refer the matter to the Crown solicitor for a legal interpretation of his position. He was however able to give Justice Roberts some comfort, indicating that if he could get Bent to testify against the Minister for Prisons he would do everything in his power to grant him a deal. The risk for Bent was that he was unable to spell out the deal until he had received advice from his Crown solicitor.

At the conclusion of the meeting, Justice Roberts rang the telephone number that had been given to him by Peter Bent.

'Mr Bent, I have spoke to the Attorney General about the matter we discussed last night. He cannot give you a guarantee that he can deliver immunity from prosecution, should you decide to provide evidence to the commission of inquiry.'

'That's not what I wanted to hear,' Peter snapped back.

'I know it's not, but let me remind you of the alternative. If you don't take the witness stand at the Inquiry, then you'll only leave yourself open for criminal prosecution. If that happens, I'll guarantee the outcome will be much worse than the option open to you at the moment.'

'You don't leave me much choice.'

'This is not about choices, Mr Bent. This is about a calculated risk you have to take about your future. Let me remind you that what you have done is criminal in the eyes of the law. What the Attorney General is offering you, without guarantees, is that you may stand a chance of walking away from prosecution. In my mind, Mr Bent, you have no choice.'

'What time do you want me at your Inquiry?'

Justice Roberts hung up the telephone and barely had a few minutes to prepare, before he had to enter the chamber for the second day of the hearing.

Michael Johnston was the first witness to be called to give evidence.

'Mr Johnston, you have told this Commission of Inquiry that you are the Chief Executive Officer of Wallshot Australia. How long have you been in that position?'

'I have been in the position for fifteen years.'

'Would you please give me a brief background on the type of services your company provides, Mr Johnston?'

'Wallshot Australia is a specialist business providing a wide range of services to government instrumentalities.'

'Would you be a little more specific? What type of services do you provide?'

'We operate exclusively for most governments in the Pacific region providing manpower support to satellite tracking stations; airports; defence establishments; water treatment plants; hospitals; communication centres and prisons.'

'That's a very impressive list of business interests you have, Mr Johnston. Do any other corporations in Australia provide the same range of services as your company?'

'No, sir. Other companies compete in segments of our market, but no other company works exclusively for government as we do.'

'Interesting! Tell me more about prisons?'

Sitting rather uncomfortably in the witness chair, Mike spent the next hour outlining to the Commission how Wallshot Australia got into the prison market.

'You would have to say your company's been successful, Mr Johnston?'

'Yes, Your Honour.'

'Have you met the Minister for Prisons?'

'Several times, Sir.'

'Are you aware of the allegations that have been placed before this Commission concerning the Minister?'

'I am, Sir.'

'Have you at any time offered the Minister an inducement for securing a contract to manage one of the prisons?'

Mike had been waiting for this question all morning and had even spent the previous night rehearsing what he would say if he was asked. Now the moment of truth had come and he couldn't get the words out of his mouth. He stuttered and stammered and gave the impression that he was guilty even before he had opened his mouth.

'Did you hear the question, Mr Johnston?'

'I did, Sir. No I haven't offered any inducement to the Minister,' he finally bleated, with his face turning bright red and beads of perspiration rolling off his forehead.

'Are you aware of anyone in your corporation that may have offered the Minister an inducement?'

This was the time he had hoped would never come. He knew that the Minister had accepted bribes from Bob Wallshot, but he did not have conclusive evidence to back his assumption. He had no right to make scurrilous accusations without hard evidence. How much did Justice Roberts know about the Minister's activities?

'Sir, to my knowledge no one within our Australian operations has offered the Minister an inducement.'

Justice Roberts appeared a little angry after Mike had shot forward his response to his earlier question.

'Mr Johnston, you're fencing with me! Take your previous answer to a wider plain. Are you aware of anyone in Wallshot worldwide that may have offered the Minister an inducement?'

It had now become impossible to avoid the Commissioner's direct question. It was pretty obvious that he knew something and he was expecting Johnston to come forward with something a little more positive than he had offered to date.

'Sir, I am not aware of any one within the Corporation that has offered the Minister an inducement, however, there have been rumours circulating within the company for some time now that Mr Bob Wallshot, the Chairman of the Corporation had offered inducements to the Minister to secure contracts. I'll remind you again, it is only a rumour.'

'Certainly, Mr Johnston, thank you for reminding me that it is only a rumour.'

The Commissioner had no more questions to put to Mike as he was obviously feeling pretty pleased that he had been able to extract from him some suggestion of Wallshot's involvement in this whole tawdry affair.

The hearing was due to be adjourned for lunch, when Justice Roberts caught everybody off-guard and sprung his surprise announcement that the Commission had a witness prepared to talk in return for immunity from prosecution. The gallery remained glued to their seats. Lunch could wait. Justice Roberts was going to bring out the final nail for the Minister's coffin.

The Commission bailiff escorted Peter Bent to the witness chair. Peter was calm and unfazed by the rumblings in the chamber. He knew that he was on show and everybody around was all wondering what revelations he was going to uncover.

'The witness appearing for the Commission will be known by the code name ZX2. Should for any reason his name be publicly disclosed, then this Commission will seek to have the offending party prosecuted. Is that understood?'

Justice Robert's use of formalities at the right time made you feel that you were sitting in a court of law and not a commission of hearing.

'ZX2, please explain to this hearing why you have come forward to offer evidence?'

Peter Bent, was remarkably relaxed as he began recounting to the Commission his experiences over the past several years. He went back to his early childhood and talked about his ambition to become a senior bureaucrat in the public service. He went on and related his experiences within various government departments and his disillusionment with life generally after his wife had died of cancer. It was after that he had discovered that the Minister of his department had been accepting bribes from Bob Wallshot.

'It was so easy, we did all the work and made the recommendations and he had the power to decide the final outcome,' he said rather angrily. 'Then after that, Wallshot paid him for swinging the contract his way.'

'Confirm to the Commission, ZX2, that you have submitted evidence to support your statement?'

'Yes, sir, I have submitted to you copies of the Minister's

handwritten notes to Wallshot outlining tender prices and copies of checks drawn by Wallshot to the Minister.'

'Please let the Commission know what your involvement was?'

For the next hour and a half, Peter meticulously detailed every event that had taken place from the moment that he first confronted and threatened to blackmail the Minister to his confession to Justice Roberts in his office a few evenings earlier.

During the whole proceeding, the Commission staff, lawyers appearing for the defence and the audience were mesmerised. They all found it hard to believe that this had been going on for so long and had it not been for Phil Black's story on Wallshot, the bribes would have still been taking place.

The afternoon had slipped away rather quickly. Justice Roberts was anxious to wrap up the hearing as he now felt that he had enough evidence to submit to the government and secure a prosecution against the Minister through the normal legal process.

He had decided not to recall the Minister, as it was going to be a waste of time and probably an absolute embarrassment from everyone's point of view to hear him constantly deny any involvement in the bribery scandal.

The Commission hearing was concluded.

As he left the chamber, Mike noticed Peter Bent sitting next to the Commission bailiff. They exchanged a glance and both smiled at each other.

$\mathcal{T}$HIRTY

There was not a spare seat left in the Senate chamber. Journalists representing every newspaper and television network had made a beeline for Washington when they had heard the news that Bob Wallshot was appearing before Harry Groves' Senate Inquiry.

The hearing would have started at ten had it not been for senate security insisting that no one else could enter the chamber, as there was no more room available. Despite this, journalists continued to squeeze past security leaving a state of absolute pandemonium at the front door to the chamber. It wasn't until the Senate clerk intervened that security finally took it upon themselves to use force to push the aggravated journalists and other onlookers back into the corridor. It was only then that the door was closed and secured from the inside.

Harry Groves and his fellow senators were aware of what was going on and remained in their suites until the Senate clerk was able to give them an indication that it was in order for them to proceed to the chamber.

The senators took up the same positions that they had occupied the previous day. They were startled by the size of the audience. Yesterday there had been little interest shown from the outside world, today it appeared that every man and woman in Washington had turned up. They had no idea how many people had been turned away by security.

The front bench was empty. Harry Groves was agitated. Wallshot had defied his orders. Not only was he not there, but his lawyer had not turned up either.

The Chairman looked at the other senators, hoping to be given guidance as to what he should do next. Groves knew it was a gamble calling Wallshot and it had not paid off for him.

The Chairman was about to adjourn the hearing, when he looked towards the chamber door. There was a scuffle as the door opened wider. Journalists were trying to get in again. In the midst of the throng, there appeared a distinguished ageing man dressed in a fine cut tailored suit, accompanied by the lawyer who had been present at the hearing the day before. Harry Groves at first did not recognise who the man was but as he drew closer to the empty bench he realised it was Bob Wallshot.

It had been over four years since he had last seen Wallshot and at first he did not recognise him. His immediate reaction was that time had not been kind to him. Although he stood upright, he walked with a falter. His age had obviously slowed him down.

The doyen of American business was not perturbed, by the commotion that was going on in the chamber. The audience was clambering to get a look at him as he pulled his seat from under the front bench and began to sit down. At no time did he face the gallery. His eyes were firmly fixed on Harry Groves.

Wallshot's lawyer sat beside him and apologised to the senators for their lateness. They had been delayed outside the building by a gathering group of television crews who all wanted to secure an interview with what they probably considered to be the most powerful businessman in the country.

The Deputy Chairman looked at Harry Groves, wondering whether he was going to acknowledge the apology. He did not and turned to Wallshot and his lawyer thanking them for attending the Inquiry.

Phil Black had arrived early and had taken up a position near the front of the audience. He had noticed that the same four gentlemen who had occupied part of the back of the chamber the previous day had turned up again and taken up the same seating.

The Chairman confronted Wallshot's lawyer asking him if his client understood the reason why he was appearing before this Senate Inquiry. The lawyer without turning to Wallshot acknowledged that his client had been briefed.

'Mr Wallshot, you appeared at the 1993 hearing into the awarding of the Island Bend Defence contract. Let me remind you that evidence given at that inquiry will be used for the purposes of determining an outcome from this inquiry,' Harry Groves said.

Wallshot and his lawyer did not answer, just listened.

'Evidence submitted yesterday suggested that your corporation has been overcharging the Defence Department for services rendered under this contract. How do you respond to this?'

Wallshot's eyes were still firmly fixed on Groves. He had not moved an inch since he first sat down.

'Accusations of that nature are unfounded,' his lawyer stated.

'This Inquiry will determine that in due course,' the Deputy Chairman responded.

'We have reason to believe that your corporation has been overcharging Defence and there has been a conspiracy between you, Mr Wallshot, your site manager, Chuck Donnington, and a Mr Bayswater from Defence procurement. And what's more we aim to demonstrate that you used a Cayman's Island company to conduct this whole illicit affair,' Harry Groves angrily blurted out.

It was not like him to lose control of his emotions. This was his way of venting his anger on the man who had eluded him for so many years. He was determined to let Wallshot know that he had him in his sights and he was ready to pull the trigger.

'I object to the manner in which you have expressed these unfounded allegations to my client,' the lawyer retorted.

'Perhaps we can start again, Mr Wallshot. Is there any substance to the allegations?'

His lawyer leant across to Bob Wallshot to get a response from him. As he edged forward in his chair to respond to the Chairman, Bob Wallshot touched him on the arm indicating that he would reply to the question.

'Mr Groves, we've known each other for a long time. Unfortunately on every occasion that we have met it has been in an adversarial way. I don't understand why you are so strongly opposed to me. Is it because I am successful and you sense that everything I do is wrong or is it because you just have total contempt for the way I stand up to you? Whatever, Mr Chairman, I have not appeared here today to listen to your unadulterated insults. I'm here to clear my name and that of my corporation and to finally get you off my back for all times.'

The attack on Harry Groves had worked. Hush in the chamber had now turned to open conversation. Wallshot had gained the sympathies of the audience. No one really cared much for politicians and Wallshot had made a hero of himself by taking the fight direct to the Senators.

'Thank you for expressing your thoughts, Mr Wallshot. I'm not here to debate what I think of you. My committee is here to determine whether or not you or anyone else in your corporation bribed an officer of Defence procurement. For the third time, sir, have you any knowledge of your corporation overcharging defence for services rendered?'

The lawyer sensed that the Chairman had been unmoved by Wallshot's address to the senators and suggested to his client that he should respond. Wallshot refused to address the senators again and demanded that his lawyer answer the question.

'My client denies any wrongdoing relating to the Defence Island Bend contract,' the lawyer quietly said.

Nearly two hours had passed by now and very little progress had been made. The committee was convinced that Wallshot was only going to speak through his lawyer. They had hoped he would open up to them, but the wily old fox had been before these committees so often he knew that the best defence he had was to say nothing.

Harry Groves was disappointed with the outcome and reluctantly excused Wallshot and his lawyer from further cross-examination. They were not asked to remain in Washington. It would have been a waste of time having them re-appear. The committee had to pursue the other witnesses, Bayswater and Donnington. These were the ones that would slip up if they were pressured enough.

Bayswater had been asked to make himself available the following day, whilst Donnington was still in town.

After the hearing Wallshot was to make his way to Buena Vista and prepare for his meeting on Sunday. He was even more determined now to press for an early execution of Incarceration.

Phil Black had half a day to spare after the Senate Inquiry came to an abrupt halt. 'What do you do in Washington with half a day to spare?' He asked. Not much, he thought, other than find a bar and drink the afternoon away.

As he left the chamber, he noticed that the four gentlemen who had been sitting up the back of the room had congregated in the corridor and were talking to Bob Wallshot. He had no idea what they would be talking about but it did confirm that Morphett was right. They did have a connection with Wallshot. Before he left he eased his way through the crowd hoping to get close enough to overhear what they were talking about. By the time he had got within hearing distance the conversation had nearly been completed as they were saying their goodbyes and patting Wallshot on the back for the way he had handled himself before the Committee. Interestingly though, he did hear one of the gentlemen say to Wallshot that he would join him at Buena Vista on Sunday. Join him for what? He was hoping that he would say!

As Phil left the Senate building his cellphone began to ring.

'Phil, it's Joe Markowitz.'

'Joe, what are you doing ringing me? What can I do for you?'

'I want to pass on some news to you. I resigned from the corporation a few days ago.'

'Was it over the short selling?'

'That and a lot of other things. I want to meet with you in New York. I think I can give you a fairly accurate insight into Wallshot's Swiss bank accounts. The information should be helpful. What do you say?'

'Mate, I'll be back in New York end of the week. Why don't we plan to meet first thing Saturday morning at my office.'

'I'll see you there Saturday.'

Phil turned the phone off. He didn't want to be disturbed that afternoon.

'Oh my God! I've made arrangements to see Joe on Saturday,' Phil said in a loud voice. 'Fran is probably coming sometime over the weekend. I need to fix the apartment up.' He looked surprised as he spoke to himself, as no one was there to answer back.

There was nothing he could do whilst he was still in Washington, he would have to wait till he got back to New York on Friday night. He had asked Fran to leave a message on his answering machine to let him know what time she was likely arrive in New York. There was no way that he would miss picking her up from JFK. He shrugged his shoulders and put the problem behind him for the time being.

He yelled for a taxi to stop. As he climbed in Phil asked the driver to take him to a comfortable bar not too far away from his hotel on

16th Street. Taxi drivers in every city in America could always be relied upon to take you to the best bar. They each had an opinion. Phil had never been disappointed in the past and he was pretty certain that he was in for a relaxed afternoon with plenty of drinking ahead of him. After all he had some planning to do.

$\mathscr{T}$HIRTY-$\mathscr{O}$NE

The Liberian registered coastal freighter had berthed in Belize City harbour the previous day. The captain of the freighter was part Cuban part Mexican and had spent most of his adult life plying the waters around the Gulf and the Caribbean. The old rusted ship had been his home for more years than he could care to remember. He knew every inch of her and as long as he treated her gently she would never let him down.

His crew was a motley bunch of undesirables, mostly refugees who had no country to call their own. The captain looked after them. Do your job and no questions will be asked, was his motto.

The day the freighter pulled into port, the captain had gone ashore to meet a man who would escort him into the Belize rainforest. Arrangements had been made for him to meet with Michael Montefiore at his jungle training camp. The only instructions that he had been given was that Montefiore had a cargo of heavy machinery that had to be delivered to a yet to be nominated Mexican port. The captain didn't need know what type of machinery was being shipped.

Over the years he had seen it all. He had worked for most of the dictatorships in the region and he even boasted about his friendship with Manuel Noriega, before his imprisonment in a Miami Federal Correctional Institution. The captain had shipped a lot of heavy machinery in his time. To him heavy machinery usually meant Russian or Chinese weapons. He had no interest in the politics of the dictatorships but made a lot of money moving cargo for them. The captain was always paid up front, so if the shipments never made it to their destination, he didn't really care. His owners had to be paid, his crew looked after and he would take his share off the top.

When he arrived at the jungle base camp he was surprised to see so much activity. The captain had never seen this group before, as they frantically assembled bomb devices and tested various types of weapons. What were they doing high in the Belize rainforest? It was not his business.

He had never met Montefiore and asked one of the men where he could find him. The man never spoke but pointed towards the hut on the boundary of the compound. Montefiore was inside the hut leaning over an old timber table carefully studying several sets of drawing plans. He had been expecting the captain to arrive and what he saw did not surprise him. He smelt of sweat and alcohol, typical, he thought, of the type of animal that would undertake this type of work. He would sell his mother's soul if there was a buck to be made.

They shook hands and eyed each other up and down for a few moments before Montefiore invited him to have a drink.

'You have a cargo of machinery you want shipping to Mexico?' The captain asked.

'I have several cases of machinery I need shipping. You're right. Can you do it?'

'Course I can do it, for the right price I can do anything.'

'I have a hundred cases. If it arrives safely you'll be paid a million US dollars.'

'My ship doesn't leave the harbour for a million dollars. This is a very expensive boat to maintain. You understand what I'm saying? I want five million dollars in my hand before I set sail.'

'You fucking pirate! Are you trying to trade with me? I'll pay you two million dollars, one up front now and the other one million when you land the cargo safely. If you don't like that we don't have a deal and you won't get back to your boat in one piece.'

'Mr Montefiore, you're a hard businessman. I'll accept your deal.'

'Good. Now listen. I want you to sail out of Belize in three days. The cargo will be alongside your boat for loading by tomorrow afternoon. My agent will meet with you and settle our account. The shipment is going to Tampico in Mexico and I want it there within seven days. Don't let me down, captain, cause if you do the seas won't be fucking big enough for you to hide from me.'

The captain had struck a good deal. If he had been pushed he would have done the shipment for a million dollars. Montefiore knew this but the extra million he hoped would buy his loyalty and he knew that his owners would only see their share of a million anyway.

Sitting in a warehouse at the Belize City docks was the one hundred crates of machinery. What wasn't known though was that this was not just ordinary machinery. Contained in each of these boxes was the largest illegal shipment of arms to leave a foreign port for delivery to the United States.

There was a range of assault rifles; AK-47/AKM and Armalite AR-15, FN MAG 7.62mm machine guns, 500 kilograms of Semtex and an assortment of detonators. There was enough weaponry, when strategically positioned, to cripple the United States of America. Montefiore's preparation was nearly completed. Immediately he received word from Bob Wallshot, the men would be transported to Mexico to meet the arrival of the arms shipment that would be leaving Belize in the next few days.

In less than forty-eight hours after Justice Roberts had concluded taking evidence in the Ministerial bribery scandal, he had forwarded a report of his preliminary findings to the Premier of the State.

The speed in which the document had been prepared had never been seen before in the brief history of CAC. Mind you this was somewhat different. Had it not been for the evidence of Peter Bent and the documents he presented to the hearing, a recommendation would have been a long way off yet.

Roberts had been in touch with the Premier to let him know the report was on its way. Despite the Premier's insistence that he debrief him over the telephone, Justice Roberts stuck to protocol advising him that he would be pleased to elaborate on any points after he had read the report.

It was the end of the week. The Premier sat in his office overlooking the harbour knowing that the Roberts report was going to have a catastrophic electoral impact on his party. He read the document again for the third time. He could not believe that his Minister, whom at one stage he had trusted like a brother, had committed such a brazen act of dishonesty whilst an officer of the

Crown. Accepting bribes was intolerable. What was even worse, he kept saying, was that he got away with it for so long. The Departmental officials would not get out of it lightly. They have to be held responsible for part of the debacle.

Justice Roberts had not been particularly kind in the manner in which he framed his report. He blamed what he termed the excesses of the eighties as the key ingredient for the Minister's flirtation with corruption and the failure of the government to have checks and balances in place to prevent events of this nature happening. He praised Peter Bent for his actions in coming forward and delivered scathing criticism for his part in the evil plan.

The report attacked the Premier for condoning the Minister's continuing personal relationship with Wallshot after the awarding of the first contract. That was a recipe for disaster, he pointed out.

The whole report was contained in less than fifteen pages and apart from a grammatical tidy up, the final report would be issued in the same context. The final recommendation to the government was that there was sufficient evidence for the scandal to be referred to the Public Prosecutor's Office for charges to be prepared.

The Premier finally picked up the phone and called Justice Roberts. He could not bring himself to thank him for the report, but did not hesitate to remind him that when it was released to the public the government would no doubt be forced to call an early election. Roberts was not a politician and expressed very little sympathy for the Premier's point of view, taking the last opportunity to remind him that it was his responsibility to protect the electorate from criminals operating in positions of privilege.

The press had got word around the traps that Justice Roberts had delivered his interim report to the government and were now looking for answers as to why its release had been delayed. The Premier's press office could not take their calls until they had been de-briefed by the Premier himself. He had no intention of making any form of announcement before Saturday morning. He argued that Saturday was usually considered a non event day for media releases and a scandal of this magnitude would be less damaging to the party. His press office was instructed to fend the media off until the following day.

The Senate Inquiry into the Island Bend Defence Contract was now in its third day.

The excitement of the previous day had somewhat tempered as the participants and the audience made their way into the Senate chamber. There was not the hustle and bustle that had been experienced the day before. Security had been stepped up, but in hindsight it probably wasn't necessary. Phil Black was there again as were the same four men that had taken up the same positions each day at the back of the chamber. They reminded Phil of the three wise monkeys, except there were four and not three. What did they do at the end of the day's hearing? Where did they go? Not once did he see them take notes. Did they have a taping device? Security wouldn't allow one in the chamber, he thought. That was a ridiculous statement! After all he had smuggled a camera into the courtroom when Montefiore was sentenced.

There were four men sitting at the front table facing the Senator's podium. One he recognised as Chuck Donnington and the other was the Wallshot lawyer. Phil guessed that one of the other men was Allan Bayswater, the Defence procurement officer who had been named by the colourful Molly Nelson and probably the other was his lawyer. It didn't really matter who was who, but it helped him fill in the time whilst he waited along with everyone else for the Senators to take their seats and get the show on the road.

Right on cue, it was ten in the morning again. The senators paraded on to the podium and took up their seats facing the sea of faces looking at them from the other side of the chamber.

Harry Groves was still somewhat annoyed with the events of yesterday. He had hoped to make some inroads and hopefully have caught Wallshot off guard. He had made very little progress in fact. One of the senators on the Committee had even approached him the night before expressing concern that he thought Groves had unfairly treated Wallshot during the hearing and that he should be careful not to treat this Inquiry as a vendetta to get even with him. Groves took considerable offence at the remark.

Those comments kept playing on his mind as he faced the chamber on the third day. Perhaps the senator was right?

'Mr Donnington, has your lawyer briefed you on the evidence

presented to this Inquiry by Ms Nelson and Mr Wallshot?' the Chairman asked.

'He has, Senator.'

'Do you have anything further to add?'

'Only one comment, Senator. The accusations made by Ms Nelson are inaccurate.'

'Why is that?'

'Wallshot Corporation at no time has prepared and submitted accounts for work not performed.'

'Ms Nelson thinks otherwise. In fact she even stated that Mr Bayswater, who is sitting next to you on your left, authorised such accounts for payment.'

'She's most definitely wrong.'

'Have you met Mr Bayswater?'

'I have on many occasions.'

'Mr Donnington, I have copies of accounts, issued by your office, authorised by Mr Bayswater for services not performed by your corporation at the Island Bend Defence site.'

Donnington turned to his lawyer sharply, seeking advice as to how he should respond to such vehement accusations.

'Senator, if you have documentation supporting Ms Nelson's claims, then you obviously do not need further testimony from me.'

'You're wrong, Mr Donnington, I would like you to tell me that you knew a fraud was being perpetuated. Or is that asking too much?'

'I have nothing further to say, Mr Chairman.'

Donnington was rattled. He was uncertain how much Groves knew. Bayswater had assured him that he had taken all the Island Bend files off Molly Nelson. Had she copied the files earlier, he wondered. Perhaps Bayswater had made a mess of that as well. He had not been successful keeping Molly Nelson quiet.

The fourth man that Phil Black had noticed earlier sitting at the front table, lifted his tall sinewy body from his chair and leant over the desk, cleared his throat and spoke directly to Senator Groves.

'Mr Chairman, I am a lawyer representing Mr Bayswater. He has asked me to read a brief statement to this Committee of Inquiry concerning the allegations made by Ms Nelson that he had fraudulently misappropriated funds from the United States Government.'

The Committee sat in silence for a brief moment, waiting for Bayswater's lawyer to adjust his reading glasses whilst he read from the prepared statement.

'Mr Bayswater is currently the senior Procurement Officer for the Department of Defence. He is aware of the allegations made against him by one of his former employees, Ms Molly Nelson. Mr Bayswater wants it known for the record that the allegations made by Ms Nelson are accurate. He has also asked me to inform this Committee of Inquiry that he will co-operate fully so that a satisfactory conclusion can be reached.'

A brief hush turned into pandemonium. Journalists scurried off in every direction, looking for the nearest exit. They had to contact their offices to file a story immediately. They could not be away from the chamber for too long as Bayswater was about to give evidence.

Senator Groves had requested a short break before the Senate Committee questioned Bayswater on the statement he had just made through his lawyer. This was no doubt the break they had been waiting for. Bayswater's statement had vindicated Senator Groves' visit to the President. He was anxious to get back into the chamber and see what more Bayswater had to say.

'Mr Bayswater, thank you for the candid and honest statement you have just read to this Committee. You have agreed with Ms Nelson's testimony that Wallshot Corporation was overcharging the Department of Defence for work not carried out?'

'Yes, Mr Chairman.'

'Who originated the false claims to the Department of Defence?'

'Mr Donnington.'

'The same Mr Donnington who just a few moments earlier, denied any knowledge of the allegations?'

'That is correct, Senator.'

'How long has this been going on for?'

'Since the award of the contract.'

'Why was a Cayman Island company used to launder the funds?'

'That was Mr Wallshot's brainchild. He believed it was in everyone's interest to move the scam offshore.'

'This Committee would have to assume, Mr Bayswater, that you received benefit along the line?'

'I did, Senator. Each time a false account was authorised by me, payment of that account was made to the Cayman's company. That would not necessarily raise suspicion as Defence did business with numerous overseas suppliers and paid funds direct to many different types of tax haven countries. The Cayman's company would transfer part of the proceeds to a Swiss bank account that had been established for me by Mr Wallshot.'

'What was your cut of the action?'

'Ten per cent of the amount paid.'

'Jeezus, you've made one hell of a lot of money, Mr Bayswater, since 1993!'

'Over ten million dollars, Mr Chairman.'

'You're telling me that the United States Government has paid over one hundred million dollars for falsely provided accounts since 1993?'

'That only covers the Island Bend Defence contract!'

'You mean to tell me that this goes beyond Island Bend? Goddam it! We can't get Congress to appropriate enough funds to educate our children and take care of the sick and you're telling me there is rampant misappropriation of funds going on within Defence. What am I doing here, Mr Bayswater? Why have you come here today and bared your soul to the world, Mr Bayswater?'

'I'm frightened for my safety. I was asked by Mr Donnington some weeks earlier to arrange for the execution of Ms Nelson. I refused to do that. I'm not a violent person. Paying her off seemed the best solution at the time. Now my family has been threatened. We need protection. By taking the course I have taken here today I am hopeful that you will arrange for my family to receive Federal protection.'

'Let me assure you, Mr Bayswater, you and your family will have help.'

During the next hour Bayswater gave the Committee graphic details of the part he had played in the conspiracy, his overseas trips, the weekends away on Wallshot's yacht, gifts for his wife and family and the property he had acquired from the proceeds of the graft. It was a frightening chain of events.

The Committee saw no further value from pressing home its advantage with Bayswater. They agreed unanimously that they had enough evidence to conclude their hearing and submit a detailed conclusive list of recommendations direct to the President.

The FBI and the US Marshall's Office were summoned by the Senate Committee to afford maximum protection to Bayswater and his family. He was now a key witness for the prosecution.

Harry Groves felt relieved when he returned to his office. He had finally nailed that sonofabitch.

$\mathcal{T}$HIRTY-$\mathcal{T}$WO

$\mathbf{F}$our days in Washington had been more than enough for Phil Black. He had a lot on his mind. Meeting with Markowitz on Saturday and hopefully hearing from Fran to tell him that she was arriving in New York over the weekend, was enough for him to deal with at the moment.

The Senate Inquiry had been an anti climax for Phil. Over the past few months that he had been working on the Wallshot story, nothing about the man any longer surprised him. Even before he had arrived in Washington he was convinced that Wallshot was guilty. It was only a matter of time before he was exposed. Harry Groves had done a superb job, he thought. Setting up the battleground, using the President as his main weapon, he had pummelled the enemy into submission. Wallshot would not take his Senate loss lying down. Phil was certain that he would be weighing up his options.

The late plane back to New York was relatively empty. Phil had been moved forward to Premium class for the short haul. Seeing Fran for the first time in over a week was occupying his mind when a man came and sat down beside him. At first he took little notice. It wasn't until he tapped him on the shoulder and spoke that he realised that someone had even occupied the seat next to him.

'Excuse me, did you say something?' Phil asked.

'I apologise if I startled you.'

'No. No you didn't. I had a few things on my mind.'

'Are you Phil Black from the *New York Herald*?'

Phil now looked at the man rather startled, wondering how he recognised him.

'Yes, my name is Phil Black. Who are you?'

'My name is not important, but what I have to say is.'

Sitting upright in his seat, Phil faced the rather large surly looking individual with a questioning look and began to listen to what he had to say.

'You have been showing particular interest recently in the personal affairs of a Mr Wallshot. If you're smart, you'll forget him. Mr Wallshot doesn't want any trouble. He has asked me to tell you that if you or your paper print any more shit about him he'll have you taken out.'

The man squeezed Phil's arm firmly making a point that he was serious about his threat. Before Phil could reply, the man had stood up and began to make his way to the back of the plane.

What was all that about? Phil asked, now feeling rather squeamish after having his life threatened. The face! He had seen the face before. Where? Of course, he remembered – it was one of the four men who had been seated at the back of the Senate inquiry chamber.

Over the years that he had been a journalist, he had been in some life threatening situations. Not once, however, had anyone gone to so much trouble to threaten him face to face. How seriously should he take this guy? What could he do? Obviously nothing until the next article appeared in the *Herald*. Perhaps I shouldn't file a story, he thought. If I don't someone else will.

The plane had arrived at La Guardia airport. Phil was one of the first passengers off. He got off the plane quickly, as he wanted to find a position in the terminal, where he could observe more clearly, the thug who had just given him the boot.

The terminal gate attendant shut the door behind the last departing passenger. Phil moved clear of his vantage point, he hadn't seen the man leave the aircraft. Where was he? Was it a figment of his imagination? He pinched himself. Yes, he had been threatened. Where had the guy gone? He couldn't just disappear. Phil turned around and made his way to the terminal exit, thinking that he had missed him in the crowd. Then he heard an announcement over the PA system. 'Wallshot Corporation welcomes passengers to flight 657 shuttle service to Washington.' Phil literally stopped dead in his tracks as the announcement was repeated. Of course, the man on the plane was a member of the crew. He had used the crew exit. That was why Phil had not seen him depart through the normal passenger terminal exit. Wallshot Corporation staffed the shuttle flights. One of Wallshot's employees had been keeping a check on him the whole time he was in Washington and had seized the opportunity on the flight to threaten him.

By the time the taxi had pulled up outside Phil's apartment, he was convinced that the threat to his life was a small price to pay for freedom of speech. He was even more determined than ever to see Wallshot nailed to the cross. There would be no point in discussing the incident with Rudy Morphett or any one else at the *Herald*. They may be persuaded to kill the story. Phil didn't want that.

He fumbled with his keys as he madly tried to get the front door open. The telephone was ringing. It was Fran.

'You OK?' she remarked.

'Yeah, I'm fine. I've just got back from Washington. Where are you? What's happening?'

'I'm in LA. The only flight I could get out of Sydney was via Tokyo. I plan to stay in LA for two nights and leave first thing Saturday morning for New York. The plane gets into JFK late afternoon. Will you be there?'

'Keep me away.'

He looked around the apartment as he hung up the telephone. There was no way that he was going to be able to have the apartment ship-shape before Fran arrived. 'She'd understand,' he said. 'No she wouldn't, she is so meticulous,' answering himself back. 'Amanda. That's the answer. Amanda can organise a housekeeper to turn the apartment upside down tomorrow. A call to Macy's will take care of a new double bed. She can do that for me as well. Fran and Amanda will get on well together.' A telephone call to Amanda that evening fixed everything. She promised to be at Phil's apartment next morning and told him not to concern himself with the detail.

The Swiss police had been called to a small village on the western side of Lake Zurich. A group of young children had been playing on the water's edge when they discovered the remains of a body floating not far from where they had been skimming rocks across the top of the glassy water.

The body had been recovered carefully as it was beginning to decompose and the authorities were concerned that fragments may fall off and destroy vital evidence. The torso faced upwards as several police officers peered over it. One of the officers had to move away as he began to feel violently ill. The decomposing body let out an unusual odour that filled the afternoon air with a sour stench.

The fingers and thumbs had been removed at the knuckles, clearly in an attempt to remove any fingerprint evidence. Both feet had been severed from the ankles. The skull had been crushed and the teeth hacked out. It was a frightful sight. Whoever had committed the murder did not want the person identified.

Television crews and journalists had turned up to the crime scene seeking interviews with the police. Murders were commonplace in Zurich, but what was unusual about this one was the horrific and brutal nature of the crime. The police were unable to provide the press with identification, referring only to its similarity to a Mafia style execution.

Some two kilometres further down the lake the waterlogged remains of an empty wallet had floated to the surface. The name of Lukas Mueller was inscribed on the inside jacket of the wallet.

Next morning at the office, Phil was thumbing through the overnight Reuters' reports. He came across one that took his eye. Not so much because he had a particular interest in a murder in Zurich, but more for they way the article described the condition of the body that was found in Lake Zurich. His first reaction was Lukas Mueller. Not as though he had ever met him. In fact he had never even seen a picture of Mueller. Rudy Morphett had spoken of him a few times during the corporate raid on the *Herald* by Wallshot. He held Mueller responsible for selling Banque de Genève's shareholding in the *Herald*, because of his connection with Wallshot's corporation. He remembered Morphett remarking at the time, that Wallshot would have Mueller skinned alive for failing him. Phil took a copy of the article, sending it to Rudy Morphett with a pencil note, "Lukas Mueller – you were right!"

Thirty-Three

The extra few hours sleep were a welcome tonic for Phil. His meeting with Markowitz was not until ten and he did not have to be at the airport to pick Fran up until late afternoon. The day had planned itself, with very little help from him.

This had been the first opportunity he'd had to take a good look around the apartment. Amanda had done herself proud. What a great friend she had been. Every piece of furniture had been moved and polished by the cleaner. He didn't want to think how much dust had been swept from behind cupboards and off the carpet. The curtains had been taken down and dry-cleaned. Flowers adorned the room. Their sweet summer fragrances reminded him of his garden in Australia. Amanda must have brought her own vases. Phil didn't remember having cut glass crystal vases in his cupboards. The bathroom was spotless. The shower was clean. The loose hair and other waste that had clogged up the drain for years, was no longer there. Without him knowing the plumber had spent most of the previous afternoon getting all the plumbing to work. The new bed had arrived from Macys. It had been made up with new silk and cotton sheets and a few cushions scattered around. It had been dark when he arrived home the previous evening and at least he'd had enough sense not to use the new bed. Crashing on the sofa was nothing unusual for Phil. The transformation had been miraculous. Keeping it this way in the future was going to be the difficult task. Fran would make sure he did not slip into his old habits.

Getting dressed didn't take long. Amanda had even pressed his sports trousers and had his casual jacket cleaned. Normally, if he had a meeting in the office scheduled for a Saturday, Phil would turn up in a pair of faded jeans, a creased sweatshirt and battered Nikes. The weekend shift would not recognise him today.

The trip to the office had not taken as long as it would during weekdays. Thank God New York was deserted over the weekend. It gave the locals and the tourists a chance to see something of the City. He never failed to call into his favourite coffee shop, which was situated just one block from the *Herald* office. Old Joe didn't recognise him at first and when he did asked him whose funeral was he going to. Joe's sense of humour was another story. Phil didn't have time for banter today, ordering a long black and two croissants.

Other than Amanda, no one else knew that Fran was arriving today. Thinking about it, he had been so engrossed in the Wallshot investigation, he hadn't even told any one else that she existed. Joe had to be told, he thought. After all he didn't want to turn up one morning with a bird hanging off his arm. The old man would be upset with him. Joe was pleased to hear his news. He went to the back of the shop and brought out a little brooch, asking Phil to give it to her when she arrived in New York. It was the same brooch that Joe had bought for his wife Maria when she arrived from Italy over forty years ago. Unfortunately Maria had died recently. Phil found it hard to accept the gift but assured Joe that he would treasure it and pin it on Fran when she got off the plane.

Arriving at the news room, he was surprised to see that Joe Markowitz had got there ahead of him. The two men greeted each other with open enthusiasm. They were like long lost brothers, hugging each other firstly and then slapping one another on the back.

'Joe, I hope you didn't mind? I've asked Rudy Morphett to join us this morning.'

'Oh no, not at all. I'd like to meet him.'

'Well how you been, mate?'

'Better now that I made the decision to leave Wallshot. My wife and I are a little uncertain as to what we'll do next. There aren't a lot of business opportunities left for me in Miami. Bloody Wallshot will make sure of that.'

'That's why I want you to meet Rudy. He has a proposition in mind for you.'

'Sounds great, let's go and meet the man.'

Rudy had been expecting Phil and Joe to join him in his office on the top floor of the *Herald* building.

'Good morning boss. I'd like you to meet Joe Markowitz.'

'Mr Markowitz. I've heard a lot of good things about you.'

'Likewise, Mr Morphett.'

'Call me Rudy please.'

'Thank you. Would you please call me Joe?'

To meet one of the greatest newspaper men in American history was a rare privilege for Joe Markowitz. To be in the same room with a legend, he found awe-inspiring. The man influenced the country's politics and it was rumoured that he made Presidents. Joe felt quite humbled to be in his presence and felt extremely envious of Phil's relaxed style with him.

'Joe, I won't beat around the bush. I want to make you an offer.'

He listened intently for what he was about to say next, smiling as he added another Aussie colloquialism to his collection of down-under phrases.

'Phil has filled you in on the story we have been doing on Wallshot. You will have guessed by now that I have no time for the man. More so since he nearly sent the *Herald* to the wall last week. By the way, I believe I have you to thank for the inside tip. It won't go any further. You have my word on that.'

'What did you have in mind, Rudy?'

'I'm proposing to put you on the payroll. I want you to help Phil develop a series of articles over the next few weeks exposing Wallshot for what he really is. The big issue for me is the way that he has been allowed to grab power from government. The thrust of the articles has to be centred on that issue.'

Looking surprised, when he heard the comment, Joe asked, 'What do you mean, grabbing power from government?'

'You obviously haven't thought this through before. Have you?'

'I guess not. I haven't got your drift yet.'

'Let me fill you in. Over the past fifteen years the United States government has been slowly going broke. To keep itself afloat it has been selling off assets and outsourcing most of its activities to the private sector. On the surface this appeared the right thing to do. You think about it though? What has happened in fifteen years? Government has very few prime assets left. How does it raise additional cash in the long term, without turning to the taxpayer? Theoretically it can't. The other thing that has happened during that time, it no longer controls essential services. It's those services that form the backbone of the country, you're getting my drift, Joe?'

Joe remembered when he first saw Rudy Morphett. It was at a New York conference. He had covered this same topic then, but very few took much notice of his ramblings.

'Government in this country has lost control of its airports. The private sector runs the FAA. It no longer provides the bulk of health care services. The country's energy stations and oil reserves are in the hands of private operators, as are communications and satellite tracking stations. We've seen the establishment of private armies, I think what you call them are manpower security corporations. Prisons and correctional centres have finished up in private hands. Education is moving that way. Think about it? Every major city in the United States is now run by the private sector, Joe, the list goes on and on.'

For the first time Joe was able to share his passion. He had on many occasions sat opposite Wallshot, whilst he spat out his theory as to why government should hand more of its services to the private sector. He was now getting an appreciation of an opposing view.

'You take all I have told you, my friend, and what does it spell out? Don't think about it. Let me tell you.'

Both Phil and Joe anxiously waited for him to continue.

'It spells out "Wallshot." Over the past fifteen to twenty years he has slowly been taking a stranglehold on government services. My research tells me that he now controls over ninety-five per cent of essential services in this country. That makes him fucking more powerful than the President. To use a cliché, do you realise that with the flick of a switch, he can bring the country to its knees! Did you ever realise that Joe, when you worked for him?'

Joe could see it all. Wallshot was capable of anything. He had seen him in action many times. Nothing got in his way.

'That's where I need you, Joe. You know the man intimately. You've worked with him. I want you to share that with us. If Wallshot is not stopped, this country is finished. And it's going to happen soon. He's got too many things going against him at the moment. He cannot afford to lose more ground. I'll have Phil outline where we are at the moment. I'm going to have to leave you shortly. Are you on board, Joe?'

There was no alternative for Joe. He believed in Rudy's theory and felt honoured to be invited to join the *Herald* team. Rising from his chair, he moved across to Rudy, shaking his hand and accepting his offer to join the *New York Herald*.

Looking down at his watch, Phil apologised to Joe that he couldn't spend the afternoon with him, as he had to be out at JFK in the next two hours. Joe understood and told Phil that he and his wife were taking in a show that evening and he would see him first thing Monday morning.

That had been a successful morning for Phil and Rudy. With Joe on board, preparation of the story on Wallshot would be made so much more simple.

The taxi driver had an effortless trip to the airport. It was one of the few times that Phil could recall a driver actually wanting to chat on about life in general. They were normally unfriendly, abrasive characters who were hell bent on getting their fare paying passengers from point A to point B in the shortest possible time The fact that they got into arguments with every pedestrian and passing motorist along the way, and on occasions abused shit out of passengers, they didn't take that into consideration. That was part and parcel of the New York taxi scene.

The arrival board at JFK said that Fran's plane was due to land in the next fifteen minutes. He felt like an expectant father as he paced up and down outside the arrivals' gate. He had managed to pick up a bunch of flowers to give to Fran. That wasn't his idea. Amanda had left a curt note for him in the apartment, to remind him to take flowers.

The arrivals gate opened. The passengers began to disperse into the terminal. Phil was feeling very nervous by now. 'There you are!' he yelled out, as he ran towards the arrivals' gate. Fran could not miss all the commotion. She had heard Phil, the second she put her nose into the terminal. She was as excited as he was. They embraced, nearly crushing each other in the excitement. He looked down at her and gave her a warm tender passionate kiss. People were looking at them, but they were oblivious to what was going on. When they had finished their kiss, the crowd applauded their approval.

Phil put his arm around Fran's waist and escorted her through the main terminal to the baggage carousel, idly chatting about nothing and everything all the way.

The trip from the airport to the apartment was uneventful, even though Phil vaguely recalled pointing out to her a few of the New York landmarks. Neither one of them was particularly interested in the sights at the moment. The trip was finally over. They had arrived at the apartment. Phil paid off the cabbie and stood out in the street with Fran and pointed up to his apartment.

'This is your home for the next few weeks,' he reassured her.

She could not have cared less. Being with Phil was all she wanted. Taking him by the hand she dragged him up the front steps to the apartment block and pushed the elevator button. Before Phil would let her into his apartment, he insisted on picking her up and carrying her across the threshold, maintaining he was superstitious. Not really! Amanda had told him to be chivalrous.

Fran was delighted with her new home and couldn't wait to spend time with Phil in New York.

Thirty-Four

The early morning sun popped its head above the distant mountain range. The reddish tinge of the sun's rays contrasted the bright blue sky. The mountains were quiet, animals foraged and the birds flew freely from tree to tree. A light easterly wind eased its way down the leeward slope and sent ripples speeding across the river top.

Today was Sunday. Buena Vista was bracing itself to meet the full onslaught of the arriving hordes. The final plan to execute Incarceration would take place here today.

Bob Wallshot had been up and about well before sunrise, pondering over the plans. Nothing had been left out. He put on his jacket and called for his ranch manager, Harry Selwyn to drive him around the perimeter of the ranch to inspect the security arrangements that he had put in place.

The four wheel drive was waiting for him by the time he was outside the ranch house. The vehicle proceeded down the western slope of the property and followed the southern boundary fence along the river's edge. A team of guards from Wallshot's security operations had been deployed at one hundred yard intervals to protect the western and southern boundaries. Each guard had been fitted out with riot helmets, tear gas, grenades and an AK-47 assault rifle. The security force, was part of the corporation's Special Services squad and were only used for the purposes of counter terrorist activity. The squad had moved into Buena Vista some seventy-two hours earlier. They were to remain on duty until Bob Wallshot authorised their departure.

As Wallshot drove past the men, they instinctively saluted the man they had come to love and respect. Every officer was an integral part of his chain of command.

The vehicle then forded the river and made its way in an easterly direction still following the boundary fence. The ranch house was now out of sight. Guards had now been posted at four hundred yard intervals, as it was felt less likely for an assault on the ranch house command post from this part of the property. Again, every man stood to attention and saluted Wallshot, as he drove past their posts. Approaching the gates at the entry to the drive that led up to the ranch house, Wallshot noticed the electronic detection cameras swivel towards them, pouncing like a lion capturing its prey. The vehicle stopped immediately. Security clearance was needed before they could drive up to the ranch house. Even Wallshot was not granted immunity from the complex security system that he had devised to protect him and his guests.

The ranch was secure.

The command post was on full alert. It housed the latest electronic monitoring and heat detection equipment capable of detecting any breach of the ranch perimeter. It was also able to monitor any aircraft within a twenty-mile radius. Wallshot had taken up his position in the command post, awaiting the arrival of his first guest, Clark Ford, the Vice President of the United States.

The signal appeared on the monitor. A craft was flying into the detection zone.

The control room operator signalled its arrival to Wallshot.

'What type of craft is it?' Wallshot asked.

'A Bell helicopter carrying four people.'

'Have them verify their presence in the control area.'

'BV control to approaching craft, identify yourselves.'

'This is United States Air Force Bell helicopter AR 2330, requesting permission to land at Buena Vista Ranch.'

'Identify your passengers.'

'I am carrying the Vice President, his Chief of Staff, a co-pilot and myself the pilot.'

Wallshot verified the passenger list and authorised the control room operator to allow the helicopter to land at the helipad adjoining the ranch house. Leaving the control room for a few moments, Wallshot moved outside to greet the first of his guests.

'Mr Vice President. Welcome to Buena Vista.'

'BW I'm pleased to be here. This is the start of a new era in America.'

'Let me escort you to our meeting room. Marina will look after you until the others arrive.'

Plans had been made for each of the guests to arrive at fifteen minute intervals. This would allow security to undertake full security checks on all approaching parties.

General Tyler had flown in and had put down at Westchester airport a few minutes early. A Special Services Commander was there to meet him and transport him and his entourage to the ranch.

Howard Lazenby had flown in from London early that morning, putting down at a small field in Maryland to refuel, before flying on to Westchester. Fred Cohen had been on vacation in the mountains. He had a property adjoining Wallshot's and made his way across, then being taken by security to the ranch house. Paul Lowenstein had been delayed. Air traffic out of Los Angeles had been chaotic. Wallshot was edgy when he heard the news. The last of the group to arrive was Judge Hardcastle. He was not as fortunate as the others, his position did not allow him to have aircraft at his disposal. He had to rely on Bob Wallshot sending the Citation down to Boca Raton to pick him up. Seeing Emily again was one of the more pleasing aspects of this early morning flight to Westchester.

By ten in the morning the Execution Committee was entrenched at Buena Vista. Judge Hardcastle was the only one who had not met the other committee members. He had been a late selection to the group. Wallshot introduced him and afterwards asked the committee to take their seats.

The meeting room had been specially built for the purpose of holding high level confidential meetings. Access could only be made by finger print control and the internal walls of the room had been sound proofed. In the middle of the room was a scale model of the United States of America, depicting every minute detail of the country's terrain and highlighting the country's major cities. This working model was to be the battleground. The wall directly in front of the scale model catered for a full size screen, similar in size to what you would expect to see in a commercial cinema. On the wall opposite the screen was a large video camera, which was going to be used for projecting target images. The room had been fully equipped with everything imaginable.

Wallshot took the podium and faced his Execution Committee for the first time.

'Our day is near,' he remarked. 'You have all committed yourselves to a better America. There is no turning back. Incarceration will be executed. America will be free again.'

The committee stood up and gave him a thunderous round of applause. The adrenalin was pumping. They had all been waiting to hear his opening remark. He had not let them down.

'Despite the setbacks I have had in recent weeks, this has made me even more determined to succeed. The final plan has been locked in. Over the next two days I will share the plan with you and then advise you on the execution day.'

General Tyler moved to the podium to join Wallshot.

'We feel honoured to be alongside you, BW. Every man in this room has had a dream to see a better America. Some of us, however, have been privileged to work with you for many years in bringing this dream to reality. We are behind you and will do everything in our power to ensure a successful execution of Incarceration.'

In support, every man in the room acknowledged their commitment to change.

'Gentlemen, the news you have all being waiting to hear: Montefiore has successfully concluded his training program in Belize. His hand picked group of terrorists is ready to strike fear into the White House.'

'How many men does he finally have, BW?' Lazenby asked.

'Including himself, sixteen. We have fifteen key targets to arm.'

'Where is the arms shipment now?' Tyler asked.

'As we speak it should be landing in Mexico. Arrangements have been made to ship the cargo by road to the nominated target areas.'

'When does Michael anticipate having the targets armed?' Cohen inquired.

'We anticipate within days.'

'What if Michael, or his gang of terrorists are picked up along the way?' Lowenstein chipped in. 'After all, every one of them is on top of the FBI wanted list.'

'Paul, there are no guarantees in life. We have done everything humanly possible to alter the identification of each man in the group. Including Michael. Time did not permit plastic surgery, but with the help of a brilliant plastic surgeon he has been able to come up with a few subtle changes. Let me assure you their mothers wouldn't recognise them.'

'Every attempt will be made to minimise the threat to life?' Cohen asked.

'Every attempt will be made, Fred, but I have instructed Michael not to let it stand in his way if he has to make a choice.'

'Have you decided on the fifteen key strategic targets to be armed?' Tyler wanted to know.

'I have. They are all key sites that my corporation is managing. That will minimise the risk of Michael and his men entering the sites. Arrangements have been put in place with key personnel to allow the trucks carrying the arms to enter the site without questions been asked.'

'When will you let us have full details on the sites?'

'Not until they are activated. For the plan to be successful, I don't propose sharing that information with anyone at this stage. The fifteen sites have been very carefully selected. Each one is of key strategic importance to the success of Incarceration.'

The reason why the whole plan had been successful to date was because Wallshot had adopted the policy of only informing the committee on a need to know basis, what was going on. They preferred it that way. Part of the overall plan included the roles that they had to play in preparing their corporations' involvement in the execution of Incarceration. Wallshot was not expected to be part of every decision that they had to make.

Clark Ford had been very quiet throughout the whole morning session. Since he had become a politician, BW had noticed a considerable change in his ability to be able to think freely. When he worked for the Wallshot Corporation he was one of the young bright lights, destined to make the very top. He was even touted to become Wallshot's successor. His wife had come from a political background and was hell bent on keeping the family tradition alive. Her father had helped Ford find the right path to the White House and with his help and her push, he had not looked back since he left the private sector. Wallshot, although very disappointed in the early days, had realised the enormous benefit of having a man in the White House working with him towards a better America.

BW sat down for a while. He had become quite exhausted having been on his feet for a few hours. Howard Lazenby, President of American Telecommunications took over the podium to give the committee an update on his activities.

'My researchers have developed a software virus that we are now confident, can be introduced into the software programs that drive the defence satellite communication network. Key programmers have been trained to install the software virus and activate it on instruction. This will bring the country's total satellite communication system to a standstill. No one from within the States will be able to communicate out and no one from the outside will be able to access the network. The enormity of this alone will have the Congress pleading for us to take the country off their hands.'

'Can the virus be reversed?' Tyler asked.

'Yes, it can. We have developed an antidote, which we will schedule to be activated at the appropriate time.'

'What about our people? How can we communicate with them?'

'The command post at Buena Vista will be the only form of communication. That will not be affected during the satellite down time. We will be using a form of high frequency wireless communication to keep us in touch with selected personnel. Keep in mind, gentlemen, we have planned for Incarceration to succeed within twenty-four hours of execution.'

'One of the more important issues we have to overcome, is how do we neutralise the armed forces during that first twenty-four hours,' BW chimed in, as he walked back to the podium. 'General Tyler, you are confident that your plan will immobilise the military long enough for us to gain control?'

'I am confident, BW. Let me give the committee an overview of the final plan. We have targeted the major military establishments on the mainland. They account for over seventy-five per cent of ground troops and most of the country's tactical air response. What we are proposing is that food rations will be contaminated twenty-four hours before execution date.'

'How do you propose to achieve that, General?' Fred Cohen asked.

'The Wallshot Corporation feeds every man and woman on those sites. They provide their total catering needs. At the point of manufacture the pre-packed rations will be contaminated with a viral infection that will cause severe stomach discomfort to every enlisted person. Providing they eat the food, no one will escape the infection. Those that do not eat the rations at that particular point of time will be quite minimal in number and of no strategic concern to our operation.'

'You're telling us, General, that the military might of the United States will be grounded for days,' Judge Hardcastle asked in dismay.

'That's correct, Judge. Let me remind you of how successful this program was in 1988. US intelligence in Europe arranged for the contamination of ration packs to the East German militia. The allies could have walked into the Soviet that day and there would have been no one there to take us out. Gorbachev's decision to end the cold war was accelerated after that.'

'Gentlemen, let me summarise this morning's activities,' BW confidently spoke.

'Twenty-four hours prior to execution of Incarceration we will immobilise the US military forces on the mainland. Our fifteen key targets will be armed and put on stand-by for activation. Wallshot special security forces will be deployed to hold and maintain key Federal government administrative buildings in Washington, New York, Los Angeles, Houston and San Francisco. The satellite tracking stations will be neutralised and I will have the pleasure of telling the President that private enterprise is replacing the government.'

Members of the committee, roared with laughter at BW's remark. The thought of the private sector managing the affairs of the country had been paramount in all of their minds for many years now. The day of reckoning was drawing near.

'How are you proposing to run the country during the interim period?' Lowenstein demanded to know.

'Ford will be appointed acting President of the new America Corporation. I'll be the Executive Chairman. Hardcastle will sit over the country's judicial system, with Lowenstein heading up the Reserve. General Tyler will be Chief of Defence and will have at his disposal the armed security force of Wallshot Corporation. Fred Cohen heads the country's energy. I plan to leave the communications to Lazenby and Michael Montefiore will be America Corporation's key international military adviser.'

The planning that had gone into this exercise had been going on now for over four years. Wallshot had covered every possible scenario.

'What fall out are we likely to experience from those Americans that are likely to reject a privatised America?' Ford asked.

'That's your job to overcome that problem. You have the respect of lower and middle class Americans, most of whom have been severely affected by the current government administration. They have little respect for the President and the congress. On the other hand they have seen you supporting their cause. To them you are the President elect.'

'International interference, BW! Tell us how you see that being minimised?'

'Most of our trading partners will be shocked by the events. That's where I see it finishing though. Remember that all the G7 countries rely on the United States for economic direction. There will be diplomatic protests. It is our job to reassure these countries quickly that nothing will change the economic structure of their respective countries. The key change is a new political direction, a change for the better. One I am confident other countries will embrace in the future. The face of America changed just over two hundred years ago. Our forefathers were criticised. The same thing will happen after Incarceration has been executed. America will get stronger and only the private sector can achieve that goal.'

Bob Wallshot sought a recess, it would give each of the committee members time to reflect on the day's activities and prepare themselves for the final stage.

THIRTY-FIVE

Michael Montefiore and his newly formed Special Services Group, had assembled at a small air field just a few miles south of Belize City. The highly trained SSG showed no signs of their previous profession as guests of the Saratoga Correctional Centre. They were a well-trained, highly disciplined group, ready to go and do battle for Montefiore. Each of the men had been given new identity papers and had been fully de-briefed on what was expected from them. They had gone over the routine time and time again. Not one small detail was left out of the plan.

Addressing the SSG, Montefiore reminded them that there was no turning back. An aircraft was due to arrive within minutes to transport them to a Mexican coastal town.

'When you joined me in Belize, not one of you had a better option in life,' Michael shouted out. 'Today, you are leaving to complete a mission, for which you have been trained. You have never asked me the reason for the mission and I have no plans to tell you now. I have been instructed to offer you a sweetener.'

The group had come to enjoy their freedom. For the first time in their lives they felt important. They were needed. They were uncertain as to what Montefiore was proposing, when he talked about a sweetener.

'You will each receive a million dollars upon successful completion of the mission. That should be enough for you to buy yourselves a new life after all this is over. You can fucking well invest it, you can spend it on whores or you can just simply piss it up the wall. It will be yours to do what ever you want.'

The group of men had been expecting a payout of some type. Not a million dollars each though. That was more money than any one of them could expect to see in a lifetime. They talked amongst themselves, each boasting what they were going to do with the cash when they finally got their hands on it. Montefiore had found the right nerve. He was now guaranteed to have their commitment to the end of the mission.

'We should arrive at our destination approximately a day before the arms shipment arrives. During that time I want you to go over your plans again and again. I want you to think about this every moment of the day from here in,' Montefiore ordered.

The sound of a twin prop DC3 freighter could be heard approaching the airfield. The plane had been chartered by Montefiore, using a contact that he had established whilst in Belize. The pilot of the plane was an old friend of his, having worked with him many years ago at Wallshot Corporation. Life had taken an unfavourable twist for him and he now found that most of his time these days was spent being involved in illegal activities in the northern part of South America. At some time or other he and his dilapidated DC3 had worked for most of the terrorist groups in the area. Working for Montefiore was just another day in his life.

The DC3 came to a thunderous standstill, just a few yards short of where the SSG had congregated. The pilot pushed open the side entry door and yelled for the men to get on board immediately, reminding them that he had to get to Mexico before dark. Immediately the last man clambered on board, the plane's engines accelerated, as it went about, facing the direction from which it had come. The pilot gave the engines full throttle. Smoke bellowed from the exhaust system as the plane began to pick up speed. The end of the man made runway was in sight. The plane's speed increased, the jungle was now fast approaching, then the pilot pulled back the throttle and she gently lifted herself over the tops of the trees. Within a few hours they would be putting down in Mexico.

The coastal freighter's captain had finally managed to load the cargo and strap it down securely in the rust filled hull of the boat. He had been given clearance to leave Belize City harbour. Not as though he really needed it. He knew every inch of the harbour and every mile of water between Belize and his Mexican destination, Tampico.

The ship encountered rough seas once it had rounded the Yucatan Peninsula and made its way across the Gulf. There had been cyclone warnings for the area. The ship's captain ignored the weather experts, saying that he was more capable of predicting weather patterns than they were. He had to get his shipment to Tampico on time, otherwise he was not paid. That was far more important to him, than the thought of having to confront a cyclone. By the time he had rounded the Yucatan Peninsula, the ship would steer a westerly course and provided he could maintain his twelve knots, he planned to be at his destination on time.

New York had turned on an exceptional summer's day for Phil and Fran. They didn't get to bed until the early hours of the morning, talking incessantly about their lives, careers and their future together. Fran had not been to New York before and was looking forward to her first day in the Big Apple.

Phil had been up early and prepared a light breakfast of orange juice, eggs sunny side up on toast and coffee. He had laid it all out very neatly on a tray and took the breakfast into the bedroom together with a red rose. She was unable to contain her excitement, chatting as she ate.

'Where are we going today?' Fran asked.

'What would you like to do?'

'A ride in Central Park; the Empire State building; lunch at the Plaza.'

'Hey hey! Hold on. We've only got one day. New York's a big city. We'll do the Empire State building firstly. That's only a few blocks away from the apartment. Then we'll get the subway up to Central Park. After that we can slip across the road and do afternoon tea at the Plaza. That sound OK?'

'That's OK, big chief!' Laughing at him as he jumped on to the bed, pinning her down by the shoulders, rubbing his stubbled chin on the side of her neck.

Within the hour they were both ready to explore New York. A short taxi ride and they were outside the Empire State. Being there early made no difference to the queue that had congregated to take the long trip to the top. Phil was convinced that it would not have mattered what time they had arrived, there would still have been throngs of people just waiting patiently to have a look see at what surely had become one of New York's most famous landmarks. They were determined not to be deterred by the large crowd and joined the slow moving line waiting to reach the ticket box. Finally they got there, only to pay their entry fee and then be shuffled to another line that was waiting to join the elevators to the summit.

They finally arrived at the top. It had been less than an hour. It was worth every moment to Phil to see the joy on Fran's face as she looked towards the Statue of Liberty. She was awestruck at the beauty of this most famous city. She put her arm around his waist and squeezed him tightly. She felt as though she had been here once before, perhaps, in a previous life. They had to move on. There was more to do and they had to get down from the top and make their way down Fifth Avenue to Central Park.

Being such a beautiful day, they decided to walk. Phil thought it was about ten blocks. He wasn't sure, in fact he had no idea, because he had never done the trip in the ten years he had lived in New York. 'Still what the heck,' he said to himself. 'It has to be quicker than taking a taxi.' Fran didn't mind. She wanted to see as much as she could. Walking was the best chance she had. By the time they had reached Central Park, they were exhausted. It had taken them over an hour. Mind you that had included one or two diversions into shops on the way down.

Fran was taken aback by the activity around the park. A carriage ride through the park, was something she had dreamt of since she was a little girl. She ran across the street, dragging Phil behind. She had spotted the carriage that she had wanted to get into. It was all white, with red and gold laced trim. The horse was a fine looking white mare with a black spot on the front of her face. Fran approached the driver, who spoke to her with an accent that was quite different to what she had been hearing during the morning. It was Irish. 'Where else would there be Irish, but in New York,' she murmured to herself.

'Where to Ma'am?' The driver asked.

'Just take us as far as you can,' Fran replied. 'And don't forget Strawberry Fields!'

Fran's idol had been John Lennon. She had been weaned on the Beatles, but her early love was John. To see the spot that Yoko had dedicated to the world, as a memorial to her husband had to be the highlight of her trip to New York. She was not disappointed. Getting out of the carriage for a few moments, she stood in silence and felt his presence move around her body. She was certain that John Lennon was there with her. Phil sensed a deep emotional interlude as he watched Fran look around Strawberry Field. It was a side of her that he had never seen before. She was obviously a person of deep emotional intellect, a characteristic, that was to bond them even closer in the future. Fran turned towards the carriage and looked pensive as she stepped inside. There was quietness for a few moments, when she suddenly burst alive and told the driver to get a move on.

By the time they had finished their long ride around Central Park it was after four in the afternoon. Neither one had had a bite to eat since breakfast that morning. Phil looked at her and suggested tea at the Plaza. Fran didn't hesitate to agree. Outside the front foyer to the Plaza, Fran laughed out aloud. It caught Phil by surprise. What the hell was wrong, he thought. She finally stopped giggling. Leaning on Phil's arm, he asked her what was all that about. She burst out laughing again and managed to get some sense back into her conversation. Finally she let Phil know that she had been reminded of the movie *Crocodile Dundee* and Paul Hogan's warm relationship with the concierge at the Plaza. She had found it quite remarkable that she was actually standing on the same steps that Paul had stood on when he did the movie. Phil was not that amused.

Afternoon tea at the Plaza was a great experience for both of them. Phil had never been inside in his life and this was Fran's first time. Phil reminded her that she had achieved more in her first twenty-four hours in New York, than he had achieved in ten years. The day had come to an end as they dawdled out of the hotel. They were both beat. Looking at each other, they unanimously agreed that a walk home was out of the question. 'Taxi!' Phil yelled.

Thirty-Six

'The final assault, gentlemen.'

The afternoon de-briefing session had commenced and BW wasted no time in getting on the podium to address his Execution Committee.

'As I told you earlier today, Michael Montefiore and his SSG will have armed fifteen key sites by declaration day. If the President has not responded to our first demand to step down as Chief Executive, Michael has been instructed to immobilise Los Angeles Airport.'

There was a momentary silence. The immobilisation of Los Angeles airport had been mentioned for the first time. The committee realised that the possible threat of the total destruction of America was now becoming reality.

'Why Los Angeles Airport?' Hardcastle asked.

'Destruction of the airport will cause minimal disruption. However, the President will know that we are serious about our threat to take control of the government.'

'What happens if he doesn't respond?' Cohen inquired.

'Heaven forbid if the man is that stupid. Let me remind you all if we have to destroy every one of the fifteen sites and bring this country to its knees, I will not be stopped.'

'You're right about one thing, BW,' General Tyler interrupted. 'Heaven forbid the President, even he's not that stupid.'

'No, you're right General. But let's not underestimate him. After all he is a seasoned campaigner. He's going to be tough opposition. We've got to make sure that we have the wood on him at all times. At the moment we have the greatest advantage. He has no idea of what we are about to confront him with.'

'When the plan is executed and we have control of the new

251

Corporate America, what happens to Montefiore's SSG?' Lazenby asked.

'Good question, Howard. The last thing we want is a bunch of reformed cons creating trouble for us after they've blown their million dollars each. Michael has been instructed to eliminate them at the appropriate time. Does that answer your question?'

'I don't need to know any more, BW. Thank you.'

'Gentlemen, you have all been very patient. What you have come here today to hear is when will Incarceration be executed. I will not keep you in suspense any longer. The execution of Incarceration will commence at 0800 hours on August 8. Just remember "888".'

The men were silent for a few seconds. Execution of Incarceration was less than ten days away. General Tyler stood up and faced BW, raising his right hand to salute him. The rest of the Committee stood and began to applaud.

'I will telephone the President at "888" and place him on red alert. If he fails to respond within twenty-four hours to our request for him and the government to step down, we will detonate Los Angeles airport and activate the software virus into the satellite communication system. If he has not succumbed to our demands within twenty-four hours, I will telephone him again. And I will keep calling him every day until he finally relents. If he's still sitting there at the end of fifteen days there will be no America left for any of us to concern ourselves about. Each day he procrastinates, another detonation will occur.'

The Committee was ecstatic that the whole plan had finally come to fruition.

The day finished on a high note. Everyone was focused on the event ahead of them. The changes they believed had to be made were only days away. They had no doubts that history would see them as conquerors. They were convinced that they had been chosen to rid America of its social and economic ills.

Mike Johnston was ready to go to work, when he heard a news flash on the morning radio. He was unable to pick up exactly what had been said as the kids were making too much noise. He yelled for them to be quiet, calling to his wife to turn the volume up. He dived into the kitchen just in time to hear the news that the Director of Public Prosecutions had decided to lay criminal charges against the Minister of Prisons for bribery and perverting the course of justice.

'Jeezus! What the bloody hell is that going to do to the company?' he screamed, hurting his hand as he thumped it down hard on the kitchen table.

'God, settle down, Mike. It's not the end of the world. You said that prosecution was inevitable,' Elizabeth replied.

'I know. The tragedy though is that all that work that we have done over the past few years, will now finish up on the scrap heap.'

'What do you mean?'

'I mean simply just that. The government will take the contracts off us. Either they'll take on the work themselves or put them out for tender again. If that happens you can bet your boots we will be excluded from tendering.'

'If that happens, where will that leave you?'

'I'm not going to wait around for that. I'll be handing in my resignation today. I can't afford to have my reputation damaged. It's going to be tough enough having to appear as a witness at the Minister's trial. There's nothing more I can do for Wallshot Corporation.'

Mike felt quite depressed. He knew it was going to happen, but he didn't realise how hard it would hit him until the news became public.

Travelling by car to work, he kept going over in his mind how he was going to handle his resignation. Should he give them a few months notice or should he just quit on the spot? By the time he had arrived at the office, all hell was breaking loose. The media hadn't wasted any time forcing themselves into the reception area. His secretary was waiting at the elevators for him. She ushered Mike through the side entry, avoiding the waiting press and television camera crews.

'I'm terribly sorry, Mr Johnston, that you had to walk into this,' his secretary said. 'When I was about to open up this morning, they were already here. I tried to keep them out. I am sorry.'

'Look let's not worry about that. You did your best. Go and ask them into the boardroom. Tell them I'll be there in a few moments.'

It was Sunday back in the States and Mike was unlikely to find anyone at the office. He didn't want to talk to Wallshot and he knew

Markowitz was no longer with the Corporation. He turned up his office directory and found the name and home telephone number of the Vice President Operations. Fortunately he caught him at home. He had never spoken to the guy before, but let him know that the Australian company was in crisis and asked for direction. As he expected the person he was speaking to could offer very little advice, only suggesting that he would get back to him as soon as possible. 'Typical,' Mike thought. He hoped it was only peculiar to Wallshot Corporation. He had known for years that there were no decision-makers within the corporation.

In disgust, he hung up in the guy's ear and moved hurriedly down the corridor to join the media in the boardroom. As he opened the door to the room, there were microphones being thrust at him from every angle. Why wasn't Fran here when he wanted her, he said to himself quietly. Pushing the microphones away he asked them to grab a seat wherever they could and he would give them a statement. It took a few minutes for them to get organised, but he was determined that he was not going to be bullied into saying the wrong thing. If nothing else, Fran had taught him how to control a noisy press meeting.

'Ladies and Gentlemen, I have been made aware this morning that the Minister of Prisons is going to face trial over bribery charges and attempting to pervert the course of justice. You know as well as I do, that allegations have been made that the Chairman of Wallshot Corporation is involved in this matter. I am unable to speak for him, but I would like to say that no one in the Australian operations had any knowledge of what had been going on. As soon as I have some more information I'll get back to you. I regret that I am unable to say any more at this stage.'

Mike had handled the situation like a true professional. Moving out of the boardroom he was tempted to answer the numerous questions that the media were throwing at him. He knew he couldn't as it might prejudice his position at a later date. Finally squeezing past the boardroom door, the noise became less deafening as he walked down the corridor and back to his office. He called his secretary in and asked her to take down his resignation effective immediately. His decision had been made.

Thirty-Seven

The weather beaten sea freighter had somehow miraculously escaped the Gulf cyclone. As she approached Tampico harbour, the noise of her worn engine bearings could be heard echoing around the surrounding hillside. The old crate reminded you of a larger version of the *African Queen*, but there would have been no way that she would have survived the jungle rivers of Africa.

The captain began to moor her alongside the wharf. Before he could put her antiquated engines into reverse, she crashed into the timber pylons and careered into the stern of a craft ahead, leaving a large gaping hole on the port side of her bow. He yelled at his men furiously to tie her up to the wharf before she caused more damage. It was his ship he was more concerned about and was nonchalant about the damage to the other vessel.

Michael Montefiore and his SSG had been waiting anxiously for the ship's arrival. She was about two hours late. He was furious, as one of the conditions that he had laid down was that she had to be in port at a specific time. Any delay had a roll on effect to other plans that had already been put in place.

Immediately the freighter was alongside, Michael jumped aboard and went looking for the captain. He found him in the boiler room, screaming at the engineer to fix the engine bearing before they set sail. The captain sensed that Michael was not particularly pleased with his late arrival but as far as he was concerned he had done a pretty good job given the unforeseen circumstances that he'd had to contend with during the voyage across the Gulf. By the time he had explained to Michael the difficulties they had encountered, he felt the tension subsiding.

The old captain was a wily old sea dog who had seen many Montefiores in his lifetime. They didn't frighten him. In fact he treated them all with contempt. He knew that there were very few ship captains plying the Gulf that would do the sort of work that he did. His clients had very little choice and most of them tolerated a few of his indiscretions.

Since the arrival of Michael and his SSG in Tampico, they had not wasted anytime in organising the removal of the weapons from the ship once she had berthed. Wallshot Corporation's Mexico City office had been requested earlier to send fifteen road transporters to Tampico harbour and to wait there until they received instructions. The trucks had actually arrived a day before the men had flown in from Belize and had occupied most of the wharf where they were told to go to. When Michael had stepped off the plane, he had immediately gone to the harbour to ensure that they had turned up. Not that he should have doubted the integrity of the Mexico City office, but he hadn't dealt with them before and he couldn't take any chances.

The trucks were in excellent condition, fully fuelled and prepared for their trip to the United States. Each truck had an American licensed driver with a Mexican side kick. The Mexican would leave them immediately they crossed the Border into the United States. His main task was to make sure that they got across the border and to overcome any language difficulties that they may encounter.

The captain was in a hurry to remove the cargo from the old sea freighter as he did not want to hang around any longer than was necessary. If the authorities detected that an illegal shipment had arrived in Tampico, they would most probably confiscate his boat and throw him and his men into prison.

Montefiore and his men were in the ship's hold sorting out how the crates would be loaded on to each of the trucks. It had been arranged previously that each truck would carry enough weapons to fully arm each of the fifteen strategic sites that had been selected for the successful execution of Incarceration.

To remove the cargo from the hold posed a problem as the men had to rely on the crane and winches that were on board the old sea freighter. How they had survived for so long was anybody's guess. They were rusted and had been very poorly maintained. As long as they did their job today, Montefiore would rest easy and be on his way to the United States by nightfall.

The first crate was lifted from the bottom of the hold. The winch creaked and groaned as the crate slowly moved up the hold wall to the open deck. There it was swung over the side and placed rather awkwardly on the edge of the wharf. The straps were removed ready for the next load to come to the top. As each load was placed on the dockside, the SSG lifted the small crates and placed them carefully into the awaiting trucks. The right selection of weapons and bomb devices had to be put into the correct trucks.

By late afternoon the task of unloading the ship had finally been completed. Apart from one of the winches seizing, leaving a load airborne for half an hour, the whole task was rather uneventful. The captain rubbed his hands together and made his way to Montefiore. He had completed his part of the bargain and was now looking for the balance of his shipping fee.

Confirming that the cargo was all there and intact he handed over the second half of the payment to the ship's captain, deducting a hundred thousand dollars for his late arrival. The captain abused Montefiore in his native tongue using language that was probably even foreign to him. When the SSG moved closer to Michael the captain knew it was a waste of time arguing over a hundred thousand. He had done well out of the assignment. Getting himself killed for a lousy one hundred was pointless. He backed off and took what he had been given, threatening that one day he would get even. Montefiore wasn't fazed by his threat.

The trucks began to leave the wharf for their trip to the Mexican border. As they roared through the outskirts of the town, the locals just stood and watched, not realising for one moment that what was being carried in each of the them would play a big part in changing the face of America.

The convoy had proceeded slowly through the night and by sunrise the following morning had reached the Immigration control point at the Mexican and US border.

Montefiore was in the lead truck sitting between the driver and the Mexican side-kick. The convoy slowed down as they approached the check point and upon seeing the signal from the immigration control officer the lead truck pulled up alongside the officer, who had now made his way to the side of the roadway. The Mexican side-kick wound down his window and greeted him. They exchanged pleasantries and the officer asked for their passports and shipment papers. Montefiore was becoming a little nervous. He didn't know the Mexican and he had no idea what he was saying to the immigration officer. The officer pored over the passports and carefully looked through the shipment papers. Any moment now Montefiore was expecting him to ask to inspect the cargo of weapons they were carrying. The conversation continued between the officer and the Mexican, the tone of their voices rising occasionally. Montefiore was beginning to sweat, his hand reaching beneath the cabin seat for the small hand gun that he had placed there, before they left Tampico harbour. Both the driver and Montefiore were unable to see the immigration officer as he had positioned himself right alongside the truck and was out of view to them. The Mexican was becoming increasingly agitated as he argued with the officer over the paperwork. Montefiore had now placed the gun inside his jacket, his hand on the trigger. He looked at the check point office noticing one other officer on duty. He was busy checking a vehicle travelling from the north into Mexico.

The immigration officer moved away from the vehicle and began to walk to the other side. As he passed in front of the vehicle's headlamps, Montefiore noticed the shoulder patch on the man's uniform. It read 'Wallshot Corporation Immigration Officer.' He immediately sighed with relief, as he released the pressure on the gun's trigger. The officer was an employee of the Corporation and had been made aware that the convoy would be passing through. He went into the check point booth and began to stamp the passports and the shipping papers. Returning the papers to the Mexican he looked at Montefiore and smiled. The ordeal was over.

None of the other trucks in the convoy was inspected. As they all roared past the immigration check point, the officer on duty closed the door to his booth until the fifteen vehicles were out of sight.

There was limited time in which to arm the key strategic sites that had been selected for Incarceration.

When Phil Black had arrived at the office of the *New York Herald*, he was noticeably high spirited. Whistling and singing were peculiarities that Phil was not well known for, particularly first thing in the morning. The people that saw his antics looked in surprise, not knowing that Phil was in love and he had just spent the best day of his life with his new found love touring New York City. Amanda was there to greet him, smiling as she asked him how things had gone.

'By the way I have two messages for you,' Amanda said. 'A Mike Johnston rang from Australia. He said you knew him. Would you give him a call? Here's his number. When you've finished go up and see Mr Morphett. He's expecting you.'

'Thanks Amanda. I'll ring Mike first and tell the boss I'll be straight up.'

Phil dialled Australia and was greeted by a warm hello from a female voice on the other end.

'Hi, I'm Phil Black, is Mike Johnston there please?'

'Yes he his, I'll get him for you. I'm his wife Elizabeth.'

'Elizabeth, how lovely to talk to you! Mike has told me so much about you.'

'Thank you Phil. I'll put Mike on.'

'Good day Phil. How are you?'

'Good day, mate. Good thanks. How are you?'

'Have been better. Phil, I said I would talk to you if things went wrong here. Well the shit has hit the fan. The Minister of Prisons is going to be prosecuted and the company is about to lose its government contracts. I thought I better let you know because the Government will be expecting Wallshot to take the witness stand at some time during the trial.'

'Yeah, I guess we all knew that this is what would happen. Wallshot is up to his neck in shit here. There's no way that he'll go to Australia and face the courts there. He'll be too fucking busy facing the courts here. I'd say Mr Wallshot is yesterday's man, Mike.'

'Phil, I've resigned from the Corporation. I was hoping to talk to Markowitz, but I have no idea how to get in contact with him.'

'What do you plan to do at the moment?'

'Nothing has been arranged. I'll have a few months off and see where the future takes me, I guess.'

'Mike, could you join us in New York for a few months? I'm doing the big wrap up on Wallshot and I'd sure appreciate your input.'

'When would you want me there?'

'How quickly could you get on a plane?'

'Leave it with me. I'll see you in New York in a couple of days.'

Rudy Morphett was in a jovial mood for the beginning of the week. Phil was sure that he had found out that the new love in his life was staying with him at his apartment.

'Come in, Phil. I believe you've got some news for me? Amanda has been gossiping.'

'Yes, boss. I should have told you sooner. But you know one thing and another. It's been a pretty busy time. An old friend of mine that I met in Australia is staying with me for a short time.'

'Is it serious, Phil?'

'Sure is Rudy.'

'I'm pleased for you. Just the tonic you needed. Good luck. Well Harry Groves rang me this morning to tell me that the President has told the Attorney General to throw everything at that sonofabitch Bob Wallshot. Harry's committee report had enough shit in there to lock that prick Wallshot away for the rest of his life. The only thing that concerns me is that he is going to get out from under all this.'

'What do you mean, boss?'

'You remember I told you that he was having a high level meeting at his ranch. Well it took place. And the most powerful men in the country were there. Wallshot is about to move. He has to do it now or face extremely serious legal action both here and in Australia. His days as a corporate giant are finished. I have also been told that he has not been able to put together the funding for his short selling. The brokers are pushing his Corporation pretty hard. They want payment or they risk losing their licences. He's in really deep shit and we gotta keep pushing the bastard to the end. I want you to spend all your time on finishing that exposé on Wallshot.'

'Boss, I've just had a call from Mike Johnston in Australia. He's left the Corporation. I've asked him to join the team. Hope you didn't mind?'

'Get whoever you need on to the job. I want the story published internationally. Thanks Phil. Get on with it. By the way I hope I'm invited to the wedding?'

$\mathcal{T}$HIRTY-$\mathcal{E}$IGHT

After the trucks had gone through the US border control, they dispersed for the pre arranged strategic locations.

Each one of the SSG had been fully de-briefed, as to the action they had to take, immediately upon arrival at the target site.

The first truck had reached its destination point, after a long arduous trip across desolate country. The Hoover Dam, stood majestically before them. Their target was to be prepared for destruction. This enormous historic shrine storing one of the largest deposits of water in the United States was to be immobilised. The impact that its destruction would have on millions of people that relied on the dam's hydro electricity generation would be catastrophic.

As the truck approached the main entrance to the Dam's administrative and operational centre, a security officer moved from behind a glass booth. The dam's closed circuit television cameras had activated and were pointing directly at the vehicle, sending live pictures back to the control centre. The officer moved alongside the driver's door and asked him to show his identification papers.

During their training sessions in the Belize jungle, the men had gone over the procedure time and time again. They knew what to expect.

The security officer inspected the paper work and was satisfied that the cargo of replacement machinery for the Dam was in order and asked the driver to take the vehicle to the Wallshot maintenance depot for unloading. The Wallshot Corporation security officer had been well briefed and had made the task easy for the truck crew.

Pulling up outside the Wallshot maintenance depot, the large folding doors began to rise. A maintenance worker in a dark blue uniform signalled the driver to park the vehicle inside the building. The truck engine was turned off and the folding doors began to close, leaving the truck and the two men alone in the large warehouse. Within a few seconds a small group of men appeared from the back of the warehouse, walking briskly towards the men and the truck. As they approached one of the men spoke.

'My name is Harry. I'm the head of Wallshot Corporation's engineering department here at the Hoover. We have been instructed to help you unload your cargo and offer you any other assistance that you may require.'

'We expected you. Your help is appreciated. There is no chance that the cargo will be detected in the warehouse?'

'No. I'm the only one who knows the security code to the building.'

'Good. Let's get the truck unloaded then.'

A small fork-lift was driven up to the rear of the vehicle. The men carefully lifted the crates on to the wooden pallet that was secured to the front of the lift. One by one the crates were methodically moved off and stored at the back of the warehouse. The whole operation took no more than two hours.

The SSG men began to open the wooden boxes. The first one had six AK-47 assault rifles. The second box had five FN MAG machine guns. The third and fourth boxes had thirty kilogram of Semtex and an assortment of detonators. The final two boxes contained the ammunition for the hand weapons.

Harry looked at the opened boxes in dismay.

'Shit, when they told me you were bringing enough detonation to wipe out the dam, they weren't wrong. There won't be a stone left by the time that goes off.'

'Listen, you nosy sonofabitch, we're here to do a job. I don't want to hear any opinions from you. Just jump when I need ya. You understand?'

The SSG men had tolerated enough. They had lost patience with Harry and let him know quickly that they weren't going to let him hinder the operation in anyway.

'Where are the plans for the dam?' he asked.

'Over here on the table,' Harry replied quickly, not wishing to antagonise the man any further.

'We've got to strategically place the Semtex so that we can detonate it from a remote area. We don't intend to be around when it goes off. Show me on the plan where you think we should anchor this stuff?'

Harry knew every square inch of the Hoover. He had been with the corporation from the very first day that the government had awarded them the contract to service the Dam's hydro-electric generators.

'There are seven likely trigger spots. Load up each of these and I'll guarantee there'll be enough water released to flood the Black Canyon.'

'I want you to escort us to each of these points. You will help us place the detonations. Let's get going. We ain't got much time!'

The men followed Harry out of the warehouse towards the foot of the dam's wall. A concealed door in the side of the dam was out of all proportion to the millions of tons of concrete that lay above it. The three men eased their way through the door. Ahead was a well lit passageway, which according to Harry made its way from one side of the dam to the other. It was the service access for the dam's engineers.

As they made their way along the passage, every now and again Harry would stop and point out where they were on the plan that he carried with him. By the time they had reached the end, Harry had highlighted the seven trigger points on the plan.

'How long would it take for us to get the explosive in here?'

'Best time would be late this afternoon. The night shift normally doesn't come into the dam passage. That'll give you all night to load her up.'

By late afternoon the men were ready to move the explosive and the detonators into the Dam's inner wall. They figured they'd do it in three stages, thus eliminating the need for them to call on Harry to assist them. They had been well prepared for the task ahead. Providing Harry kept the access to the passage free, the rest they knew would be a piece of cake.

During the night they positioned the Semtex at the seven trigger points. Each point was wired to a frequency signal that would be activated from a control point well clear of the Dam.

The first of the fifteen key strategic sites had been armed. The

Hoover Dam was ready to be destroyed immediately the signal was given.

Around other parts of the country fourteen trucks were slowly making their way to their designated targets.

By nightfall, Montefiore had planned to have the west coast trucks in place at the San Diego Naval Station, Mather Air Force Base in Sacramento, the Oakland Military Base and Los Angeles International Airport.

The San Diego naval base was Montefiore's prize. He had been the West Coast manager for Wallshot Corporation when they were awarded the contract to secure the naval base and feed the personnel. That was many years ago but at that time he had walked every inch of the establishment and had formulated in his own mind what action was now needed to immobilise the Pacific Naval Fleet of the US Navy. The other three locations were going to be much easier to prepare as the Corporation had a controlling presence at each of the sites.

Two of the trucks that had been in convoy with the Hoover Dam truck had now arrived at the country's largest nuclear and oil reserve site.

The corporation had been managing these sites for several years and in fact had just rolled over the oil reserve contract for another fifteen years.

The national oil reserve site had been chosen in the seventies to house the country's oil reserves. The government at the time had made that decision following the international Arab oil crisis of the early seventies. The government was not going to be held to ransom again, particularly by a group of unstable Arab nations. Stored under the ground was the equivalent to seven hundred and fifty million barrels of crude oil. Enough oil to keep the American economy going at full steam for three months. Detonation of this site was planned as a last resort only.

The other trucks had checked in during the day as arranged. Each vehicle was to check in with Montefiore at two hour intervals and give its co-ordinates. This was the only way that he knew the exact location of each vehicle and also it allowed him to monitor the destination arrival times.

Tomorrow the trucks were due to arrive at the Hartsfield

International Airport in Atlanta and the Miami International airport. By late tomorrow night, the remaining trucks would be positioned at O'Hare International airport, Vernon Nuclear energy site, Mississippi River Nuclear energy site, Newark International airport, United Nations building in New York and finally the Pentagon in Washington. The task after that would be to prepare each site for destruction. Two days only had been allowed.

It was noon on the second day since they left the Mexican border. Montefiore began picking up the coordinates signal from each of the trucks. As they checked in he plotted their position into his lap top computer. Fourteen had checked in and he had them each logged into the program. The fifteenth truck was late. He checked with the previous positioning and according to his information they were within twelve hours of Atlanta International airport. Why hadn't they logged their coordinates in at twelve noon? The SSG man on board was Mickey Ryan, the Irish terrorist. During training in the Belize jungle, Ryan had become Montefiore's right hand man. He commanded the respect of the other escaped prisoners. They looked up to Mickey for support and direction. None of them cared for Montefiore. They never trusted him. They trusted Ryan though.

Montefiore re-programmed his coordinates to see if he could pick up their signal. They could be having difficulty getting through. He tested the function again. The program was working perfectly. Something had gone wrong. What was it? Had they been picked up by Highway Patrol? What if they had run off the road? The probabilities were endless. Montefiore did not deal in probabilities. He only dealt in facts. Checking his watch it was now twenty after twelve, still no response. Something is definitely wrong, he said to himself. The next check in time was two that afternoon. He would have to wait until then.

Parked in downtown San Diego with fifty kilograms of Semtex on the back of your truck was not Michael's way of spending a pleasant afternoon. He was agitated. He had not heard from the Atlanta truck. It was now two in the afternoon. The signals began to come through. Codes were received from all trucks again except Atlanta. He waited a few more minutes, still no response. The truck had gone down. 'Don't panic,' he kept saying over and over to himself. There was no signal of any sort. He was unable to intercept the emergency signal band. The transmitter in the truck had been disconnected. He was convinced of that. Mickey Ryan had gone rogue. Why had he done it? He had no way of getting the answer. All he could do at this late stage was to get in touch with Wallshot at the Buena Vista ranch control station and advise him that one of the trucks had gone down.

'BW, it's Michael.'

'Has something gone wrong?'

'I'm uncertain. I need your help. The truck headed for Atlanta International airport has gone missing. I've lost its signal.'

'What do you think has happened?'

'Could be a number of things. Your guess is as good as mine.'

'What does your gut tell you, Michael?'

'He's changed his mind. He's not heading for Atlanta.'

'Where is he going, if he's not headed for Atlanta.'

'I have no idea. Last time I heard from him he was in Arkansas. He was heading east then.'

'When's he due in Atlanta?'

'Within the next twelve hours.'

'The best we can do at this late stage is to pray that he's still on his way and there's been a malfunction in the equipment. In the meantime I'll have our security road patrols on full alert. We'll intercept him if we spot him.'

'How's the plan going, Michael?'

'On target. Hoover is armed and we'll have the East Coast sites armed shortly. The others I anticipate completion within the next two days.'

'Keep me informed if you hear any more on the Atlanta truck.'

Thirty-Nine

The trip from New York to JFK International airport was now becoming familiar territory for Phil. He was on his way out to pick up Mike Johnston who was due in from Los Angeles late that evening. Fran was not going to be left at the apartment. When she found out that Mike was coming into town, she wanted to be with Phil when he picked him up.

They didn't have to wait long. Mike's plane had been fifteen minutes early and he was one of the first passengers off when it arrived. Fran was the first to spot him, running over and planting a warm friendly kiss on the side of his cheek. Phil was not quite as amorous. He furiously shook his hand and welcomed him to New York. Fran couldn't stop chattering. She wanted to know what had happened back in Sydney. Had the company lost its contracts? What happened to the Minister of Prisons? She kept firing questions at him. Phil pulled her away and asked her to tone it down a bit, reminding her that Mike had been flying non stop for twenty-four hours. She got the message and let Phil and Mike do all the talking as they travelled back to the city. Phil had found a hotel for Mike, just half a block from the *New York Herald*'s office. When they arrived at the hotel, Phil promised to be there at seven in the morning to pick him up.

Right on the dot of seven, Phil had arrived at the hotel. He asked the bell boy to ring Mike's room. There was no answer. 'Ring again,' he asked him. He did, still no answer.

'You looking for me, Phil,' the voice said.

Looking around sharply, Phil saw Mike standing behind him, dressed and ready for work.

'Shit, you're all ready?'

'Well you told me to be here at seven. Here I am. Let's go we've got work to do, Phil.'

The sort of enthusiasm that Mike generated was good for Phil's motivation. He needed someone to keep pushing him.

When they arrived at the office, Mike was beside himself when he saw Joe Markowitz sitting behind the desk, with his feet up eating a croissant.

'Christ, Phil, you never told me Joe was working with you!'

'Mate, us journalists have to have something up our sleeves. Besides if I'd told ya, you may not have come.'

'You wouldn't have kept me away.'

Phil was ready to work. He now had the strongest possible team working with him to nail down the Wallshot story.

Phil had a whiteboard in the room where he had laid out in detail, the information that he had been able to get his hands on to date. This was no ordinary whiteboard. It was the biggest one that Mike had ever seen and was covered with cryptic comments about Wallshot.

'There are two major areas that I have not been able to cover at this stage,' Phil said. 'And that is why I wanted you two guys involved.'

'Mike, I want you to research the Senate hearings for me over the last ten years and give me a comprehensive brief on each one. I then want you to meet a friend of ours, Senator Harry Groves, who was the Chairman of the committees. He'll give you his views as to why Wallshot was never prosecuted.'

'What can I do for you, Phil?' asked Joe.

'Where you will be most valuable is giving us a full run down on the Swiss bank accounts and the off-shore companies. Can you handle that?'

'I'll let you have everything I know and more if I can.'

'Finally, I hate to have to say this to you guys but I'm under a bit of pressure from the boss. He wants the story finished by the weekend.'

Phil ducked as he felt a book go flying by, just missing the top of his head by inches. Had Joe been a split second sooner it probably would have collected. They both took the deadline comment in fun and promised to give Phil all the cooperation they could to have it finished by the end of the week.

San Diego naval station was not an easy place to get into. Montefiore and the driver had tried several entrances but each had been closed. The only way that they could now get into the base was literally through the front door. Michael had hoped to avoid the main entrance. Getting past security was not the problem, the Wallshot Corporation security had been pre-warned to expect a shipment of cargo and had been given full detail as to how it would arrive. Michael's concern was the Naval Base Shore Patrol. Ever since Wallshot security had been on site, the Shore Patrol had resented their presence. They were firmly of the opinion that security was a naval function and not one for private enterprise. Shore Patrol would occasionally stand alongside security and watch what they did, questioning their actions and do everything possible to trip them up. Michael didn't want to go through the main gate and be confronted by those Shore Patrol mongrels.

The truck turned the corner and slowly made its way towards the large boom gates. There was a lot of activity around both the entry and exit gates, a quick look and all Michael could see was the Wallshot security officers on the front gate. He told the driver to move forward and stop at the boom gate. The security officer asked for identification, which the driver passed to him. The officer looked up acknowledging to the driver that he had been expecting them. The papers were returned and the officer ordered the driver to take the truck to Compound C where they would be met. The boom gate was raised, the truck began to move slowly into the Naval Base.

Suddenly there was a yell from the other side of the truck to stop. There was nothing else the driver could do but comply. The security officer noticed what had happened and ran to the front of the vehicle, yelling at the Shore Patrol officer to let the vehicle through. The Shore Patrol officer had the right of veto over the security officer' authorisation. The two men stood toe to toe, looking at each other with the utmost contempt. Michael was beginning to get nervous and warned the driver to be ready to turn the truck around and hightail it out of here if they had to. The confrontation between the two men continued. Michael's assessment was that the Wallshot security officer was not fairing too well. By this time, Michael had pulled his AK-47 from under the cabin seat and placed it on the floor under his feet. If they had to bolt for it he intended going out in a blaze of glory.

Other vehicles had begun to pile up behind the truck. The Mexican stand-off between the two officers was causing considerable congestion at the main gate. Suddenly a break through, a naval commander who had been leaving the base had noticed the skirmish between the two men, parked his vehicle and walked over to see what he could do to break the stalemate. This was not unusual. He had seen this happen many times before. He pulled the two men to one side and spoke to both of them in a terse manner, threatening to report both of them for infantile behaviour. In the meantime the beads of perspiration were beginning to trickle down Michael's back. What was going to be the outcome? Conversation between the three men stopped. The Commander made his way to the truck and asked to see the identification papers. He inspected them for a few seconds and then returned to the two men, telling the Shore Patrol officer that the papers were in order and instructed him to immediately let the truck through.

The ordeal was over. They were now inside the San Diego Naval base. The program to arm the targets could now be accomplished.

There had still been no signal response from the truck heading for Hartsfield International airport in Atlanta. Montefiore was now convinced that Mickey Ryan had made the decision to make a run for it. He couldn't understand why as he was the only member of his SSG that he thought he could have trusted. What about the others, were they likely to do a bolt? He thought perhaps not!

The West Coast sites were nearly ready and the trucks would be rolling into the other target areas within the day. Each of them had religiously signalled in every two hours as instructed. 'If anything was to go wrong with them, surely it would have happened by now,' Michael murmured.

The San Diego Naval base was a complex site, having grown topsy turvy over many years. The original plan for the site was quite simple. There were deep water channels carved out of the shoreline, interspersed with dry dock facilities. The support facilities were built right alongside the docks. Over the years the Department of Navy had to expand its base requirements to cater for the increased US Naval presence in the Pacific. That's where the planning went wrong, wherever they could find a spot, up would go another building.

Michael had carefully plotted the base targets that he needed to arm. He knew it would be an impossibility to take out the complete site, but he was confident that he could immobilise the critical points for several months.

Walking around the base with his security tag pinned to his jacket he was afforded security clearance to all restricted and non restricted areas. Very little had changed since he worked on the site back in what he called the good old days.

To bring a halt to the base, he considered he would have to arm the central communications area, administration and the fuel storage tanks. Knocking out communications would effectively sever all contact between the base and the Pacific Fleet. That would allow sufficient time for Wallshot and his new Corporate America to become ensconced in Washington.

An old friend of Michael's met up with him. He had been asked to escort him around the site. The guy had worked for Michael previously and was well known and respected by all naval personnel at San Diego. No one would ever have expected him to be part of a conspiracy to overthrow the government.

They stored the weapons in a concealed part of the main warehouse. When Michael saw the amount of armaments stored he thought that he shouldn't have taken the risk to bring their supply. There was enough hand weaponry stored to fit out the whole of the US Navy.

Dressed as maintenance personnel, Michael and his friend moved into the communications area to service the electrical wiring for the computer based technology that formed part of the hardware that kept communication open with the Fleet. No one suspected what they were up to, as most personnel in the centre were accustomed to maintenance men roaming freely around the site.

Michael's friend worked with the tools going about his job as normal. Michael was alongside him, carefully positioning ten kilograms of Semtex and wiring the detonation to the main communications hardware. At one stage during the operation one of the naval personnel came over and spoke to them and asked them how long they would be. The maintenance guy grumbled and told him they would be there until they're finished, no longer. The naval personnel walked away scratching his head, none the wiser.

With the Semtex in place at the communications centre they systematically moved through the compound to the fuel storage depot. There were over sixty white storage tanks containing everything from high-grade benzine to diesel fuel and crude oil. Each tank grouping was interconnected by a pipe system with flow valves situated every twenty yards. Getting access to the storage tanks did not pose a problem for Michael and his friend as they were both security cleared. Moving around within the area had its difficulties. There were an unusual number of personnel in the restricted area re-painting the tanks. Michael had to create a diversion. A diversion that would give him sufficient time to locate Semtex and detonators at the base of four of the high benzine storage tanks. He opened a flow valve, gallons of benzine began to pour out of the tank, Michael's accomplice brought his seven-pound hammer across the face of the valve, smashing it beyond recognition thus preventing anyone being able to turn it off. They yelled out for assistance. The painters near them stopped what they were doing and came to assist. There was nothing they could do as hundreds of gallons of benzine kept pouring out of the damaged valve. A siren went off. Michael had discreetly moved away from the panic stricken group and began the arduous task of arming the high benzine tanks. He needed about twenty minutes. Was the diversion going to give him sufficient time?

As he furiously worked away, carefully positioning the explosive and loading the detonator a naval person in uniform saw him and ordered him to get out of the danger area. He ignored the command and kept on going. The person ran towards Michael, yelling at him again to get his ass out of there. Again Michael ignored him. Panic had now set in. The valve could not be fixed immediately. The fuel had to be turned off at the main flow valve. The site engineer had been called for. Michael felt a hand grab him buy the scruff of the neck and pull him to the ground. He looked up. It was the same person who had ordered him to remove his ass from the site.

Michael looked around quickly. There was no one else nearby. He stood up and pulled out a large knife and thrust the blade under the rib cage into the person's heart, twisting the knife as the man dropped to the ground. He was dead.

Michael dragged the body a few yards to a small storage unit. He opened the door and dumped the dead man inside. He had two more tanks to arm. Pandemonium surrounded him. He was ignored as he went about his task. Someone yelled out that the fuel was off. One more minute and he would be finished. Michael's accomplice had been watching him very carefully throughout the operation and as calm was restored, Michael casually walked past the crowd that had congregated oblivious to what had taken place during the last twenty minutes.

Loading up the administration sector was a piece of cake compared to what he had gone through. How long would it be before they discovered the mutilated body was anybody's guess? Probably a few hours! Michael had to be off the base before they found him. He couldn't afford to be caught. The operation although successful, concerned him that he had come so close to losing it out there. One slip and Incarceration would have been jeopardised.

Forty

The arming of the other sites had not been as dramatic as the San Diego Naval Base. The task was now completed except for Hartsfield International Airport. Four days had passed since Montefiore had his last communication signal from Mickey Ryan. He had heard nothing either from Wallshot. How had Ryan managed to fall off the end of the earth without been seen or heard from?

The *New York Herald* morning headline was not particularly kind to Wallshot. Rudy Morphett had fired his most scathing attack at the corrupt business mogul, accusing him of bribing officials at the highest level of government. Morphett demanded that the government take immediate action to indict him following the revelations of the Harry Groves Senate Committee findings. He went on further to demand that Wallshot should face extradition to Australia to face criminal charges that were about to be laid against him in that country.

Wanting to bury the hatchet as far as he could, Morphett put pressure on the Texas government to commence legal action against both Governor Sharp and Wallshot for corrupt activities against the State of Texas and the people of America.

The article took up three full pages of the *Herald* and by mid morning the newspaper stands had run out of copies. Morphett had to authorise a further run of the morning edition to satisfy the insatiable appetite of public demand.

The White House Chief of Staff called Rudy Morphett. He had been instructed by the President to set up a time for them to meet. The Chief of Staff had expressed to Morphett that the President was vitally concerned with the venomous attack that his paper had made on one of America's leading business tycoons. Morphett was unaccustomed to bowing to political pressure and maintained that his responsibility was to the people of America.

Agreeing to meet with the President was not high on Morphett's list of priorities, but the Chief of Staff insisted that he wanted to meet with him urgently. Arrangements were made for Morphett to see the President later that afternoon. A condition of the meeting laid down by Morphett was that he be allowed to bring along Phil Black, Mike Johnston and Joe Markowitz. The Chief of Staff didn't agree at first. He saw no benefit from those people being present. When Morphett insisted that they had to be there otherwise there was not going to be a meeting, the Chief of Staff relented and invited them as well.

Rudy summoned Black, Markowitz and Johnston to his office. He told them about the conversation he had just had with the White House and asked them to be on standby for an afternoon meeting with the President to discuss the Wallshot expose.

'Sounds as though today's story has hit the target,' Phil said.

'The President's worried,' Rudy replied. 'I got an indication that he wants us to drop the story completely. He believes that there could be a run on Wall Street if we continue to headline Wallshot. He's also concerned that it may rub off on to other government contractors.'

'Shit, what is he trying to do, protect a corrupt business community?'

'Not exactly! As it involves the government he doesn't want his administration undermined. He needs to handle it in his own way.'

'You've caved in to him, boss.'

'Listen Phil, I have not caved in. That's why I want you guys there. To back me up! You know more about Wallshot than I do.'

Morphett was a little hurt by Phil's cynical comment and turned to him and said sharply, 'Don't you ever accuse me again of backing down. I didn't take too kindly to your remark, mate,'

'What do you want us to do, Mr Morphett,' Mike asked.

'Simple! Let's see what he has to say firstly. Then if we have to I want each of you guys to give him a full account of the work you've done to date. Phil, you talk about the Aussie affair. Mike, you can cover the operational issues, whilst you Joe, have to lay it right on the line about the Swiss accounts.'

Mike was feeling somewhat nervous by the time the meeting with Morphett had finished. Never in his wildest moments would he have thought that a few days ago he was sitting at home contemplating his future and here he was this afternoon going to The White House to debrief the President of the United States.

The *New York Herald*'s chauffeur driven limousine slowed down as it approached the entrance gate to the White House. Security was expecting Morphett and his guests. Security telephoned control to let them know that the vehicle was proceeding to the West Wing of the building. As the vehicle came to a stop the Chief of Staff, Freddy Hayes was there to meet the four visitors. After exchanging pleasantries he then escorted them through the west wing to the Oval Office. The President was there to meet them and shook each of their hands very firmly, thanking them for coming at such short notice.

The President had asked his Chief of Staff and Secretary of State, William Franklin to join the meeting.

'Gentlemen, thank you for coming to see me at such short notice! I'll cut out the idle chit chat and get right down to business. We're all busy men and I'm sure you don't want to hear a pile of political crap from me.'

The President's opening remarks took Rudy a little by surprise as he was expecting him to soften them up firstly before he put the hard word on them.

'I've asked you here to talk about Bob Wallshot. I want to share with you some concerns I have about this man and his corporation. In return my advisers have informed me that you have been doing a considerable amount of research on him, some of which I think I will find very helpful. Nothing goes outside this office. Do we have a deal?'

'Mr President, you have a deal. We are in a position to share our information with you.'

'Good let's get down to tin tacks. You're aware of the Senator Harry Groves recommendations, I presume?'

'Yes we are, Mr President.'

'Well, Harry was in my office some weeks ago and I gave him the green light to re-open one of the closed files on Wallshot. You know the outcome of that? When I authorised Harry to re-open the file, I also said that if he was successful he could open the other closed files. Truth is I don't want him to do that now.'

'Why's that, Mr President?'

'Your newspaper article today sent Wall Street plunging over four hundred points. Wiped over twenty per cent off the value of Wallshot stock alone. It is not in our interest to see further falls. I have to talk up the market and tell the investing public that this is a one off case only. Wall Street now thinks that the whole government is corrupt and is just waiting for the next *New York Herald* exposé. How much more do you have on Wallshot?'

'Enough, Mr President, to send his corporation to the wall and Wallshot with it.'

'Christ, that's a pretty powerful position you're in. I hope you're on my side when I run for the Presidency next term?'

'Oh yes, Mr President. But you did say that we are not here to talk about politics,' Rudy quickly replied. 'We'll give you an overview of how much we know, then perhaps we can talk about a mutually beneficial strategy?'

'Let's hear your proposition.'

Over the next hour they gave the President and his advisers a comprehensive overview of what they knew about the workings of Wallshot and his corporation. Morphett even went on to share his theory with the President that he suspected that Wallshot was up to something sinister and was ready to strike at any moment. The President found that a bit hard to swallow but became more convinced when Morphett told him that the Vice President had met with Wallshot several times recently at his ranch in South Carolina.

'Freddy, is that true about Vice President Ford?'

'I have no idea, Mr President. I'll have it checked out immediately.'

'What the blazes is that sonofabitch Ford up to?'

The President pulled himself out of the sofa and went to his desk to sit down. He leaned back in his chair and thought for a few moments.

'Mr Morphett, I think it was appropriate that I called you in to see me this afternoon. Having listened to what you and your staff have told me about this man, I have every reason to be extremely concerned. We have to deal with this matter very carefully. Don't you agree?'

'I agree, Mr President. You have a real dilemma on your hands.'

'I would like you to cease further reporting on Wallshot. Give me enough time to get the market settled down. I'm proposing to call a press conference later this evening to tell the public that I have everything in hand. Knowing what I have learned from you guys today, we have to put a strategy in place immediately to stop this train from running away from us. I have asked the Secretary of State to review all government contracts with Wallshot. If I have to pull the contracts off him it has to be done in such away that I don't have panic and pandemonium. Will you help me?'

'Mr President I have a responsibility to my readers but I do agree that I can't let that influence my responsibility to the government firstly. I would suggest that we work to putting a firm strategy in place within the next forty-eight hours. You agreeable to that, Mr President?'

'We have a deal, Mr Morphett.'

$\mathscr{F}$ORTY-$\mathscr{O}$NE

"888"

'This is the White House, how may I help you?'

'I wish to speak to The President please.'

'Just a moment I'll connect you with the President's office.'

'This is Jenny Shevak speaking. I'm The President's deputy press officer. May I help you?'

'I want to speak to the President please. Now!'

'I'm sorry, sir. The President is not available to take your call. Perhaps I can help?'

'This is Bob Wallshot speaking and I demand to talk to the President immediately.'

There was a moment of silence as the telephone was put on hold.

'Mr Wallshot, this is Chief of Staff, Freddy Hayes. I understand you want to talk to the President. I'm sorry, sir, the President is busy at the moment.'

'Mr Hayes, I will not ask again. Put the President on the line right now, or I will not be held responsible for what happens next.'

The tone of Wallshot's voice was sinister. Hayes remembered the conversation that the President had with Rudy Morphett. Morphett maintained that Wallshot was about to do something. Was this it? Why had he insisted so strongly in talking direct to the President?

'Just a moment, Mr Wallshot, I will have the President interrupted.'

The wait was only seconds.

'Mr Wallshot, this is the President. I understand from my Chief of Staff that you wish to talk with me?'

'I do, Mr President. Firstly I would suggest that you tune your television receiver to Channel 88. Then secondly you listen to what I have to say.'

The President was about to argue the point with Wallshot when he thought better of it for the time being. Signalling to Hayes, he asked him to tune the receiver into Channel 88, at the same time activating the voice recording control on his direct telephone line.

'Mr Wallshot, we are tuned in to Channel 88. What should I be looking for?'

As he uttered those words, a picture appeared on the screen. It was Wallshot sitting down at his desk at the Buena Vista ranch with the Vice President Clark Ford sitting alongside him.

'Mr President, you are obviously acquainted with my guest, the Vice President.'

The President was speechless. He couldn't believe what he was seeing. The Deputy Chief Executive Officer of the United States sitting beside one of the country's leading power barons. A man who very shortly was to face the judicial system on criminal conspiracy charges.

'Mr President, I want my opening statement to be precise and very clear to you.'

The President waited anxiously for the charade to begin.

'I am the founder of a new political group in the United States. The group is known as Corporate America. As the name implies we represent a new wave of thinking in this country. Corporate America believes that it is time for change in the political and socio-economic structure of the United States. To achieve our goals we believe that you and your government should step down immediately and make way for private enterprise to take political and economic control of this great nation of ours. We intend to bring about change, with or without your cooperation, Mr President.'

Not believing what he was hearing, the President turned to his Chief of Staff looking for assurance that it was only a dream. Wallshot's brazen attitude in threatening the government was intolerable.

'Mr Wallshot, do I hear you right? Are you threatening the people of the United States? And what the hell are you doing there, Ford? Are you part of this treasonable conspiracy?'

On instructions Ford continued to sit not answering the President's questions.

'My demands are very simple. So simple that I have no intention of repeating them to you. However, I will provide you with a concession. You now have twenty-four hours in which to step down. Do you understand?'

'You arrogant sonofabitch, Wallshot! Who the fucking hell do you think you are? I'll have you arrested immediately for treason. And I'll personally pull the switch when they fry you.'

Remaining calm, Wallshot fired his last salvo at the President.

'You have obviously not understood what I have said to you Mr President. Will you and Congress step down within twenty-four hours?'

'Go fry your ass, Wallshot!'

'Mr President, if you and your government do not step down within twenty-four hours, you can then hold yourself responsible for one of this country's greatest disasters.'

The television screen went dead. Wallshot had disappeared. The President, with sweat accumulating under his arms and dripping down his body, picked up the phone and telephoned the Director of the FBI telling him in an incoherent manner details of his conversation with Wallshot.

The President slumped into his chair and spoke to Hayes.

'Christ, Freddy, this is fucking serious business. Rudy Morphett was right about Wallshot. He wants to run the fucking country. I can't give in to his terrorist threats. How do you prepare for something like this? We're going to have to mobilise all of our resources to find this useless shit and stop him from bringing this country to its knees. Call an emergency meeting of Cabinet. Tell them to assemble here immediately. This is out and out war. And we know very little about our enemy and what his strategy is. Get me everything you can on him. Have Morphett and his colleagues join the cabinet meeting. We have twenty-four hours to neutralise him and his bunch of terrorists.'

The Secretaries of State and Defence and the Joint Chiefs of Staff had wasted no time in getting to the White House Cabinet Room. They had been given a de-brief by Freddy Hayes. It was enough to place them on full alert and to be at the White House immediately and to be fully briefed by the President. Rudy Morphett, Phil Black, Mike Johnston and Joe Markowitz hadn't left Washington since their earlier meeting with the President. Morphett had been having discussions with the Board of the *Washington Post* concerning a possible merger between the two papers.

The President got straight down to business. Time was at a premium and he emphasised that to his Cabinet Committee. No detail was left out. The recorded television broadcast between Wallshot and the President was played back to the Committee. Everyone in that room was now as up to date as the President was.

They each took turns in looking at one another as they sat there for what appeared to be a lifetime before finally Morphett spoke.

'That sonofabitch has finally played his trump card. I was right, he did have something up his sleeve. I would have never imagined in my wildest dreams that he planned to privatise the United States.'

'Well, we all know what his intentions are,' the President said. 'And we have less than twenty-four hours in which to put a stop to his terrorist demands.'

'Have the FBI been able to locate where the television signal came from, Mr President?'

'Not yet but they are close. The Director tells me it's somewhere in South Carolina.'

'Mr President, we obviously know that the Vice President is involved in this criminal conspiracy. Do we know who else is supporting them?'

'We have a fairly good idea, thanks to Mr Morphett's journalistic skills. He has reason to believe that Wallshot has been having regular meetings with a group of prominent Americans. No doubt these meetings were being held to plan this coup.'

'Who are they, Mr President?'

'Paul Tyler, Paul Lowenstein, Howard Lazenby, Fred Cohen and Judge Robert Hardcastle.'

'Christ, that is the most powerful force of businessmen that he could have ever assembled in this country. Paul Tyler worries me though. He has a comprehensive knowledge of all our defence strategies.'

'Gentlemen, we haven't got the time to be sitting here contemplating our navels. We have to come up with a solution to overcome this catastrophic crisis we are facing. I'm proposing that we have our total mainland armed forces on standby to repel any mass terrorist attack on our military establishments.'

'Mr President, I have some bad news, I've been told by my military commanders, that our ground troops are calling in sick. Apparently some vicious virus has struck the major part of our force and has immobilised our ability to react to a situation like this.'

'What about the navy and fly boys?'

'Same thing there, Mr President.'

'Could Wallshot have got to our troops before he planned his call to me?'

'Highly possible, Mr President. Remember we did it behind the Iron Curtain in the late eighties. I suspect the food has been contaminated. The sick call should be over in twenty-four hours if it is only contamination. We won't know until we get test results back.'

'How would Wallshot contaminate the food?'

'Mr President, I can answer that,' the Secretary of State replied. 'Wallshot Corporation has the food contracts for every one of our bases on the mainland.'

'You mean to tell me that one Corporation has effective control over the military might of this nation?'

'I'm afraid so, Mr President.'

'I cannot believe that we have allowed one man to rule this country for so long. Morphett was telling me that he also controls every major international airport, our nuclear energy sites and our oil reserves. Gentlemen, let me go on to tell you that is just the tip of the iceberg. His corporation has control of nearly every government service in this country. Have any of you stopped to think for a moment what that means? Well if you haven't I'd suggest that you think very carefully, because Wallshot is in a more powerful position at the moment than the United States Government is!'

'His Achilles heel is cash, Mr President.'

There was silence for a moment. The brains trust of American politics turned their heads to this lone voice at the far end of the Cabinet room oval table.

'Thank you for that, Mr Markowitz. Would you elaborate for us please?'

'Mr President, as a former Chief Financial Officer of Wallshot Corporation I had more than just an understanding of Wallshot's financial affairs. The success of his international operations has been the cash advance policy that he has adopted with government agencies around the world. If that were to stop, his business would crumble.'

'What you're saying is that he's spent the cash before he has actually earned it.'

'That's correct, Mr President.'

'If that's the case then all we have to do is stop paying his contracts immediately and kick the corporation off every government site in the country.'

'The theory of that is sound, Mr President. But you're too late for that plan of action'.

'Why's that?'

'Firstly Wallshot has been planning this day for a considerable period of time. I'd even suggest probably as long as fifteen or twenty years. You see his cash funding is provided by offshore foreign banks. You can't touch that, Mr President. Secondly, if you cancel his contracts immediately you will be held responsible for bringing the country to its knees. You will not have sufficient time to be able to put a replacement strategy in place. He's checkmated you, Mr President.'

'I like your balls, Mr Markowitz. You're the only one who has made sense here this morning'.

Sitting back in his chair, Joe felt pleased with his contribution and even more pleased with the accolades he had received from the President.

'Gentlemen, Mr Markowitz has perhaps found an open door for us. Where we sit at the moment is that there is very little we can do until Wallshot comes back to us at eight, tomorrow morning. I'm sure you all agree that we continue to maintain the policy of the Government that we will not succumb to terrorist threats. What will be his reaction to that? We have to wait and see! In the meantime we have every agency working around the clock to put protective measures in place at the key strategic sites around the country. Maybe we are too late for that, but I don't think we have an alternative. Finally we have to have a solution as to how we can stop his feed line coming in to the States. His cash arm has to be severed. Mr Markowitz, I'm hoping you can help us find that artery.'

The Cabinet Committee scurried out of the Cabinet Room to

implement the President's plan of attack, each person knowing that the odds were stacked against them succeeding. Until Wallshot came back to them tomorrow morning they had no idea what they would be dealing with.

$\mathcal{F}$ORTY-$\mathcal{T}$WO

The FBI had not been successful in tracing the broadcast transmission to the President's office. South Carolina was the best they could come up with. There had been insufficient time to pinpoint the exact location of the transmission.

The President was alone in the Oval Office replaying the Wallshot tape over and over again. He kept asking himself, what was he hoping to gain from this act of high treason? How long had the Vice President been involved in the conspiracy? He felt his judgement was clouded by the events of the morning. He was convinced that there was no way that Wallshot could pull this off. The chink in the armour had to be staring them in the face. What was it?

The Secretary of Defence had cancelled all leave for military personnel. For those that were not confined to sick bays, and there were very few, they were put on red alert. No explanation had been given other than an un-scheduled exercise had been called to determine troop readiness for a catastrophic crisis that may hit the country unannounced. FBI, CIA and other Federal Investigative Services were working around the clock to put preventative measures in place at all key strategic sites. The task was daunting and could never be achieved to total satisfaction, but it was necessary to do what they could in the short time frame they had left.

The President asked Rudy Morphett to visit him again at the White House. Morphett understood the pressures of business and had a real appreciation of what the President must have been going through right at that moment. He had no hesitation in dropping what he was doing and made his way from the hotel, where he had been stopping in Washington, direct to the White House.

When he arrived at the Oval Office, Morphett was surprised to see the President in a reasonably relaxed mood.

'Mr Morphett, I've had some news from the Director of the FBI that I'd like to share with you in confidence.'

'Let me assure you, Mr President, that anything you tell me inside these four walls remains within these walls.'

'You'll recall the break out at Saratoga prison some time back?'

'How could I forget it, Mr President. Wallshot's private prison!'

'Yeah! One of the escapees was an Irish –American. His name was Mickey Ryan. The agency told me that he headed their most dangerous list. Apparently he had been one of the IRA's lead hit men. He would do a job in Ireland and return to America where he knew he couldn't be picked up for his crime. Well it appears that he had a connection with Michael Montefiore. You know that Montefiore escaped from Saratoga at the same time and I'm sure you also know that he was like a son to Wallshot.'

'I would have never realised that the FBI had such a dossier on Wallshot and his connections.'

'Oh yes, Mr Morphett. After this is all over, I hope I get the opportunity to share our dossier on you! Anyway let me go on. Montefiore was imprisoned because of his sabotage of that Jumbo 747 in Miami. The FBI have told me that one of the men that was killed on that day was Mickey Ryan's twin brother. Ryan was serving a life sentence in Saratoga and when he found out that Montefiore had been transferred there, rumours had it they he wanted to get even.'

'The plot gets deeper, Mr President.'

'This is only the beginning. The warden at Saratoga, according to a report prepared for me by the FBI, helped Montefiore mastermind the escape by providing him with plans of the prison compound and the files on each of the men that escaped with him. The prisoners who escaped with Montefiore were all hand picked because of their weapons and bomb experience.'

'I guess what you are going to say is that this Mickey Ryan found himself as part of Montefiore's escape plan?'

'You're exactly right, Mr Morphett. Now here's the punch line. Before Montefiore had taken up residence in Saratoga, Ryan had agreed to cooperate with the FBI and the British government on naming key IRA operatives. For that information his sentence was going to be squashed. Ryan was due for release from Saratoga two days after the escape.'

'What a bizarre story, Mr President. Why would Ryan have crossed the line when he knew he was going to be freed in two days?'

'That's what I've been asking myself and that is why I wanted to share this with you. You have done so much background on Wallshot I was hoping you could shed some light on it for me.'

'I'd have to say, Mr President, that Ryan took a calculated risk. Let's face it, no one has heard from Montefiore or the escapees since they left Saratoga. My guess is they've been held up some-where offshore. They have to be part of Wallshot's plans, there's no question about that. What part are they playing? I guess we'll know more about that when he contacts you tomorrow morning.'

'Let me add something, Mr Morphett. For Wallshot to gain control of the government he has to have something to threaten us with. I'll put this scenario to you. What if Montefiore and the guys who escaped with him from Saratoga are back on the mainland and have armed a number of key strategic sites, which when activated could bring the country to its knees.'

'Mr President, that's preposterous!'

'Not necessarily! We can assume Wallshot has found a way to immobilise the armed forces until he is ready to talk to me again. If he is capable of doing that then he's capable of making it very easy for me to make that final decision.'

'Mr President, the irony of all this of course is that if your scenario is accurate then Montefiore has a loose cannon in his midst. That would be the only logic for Ryan to join forces with him, otherwise he'd be a free man today.'

'You're exactly right, Mr Morphett. I'm confident that Ryan is going to have his revenge. Don't you agree?'

'I hope your gut instinct is right, Mr President.'

Cabinet and the President had been in conference right throughout the night ploughing through mountains of information that they were receiving from the numerous government agencies. They had to be prepared as best they could for the television transmission that they were expecting at eight from Wallshot. Morphett, Black, Johnston and Markowitz had joined the Cabinet discussions in the early hours of the morning having prepared as much information as they could on Wallshot and his corporation.

The President paced the floor, throwing 'what if' scenarios at each of the cabinet members. They all unanimously agreed that they would not give in to terrorist threat and would continue to negotiate for a successful solution.

The President had contacted each of the premiers of the G7 nations and alerted them to the crisis that the country was facing. Each of the G7 members had shown total support and were prepared to ship in troops and other support services to America should the crisis worsen. Boris Yeltsin had telephoned the President direct and offered to realign the Russian satellite tracking stations in America's favour should the President request. International support was overwhelming but the President insisted that no active or covert action should be initiated by a foreign power until he had exhausted all avenues.

The eight bells rang on the cabinet clock.

It was eight o'clock.

The television receiver was tuned into Channel 88. It began to flicker.

A group of men appeared on the screen, there was Wallshot, Tyler, Ford, Lowenstein, Lazenby, Cohen and Hardcastle. The FBI immediately began to search for the location of the signal. Standing directly behind Wallshot was a younger man who appeared extremely nervous and anxious.

'Mr President, I don't propose introducing you to my colleagues. I am sure you know who they all are. It has been twenty-four hours since we last spoke. Have you reached a decision, Mr President?'

'Myself and my cabinet have been in deep deliberation since we last spoke and we are all in agreement that we will not succumb to your threats. Let me remind you, Mr Wallshot, that America does not take kindly to your type and I can promise you that if it's a revolution you want, it's a revolution you'll have. I will not hand over myself and my government to terrorist sonofabitches like you and your slimy bunch of whores. That's my answer to your demands!'

'You have made your position quite clear, Mr President. In less than sixty seconds Los Angeles International airport will be destroyed beyond recognition and a software virus will be introduced into the defence satellite communication network neutralising communication with all US military establishments.'

Wallshot turned to the young man standing behind him and said, 'Michael, execute the order now.'

'Mr President, I will telephone you again at this time tomorrow morning. You will have come to your senses by then, I'm sure.'

The television screen reverted to a black and white flickering transmission signal. The broadcast had been terminated.

The FBI still had not been able to locate the signal. They needed a few more minutes but it was too late.

The Presidential press officer burst into the Cabinet Room.

'Mr President, Mr President, we've just had word from Los Angeles that there has been a series of explosions at the international airport of cataclysmic proportions. We are not certain of the extent of the damage at this stage. We're awaiting further reports. My guess is that it has been wiped off the face of the earth.'

'Get me the Governor of California on the phone immediately,' the President yelled.

The Cabinet members were in shock. Rudy Morphett was the only one who had had time to compose himself, he knew what Wallshot was capable of. This was only the beginning. The President looked at his advisers in dismay searching their faces looking for answers. There were none forthcoming. The Secretary of State told the President that they needed to give serious consideration to turning over the government to Wallshot's Corporate America, before he brings the country to its knees. The President wasn't prepared to entertain that as an option at this point of time.

'Governor, my office has signalled me that you've had a serious of explosions at the International. Can you confirm that?'

'Mr President, I don't know what the hell is going on as yet but I believe that we have had a terrorist attack on the airport. It appears that the communications centre and the control tower are out so we are not getting an accurate picture at the moment. Let me come back to you as soon as I know more.'

'I want to know the extent of the damage immediately. You hear me, Governor?'

'As I said, you'll know as much as I do when I find out what's going on out there.'

'Well, you all heard that,' the President said to the Cabinet. 'That stupid bastard is playing for keeps. I can't let the country know that we are being held to ransom by a bunch of corporate terrorist thugs. We've exactly twenty-four hours to sever his Achilles heel. I want everybody working around the clock. That of course includes you and your colleagues, Mr Morphett.'

FORTY-THREE

Markowitz and Johnston had been given an office in the West Wing of the White House. They were expected to provide the President with a schedule of weaknesses that either Wallshot or the Corporation may have. There was nothing they could do to assist with the crisis that had occurred at Los Angeles and there was possibly nothing they could do after the eight o'clock call from Wallshot the following morning.

They were both convinced the Corporation was doomed if the government survived the crisis. Wallshot, if found guilty, would be sent to death row for treason and the international operations would probably suffer the same fate as the US domestic operations. The one thing that they were having difficulty putting together was how could they accelerate the process in less than twenty-four hours.

'Joe, we know that Wallshot commands enormous respect and loyalty from his staff,' Mike said. 'His employees won't turn on him. Correct?'

'We both know that most of them will follow him across a bed of hot coals.'

'We also know that Montefiore will do everything possible to ensure that Wallshot has the upper hand at all times during the negotiations with the President. Do you agree with that?'

'Yeah, I do. Where is this line of thinking taking you, Mike?'

'We know his strengths. How strong are his strengths? Consider his major weakness!'

'Of course,' Joe responded surprisingly. 'What has he done all his life? How has he succeeded? He's bought people's loyalty.'

'That's right, mate. And the only way he has done that is with cash. Cut off his cash supply and loyalty disappears. How do we do that, Joe?'

'I have a solution, which the President would be interested in listening to. Firstly see if you can get hold of Morphett and Phil Black. I'd like to run it past them before we discuss it with the President.'

The other two guys had been in the East Wing poring through documents and bundles of press releases, hoping to be able to get a break through. When they received the call from Markowitz they were quite happy to drop everything to talk with them about a possible solution. Mike and Joe ran through a scenario with Morphett and Black convinced in their own minds that it could work if the President was prepared to take the gamble. They both agreed that there were elements of risk but it was the best solution they had at the moment. If it failed then the time would have been lost and the President would have to relinquish power to Wallshot.

The President didn't hesitate for one moment to summon a Cabinet meeting when he heard that Markowitz wanted to put a proposition to them. At that time they had no other answers.

'Mr President, the way I see things at the moment, nothing appears to be going your way. Would you agree?'

'It doesn't look good, I must confess.'

'Well what I would like to propose is a gamble, the downside being you turn over America to Wallshot and his terrorists.'

'We still have to hear your proposal, Mr Markowitz, but looking at Cabinet I'd say you have our attention.'

'Thank you, Mr President.'

'Mike Johnston and I know Wallshot and the way his corporation works better than anyone here, the thing that Mike and I are convinced about is that if his cash supply is cut off, the corporation falters and his employees walk away. You now know that he has spent a lifetime bribing corrupt government officials. How has he done it? He's opened overseas bank accounts for them. He's given them unlimited travel. He has poured money into their pockets. You can only do that and expect people to remain loyal if you have the cash to do it. Take it from him and he's vulnerable.'

'That's fine, Mr Markowitz, but how do we cut down the money tree?'

'I believe that is where I can help? The corporation has very little onshore cash, most of it is kept in various accounts in Switzerland. Neither you nor the Federal Reserve can touch the cash there. The only way that Wallshot could have mounted this campaign would have been to promise a hell of a lot of people a hell of a lot of money to stick by his side until all this was over. You agree?'

'Keep going, Mr Markowitz!'

'We freeze the Swiss accounts.'

'Hold on, you stated earlier that neither I nor the Federal Reserve could touch his accounts in Switzerland.'

'That's correct, but if the United States Government was to renege on the guarantees that it has given the Swiss Feds for loans they have given to Third World countries, the Swiss banks would be at our mercy. If they didn't cooperate there would be a run on the banks. The consequences would be catastrophic. I'm sure you could imagine what would happen!'

The President looked at the Cabinet members and asked their opinion. To a man they all agreed that it was an alternative worth pursuing.

'Mr Markowitz, your proposal has the support of the government. What do we need to do to execute your plan?'

'I assume that the Swiss Federation President is aware of the events that have taken place here in the last twenty-four hours or so?'

'He does and he has offered to support us in any way he can.'

'Good. The door is open. I have the Wallshot Swiss account numbers and the secret access codes. You, Mr President, are going to have to convince the Swiss President of the plan and have him ready to shut down the accounts immediately. If he bucks and shoves remind him of the guarantees the US government has given on Third World loan accounts. That'll bring him to his senses. Once you have secured his commitment, we can then place that on the table when Wallshot rings tomorrow morning. I'm confident that will stall him for a day or so. If it doesn't, Mr President you will have to make one hell of a decision for the people of America.'

The President didn't hesitate for one second. He had his Chief of Staff get the Swiss Federation President on the phone and took the call in the Cabinet Room where everybody was able to hear the conversation. The Swiss President was extremely sympathetic at first but as the conversation went on he became somewhat reluctant to help the US President solve his dilemma, arguing that the Swiss had once told Hitler that the Germans could spend time in their country but threatened to ruin his victory march if he touched the Swiss banking community. That was probably the only good advice Hitler ever listened to. The US President was losing patience with the man's arrogance and finally threatened him with withdrawal of US guarantees for Third World country advances. The Swiss President's silence was noticeable. He rejected the threats at first but began to soften his stand when he began to realise the consequences of the US threat to remove its government's guarantees.

The President waited for a few moments for his counterpart to take in what he had just been told. The pause was like a lifetime as the Cabinet and the men from the *New York Herald* sat on the edge of their seats waiting for his decision. The President put down the phone gently. He looked at his advisers.

'That sonofabitch has agreed to put an immediate stop on Wallshot's funds leaving Switzerland.'

Everyone in the room fell backwards in their seats, smiling for a brief moment, believing that this might be the start of the victory path for them.

Right through the night the President and his advisers prepared for their next confrontation with Wallshot. The scene was set. The Swiss banks would turn off the money to fund his terrorist activities; Morphett would lead with a *New York Herald* headline denouncing the criminal activities of Wallshot but making certain that there was no reference to his plot to overthrow the US Government. The President couldn't afford to publicly state that the country was in crisis. Enough damage had already been done in Los Angeles. The newspapers were hyping the public into thinking that a wave of unknown terrorists were sweeping the country selecting targets at random for destruction. Whilst all this was going on the President had not responded by pulling the nation together as a cohesive unit. His problems were greater and he was unable to share them with his fellow Americans.

The second day had passed and it was fast approaching eight again. The Cabinet members and the *New York Herald* staff were extremely exhausted. They had been working without break to put in place what they hoped was the plan to destroy Wallshot.

The President's Chief of Staff turned the television on again. On the dot of eight Wallshot appeared as he had promised. He was by himself on this occasion and made absolutely no reference to his co-conspirators when he began speaking to the President.

'My patience is running out, Mr President. What is your decision?'

'My position has not changed, Wallshot. As long as I am President I continue to maintain the view of this government that we will not give into terrorist threat.'

'You stupid man. Who the hell do you think you are? I can destroy this country on one command. Do you realise what that can mean?'

'What it means to me, Wallshot, is that you are a very sick old man and you have no tolerance for the changes that have evolved in our society. Do you think I like what has gone on? We have to live with it and manage the problems as best we can. This is not 1945, Wallshot. This is the beginning of a new millennium.'

'Corporate America will change all that.'

'You'll change nothing if you execute your threat. You admitted yourself there will be no America left if you give the command. Is that what you really want?'

'There has to be subversion and anarchy before you can gain control. I will rise as the saviour for mankind.'

The President and his advisers were shocked by Wallshot's outburst. He had finally made his position known to them. His strong desire to rid America of its wrongs had possessed him beyond belief. He and his followers had to be destroyed, otherwise there would be no tomorrow.

'That's enough! I will give the order for the Hoover Dam to be exploded within the next sixty seconds. I will talk with you again this time tomorrow. That will be the pattern until you come to your senses.'

'Wallshot, before you turn us off, let me remind you that your game is nearly over. The President of the Swiss Federation has agreed to freeze your Swiss bank accounts. You have no funding left for your terrorist operations. You know what that means don't you? Every day this stalemate continues it means one day closer to me getting my hands on you and it's also one day more that your activists don't get rewarded. They'll desert you in droves. You're finished, Wallshot!'

'You are more stupid than I thought, Mr President. There is always a contingency plan. The other members of Corporate America will fund the operation through to the end.'

'No they won't, Wallshot. Your so-called friends that you introduced us to have had their corporate and personal banking accounts frozen as at six this morning. The Federal Reserve has taken that action on my instructions. Mr Wallshot, give this useless game up and surrender yourself to the authorities.'

The transmission went dead. Wallshot had disappeared. The FBI Director knocked at the door and entered the Cabinet Room.

'Mr President, we have a breakthrough. We've pinpointed the signal to a ranch in the Blue Ridge Mountains of South Carolina.'

'Mr President, I'm sorry to interrupt the conversation. Wallshot has his ranch in the Blue Ridge Mountains. It's a place called Buena Vista,' Markowitz blurted out.

'A great job, Mr Director. We've found the man. Now take him out before he does more damage.'

The telephone rang in the Cabinet Room. The Chief of Staff picked it up, he listened attentively to the voice on the other end. He could no longer contain his emotion and yelled out for the person on the other end to bring him as much information to him as he could immediately.

'Mr President, I've just received word that Wallshot has blown up the Hoover Dam. The damage is beyond anyone's wildest imagination. The Colorado River is pouring through the valley and threatening to wipe out Las Vegas. The Mayor has declared a state of emergency and ordered the city folk to evacuate immediately to higher ground. Hundreds of thousands of lives will be lost if they don't.'

'God what is happening? Will this ever stop! Send what force we can to the Blue Ridge Mountains. Wallshot has to be closed out immediately. We have to assume he's using his ranch as a command post. If that's the case we need to get inside before he triggers another target area that he has loaded for detonation. Whatever you do, don't send the fly boys in. Wallshot knows more about security than all of the military does collectively. Remember he has spent his life as a covert operator. If he spots anyone approaching the ranch you can bet your boots that he'll have you pinpointed, if that happens there is no saying what he is prepared to do next.'

The President was still unable to read what Wallshot may attempt to do next. Although his whole behaviour was irrational he had acted in a rational manner to date. He had been consistent. When he said he would do something, he would do it. He had not deviated once from his carefully laid down operational plan. The government now had the element of surprise on their side. They knew his location. They knew he had no funding to keep his operation rolling. They also knew that very shortly when it became known that his funding had dried up, the whole operation would begin to disintegrate. The President was banking on the fact that he would get his eight o'clock call tomorrow with further threats of reprisal. Wallshot would not be expecting the Federal authorities to be turning up on his doorstep.

An elite group of battle trained commandos were transported by helicopter to the foot of the Blue Ridge Mountains. This was the country's best, they had served on many fronts and were seasoned campaigners, in covert and subversive operations. They were code named, 'Blue Ridge.' Their terrain maps had put them at twenty-five miles west of Buena Vista.

It was nightfall and they planned to be at the ranch boundary by three the following morning, believing that five hours, before the next transmission, would be sufficient time for them to penetrate the command post and secure the premises.

They began the trek to the foot of the Buena Vista ranch.

Las Vegas had been devastated by the torrents of water that had penetrated the southern end of the city. Fortunately nature had taken a turn for the better and the fast flowing spillover from the Colorado River had just about run out of intensity by the time it had reached the city. Although there had been extensive property damage the Mayor of Las Vegas had made a preliminary announcement that an estimated five thousand people had lost their lives in the inexplicable disaster that had occurred.

$\mathcal{F}$ORTY-$\mathcal{F}$OUR

The President was caught unawares. A flash news report had just been broadcasted. The United Nations building in New York had been bombed. The report blamed a militant unknown terrorist group. It was unknown if Wallshot had orchestrated the devastation. The pressure was mounting on the President to accept the terrorist terms. He had no way of getting in touch with Wallshot to determine whether or not he had authorised the bombing.

The City of New York was in chaos. The lower front section of the building had been torn away from its steel structure. Tons of rubble had piled onto the street. People and vehicles were crushed as the concrete walls collapsed. Fortunately it was early evening when the explosion detonated. Most of the office workers had already left for the evening. Those that had remained had been killed instantly.

The President sat glued to his television screen as the CNN cameras panned the building. He felt sick, knowing deep down that Wallshot had caused the disaster and he was not in a position right at that moment to warn the people of America what was happening. 'Three catastrophic disasters in the space of a few days,' the CNN reporter shouted out over the noise of the sirens of the emergency vehicles that were arriving at what was left of the United Nations building. 'The people of America demand an answer,' the reporter went on to say. 'The government should tell Americans as to what action is being taken to stop this unprecedented terrorist attack on mainland America.' The President listened motionless, his heart going out to the families of those people that had been killed in the attack. He knew the reporter was right. Americans did deserve an answer and perhaps by tomorrow morning at eight o'clock he may well have to give them one. All he needed now was time. Time for 'Blue Ridge' to succeed.

The Secretary of Defence gave the President an update on operation 'Blue Ridge.' The commandos were now within a mile of the ranch boundary. They had been able to cover the assault on the mountain range without detection. The camouflage they were wearing was covered in a protective coating similar to the material that was used to line US stealth bombers. The final attack on the ranch would take place just before sunrise.

The President looked out of the window of the White House thinking to himself why he had got into politics. He reflected on the days of John F Kennedy when he was faced with the Bay of Pigs crisis. He thought that perhaps he stood at the same window wondering what the next course of action was. Spreading panic made no sense. JFK had remained visibly calm right through the whole incident. 'That is what I have to do,' he kept saying to himself. 'The enemy will falter.'

The sun began to pop its head up over the eastern horizon. He had received no word from the Secretary of Defence that the mission had been completed. Waiting fifteen further minutes, the morning sun was now in full view, still no answer.

The Chief of Staff was called to his office and asked to send the Secretary of Defence to the cabinet room immediately.

The news was not what he wanted to hear. Contact had been lost with the commandos. The President was now standing in 'no man's land'. Had they penetrated the ranch and captured Wallshot and his terrorists? This was the first question he asked himself when he heard the news from the Defence Secretary, or had they been caught and possibly executed? In sheer frustration he stamped his fist so hard on the table that he cracked a large ornamental glass vase.

Time had slipped by so quickly since the early morning sun had popped its head up. It was approaching eight o'clock. The President turned the television receiver on. The cabinet members had all arrived. They stood around the room waiting patiently for Wallshot's broadcast.

The chimes struck eight. Again the screen began to flicker. Wallshot was true to his word. He sat at his desk peering at his audience, appearing calm and quite oblivious to everything that had been going on.

The President was outraged and yelled at him, 'You miserable sonofabitch, what right did you have to kill all those innocent people at the United Nations building?'

'Mr President, the people of America will judge you on your decisions, not me. You have failed them. We are now into the third day and still you continue to treat me with contempt.'

'What the hell do you want?'

'Your public resignation and that of Congress by noon today. And by the way, that was a stupid thing you did sending in commandos to destroy our operations. They were detected at the boundary and annihilated. We had been monitoring their progress throughout the night. My command post is impenetrable and I know you won't use air power for fear of what further damage you may trigger to sites I have armed around the country.'

'You lying weasel, you have not killed those commandos.'

'Michael, bring in the body of the commando colonel, we picked up at the boundary fence.'

Montefiore had placed the colonel's body into a chair alongside Wallshot and propped it up by holding onto his head and pointing it towards the recording camera.

'You see what I mean, Mr President. You continue to under-estimate me. Your resignation by noon, otherwise I will detonate a further three sites. These will be far worse than anything you have seen so far.'

Before the President could respond, the screen had gone blank. Wallshot had disappeared again to the confine of his protected command post.

The time had arrived for cabinet to make a decision. Their plan to send in commandos had failed. Three strategic sites had been destroyed with increased threat to further sites. Wallshot was determined to see this through to the end. The President was under enormous pressure from Congress to face the public and give them assurances that the government was doing everything in it power to locate the terrorists and bring them to justice. The truth was of course that the President knew who the terrorists were and he had been able to do very little in bringing them to justice.

The time had come for him to face Congress and the Senate to tell all. He had less than four hours before Wallshot would re-appear. Cabinet members realised that they were powerless and reluctantly agreed with the President that he had to tell them of Wallshot's demands.

Both houses were sitting at the time and having them available to be addressed by the President was a matter of formality only. He instructed his staff to advise the Speaker of the House to arrange an emergency meeting of both Houses

The President asked his staff members into the Oval Office. He informed them of his decision to resign as President and explained that he had now been given no choice. It was in the best interests of America. The staff understood the predicament he was in but they knew him well enough to know that his first love was for America and he would do absolutely nothing to harm his beloved country. It had been hurt enough already.

The secret service agents escorted him to the waiting limousine. This would probably be the last time that he would leave the White House on official business. The limo made its way out of the grounds of the White House to Capitol Hill. Those few minutes were to be the longest in the President's life.

Arriving at his destination the President, flanked by secret service agents made his way to the Congress chamber. As he entered the chamber, Congress and Senate members of both sides of the house stood and applauded. The Speaker of the House invited him to the podium to address members. As he walked up to the dais he noticed the seat of the Vice President was vacant. Only he knew why he wasn't there this day. Shortly the whole of America would know.

He paused for a moment before he reached down to turn his notes over. He looked up at the sea of faces, cleared his throat and began to speak.

Without warning his Chief of Staff who had accompanied him into the chamber, unceremoniously ran from the side of the chamber towards the President. The secret service agents who were discreetly positioned around the chamber ran forward to impede his progress. He pushed his way past the first agent and had now reached the podium. The President stopped his speech, looked at his friend and beckoned for him to come forward. An agent grabbed him by the arm and escorted him to the President's side. There was a hush in the chamber. Congress and Senate members were in dismay as they witnessed what they thought was an attempt to assassinate the President.

The President stepped down from the podium to be confronted by his Chief of Staff that he should delay his address for one hour. He asked him not to ask for the reason right at that moment but said that he would explain, immediately they were able to secure a private room. The President had always trusted his Chief's judgement and saw no reason to have a change of mind now. He turned to the Speaker and asked him to apologise to the Joint House on his behalf and advised him that he would return in one hour to continue his address.

The Chief of Staff had just told the President the most incredible story that he had ever heard in his whole life. The blood drained out of his face as he went ashen white. 'There is a God,' he thought.

'Call an emergency meeting of Cabinet,' the President ordered his Chief of Staff, Freddy Hayes. 'I also want the representatives of the *New York Herald* there as well.'

The cabinet members had been in the Congress Hall when the President suddenly left the chamber. They had assembled at his request within minutes, followed a few minutes later by Rudy Morphett, Phil Black, Mike Johnston and Joe Markowitz.

'Mr President, we only have a few minutes before Wallshot contacts us again. He is expecting your decision and you haven't addressed the Joint House yet! What's going on?' Secretary of State demanded to know.

The President remained calm as the questions were thrown at him like baseballs.

'Gentlemen, if you've never prayed in your life, do so today. As you know our defence satellite tracking system was immobilised by Wallshot. Thanks to our Russian friends, Yeltsin altered the course of his spy satellites to spy on America. The CIA had given the Russky's the coordinates of Wallshot's ranch and they had been monitoring events there for the last few hours. Apparently all hell has broke loose there during that time.'

303

The President was exhausted. He had to sit down. He was given a glass of water whilst he composed himself.

'The Russian secret service mounted a joint spy operation with the CIA. They witnessed the tragic events that unfolded early this morning when Wallshot's armed guards unexpectedly killed our commando squad. What transpired after that you will never believe,' he said with great excitement reflecting in his voice.

'The approach road to Wallshot's ranch was unsecured until it reached the boundary gate. A heavy truck was making its way along the approach road, apparently at great speed. It failed to stop at the entrance gates, instead ploughing its way through the security cordon and making its way to the ranch house. That's when all hell broke loose. The distance from the gate to the house was about a mile. The truck was in full flight and nothing was going to stop it, despite numerous attempts to bring it to a standstill.

'Wallshot had prepared his command post like an electronic fortress. What he hadn't planned for was a perimeter breach by a speeding truck. As the truck was in sight of the ranch house and was only metres away it accelerated and ploughed into the building, exploding on impact and destroying everything around it, including the ranch house. Nothing is left.'

'Jeezus, Mr President, if it hadn't been for those fucking Russkies, you would have just delivered your resignation to the Joint House.'

'No, Mr Secretary, if it hadn't been for the driver of that fucking truck, we would have all been on our way out of politics.'

'Mr President, I gather from what you have just told us that the driver of the truck was killed in the explosion.'

'Gentlemen, I said go and pray today. By some inexplicable miracle the driver managed to jump out of the vehicle just moments before the truck accelerated into the building. Miraculously he was not killed but early reports say he is in a serious but stable condition.'

'Do we know who the driver was, Mr President?'

'Yes, I have been told it was Mickey Ryan, the Irishman who escaped from Saratoga a few days before he was due for release. He has his revenge now. Michael Montefiore appears to have been killed in the explosion.'

The meeting room clock struck twelve noon.

'Mr President, you have to go and address the Joint House. What are you going to say to them?'

'Very simply that as President of this country I have been appalled by the acts of terrorism that have occurred and I'm pleased to tell the Joint House that the terrorists have now been brought to justice. I propose releasing a full report to the American people within twenty-four hours, naming everybody that was involved.'

$\mathscr{F}_{\text{ORTY-}}\mathscr{F}_{\text{IVE}}$

The events of the last few days had taken an extreme toll on the health of the President. His advisers were encouraging him to take a vacation and do a spot of fishing at his country home in Maine, but the Wallshot affair was not finalised and until it was he had no intentions of leaving Washington.

The FBI had spent several days sifting through the remains of Buena Vista. They had discovered the remains of seven bodies, six of which had been positively identified by dental records. The agency confirmed that Wallshot had been killed when the truck laden with Semtex had hit the ranch house. The other bodies were identified as those of Lowenstein, Tyler, Lazenby, Cohen, Hardcastle, and they assumed that the seventh body was the Vice President, Clark Ford, even though a full set of his teeth were not able to be matched with known dental records. Everybody was accounted for except Montefiore. The FBI was uncertain as to whether or not he was at Buena Vista at the time of the explosion. There appeared to be no evidence that he was.

At Wallshot's office the FBI had pulled the place apart. They were looking for any records that he may have kept identifying the location of the sites that his terrorists had armed for destruction.

Buena Vista had buried its secrets when Mickey Ryan ran the truck into the building.

Their luck changed when Wallshot's secretary, Marina, turned up at Wallshot's Miami office to empty her desk. She hadn't been expecting an investigation and when asked how much she knew about Wallshot's activities she broke down and confessed what she knew. It wasn't much, as Wallshot had kept most things from her and others. The most helpful information she was able to pass on to the FBI was his confidential computer access codes. She had never used them in the past and told the FBI that she came across them one day purely by accident. Her story was plausible, but only just.

Accessing his computer they found one of the most extraordinary schedule of files that they had ever seen. Scrolling through each file one by one there was documented a detailed account of every illegal activity that he had been involved in for the past twenty-five years. It listed the corporation's covert activities, some of which had been undertaken in conjunction with the CIA. There were lists of people that he had corrupted over the years and the bribes that he had paid. The schedule of assassinations was the most interesting. A check of the names still showed the people assassinated as missing persons assumed dead. There was no longer any doubt at all.

Then came the most important file. The one that no other person had ever seen. His plan to overthrow the President and the Government of America, code named Incarceration.

The planning of Incarceration had been spawned on the day General Douglas MacArthur had died.

The opening line of the file read, 'The work of a great man is not finished until I have fulfilled his dream.' The words were chilling. It described in graphic detail every event that had taken place in his quest to execute Incarceration and finally the information the FBI was looking for stood before them. The listing of each of the armed fifteen sites with the word execution alongside Los Angeles Airport, Hoover Dam and the United Nations building. He had included the minutest of detail in his reports.

Searching through the Incarceration file they came across how each of the sites had been armed. They were now sitting on twelve of the most lethal weapons in the country, which could be triggered accidentally at any time. An immediate plan was put in place to disarm them and close down all the sites until the project had been finalised. Nothing could be left to chance.

A modern day Adolf Hitler had been close to securing the ultimate prize – the United States of America.

Some days later the remains of a Citation jet had been discovered on a wooded mountain top not too far from Westchester airport. A search of the remains by local authorities had discovered two bodies. One had been identified as Michael Montefiore. There was sufficient evidence at the crash site to determine that the plane had exploded in flight. Montefiore and the pilot would have died instantly. How did the Citation explode? Perhaps Mickey Ryan had the answer!

By the time Phil Black returned to New York he had not seen Fran for close on a week. It was time for decisions. He wasn't prepared to put off the inevitable any longer, asking her if she would marry him next week in New York. There was no hesitation. Her answer was, 'Why wait so long?'

Phil's only concern was that after the wedding how would he break the bad news to Rudy Morphett that he was returning to Australia to live. He quietly said to himself, 'It's time for a change, c'est la vie.'

The Wallshot Corporation was delisted from the New York Stock Exchange and the Federal Authorities took the unprecedented step of liquidating the corporation and distributing the surplus cash to the families of the victims that had been killed in the Wallshot bombing disasters.

Mike Johnston stayed on in New York for a while longer and helped the *New York Herald* put together the final chapter on the Wallshot exposé. The paper won the country's leading literary prize for its work.

The biggest surprise of all was Joe Markowitz's appointment to the Presidential Staff. It appeared that the President had been extremely impressed with the way that he had conducted himself throughout the whole sordid ordeal. His job was that of Special Adviser to the President on the privatisation of government agencies. Congress had passed legislation forbidding private enterprise controlling more than five per cent of government services.

The *New York Herald*, much to the delight of Rudy Morphett merged with the *Washington Post*. Rudy received a Presidential commendation for the work he had done in exposing Wallshot. He is now waiting on government approval to buy into the US Satellite tracking system.

The President of the United States took a well deserved rest at his country home in Maine, knowing that when he returned to the White House he would not be facing such a tough battle to run for a second term. His approval rating after the Wallshot affair had risen twenty points, enough to secure him the ultimate prize for a further four year term – the United States of America.